MAGE'S NEMESIS

A LIGHT MAGE WARS NOVEL

NANCY NORTHCOTT

ISBN:978-1-944570-21-7

Copyedits by Ann Wicker, East Oak Media

Cover by Lyndsey Lewellen Llewellen Designs

Published by Rickety Bookshelf Press

info@riockrtybookshelfpress.com

CHAPTER ONE

Brunswick, Georgia
Present Day

THE PAST, TASHA MURDOCK FIGURED, SHOULD HAVE THE DECENCY to stay buried.

Unfortunately, her past was not cooperating. Particularly not the part bound up with the six two, chestnut-haired, smart-as-the-devil and handsome-as-homemade-sin bundle of bad memories known as Carter Lockwood.

Pacing her potential client's elegant study, she frowned at the memories plaguing her. What sneaky jab of fate had landed Lockwood in this area?

Granted, going into mage law enforcement was a reasonable choice for a mageborn former naval officer. But there were nineteen shires, as the mageborn called their secret governmental districts, in the US. Why couldn't he have gone to work in some other one?

Instead, he'd landed here in the southeast and turned up, on duty, heading the mage security detail for her friends' archaeo-

1

logical excavation this past November. Until then, she hadn't seen the man for ten years. She'd managed to bury the memory, the old hurts, and hadn't even thought of him in forever.

Now, after just that one encounter three months ago, the big jerk popped into her thoughts whenever her guard was down.

Even worse, the battles at that excavation site had shown how superbly Lockwood wielded both magic and a broadsword. The combination was sexy as...

Crap. She was doing it again. Letting him distract her.

Head in the game, Tasha.

While the prospective client kept her waiting, she should be refining her pitch to show that her company, Murdock Custom Builders, was the best choice for this job. The economy was booming now, but after struggling through the recent downturn, she wouldn't take success for granted. Her eleven employees sort of counted on being able to eat regularly.

Besides, the Colliers, the potential clients, were well connected socially and could open important doors.

So. Back to business.

She turned to survey the space. Bumping out the end of this long, narrow room would make the space look even narrower, but that was up to the client. On the phone, the woman had said they wanted more room for entertaining.

That might mean they planned to ditch the gorgeous floor-to-ceiling shelves along one wall. That would be a shame. To get a closer look, Tasha walked over. She set her leather tote on the wide, mahogany desk, careful not to disturb the papers strewn on it. The shelves were burnished walnut and in great shape.

But some people tossed out very nice things on a whim. That was always baffling, maybe because she'd grown up cherishing anything nice her family could scrape together the funds to buy. She made a lot of money supplying replacements, though, so she wasn't going to complain.

Gently, she stroked a wooden shelf. Her mageborn senses hummed with the powerful energy in the wood, muted now

2

that the tree was cut but still present. If the client tossed these, she might be able to find a home for them.

She drew her tablet and tape measure out of her tote and set the tablet on a clear corner of the desk. Humming, she started measuring shelves. Seven feet high by four wide. She grabbed the tablet and jotted that down.

"What are you doing in here?" a woman's voice behind her demanded.

Tasha turned toward the sound. A petite, fiftyish white brunette glared at her from the doorway. Magic crackled in the air, confirming what Tasha had heard from the client who referred her, that Geneva Collier was mageborn. Her husband supposedly also was.

Tasha raised her brows and kept her voice cool. "You must be Mrs. Collier. I'm Natasha Murdock. I was asked to wait for you in here."

"Oh, of course!" The woman relaxed, smiling broadly. "I'm so sorry. Yes, I'm Geneva Collier. Our new maid seemed clever enough when we hired her, but she can't seem to learn the house. The room we want you to expand is this way."

She stepped back and gestured to the side. Tasha stuck her tools back in her bag. As she walked out of the room, Geneva darted a glance back into it.

"Something wrong?" Tasha asked.

"No, nothing." The other woman smiled, but she looked distracted.

Following Geneva, Tasha mulled her pitch. Getting this job could lead to something even more important than building a financial cushion. Despite having moved to Brunswick, Geneva Collier remained a mover and shaker on the steering committee of the Savannah Christmas Cavalcade charity. She'd chaired it for three years. Tasha had never been able to land a slot in any of the homes showcased during the holiday season. She wanted one badly.

Putting on an impressive display at one of those houses

would bring business rolling in. She could take her firm to the next level, would be able to hire—and keep on her payroll—some of the skilled craftsman she now subcontracted. Having them committed to her company would give its rep a serious bump.

But everyone knew a good presentation wasn't enough to win a slot. Someone the selection committee trusted had to vouch for you.

Geneva ushered Tasha down a hallway and into a large room furnished in heavy, upholstered pieces, a mix of brown leather and green-and-gold-striped velvet. French doors opened onto a terrace. A fireplace and the bar for an open-design kitchen bookended the room.

With a sweep of her arm, Geneva said, "This is the room we plan to redo. We want to extend it by fifteen feet and open it up completely, no posts or anything in the way."

"I can see the potential." Tasha eyed the eight-foot ceiling and the yard beyond the doors. This room was much wider than the other. "Because this is an external wall, and thus load-bearing, an opening that size will require support posts or a steel I-beam header to span the opening."

"Our architect said something similar." Geneva frowned. "We don't want our guests having to dodge around pillars."

"Opening this up will certainly create a gorgeous space, but building codes require support in a situation like this. I'm sure you want to do everything by the book since cutting corners can lead to serious structural problems later."

Judging by the woman's crestfallen face, she was lying when she nodded, but that was too bad. No matter how much Tasha wanted this job, Murdock Custom Builders did nothing that wouldn't hold up for a very long time.

"There are various things we can do," she assured her hostess, "to dress up the support posts. The I-beam I mentioned can span this space, but that requires a more involved installation than you might want. I think you might like the look of the posts if they're done well. We can make them consistent with the style of your house."

Geneva pursed her lips. "You come highly recommended, but we have some doubt about hiring such a young woman for such a big job. Have you handled many like it?"

Not this again. At thirty-two, Tasha didn't consider herself that young. Years of good, solid work had made such comments mostly history, but she ran up against these attitudes every now and again.

She kept her smile in place. "Thanks to my work in the US Navy's construction arm, the Seabees, and with the former owner of my company, I have more than a dozen years of construction experience that runs the gamut from concept to move-in. As well as decorating experience, of course."

"Hmmm." Geneva turned to the wall she'd indicated. "How soon can you give me an estimate?"

"If we settle the details today, I can have a construction estimate and rough sketches by the end of the week. You said you wanted redecorating, too, and the cost of that will depend on what you select." And how often she changed her mind.

"We want only the best, of course. Now that my husband has become a vice president at his brokerage house, we'll be entertaining a great deal. It's important to present an elegant home. So what do you think that would run?"

"It depends on the materials in the addition," Tasha repeated, "and whether you want to raise the ceiling as well as the décor you want, from paint to furniture to flooring to wall or window treatments. I can't make even a ballpark guess until I know more about what you would like. Do you have anything in mind?"

"Not yet." Geneva added, "I'll need to call my husband and see if he wants me to ask you anything. He'd hoped to be here by now, but he was delayed. Sit down, and I'll have our girl bring you something. How about coffee?"

"Thanks, but I'm fine. I have to be over in Fargo later this afternoon, so I'll go ahead and take some measurements."

"Oh. All right, then."

Geneva frowned as she bustled away.

Yeah. That went so well.

At least Tasha could use this waiting time. She pulled her tablet and tape measure back out of her bag and got to work, jotting down the measurements for the wall that was going to go.

This bumpout needed to blend with the existing structure to avoid looking like an afterthought. Which way did the roofline run?

She walked outdoors to the patio and took in the multiple gables going in different directions. Then she closed her eyes, envisioning how an addition could meld naturally with the current lines of the house.

Instead of the image she wanted, she flashed on a memory, Carter Lockwood nailing shingles on a roof in India. Their Seabee unit had been sent in for typhoon relief. A lieutenant wouldn't ordinarily be on the roof, but a storm was coming in, and one of the guys had fallen and sprained his shoulder. So Lockwood had pitched in.

Because they'd spent a lot of time doing heavy work in subtropical heat, all the guys had shed their outer shirts as soon as possible. But not all the guys were as ripped as their company commander. Even now the image of him with sweat darkening his chestnut hair almost to black and making the regulation tan tee stick to his superbly toned body, made her mouth go dry.

Damn it.

What was keeping Geneva? She'd been gone almost ten minutes.

Tasha made more notes, then quickly sketched the roofline. As she went back inside, she glanced at her watch. Only a short time until she needed to leave. She didn't want to offend or disappoint Geneva Collier, but being on time for appointments was a key part of her company's appeal. Wasting the time of an existing client for the sake of a possible one was never smart.

She needed the room's layout and dimensions to estimate materials, so she set about measuring the space. Next came cell phone photos, including the existing furniture. The current look was dark and heavy. Would Geneva want that or something lighter and more contemporary? The latter would be better, especially if they weren't raising the ceiling.

The upholstered pieces in here were rock solid. Recovering those would ease the budget and still give a lighter vibe if she used the right fabric.

Geneva strolled into the room. "My husband is on his way and very much wants to discuss concepts with you if you can wait."

"I'm afraid I can't. I'm due over in Fargo. But I can come back later in the week."

Geneva hesitated. "We might want to redo the entire downstairs. You could give us a discount for a big purchase like that, couldn't you?"

"We could work something out."

Once Tasha had the job, she would steer the conversation around to the Christmas Cavalcade. Planning for that would kick off in June. This being late February, she had time to redecorate everything if Geneva could make decisions quickly. Some clients couldn't. The final results should be *elegant* enough to impress Geneva and her friends.

"I'll show you around before you leave. We can discuss alternative visions. My husband also wants you to look at the wine cellar. He's considering updating it."

A wine cellar. Most likely a small, enclosed space.

Tasha's heart jolted, but she made herself smile. "My construction supervisor is an expert on wine cellars. I'll want him to look at that. He can come by later in the week, and we'll come up with some ideas. I can't be late for my next appointment, though. It's a long drive."

No matter how much she wanted this job, it was still only a possibility. Every client's time was valuable, and she couldn't work with one who didn't respect that.

Geneva frowned but didn't argue.

"Think about what you want," Tasha added, "and shoot me an email or give me a call."

At least when she was busy, her mind stayed on task instead of straying to Lockwood. She just had to keep it that way more often.

TASHA STARED at the road unwinding in her headlights. Too bad there was nothing to look at along here besides dense, shadowy stands of commercial timber. The long drive on the mostly deserted Georgia 94, better known as South End Road because it ran along the southern edge of the vast Okefenokee Swamp, offered too much opportunity for that pestilential man to invade her thoughts.

She sighed. It wasn't as though there'd ever been anything between her and Lockwood. Aside from their both being mageborn.

And the sizzling little current that arced through the air whenever they were in the same room.

Not that either of them had let that matter. He'd been her CO, and even if he hadn't been—

Her cell phone rang. *Yay, a diversion!* She engaged the car's wireless audio. "Hello."

"Hey, Tasha, it's Lorelei."

"Hey there. How was your day?" Tasha kept her tone breezy. Lorelei's boyfriend had died in an auto accident almost two months ago, and she had some days when she was fragile.

She didn't want to be hovered over, though, and Tasha could relate.

"It was long. The Problem Bride decided that no, she doesn't want rose petals in the sachets she's giving the wedding party after all. She now wants lilac."

Tasha grimaced in sympathy. "Did you tell Bridezilla we don't have lilacs blooming in late February, even in south Georgia?"

"I suggested this might cause a delay in having the sachets ready, but she's adamant." Lorelei sighed. "At least she didn't balk at the rush fee."

"What a pill, though. I'd ask you over for wine, but I won't be home for a couple of hours. I'm on South End Road, about ten miles from the turn north. Had to go check a job site and meet with a client in Fargo."

"That's a long drive."

"Tell me about it."

"You know," Lorelei said, "I didn't realize how cathartic it was when we used to go with the guys and take out ghoul nests. I could really use a chance to transfer all this built-up frustration."

Tasha grinned at the dark countryside. "I know what you mean."

She and Lorelei had been part of Griffin Dare's rogue covert ops team during his renegade years. Taking out the settlements, or nests, of the dark magic users known as ghouls did a lot more to improve the world than either of their day jobs.

The humanoid, sallow-skinned ghouls were the Light Mages' deadly enemies. Unable to reproduce among themselves, they kidnapped mages and Mundane, or normal, humans as breeders. Their retractable talons could suck out life energy or magic or inject searing, deadly venom into their prey.

"It's good Griff cleared his name and has his life back," Lorelei said, "but sometimes I miss those days."

"Me too." Tasha had enjoyed the camaraderie along with the

knowledge that she was doing something that seriously mattered.

But stopping the raids had been part of the price for good relations between Griff and the mage governing Council. He got to return to the fold of mage society, and the Council got to be seen taking the lead in operations against the ghouls.

"We could spar at the gym tomorrow," Tasha offered. "I could use a workout with my saber." Firearms had greater stopping power, but only a bladed weapon imbued with magic could destroy a ghoul's life energy. Raids or no raids, she wasn't going to let her skills go rusty.

"I could too. So—"

A fist-wide bolt of silver mage energy flashed out of the darkness and slammed into the underside of her truck. The radiator blew with a gush of steaming water, and the truck jolted to a stop, flinging Tasha forward against the shoulder belt.

She shielded to limit the airbag's punch. It deployed, then deflated quickly, but she kept her shield, a green aura, around her.

Extending her senses, she caught the nauseating prickle of ghoul energy. A lot of it. Shadowy, bulky shapes moved in from both sides of the road.

Then seven muddy yellow shield auras flared to life.

Oh, shit. She'd never taken on such a big group alone. No avoiding it, though. She couldn't translocate into the dense timber lining the road, and there was nowhere else to go but along the road, where she would be clearly visible. And easy for them to run down with a car.

"Tasha!" Lorelei's voice came from the speakers. At least the connection had survived. "What's going—"

"Ghoul attack." Tasha snapped, reaching behind the seat for her saber. "Call the Wayfarer patrol. Seven ghouls and a traitor mage. I need backup."

The nearest backup was the mage patrol in the town of

Wayfarer, more than thirty miles away, but worrying about that wouldn't do any good.

Tasha waited until the ghouls surrounded the truck, then reached for the space between life and death and visualized the road about a hundred yards behind her. She poured power into the shift, and reality jerked sideways in a wave of wrenching cold.

Shielding didn't survive translocation. Emerging from transit, she dived and rolled as her protective aura reformed. Too bad she lacked the power to translocate out of visual range, so they couldn't follow her. No time to worry about that, though. The ghouls had sensed her and were turning.

She was going to need a lot of luck to survive until backup arrived.

～

CARTER DRUMMED his fingers on his steering wheel and watched the thin ribbon of asphalt unreel under his headlights. Sometimes hunches paid off, and sometimes they didn't. If his family had possessed a true precog gift—but they didn't, and that was that.

So here he was, miles south of the small town of Wayfarer, because of a vague feeling that he should drive down this way. After his daily shift as head of the mage patrol there, a group that had to be kept secret from the non-magical residents, who were known as Mundanes, he normally went back to his home in Brunswick.

But not tonight. Instead of turning left out of their little base and heading north, he'd turned right. And kept going.

All this empty countryside gave him too much time to think about the woman he'd never gotten out from under his skin.

He scowled at the road. He'd managed to forget about Natasha Murdock, mostly, until they'd met again last

NANCY NORTHCOTT

November. Who knew she'd be a friend of the mage archaeologist whose project he was assigned to guard from ghouls?

Or that she would pop into his head with annoying frequency even though they hadn't seen each other in almost three months since that project wrapped up?

That day in November, he'd been idiotically glad to see her. Probably grinned like a fool. *Hey, Red,* he'd said, using her nickname in their Seabees company. *Good to see you.*

Jackass. He should've realized the pleasure would be his alone. After all, he was the one who'd reported her misuse of building supplies in the Seabees. The navy hadn't cared that her intentions were good, and they'd busted her rank. If he'd had any warning, he might've thought of that before he opened his idiot mouth.

But no, he'd let that instant flash of happy surprise, of hope they could start fresh, get the better of him. She'd slapped him down fast, with a whipcrack in her voice that had her friends closing ranks around her instantly.

That feeling of being on the outside had punched him in the gut, especially because doing his job required working with those same friends. He'd thought they were becoming his friends too.

In the interest of protecting the archaeology project, the two of them had struck a civil but distant accord. That should have been that.

But it wasn't.

So he was a dunce. There were worse fates.

His cell phone beeped, signaling a text. The dispatcher for the Wayfarer patrol would've used the radio. This could be a friend wanting to chat and seeing if he was clear first. Or one of the kids he unofficially mentored could need help.

The in-dash screen read, "Jaybird."

"Read text," he ordered the car system.

"From Jaybird," the mechanical voice responded. "Got 87 on science test. Thx."

Carter relaxed. He'd been half afraid the seventh-grader's dad had gone on a bender again.

Carter had met the Jeremy Hayes while investigating reports of dark magic use and found him dabbling with blood spells. He'd wanted to make his father stay sober and calm by keeping his drinking buddies away. His mother'd deserted them, so no help there. Reporting the boy was standard procedure, but Carter, product of two responsible and loving parents, hadn't been able to do it.

Not then and not when other troubled kids, mageborn or Mundane, had come across his radar.

The mage system that would haul those magically gifted kids in for examination and counseling, possibly in detention, wouldn't do anything to fix their home situations. It wasn't set up for that. Nor would the Mundane system help the other kids, ones it had already failed.

If anyone at the Collegium, the mages' secret headquarters, found out what he was doing, his ass was in a sling. There would be much talk of undue interference and even legal liability. But that was a problem for later.

There was no other traffic, so he stopped his low-slung, red Gyrfalcon where he was and texted Jeremy back. *WTG, my man. Burgers on me next chance we get.*

All those off-duty hours Carter had spent hunched over a science textbook with Jeremy had paid off.

You rock came back to him, and he smiled.

Starting forward again, he almost made a U-ey, toward Wayfarer and his home beyond it in Brunswick, but that itchy urge still pulled him south.

Maybe there was something going on that would turn this wild goose chase into a wise choice. "Call dispatch," he told his phone.

Even as the phone rang, the voice of Ginger Wilson, the Wayfarer patrol's dispatcher, crackled over his radio. "All units, all units. Mage under attack on South End Road, ten miles west of Okefenokee Parkway. Seven ghouls, one traitor mage reported on-scene."

Fuck. Those were deadly odds, especially for a civilian. His hunch had been valid after all.

Carter keyed his mic. "Lockwood here. I'm on the parkway now, a dozen miles north of St. George. I'm rolling. Ginger, send me backup."

He stomped on the gas, and his sports car leaped forward. Drawing on mage reflexes and driver training, he pushed his speed up near a hundred miles an hour—not as much of a risk on this little-traveled road at night as it would be elsewhere.

Yet the speed did nothing to ease the sick feeling in his gut. The beleaguered mage was in the pocket of Georgia that stuck down into Florida. That was better than being on the other side of the Okefenokee, but he was twelve miles from the turn onto South End Road in St. George. Then another ten miles to reach the victim.

Unless whoever it was had hellacious combat training, help would arrive too late.

TASHA'S back burned from venom-infused talon slashes, and her sword arm ached. A venomous puncture on her left arm had it cold and throbbing. Blood from triple slashes across her chest stuck her shirt to her, and venom poisoning had her fighting chills and nausea.

Three down, four to go, but she couldn't last much longer.

At least the mage had hung back for some reason—and thank God for small favors—but if he chose to enter the fight, she was dead.

Needing the truck as a barrier, she'd worked her way back to it. Now behind her, it blocked more than two of the surviving ghouls from attacking at once. Tasha side-kicked the big, burly male ghoul on her right in the gut, driving it backwards as her strike punched through its shields.

Its companion lunged.

Slashing left, she shouted, *"Morere,"* the Latin command to die, to amplify her power. Her blade sliced through the charging ghoul's shielding and opened a gash in its torso.

But another ghoul was moving in. Yet another, a burly female, vaulted into the truck bed. It could blast her from there.

Fuck.

Tasha translocated to the truck's far side, diving and rolling as she emerged and re-formed her shields. She gained her feet and blasted as much power as she could through her saber, amplifying it, at the big female ghoul in the truck bed.

The bolt slammed into the ghoul, disintegrating its shields and shoving it out of the truck. With luck, that blast and the fall had at least knocked it out.

But Tasha's shields flickered. The translocation and then the blast had nearly drained her. And the ghouls were still coming. Fear prickled along the back of her neck. She tightened her grip on her saber.

Drawing power from the life energy in the surrounding woods, she reinforced her shielding as the ghouls scrambled around the truck. She blasted another ghoul, knocking it six or eight feet but not killing it.

Recharging again, she backpedaled to the road's edge. The steep drop-off to the drainage ditch should protect her rear.

A sweeping, fist-wide blast of green energy from her left hand knocked back two ghouls. She ran at the third, shouted, "Morere," and aimed a slashing stroke at its head. Her sword pierced its shielding but only opened a shallow gash.

Still, the ghoul reeled away, out of the fight for now.

The other two split up, one to her left and one to her right. She blasted them both.

Wheeling toward the one who'd gotten the milder bolt, the one from her bare hand, she sensed the crackle of magic energy.

Spaced out on each side of the road and a few dozen yards to the east, three more ghoul shields flared into view.

Shit. Tasha swallowed against gut-wrenching panic. She couldn't take this many. Especially not with the injuries she already bore.

The traitor materialized in front of her, a drawn claymore held upright before him. Silver mage power reflected off his rugged face and dark hair, and she recognized him from Griff's sketch. He'd been part of the attack on Will and Audra last year.

Disgust drove out fear. Tasha pulled power from the woods.

If she died here, she was taking this bastard with her.

Grim-faced, he thrust his blade at her. Tasha sidestepped, batting it away, and sliced below it.

Miraculously, he recovered in time to block. He pivoted into a kick. It slammed into her hip, and she stumbled backward, to the brink of the ditch.

Ghouls flanked her, but they weren't attacking. Leaving her to him.

Fucking traitor bastard.

He knocked her blade aside, blocking it with his, and stepped in to grab her shoulder with his free hand. His energy melded with her shields, and they...winked out?

The other ghouls closed in. Talons raked her back and dug into her arms. Venom slid its icy poison into her veins.

Tasha screamed. Her knees crumpled, only the taloned grips of her attackers holding her up. The saber fell from her shaking fingers.

The mage caught her jaw in his hand, and she couldn't draw power. What was he doing? His brown eyes raked over her with disdain. "You're beaten. Surrender."

So they could make her a breeder? Or a snack? "Fuck you."

"That can be arr—"

An engine roared to her right. Headlights cut through the night. The ghouls shot bolts of muddy yellow energy at the low-slung, red car, but its blue aura deflected them.

Exultation roared in Tasha's veins. She wrenched free of the distracted ghouls. Agony blazed along her arms as the talons tore loose, but she shielded again as she dived for her saber.

Mage power shot over her head, fist-wide bolts of blue energy slamming into the ghouls who'd flanked her. They stumbled.

The traitor mage wheeled to face the threat. Gaining her knees, Tasha pulled power from the woods and poured it through her blade at his scuzzball back.

He staggered.

Oh, yeah. Combined power drain and pain had blackness licking at the edges of her vision, but she blasted him again.

A flare of blue lit the night on the other side of the truck. A rough ghoul cry mingled with a man's shout of "morere," and Tasha grinned.

But the ghouls were recovering. She blasted one, and black spots danced in front of her eyes.

Recharging, she bore down and blasted the other.

A man's shape, visible in the blue glow of his broadsword, came around the truck. The ghouls charged him.

Except for the one that reached for her. Hell, no, she wasn't turning hostage. Tasha put everything she could muster behind a groin thrust and shouted, "Morere."

The strike connected. The ghoul fell.

But the world spun. The newcomer's flashing blade blurred.

Somewhere, a voice shouted, "Go, go, go!"

Mage energy washed over her open senses. Blinking, trying to focus, Tasha forced her blade up.

"Hey. Easy," a man's voice said.

Familiar, but who?

"I'm on your side, so—Tasha?"

Her rescuer knelt a few feet away and held his blue-glowing blade near his face. Tasha's heart jumped in the instant before chagrin took over.

She'd been saved by Carter Lockwood.

CHAPTER TWO

"UH, HI." CARTER'S DEEP VOICE GENERATED UNWELCOME HEAT deep within her. He stood, offering a hand. "We should get out of the road in case they come back. Can you stand?"

"Thanks for the save, and yeah. I can." Damn if she was letting him carry her, but she wasn't too proud or too stupid to grip his hand. The shivers inside her when she touched him were probably coincidental, likely from venom sickness.

He tugged her upright. The blackness threatened her vision again, but she stayed on her feet. Was the world tilting?

"Whoa. Need a sec," she said.

"We might not have it. Hold on to me, and we'll walk to my car, nice and easy. Your truck's front is bashed in. It's not drivable."

"I figured." The ghoul retreat could've been a ploy, a way to buy time and regroup. Tasha gripped Carter's bent arm, her fingers in the crook of his elbow below the hard curve of his biceps. The warmth of his skin came through his long-sleeved T-shirt.

Geez, Tasha. What kind of idiot notices things like that at a time like this?

Swallowing a scowl, she leaned on him as they walked

18

around her truck and past ghoul corpses. Embarrassing, but less so than keeling over and having him pick her up.

Mages who'd fought together traditionally embraced afterward, sharing energy to bolster each other's power. But that would be beyond awkward for him and her. Lockwood earned major tact points for not suggesting it.

"You kicked ass," he said, glancing at the bodies in the road. "With a little better odds, you wouldn't have needed me."

She acknowledged the compliment with a nod. "Appreciate it, though." Owing him for anything lodged in her throat like a boulder, but fair was fair. A wave of nausea rolled through her. Tasha swallowed hard against it.

"Hey, I'm just glad I was close enough to reach you. Still, that's damn impressive for a civilian."

Griff and his second-in-command, Will Davis, had drilled everyone on their little squad to lethal levels. Even their team medic, mage physician Stefan Harper. Attacking a ghoul nest with any less proficiency was suicidal.

That wasn't Carter's business, though.

The red sports car stood a few yards ahead, its engine idling and its driver-side door open.

Tasha shook her head. "Should've known...you...would drive a penis car."

As soon as the words were out, she realized how ungrateful, even insulting, they were, and she groaned. "Sorry. That...didn't mean it...the way it sounded."

"No sweat." He flashed her a grin. "I took it as a compliment to my manhood."

Nice comeback. The last thing she needed was a reason to warm to him, but Tasha mustered a grateful smile. The world was still not quite in focus. She drew more power, and her vision steadied, but her wounds burned.

Opening the passenger door, he said, "Watch your head" and steadied her with a hand at her elbow as she sank onto the low, gray seat. She propped her saber against the doorframe within easy reach. The ammonia stink of dead ghouls wasn't as strong over here.

Headlights to the east split the darkness. The car stopped about thirty yards away. A moment later, the radio crackled.

"Carter, I think I see your red bullet," a man's deep voice said. "Over."

Grinning, Carter reached past her and grabbed the radio. "Roger that, Roland. No imminent threat, but we need to clear the scene and get someone to the infirmary. Come on in."

A black Dodge Charger rolled up. Mundane eyes would see only the car, but mageborn ones would pierce its surrounding glamour and see the white, eight-pointed star with Deputy Reeve printed across it on the front door and the narrow, green light bar on its roof.

A six-foot guy built like a linebacker emerged. As he surveyed the scene, he rubbed his hand over his blond buzz cut and whistled.

Fighting nausea, Tasha mustered a weak smile for Deputy Wade. Along with Carter, he'd been part of the battle to protect that archaeological dig.

"I got backup rolling," he said. His glance ran over her. "Damn, Tasha."

"Yeah," she muttered.

Carter patted her knee, sending an unwelcome flash of heat to her core. "Sit tight while we make sure they're all dead. Then I'll get the kit. Soon as we finish this and Roland's backup arrives, we're out of here. If the ghouls come back before then, you stay in the car. I'll shield it."

In no shape to do much else, Tasha nodded.

Carter and Roland made sure all the remaining ghouls were dead. Then Roland started stacking bodies to burn. Weary as Tasha was, she still caught the wash of the two men's extended senses. They were staying alert for ghouls to return.

Carter walked back to her. "The ghouls translocated out."

"All?" Her gaze locked with his grim, gray one.

"The living ones, yeah."

No wonder he looked so dismayed. Ghouls couldn't translocate, so the mage traitor must've shifted them out with him. Translocating something you weren't touching took far more power than translocating yourself. Shifting yourself and three ghouls...

Tasha grimaced. "His . . . power must be off . . . the scale."

"So it seems." Carter scowled. "Let me get the first-aid kit out of the trunk. It's easier if I work on you with this door open, but we'll shut it at the first sign of trouble."

While he walked around the car, Tasha tried to pull her muddled brain together. When Carter returned with a big, red first-aid kit in hand, she told him, "There's something else.... He grabbed me. My . . . shield just died. I've never . . . heard of that."

"Me neither, but . . ." he said slowly, his gaze losing focus.

"What?" she asked.

"In the fight at the farmhouse—Davis said a section of the ward around the property suddenly just dropped. Then a mage who looked like the one here tonight waltzed through it. At the time, we figured it was overtaxed, but maybe not."

"All we need is a foe who can . . . walk through a ward."

Before Griff lost his magic, he'd been able to attune it to a ward and slide through it, but it wasn't easy. Killing the ward would be even more difficult.

"I'll put all this in my report, but we can worry about that later. For now, let's get you fixed up."

Another deputy reeve in a black Charger rolled up. A woman Tasha didn't know climbed out. With a nod at Carter, she went to help Roland.

Carter knelt in front of Tasha and balanced the first-aid kit on one knee. "I'm sorry, but we're going to have to lose your shirt. I have a blanket you can wrap around you when we're done."

Tasha bit back a curse. This just kept getting better.

He was right, though. Besides, things could be worse. She could be dead.

She reached for the shirt's hem, pulled upward, and sent pain flashing through her back, shoulders, and arms. A choked groan escaped her.

"Wait." Carter touched her hand—gently and for only a second, but her pulse kicked again. "It's ruined anyway. I can cut it off if that's easier for you."

Tasha nodded. "Thanks."

He made mercifully short work of the job, and his brisk efficiency eased the awkwardness of being shirtless in front of him.

"I have poultices to draw the venom," he told her, ripping one open. "They need about ten minutes to work. Won't draw it all, but they'll pull enough to make the ride to the Collegium infirmary less miserable. Then I'll bandage the wounds and we'll roll."

Everything he said was sensible, but the little quivers inside her from the idea of having his hands on her made it seriously unwise. All that venom must be screwing with her common sense.

"I can . . . make it to the infirmary," she said. It was probably an hour and a half from here.

Carter shrugged, his face expressionless. "Standard procedure. It won't take long, but it's your call."

If she refused, he would think she didn't trust him. He didn't deserve that.

"Go ahead," she said. Maybe the darkness would hide the heat rushing to her cheeks.

"This'll sting," he warned, but his power flowing over her skin, stopping the bleeding, cleansing the blood and venom, felt soothing.

Carefully, he applied the first poultice to the four gouges on her right inner arm. Venom sliding from the wounds burned. Tasha hissed.

With a muttered *sorry*, she set her jaw.

"You're doing great."

He tended her other arm wounds. With a poultice in his hand, he paused, then looked up at her. "Your back's bad, but the gashes on your chest look deeper. We should probably do those next. When we come to the lower gash, I'm going to lay this over the wound in the center. Since I'm not a doctor, though, I think it's best if you smooth it down under your bra."

Across her breast, he meant. The thought of his hands there should not be appealing in any way, let alone make her feel fidgety. Tasha kept her face bland with an effort. "Right."

On top of his nick-of-time-rescue points, he'd earned another one for chivalry.

While he worked, she tried to ignore him, to think about something else. Too bad her uncooperative memory kept focusing on him. On how he'd always been generous with praise, verbal and written, while holding the sailors he commanded to exacting standards.

He'd been an approachable, capable company commander. Despite the mutual attraction they had to ignore, they'd gotten along well until she'd stupidly used leftover supplies to repair a school, not knowing they were earmarked for a local strongman. Lockwood had uncovered the problem and, responsibly, reported it. The camaraderie between them had disintegrated.

"Okay," he said. "I'll grab that blanket and then do the bandages. We'll get your stuff out of your truck too." He patted her hand this time, sending heat zinging up her arm and down into her core.

Her nipples tightened. At least he'd turned away and wouldn't see.

Tasha swallowed a groan. An hour and a half in the car with him suddenly seemed like a torturous eternity.

～

Touching Tasha had been a mistake, but what choice had there been? Her wounds had needed tending.

Carter glanced sideways at her. Sitting gingerly away from the seat back, she stared out the window.

The sight of her elegant profile, the straight nose, determined chin, and generous mouth, stirred soft warmth in the middle of his chest and lower. Her boy-short, auburn hair was sweat-matted and tousled, and her blue eyes looked pain-fogged in her pinched face. She had to be in considerable pain.

Fury tightened his hands on the wheel. Ghouls were bad enough, but traitor mages . . . The torments of every mythical hell were too mild to pay them back.

Anyway, her wounds had needed treating, and he'd be damned before anyone else put hands on—

Whoa. Where had that come from?

Who touched her or didn't was not his business. Was way outside the realm of anything that even remotely resembled his business. He and Tasha weren't even friends. Never really had been.

And yet . . .

His jaw tightened. She'd been under his command, and he looked out for his own. Whether or not they wanted him to.

And maybe he still felt bad about the way things had worked out, even though he'd had no acceptable alternative.

Anyway, she was a civilian now, and that made him and every other deputy reeve responsible for her safety. That was probably why seeing those gashes on her chest and back, the gouges on her arms where she'd pulled away from piercing talons, had sent icy rage rolling through him. He'd managed to throttle it back to a simmer while he tended her, but it blazed again now.

Once he handed her off to the docs, he was going to the gym in reeve country, as the deputy reeves called their part of the Collegium, and pounding the shit out of something.

Music blared from her bag on the floor, something with

brass and drums.

"Hell," she muttered. Carefully, she reached for it.

"I got it." Watching the road, he grabbed the oversized, tan leather tote and set it on her knees.

With a nod to him, Tasha fished out a phone and swiped the screen. "I'm fine, Nate."

Nate? Who the hell was—

"Yes, really," she insisted.

Unless the guy was stupid, he had to hear the stress under her cheery tone.

"A run-in . . . with ghouls."

If she was using that word, Nate Whoever must be cleared to know about the mage world, or else was part of it.

The guy's words were indistinguishable, but his outraged tone came through. *Welcome to the club, buddy*, Carter thought as Tasha winced and held the phone away from her ear.

"I didn't call you because . . . nothing you can do from . . . wherever in South America . . . you are."

More outrage, and then she said, "I've had first aid. I'm on . . . the way to the Collegium infirmary…with a deputy reeve."

The outrage dropped to a rumble. Tasha rolled her eyes. "Yes, really and truly. No, you don't need to come. What . . . are we, twelve?"

With a sigh, she held the phone out to Carter. "He wants to talk to you."

That the guy wouldn't take her word for being okay said a lot about her, but Carter would worry about that later. Trying not to resent this Nate for knowing her so well, he took the phone.

"Sorry," Tasha said, wrinkling her nose.

"It's okay." Into the phone, he said, "Lockwood."

"Hey. Please identify yourself."

Blunt and straightforward. Maybe military?

"I'm Southeast Deputy Shire Reeve Carter Lockwood, badge number 87693. To whom am I speaking?"

"Good to meet you. I'm Nate Murdock. The bullheaded woman riding with you is my twin."

As Carter swallowed a completely irrational wave of relief, Nate continued, "What's her real status?"

"She gave you the high points. She has five venomous slashes across her back, one of them pretty deep. The three on her chest are worse. Four gouges on each arm."

Murdock didn't need to hear that she was periodically shivering from the venom in her system. Besides, he would assume that if he understood the effects of ghoul venom.

"Fucking bastards."

"Yeah, pretty much. Despite all that, your sister kicked ass. Faced off against ten ghouls and killed four before I got there. If they hadn't had quite so many ghouls and a traitor mage along, she might've nailed them all."

He'd forgotten that while he was working on her. The fact she'd done so signaled serious battle experience, as did her capable help in safeguarding Will Davis's archaeological dig last November. Carter would bet he knew where she got that training.

"She never does anything halfway," Nate commented. "So you're headed for the Collegium?"

The Collegium was the mages' headquarters. As the regional, or shire, center for mage government, law enforcement, magical studies, and archives, it was a hub of activity, but Mundanes knew it as the Georgia Institute for Paranormal Research.

"They're expecting us," Carter replied. "A night in the infirmary, and she should be as good as new."

A brief silence, and then, "Thanks. I mean it. Thanks for looking out for her."

"It's what we do. I'm giving her the phone back." He passed it to Tasha.

Affection warmed her voice as she said, "Satisfied? Call you in . . . the morning. No. Nothing you can do." After a short exchange, she and her brother signed off. She dropped her phone back into her purse.

Carter snagged the bag before she could and put it back on the floor by her feet. "I'd forgotten you had a twin."

"We didn't exactly . . . keep in touch."

The reasons they hadn't surged to the fore. The silence in the car grew tense.

Tasha cleared her throat. "He was an Army Ranger. Now . . . does extractions from . . . nasty places."

"Tough work."

"He's good at it." Pride rang in her voice.

Being jealous of her brother was another dunce move. Pushing down the idiotic feeling, Carter said, "Weird that he happened to call now."

"Not really." She sighed and rubbed her forehead. "It's a twin thing. We . . . always know when the other one . . . is hurt. He would've . . . called sooner, but was . . . in the middle of something."

"I'm glad he made it out okay."

"Me too."

"Speaking of making it out," he said, watching her from the corner of his eye, "the average mage would've been dead long before I got there tonight. On top of that, I remember you held your own in the battle in the swamp last November. So I guess everything I've heard about Dare's covert ops team is justified."

Shivering, she clutched the blanket tighter. "Sorry, what?"

"You know what I mean. You have no official training, but you're on the front line whenever one of your friends is threatened. And you're damn good. That means an expert trained you. One like, say, Griffin Dare. After the battle in the swamp, I watched the video of his trial. When that bastard traitor challenged him, you were one of the first to rush down from the seats and stand with him."

If Carter had envied the loyalty she gave Dare, that was his secret. "The reports he turned in to the shire reeve's office about his covert ops didn't name anyone but Will Davis and Stefan Harper, but it's obvious you were in that group."

The edgy crowd, like the kids he'd secretly envied in high school. Being student body president, basketball team captain, and an honor society member did him no good with those kids. He'd always suspected they had more fun than he did, and raiding ghoul nests when the shire reeve's office was hamstrung by traitors would've been definite fun despite the risks involved.

Her stare seemed to bore into him. After a long moment, she relaxed. "That was Griff's choice. Not everybody wanted to welcome him . . . back into the mage fold, and he doesn't want . . . anyone who supported him in his years on the run . . . catching flak. Will and Stefan wouldn't have . . . been named either, but they had access . . . to the reports before they went in."

Considering that Davis was the Collegium's Assistant Loremaster—known to the world at large as the assistant archivist—and Harper was its chief physician, Carter could see why Dare had worried about fallout. But his friends—also the ones most likely to be in it with him early—hadn't cared.

That kind of loyalty was rare.

"Those reports," he said, "describe some pretty impressive raids."

Tasha shrugged, then winced. "Somebody had to do it. . . . Shire reeve's office wasn't."

"I hope we are now," Carter said.

The shire reeve at the time, Valeria Banning, had thrown her lot in with Dare after he rescued her from ghouls and proved her department had a rotten core. Now they were married, and she headed a task force to keep traitor mages out of the Collegium. Griff, also a former shire reeve, was her top deputy.

"Same here." Tasha shifted in her seat. "How's . . . your family?"

"Not much changes." He flashed her a grin. "My sister just

had her third baby, a girl. My dad threatens to retire but never does, and my mom can always find a new committee to serve on."

"Sounds nice."

He made a noncommittal noise. That *nice* life could also be suffocating. And it, too, came with a price. "Your folks?"

"Some old same old," she said, her voice wry under the pain.

That sounded like a deflection. Maybe it was best to return to business. "I'll type up a report based on what you told me and have it ready at the front desk in reeve country tomorrow morning. You can make any changes and then sign it. There's no need for you to mess with that tonight."

"Appreciate it." Tasha cast a wary glance his way. "I'm still in touch with . . . some of the guys. Are you?"

"Some." Odd that she'd want to rake up the past. Unless maybe she was trying to smooth it over. But that encounter last fall had taught him not to hope. "Did you know Chalmers got married again? Seems to be working this time."

"I did. It's good. His divorce...hit him hard." Tasha shook her head. "Carter..."

"Yeah?"

She hesitated. "Nothing. . . . I need to call Lorelei."

"The Lorelei who also helped out at Davis's project last fall?"

"Yes. I was on the phone with her when...ghouls struck. She'll worry...until she hears."

"Sure." He grabbed her bag for her again.

They'd already passed the outlying buildings of Kingsland and were almost to the interstate. "Won't be long once we hit the highway," he commented.

He was more than ready to turn her over to the doctors. Maybe he was a chicken as well as a dunce, but he felt entirely too aware of her over there. Too focused on her. The sooner they could go back to their usual polite distance, the better.

CHAPTER THREE

At last, the headlights caught pillars of gray stone, the Collegium gateway. Wrought iron letters in the arch over it read, Georgia Institute for Paranormal Research, the name the Collegium used in the Mundane world. Tasha welcomed the sight. Not long now until she could escape this car and her feeling of obligation to Carter.

Not to mention the disquieting, continual awareness of him sitting there. So he was a good-looking guy. So what? Lots of guys were, ones whose pasts did not intersect with hers in painful ways.

Carter turned in between the pillars and braked. A tall, sturdy-looking woman stepped out of the hut on the left. Her khaki trousers and brown jacket, with an eight-pointed star on the left chest, marked her as a deputy reeve.

Carter rolled down his window. "Hey, Nell."

"Hey, Carter." Brown-haired and thirtyish, she peered inside and nodded at Tasha.

Magic rolled through the car. Tasha cast Carter a questioning glance. He answered with a tiny headshake.

"You're clear," Nell said and stepped back.

"Thanks. How about buzzing the infirmary and letting them

know we're here? They're expecting us."

"Will do. Good night, y'all."

Carter headed down the drive. It curved through a stand of palmetto trees mixed with Spanish moss-festooned live oaks. As the car emerged from the trees, the main building came into view. Four stories tall, it had lights in the forward-jutting end wings that were staff and student quarters and in the central door that opened onto the main lobby.

"Since the attack last fall," he said, "we magically scan every arrival."

It was a sad commentary that even cars driven by deputy reeves needed checking. But traitor mages could glamour themselves to look like anyone. And last summer's exposed traitor had been in a position of trust. So the magical check made sense.

Carter swung left, toward the main parking lot, but drove through it to the boxy, four-story infirmary. He stopped beside double glass doors on the ground level. The doors slid open. A woman in green scrubs pushed a wheelchair toward the car.

"I can walk," Tasha said, but Carter was climbing out of the car.

He stuck his head in as the woman opened Tasha's door. "Venom wounds take a lot out of you—as I think you know—so humor us, okay?"

"I'm Susan Wells," the woman said, smiling. "If you'll have a seat, Ms. Murdock."

Tasha slid to the edge of the bucket seat. When she stood, her knees wouldn't lock. Carter and the nurse each caught an elbow. Nurse Wells steadied the chair, and Carter helped Tasha into it.

Her cheeks burned with embarrassment, but at least no one she really knew would see her like this. Except maybe Stefan, if he was on duty tonight, and he'd seen others in worse shape.

Without comment, Carter snagged her saber from behind the seat.

"Thanks again," she told him, "but don't . . . let me keep you."

"I'll see you settled. Anyone you need to me to call? Anything I can get you?"

"No, thanks." She glanced up at him as they entered the building. "If you…wait a minute, I'll…give your blanket back."

They turned left into what looked like a waiting room. Inside an open pair of double doors at the far end stood a narrow desk and computer terminal. Beyond them lay a brightly lit area lined on each side with blue-curtained booths. Various rolling stands and monitors stood against the end wall.

"This is as far as you go, Deputy Lockwood," the nurse said. "I'll bring the blanket out to you in a minute."

He nodded. "Good luck, Tasha."

She thanked him again. He passed her the saber before turning away. For a moment, she had an insane desire to call him back.

Resolutely, she turned her attention to the narrow bed in the curtained booth before her. But the image of his lean hips and taut butt in faded denim taunted her.

Great. Just great. Venom was affecting her judgment.

The nurse helped her onto the bed and into a gown. "Dr. Cooper's on duty," she informed Tasha. "He'll be in shortly. Meanwhile, I'm going to check your dressings."

"Okay."

Regret shadowed Ms. Wells's eyes and softened her voice. "Sorry, but it's going to hurt."

"I figured. But…thanks for the warning." At least pain would distract her attention from a guy who could have no real interest in her.

No matter what kind of purely hormonal reaction he aroused.

~

As PROMISED, an hour of having the venom magically drawn out and the wounds healed was not fun. Tasha gave herself a point for stoic silence.

"All done," Dr. Alex Cooper finally said. With that handsome face, golden-brown hair and hazel eyes, he could have qualified to be a cover model if he hadn't chosen medicine instead. But Tasha kept thinking of chestnut hair and gray eyes.

"We'll keep you overnight," he said, "as you're probably about done in by now. Barring any unforeseen complications, you can go home in the morning. It would be better to take it easy tomorrow if you can."

"That's doable. Thanks, doctor."

"All part of the service," he replied, echoing something Stefan Harper often said. "Nurse Wells will wheel you up to a room."

The nurse pushed through the curtains almost immediately. "Let's get you to bed, Ms. Murdock." She set Tasha's saber across the bed's foot and deposited the plastic bag with her tote and remaining clothes by Tasha's knees. "You've had a long day."

Something clicked near the floor, and then the nurse wheeled the bed out of the curtained booth. By now, Tasha was too tired to care about looking feeble.

They rolled out of the ER and into the waiting area. She was zoning out when a familiar voice said, "There she is."

Forcing her eyes open, she saw Will Davis fall into step beside the gurney. His streaky blond-and-brown hair looked no more disheveled than usual, and his beard scruff was about normal thickness. His arctic blue eyes, though, were dark with concern.

He covered her hand with his. "You okay, *amica*?"

Tasha smiled at the Latin feminine form of *friend*, his special nickname for the women who were closest to him. "Better than the ghouls," she replied.

"Damn straight."

"How did you know I was here?"

"Carter called me. Thought you might like to see a friend at the end of a hellish day."

Now she had to give Carter another thoughtfulness point. He was really piling them up. Damn it, she did not want to like him.

"Anything I can do for you?" Will asked.

"I'm good, thanks. I talked to Lorelei on the way here. She's bringing me some clothes in the morning." The main thing Tasha needed right now was sleep. But she'd promised to call her friend again once she was in a room in the well-protected Collegium and, in Lorelei's view, absolutely safe at last.

They swung into the elevator. Pushing the button, Nurse Wells turned a stern look on Will. "It's not visiting hours, so once we reach the room, you're out of here."

He grinned at her. "Got it. Even I can see Tasha needs her sleep."

With a gentle squeeze of Tasha's fingers, he said, "I'll be back in the morning. If you think of anything, give me a shout."

"Right. Thanks." His position as assistant loremaster rated an apartment in the main building, so coming back wouldn't inconvenience him. Though it was anyone's guess how long he would stay there, now that he and Audra Grayson, the archaeologist he'd met last fall, were serious.

Tasha stifled a sigh. Everyone seemed to be pairing up these days. If a confirmed, determined player like Will could fall, anyone could.

Carter's face flashed into her mind, and she scowled. *Idiot.*

"Okay?" Will asked.

"Yeah, just . . . this is going to blow a hole in my schedule."

The elevator stopped, and the nurse wheeled her out.

"You know," Will said, "I can drive a nail if you need another hammer."

"Yeah. Thanks. But it's mainly client meetings, and no one

else can do those." She needed those people's business. Nothing she could do about it now, though.

At the door of a room, Nurse Wells turned to Will. "Good night, Dr. Davis."

"Good night," he said cheerfully. "Take care of my friend. Amica, see you in the morning." He kissed Tasha's forehead and sauntered down the hall.

Switching Tasha to the bed in the room took only a few minutes. As the door closed behind the nurse, Tasha picked up her phone and summoned the last dregs of her energy. Lorelei worried more than she had before Ken's death. Reassurance was the order of the day.

Tasha tapped her friend's number. Lorelei answered immediately.

"How are you?"

"Alive and more or less well." Trying for humor, Tasha added, "Wish I could say the same for my truck."

"You're sure?"

"Yes. It was dicey for a bit, but the deputies got there in time. Thanks for making that call."

"I'm glad I could help, and I'll see you in the morning. Eight thirty okay?"

"Should be fine. Thanks, Lorelei. You'll be a lot more comfortable company than on the trip in."

Tasha winced. *Idiot.* Fatigue had let her mouth run away with her.

"What do you mean? Don't tell me the deputy reeves weren't cooperative. If they—"

"They were fine. He was. Lockwood."

A moment of silence, then, "As in Carter Lockwood?"

"Um. He was the closest deputy."

"I see. Y'know, if there were nothing to tell, you wouldn't have mentioned it. So be prepared to spill in the morning."

"Not much to spill." Or there wouldn't be by the time she had some rest and regained her perspective. "But okay."

She and Lorelei signed off, and Tasha turned out her light. Snuggling down in the bed felt better than anything had in a long time. Surely rest would do the trick.

Yet she couldn't help contrasting Carter's kind, almost friendly attitude with the way he'd been the last time they'd been alone together. The day he discovered her unauthorized use of leftover supplies in Bangladesh was burned into her memory.

Summoned into his office, she'd stood at attention. He hadn't said to stand at ease. The stiff posture kept her from seeing his face, but she'd glimpsed it on her way in. His eyes, which could be soft as morning fog when he was thoughtful or bright as a new coin when he was amused or intrigued by something, were granite, his face equally stony.

"I've never been as disappointed in a sailor as I am in you, Murdock," he stated.

She listened with a sinking feeling that turned into sick gut knots as he detailed his findings in a cold, emotionless tone.

He concluded, "This has created a political shitstorm. I never thought you were so damn stupid."

The words had burned themselves into her brain, his opinion more searing than any threat of punishment.

When she'd tried to argue that the girls' school was more important than a single room in the local strongman's compound, which she hadn't known about anyway, he'd told her in a flat, disgusted voice, "That decision isn't for people at either of our pay grades." Shaking his head, he'd muttered, "unbelievably stupid" and dismissed her.

He couldn't have been more different tonight. He'd been almost like the old Lt. Lockwood, considerate and supportive.

Of course, he didn't have to work with her now. Wasn't responsible for her. He could afford to be kind in these circumstances.

Carter had done his job. Just as he'd done it when he'd ruined her career, as she'd believed he'd done back then. Over time she'd come to realize she'd been wrong, that her choices had ruined her career, and he'd only done his duty.

Tonight, he'd been polite and professional, no more.

So by morning, she would have him back in his proper place, someone she once knew and occasionally, casually, met. That was all.

"SPILL." Looking expectant, Lorelei swung the gray backpack she carried onto the visitor chair. The petite brunette set her big, blue tote on the floor next to the chair with a faint *clunk*.

Standing five three without spike heels, blessed with a tip-tilted nose and generous mouth, she looked like most people's idea of a pixie. But most people didn't know pixies, before they died out centuries ago, had definitely inhuman features.

Tasha smiled and gestured to the bag. "Got your crossbow in there?"

"You know it." Blue eyes intent, Lorelei perched on the edge of Tasha's bed. "What happened between you and Carter last night?"

"Aside from his saving my butt, nothing."

"Uh-huh. You don't usually mention him."

"I'm not usually around him." Her disappointment that he hadn't checked on her this morning was a warning sign. Danger could bond people. Where he and she were concerned, better to nip it in the bud.

Lorelei made a rude noise in her throat. "We were around him every day for over a week in November when we were guarding Will and Audra and their excavation. You mostly pretended he wasn't there."

"It's harder to do that after someone saves your life. Which was mortifying in its own right."

"Why?" Lorelei cocked her head, her sleek, brown bob

37

swinging with the movement. "He's a deputy reeve. It's his job."

Tasha studied her friend. Maybe if she talked to someone, she could stop thinking about him all the time.

"There's more to it than I told you, about him and me and the navy, I mean."

"I figured."

When Tasha raised her eyebrows, Lorelei grinned. "You told me the two of you served together and clashed just before you got out. That wasn't enough to explain why, on the rare occasions you both were in the same room for more than ten seconds, I noticed him watching you. When you weren't watching him, and don't try to tell me you didn't."

Tasha grimaced. "I hoped no one noticed."

"I wouldn't put money on my being the only one who did."

"No." Tasha rubbed her hands over her face. "There was always this...zing between him and me. We couldn't do anything about it, though, because he was my CO."

"So it sort of hovered there in the background."

"That's a great way to put it. In my early days in the unit, he often corrected the way I was doing things—in a constructive way, but I started to see him as my nemesis. Then I realized he only made suggestions to those of us relatively inexperienced with construction, and never to the slackers. I took his input as a mark of approval."

"Sounds like it."

That had been a good feeling. While it lasted.

Tasha blew out a breath. "Anyway, I had a tendency to skate around some of the less reasonable bits of navy regs. The final time, I sort of commandeered some leftover supplies to repair a girls' school. But that took the materials away from a relatively minor repair for the local grand pooh-bah, who was not pleased. He made a stink, a big one. Lockwood figured it out."

"He reported you. Became your nemesis again."

"In a nutshell." Tasha ran her hand through her bangs. Just

thinking about this brought back the embarrassment she'd felt. "At the time, I blamed him. Thought he should've covered for me. After all, this was a much worthier cause."

"You don't blame him now?" Lorelei asked.

Tasha sighed. "Let's just say I grew up. I realized not reporting what he'd found would put his career on the line, maybe even reflect on our company."

"What happened to you? Did you have a court martial?"

Tasha shook her head. "Captain's mast. Nonjudicial punishment. In the end, I got busted." Even after all this time, the words tasted bitter. "I was a petty officer second class, so my job rating and rank, combined, made me a builder second class. Had it in mind to make chief petty officer one day. I was taking online courses to get a college degree and improve my chances to qualify. Instead, I dropped back down to third class. The competition for promotion is fierce in today's leaner, meaner navy. I knew then I'd never make chief."

She also hadn't wanted to spend any more time around Carter. Or the other sailors who could've suffered for her choices. But especially not around him.

"I didn't re-up when the time came," she concluded.

"So being around him is awkward." Lorelei nodded. "That's understandable."

With a shrug, Tasha said, "Two things still rankle. First, that damn zing is still there whenever he's around. Second, maybe harder to get over, was his attitude. He didn't even seem particularly sorry for what he had to do. I guess he figured I didn't deserve his concern. Hell, maybe I didn't. He was just so cold, even when I explained why I'd done it. So having him be the one to save my ass last night really burns."

What still burned more, even after all these years, was the knowledge she'd disappointed him. Lost his respect. Only when it was gone had she realized how much she valued it.

Lorelei opened her mouth, but a knock on the door forestalled her.

"Come in," Tasha called.

Will pushed open the door and grinned. "Hey, y'all. Look who I found wandering the halls."

Behind him came Griffin and Valeria Dare. They were both tall, Griff a couple of inches over six feet and Val about five eight. His black hair and blue eyes were a striking contrast to her tawny hair and hazel eyes, but they wore matching expressions of concern.

"Thought we'd see if you were back to ass-kicking condition this morning," Griff said.

"Test me and see," Tasha replied.

Griff smiled. "You sound like yourself. So give me a hug."

After greetings had been exchanged all around, an awkward silence fell. Griff, Val, and Will seemed to be trading *Who goes first?* looks.

"What's going on?" Tasha asked.

Val said, "I looked at the draft of your statement about last night and at Carter's report. It said there were ten ghouls, total, there as well as the mage."

As director of the task force on traitor mages, she was also a deputy reeve and so would have access to the records.

"That's right," Tasha said.

Val looked at Griff before she said, "Ghouls don't hunt in packs that big except for two reasons. They're either planning to capture a mage or they're looking to grab several Mundanes."

"Killing a mage is easier than capturing one," Griff put in.

A chill ran down Tasha's back. "South End Road is an odd place for either one of those things. It doesn't get a lot of traffic during the day. Has even less at night."

Lorelei wore a worried frown. Tasha looked from Griff to Val to Will, all of whom had grim expressions.

"You think I was targeted," she said slowly.

Will responded, "We're about as sure of it as we can be without a prisoner to interrogate. So, amica, what do the ghouls want from you?"

CHAPTER FOUR

AT THE REAR OF THE MAIN COLLEGIUM BUILDING, IN THE GROUND-floor complex known as reeve country, Carter was also wondering why ghouls would target Tasha.

"She builds houses or office blocks and decorates them," he told Deke Jones, the Southeast Shire Reeve. "What about that would draw ghoul interest?"

The two men sat in Deke's office, Deke on the battered leather sofa and Carter in an armchair by it. Each had a mug of coffee that'd grown cold while they puzzled over the problem.

A worried frown twisted Deke's dark brown face. "Maybe they need someone else to build their nests. Somebody's gotta put up their housing and their breeding sheds, but kidnapping a Mundane builder would be easier."

"Yeah." Ghouls always took the path of least resistance.

Carter shook his head. "Somebody needs to talk to her about this—see if she knows why they would target her."

He was not going to be that somebody. Natasha Murdock had been on his mind way too much lately. The best method for getting her off it was to step away.

"Still," Deke said, "a big pack of ghouls and a mage on a road as deserted as that one...they had to be hunting her."

"You get no argument from me." Frowning, Carter sipped cold coffee. "If we have somebody in Savannah drive by her shop and home, maybe—"

Deke's desk phone buzzed. He stepped around Carter and grabbed it. "Yes, Ron... Yeah, just a minute."

Turning to Carter, he held out the handset. "It's for you. Guy in the garage where you had Ms. Murdock's truck towed."

"If he's calling me instead of her, that can't be good." Carter leaned over for the phone. "Hey, Dave. Let me put you on speaker so the shire reeve can hear, too." Carter punched the button, laid down the handset, and asked, "What's up?"

"Weirdest damn thing, Carter. I went out a few minutes ago and saw a guy messin' around that truck we brought in last night. I was about to ask could I help him when he just up and vanished. Like he translocated."

There were advantages to having a mageborn mechanic. A Mundane would wonder whether he'd seen anyone at all. "Do you think he spotted you, Dave?"

"I dunno. Mighta heard the office door shut behind me."

"Well, you're right. It's weird."

"Gets weirder. That made me uneasy, so I checked the truck over. Found this little round thing under the back bumper. Looks like one of them trackers they use on TV."

Carter exchanged a grim look with Deke. "Can you take a photo of it and text it to me? You have my phone number, right?"

"Yeah. I called, but you didn't pick up. Then I tried the office."

"I had it on silent because I'm with the shire reeve."

"Okay. Hang on." A moment later, Dave added, "Sent the photo."

Carter pulled out his phone. Holding the phone so Deke could see, he checked the newly arrived text, then enlarged the photo.

"Damn," Deke said.

"It's a tracker, Dave," Carter said, "like you thought. Do you think you could identify the mage who put it there if you saw him again?"

"Might could."

"Stand by. Shire Reeve, do we have that sketch of Dare's from last November?" Griff Dare, who was a successful artist when he wasn't chasing ghouls, had spotted a traitor mage watching the farmhouse that was the archaeology team's headquarters. His sketch of Ross Graham, an Inverness mage who'd done some jobs for the North Sea Collegium before mysteriously dropping off the grid, had been as good as a photo.

Deke stepped behind his desk and called up the file. "Sending it to your email, Carter."

"Roger. Dave, I'm texting it to you. Stand by."

The operation took a couple of minutes.

"Got it," the mechanic said. A moment later, he whistled. "That's the guy. Damn, that's a good likeness."

"It pays to have a witness who's an actual artist."

"So what do you want me to do with this thing, Carter? Should I stomp on it?"

Judging by his enthusiastic tone, Dave liked that idea a lot. Carter grinned at Deke, but the grin faded as an idea struck. "For now, Dave, put it back where you found it. I'll get back to you."

They signed off. Deke's brown eyes took on a satisfied glint. "You want to bait a trap with that truck."

"Damn right. Something else odd—the front grill and the radiator are pretty much toast. But those are relatively easy fixes. It's almost like they wanted the car repairable."

Deke shrugged. "Maybe that was a backup plan if they couldn't nail her last night. Easier to find someone if you know what she's driving."

"Yeah, but was that thing on the truck yesterday? Or was that bastard putting it on when Dave spotted him?"

The intercom buzzed again. Deke answered it, listened for a

minute, and said, "Send them back." Hanging up, he told Carter, "Ms. Murdock has signed her statement. Now she and her friends want to talk to me, and I want you in on that."

So much for staying away from Tasha.

Deke opened his office door. A moment later, a small group walked in. Lorelei Martin, Will Davis, and Tasha came in together. Griff and Val Dare, both former shire reeves, brought up the rear. Seating them all used the sofa, both armchairs, and Deke's desk chair, but they managed.

"What did you want to talk to me about?" Deke asked.

"We think I was targeted for some reason," Tasha said.

Someone who didn't know her might think she was eerily calm, but Carter recognized the tension around her eyes. It'd been there the day he told her he'd uncovered her unauthorized and politically poisonous repair job.

"We think so too," Deke said. "Any idea why?"

"Not a clue. I did my usual rounds of clients and job sites yesterday. Not everything went smoothly, but that's par for the course. I dealt with a mix of Mundanes and mageborn." With a wry smile, she added, "No ghouls until the encounter on the road."

Deke glanced at Carter, who said, "We have further indications that you were targeted, Tasha." He told her about the tracker on her car.

"We've been trying to get her to move in with us until this is settled." Griff shot Tasha a grim look. "Ready to reconsider?"

"No." The word sounded flat and definite. "I won't bring my troubles to your door."

"We may be able to solve this fast and make that unnecessary," Carter said. "We want to use your truck to bait a trap."

The sudden, fierce glint in her eyes jolted his heart and stirred his blood.

"I'm in," she stated.

"Your truck is in," Deke countered. "You're not."

"I can hold my own." She lifted her chin as though daring him to disagree.

"After the battle in the swamp in November," Deke told her, "I don't doubt it, but I have enough deputy reeves to handle this without calling in civilian volunteers."

"Ghouls may be irrational and anger-driven," Tasha said, "but that mage is no idiot." Looking to Will as though for confirmation, she added, "He's smart enough to verify that I'm there before they attack."

"She's right," Will admitted, exchanging a frustrated look with Griff. "You can get your people in place, Deke, and then I'll go in with her."

Deke frowned at him. "When I said no civilian volunteers, I wasn't just blowing smoke, Davis."

Carter said, "If the mage is there, he'll detect a strike force, even if we screen ourselves magically. The best move is to translocate in when they attack. But I agree with Deke, we shouldn't risk anyone but reeves. Tasha, we can get a double for you."

"No." Tasha shook her head. "You can't be sure that mage won't know the difference. He not only fought me, he touched me."

Fury ignited in Carter's veins, as fresh as it'd been when he saw her wounds last night.

Tasha's eyes flashed. "These bastards wrecked my truck, slashed me up, and scared the crap out of me. I need to be part of taking them down."

"For what it's worth," Val said, and her rueful demeanor had the air of *one shire reeve to another*, "she's got a point. This mage may be able to tell she's not in the house. We could avoid that by warding it, but that might make them suspicious, maybe spur them to bring in a bigger group."

"You recommend I let her do it?" Deke looked first at Val and then at the other former shire reeve in the room, Griff.

"It's the most likely move to succeed," Griff said, "though I agree it sucks."

"If it were me," Lorelei Martin said, her blue eyes hard, "I'd be scared spitless, but I'd still want to be the one in my house."

Deke scowled, and the silence grew heavy. At last, he said, "I wish I could find some reason not to agree, but I can't. Lockwood, I'm putting you in charge. Let's make a plan."

TASHA'S CABIN on the Big Satilla River had fewer neighbors than her Victorian fixer-upper across the street from Forsyth Park in Savannah. It was a safer place to stage this operation. But the cabin was the first place she'd ever owned, her first real home after the navy. She'd never had people here who weren't friends or employees.

Carter's presence was necessary now, though.

As planned, they arrived in the late afternoon. Tasha watched Carter set Stefan's guitar case on the blue denim couch and flip it open. Instead of a guitar, it held their swords and his radio. He passed her the belt that held her saber before shrugging into the behind-the-back shoulder harness for his broadsword.

Buckling on her weapon, Tasha hastily averted her eyes. There was something about him standing there wearing that badass sword harness that drew her attention like iron filings to a magnet.

She needed a distraction, and she had the perfect excuse, food.

Heading through the great room, past the dining area to the kitchen, she asked, "Would you like a sandwich? I have some chips and some wicked salsa, too, if you want them."

Having Carter here, in her sanctuary, felt weird. Out of synch with reality somehow.

She had to give him credit for working quickly. They'd

hatched their plan this morning and put it into effect, complete with repairs to her truck, in a few hours.

"I don't want to put you to any trouble," he replied.

He'd hooked the radio to his belt. Now he stood at the edge of the sitting area's round, braided rug, near the dining area, looking as though he didn't know what to do with himself.

"I'm having a sandwich." She took bread, sliced turkey, and ham from the refrigerator and set out condiments. "It's no trouble to fix another."

"Let me make it." With a rueful smile, he walked around the leaf-green counter and into the kitchen. "It's getting dark, but the ghouls may wait until full night before they attack. I should've brought a book."

Ghouls were stronger at night and thus more active then, so Tasha and Carter had timed their arrival for dusk. In the woods about quarter of a mile away, outside the range where any mage near the cabin should sense them, Val waited with a squad from her task force and a squad of deputy reeves. Both squads wore combat gear, the fatigues bespelled to reflect their surroundings. Unless the Scottish traitor had better extended senses than anyone ever had, he wouldn't detect them.

Overhead, Will and Griff hovered in a magically silenced Black Hawk helicopter with Josh Campbell, a mage who happened to be a US Army combat veteran, at the controls. Their sensors scanned for magical energy approaching the cabin.

"We can kill an hour or two if need be," Tasha said.

As Carter surveyed the food she'd set out, she took forest-green plates from the cream, glass-fronted cabinet. Having him at her elbow made her conscious of her every motion. Did she look competent?

Gah. *Idiot.* Now she was worried about looking competent making a sandwich, of all things. His opinion was no longer relevant. Maybe she was unconsciously trying to compensate for his last impression as her CO, but that was surely a futile effort. *Get a grip, Tasha.*

"If all else fails," she added, "I have board games. And a deck of cards."

"I could go for gin rummy."

"That works."

With just the two of them here, she couldn't help noticing the broadness of his shoulders and his solid, athletic build. She'd always noticed, but he was as much out of reach as he'd always been. He'd made his opinion of her clear that awful day.

She wrenched her attention back to the food. They assembled their sandwiches and fixed glasses of iced tea in silence.

Following Tasha to the table, Carter said, "I realize you'd rather have Will here. Deke's serious, though, about wanting to rebuild the shire reeve department's morale. The more we rely on civilians, the harder that'll be."

"I get it." Tasha set her food down and grabbed napkins, blue with red flowers to coordinate with the armchairs, from the matching oak sideboard. "After working together in November, I don't have a problem with doing it again. If you don't."

"No." He came around the table to hold her chair.

Surprise brought heat to her cheeks, but refusing would add to the awkwardness in the air. With a word of thanks, she let him seat her.

"What do you like to do in your spare time?" she asked.

"I fish," he replied, taking his seat. "I live on the water and have a dock it seems like I'm always fixing. Have a little sailboat I take out overnight if I'm inclined. What about you?"

A sailboat and a house on the water. Pricey. But maybe he'd fixed one or both up the way she'd redone this cabin.

"I help out at the Wayfarer community shelter," she replied. "And I like to sew."

"Seriously?"

When Tasha raised an eyebrow, Carter said, "Didn't mean to

be rude. It's just that you were always so active, so physical. I didn't think you'd be into something so...sedentary."

"So domestic?" she asked softly. Really, there was no reason for her to feel stung. No one in the navy had ever seen that side of her. And the skill was useful to an interior designer.

He shrugged. "Maybe. No offense intended, though."

She nodded acknowledgement. "I like making things. My first job was in a home interiors store as a clerk. I discovered I had a knack for making pillows and throws, so the owner let me sell them on consignment."

"How'd you move from that into construction?"

"Nate helped our dad around our place. My folks didn't think that was a good job for a girl, though, so I could only watch. Except when I helped Nate do something for our grandmother. From him, I learned how to cut a board, miter a corner, and drive a nail, as well as some basic plumbing and electrical stuff. I had to wait until I joined the navy to actually do those things often. I was thrilled to land in the Seabees. That was my first choice."

"You were great at it," he said, eying her warily as they ventured onto this very thin ice. "I figured you had experience."

"Just enthusiasm. How did you end up a sailor?"

"You may remember I grew up in the family construction business. I liked building things, but I wanted to see the world beyond Gulfport, Mississippi."

"The navy will do that for you."

They ate in silence for a few minutes. Tasha eyed Carter. He was looking around at the exposed log walls, flowered chintz curtains, and upholstered furniture with fat cushions in warm blue and marigold yellow with accents in burgundy. The patterns mixed flowers and stripes.

The great room took up this entire end of the cabin, its furniture upholstered in chintz and denim, with a big plate glass window at the far end. French doors leading to the deck she'd built offered a view of the river. She was proud of it all.

But what would someone from his hometown's leading family see? A cozy haven? Or a cobbled-together assortment?

She pressed her lips together. Old insecurities died hard. His opinion was not her problem.

"Did you make any of these cushions or curtains?" he asked.

"All of them." Pride rang in the words, and that was fine with her. She'd worked hard to get this place just like she wanted it. Like the kind of place a kid from a rundown trailer would never be expected to own.

"Great job," he said. "It all goes together. How do you know what colors go with what?"

Tasha smiled. "A color wheel and practice."

When she hesitated, he asked, "What?"

Tasha blew out a hard breath. "I realize this was probably not your first choice as an assignment. I figure there's a chance the shire reeve tossed you into it because you'd already handled the initial encounter. So, for what it's worth, I appreciate it."

Even if she was far too aware of him sitting there. Too conscious of his square, long-fingered hands, ruggedly handsome face, and sheer masculine presence.

He shrugged again. "I like to see things through. Pissed me off, what they did to you. Whatever else, we're both mageborn. We need to stick togeth—"

"Incoming," Griff's voice snapped over the radio.

With a *kra-kow* of magic and the high-pitched sound of shattering glass, the French doors exploded inward under a concerted blast of muddy yellow ghoul power. An instant later, the front door blew off its hinges. Ghouls poured inside.

Adrenaline chilled Tasha's veins and flung her to her feet. She and Carter shared a look of determination as they spun shielding auras and drew their swords.

"Get in the kitchen," he ordered, "and stay down."

Oh, as if. "I've got the back," Tasha snapped as more ghouls rushed in.

She ducked a bolt of muddy ghoul magic and vaulted the

couch to engage the nearest ghoul, a burly, blond male whose grin showed jagged teeth. Behind her, magic sizzled in the air as Carter met the intruders at the front door.

Tasha dodged a swiping stroke of talons and sliced upward under it, spinning away before the ghoul could recover its balance.

An inrush of energy heralded six deputy reeves translocating in. One gutted the ghoul Tasha had sliced as another ghoul charged her. She wheeled into a roundhouse kick at its head.

A woman deputy shouted, "Morere," and skewered the ghoul with her broadsword. To Tasha she said, "Get clear. We got this."

Someone grabbed the back of Tasha's shirt. Before she could turn, reality shifted sideways. A flash of cold darkness, and then she emerged from transit in her kitchen. Sword up, she spun around. Just in time, she recognized Carter and pulled the strike.

In her great room, the new arrivals took on the seven surviving ghouls. Furniture splintered, and the air crackled with magic bolts of green, blue, and muddy yellow.

Glaring at him, she demanded, "What the hell?"

"Deke told you to keep your ass out of trouble. Now get behind me and stay there."

"Like hell." She pushed past him to join the fight.

He caught her arm and jerked her back. "Don't make me put you down."

"Oh, like you could."

Their gazes locked, hot and angry, and that damnable sizzle flared again. In a heartbeat, she felt the heat and strength of the hand gripping her arm. Felt her breasts brush his hard, muscular chest. Leaning in would be so easy.

So crazy while a fight raged so near.

"Let go of me." Hating the high, shaky tone of the words, she shoved at him with her free hand.

"Clear," someone called from the great room and broke the spell.

Carter released Tasha, who shot him her best icy look and turned on her heel to survey the damage.

"Clear," a man called from the hallway to the bedrooms.

"All clear," came from outside. "Helo confirms."

"You don't give me orders anymore," Tasha told Carter softly.

"When I'm responsible for you, I do. Get over it."

He hadn't been so damn protective when her career was on the line, but she'd die before she said so.

He brushed past her, but the sight of her great room froze her in her tracks. Not one piece of furniture had survived the fight unscathed. Not the sofa she'd bought secondhand and reupholstered. Not the dining table and sideboard she'd salvaged from a dump and refinished. The windows were all broken, and a chunk of wall was missing from beside the big plate glass window at the end.

Tears stung her eyes. Compressing her lips, she blinked her vision clear. She was alive. Unhurt. There'd been no "mage down" calls, so no major injuries. That was what mattered. She could fix the material things.

But oh, the hours of work that'd been wiped out. This better have been worth it.

She walked up to the confab in the great room. "Did we get a prisoner?"

CHAPTER FIVE

CARTER CAUGHT UP TO TASHA, WHO WAS LOOKING AT THE GROUP in general. He seemed to be the only one here she knew, since she didn't address anyone by name, yet she avoided eye contact with him.

Fine. If she was pissed because he'd kept her from an unnecessary risk, that was too damn bad.

Thanks to that encounter in the kitchen, aggravating awareness of her hummed through him, but he put it aside.

"We caught a couple," he replied, his voice level. "We were just about to question one." Into his radio, he said, "Lockwood to backup squad. The mage didn't show. Over."

"Roger that," Val Dare's cool alto said. "Helo confirms." Wryly, she added, "They might come back, though, so we'll stay as long as you're there."

Carter hooked the radio back on his belt and walked around the shattered sofa, his sword in hand because he'd had no time to clean it. Tasha followed with her saber drawn. He didn't like her being so close to a ghoul, even a mortally wounded one, but she had a right to hear what it said.

He knelt by the big male groaning behind the couch. "You know we won't save you." That would be like saving the copperhead that'd taken up residence in your back yard. Sooner or later, you'd have to kill it anyway. "But we can make your death faster."

The ghoul spat at him, sending a whiff of ammonia through the air.

"Why are you attacking this mage?" Carter demanded.

The ghoul ignored him and grinned up at her. "So . . . fuck-able," it said.

"That's what you say about every mage or Mundane woman," Tasha told it, her voice flat. "What else?"

My interrogation, Carter thought, but he couldn't help admiring her composure. Hell, if the things had been after him, he'd probably barge in too.

"Bet you'd...like to know." The ghoul coughed blood and died.

"Shit," Carter muttered. He glanced up at the tall, brunette woman holding her combat helmet under her arm. Her gear was ensorcelled to reflect its surroundings, which usually meant forests. Seeing Tasha's wrecked living room on her instead felt weird.

"We have any others?" he asked.

"Let me check." She touched the mic on her headset. "Danvers to Lennox, any prisoners? Over." Her voice crackled from the radio at Carter's belt.

"One, but it's dead," came the reply in a man's gravelly voice. "About a minute ago."

"Well, hell," someone behind Carter commented before he could.

"Okay, people," he said as Danvers acknowledged the info, "let's get the cleanup done."

They would burn the corpses outside and bury the ashes. Magefire would destroy even the bones. There would be nothing to point to the existence of the ghouls.

Carter rose. Tasha had turned, surveying the cozy room's wreckage, and the naked grief on her face twisted his heart.

"I'll send someone into Brunswick for lumber," he said. "We'll get the windows and doorways boarded up before we leave."

"Thanks, but I can do it."

"This was a Collegium operation. The Collegium not only helps but pays."

Denial bloomed in her eyes, and she opened her mouth. A moment later, she shut it. Aware of deputies carrying bodies out, Carter waited.

"That's a big help," she said. "I'm sure Will, Griff, and Val will come back and help after they change and grab a car."

She looked sick at heart, and the sheen in her eyes might be tears. But he forced himself to stand by, to keep his hands to himself. She wouldn't want comfort from him.

"I know it's not much help," he said, trying for a light note, "but now you have a great excuse to redecorate."

With a choked laugh, she said, "Yeah. There's that."

He longed to touch her, to just grip her shoulder as a gesture of support. Better not, though. That kind of support was for Griff Dare or Will Davis or Stefan Harper, men she considered actual friends. But he couldn't just walk away.

"It was beautiful," he said, "because you made it that way. You will again."

Biting her lip, she nodded. "It . . . This place means something. I . . ." With a shake of her head, she stopped.

That seemed like his exit cue. "I'll be outside if you need anything."

She nodded again.

He had almost reached the door when she called his name. He turned to find her regarding him with the steely look he'd come to know so well.

"I won't hang back while others risk their lives for me," she said. "I appreciate everything you've done, but I'm not in your chain of command anymore. You don't give me orders."

"I'm a deputy reeve. You're a civilian. That makes your

safety my responsibility, so yes, you will do as I say at the first sign of any threat."

Her eyes flashed. Perverse of him to find that encouraging, but it meant she was recovering her poise.

"If you don't like that," he added politely, "I'm sorry, but that's the way it is."

He walked outside, but he could've sworn he heard her say, "You wish." He ignored her, though. Sometimes silence was the best weapon of all.

Yet he couldn't quite stifle a twinge of regret as he took the tracker off her truck and smashed it. The little truce they'd formed was blown to hell now.

Too bad he couldn't walk away—wouldn't—until she was safe. That might not be his smartest decision ever, but it was the only one he could make.

~

TASHA LET Carter usher her into the shire reeve's office. Val had insisted on tagging along in her capacity as head of the task force on traitor mages, but Tasha suspected she'd done it mostly as moral support. When Tasha sank onto the worn couch, Val took the seat beside her, leaving the armchairs for the two men.

Looking around the room, Tasha had a strange sense of disorientation. Surely it hadn't been only a few hours ago that they'd plotted today's trap with such confidence.

"I'm sorry about your house," Deke Jones said to Tasha. "Send the invoices for repairs through this office."

"I'm grateful." She hadn't expected such a boon. It meant she wouldn't have to dip into the repair fund for the Savannah house, money she'd been saving for a while, to fix the cabin. Although business was good, she kept her personal salary at rock bottom so as to put more into the business. You never knew what life might throw at you.

Deke glanced at Val. "We have to decide what to do next."

"I can't imagine why they're so interested in me," Tasha said. "Maybe it's a mistake and today discouraged them. But I'll be extra careful."

"It's not likely to be a mistake," Carter responded. "You know something or saw something or have something that matters to them."

Tasha shook her head. "I don't. I just don't."

"Maybe you don't know you do," Val said. "Or they're wrong in thinking you do."

"I see the logic in that." Rubbing a hand over her face, Tasha added, "I've been racking my brain, but there's just nothing."

"Nothing you can pinpoint," Deke qualified. "There is something, or they wouldn't be after you with such determination."

Tasha spread her hands and gave him her best *I got no clue* look. "It's been a long couple of days, and I'd really like to get home."

"You shouldn't go home," Deke began.

Val, knowing Tasha better, winced as Tasha bridled at the flat tone.

The shire reeve finished, "You shouldn't go anywhere you're expected to be."

"On the one hand, that makes sense," she conceded reluctantly. "On the other, I have a business to run, which means clients to see and jobs to supervise. I can't just hole up somewhere."

"I was thinking of here," Deke informed her.

When she gaped, he added, "We stepped up security since the ghoul attack last fall. You'll be safe in the Collegium. You can run your business by videoconference."

"I can't. I have to put together project boards—furniture photos, fabric swatches, carpet and drapery samples. Flooring samples. I can't do that shut up in here."

But they were right. What was she going to do? If she didn't keep on top of the various projects, little things like meeting a payroll would become a challenge.

She looked at Val, who said, "If I were hunting you, I'd watch your house. You could at least sleep here. You can stay in our apartment and not bother with a guest unit."

Val and Griff had an apartment at the Collegium because of her task force position. They used it only when she had to be here, though, preferring the old farmhouse they'd renovated outside Wayfarer.

Being underfoot with newlyweds—because they would be here some of the time—did not sound like a great plan.

"Or," Val suggested, "you can stay at our place in Wayfarer. It has multiple layers of warding and concealment, and you could have privacy in the barn."

"I'm not bringing my troubles to you, as I've already said. That property's concealed for a reason."

Reminding Val that she and Griff both had targets on their backs because of being former shire reeves and because of his zealous destruction of ghoul nests during his renegade years shouldn't be necessary. "I won't be the cause of the ghouls finding you."

"Griffin and I are confident the concealment will hold."

Love for them both welled into Tasha's throat, and she shook her head. "Last resort only, but thanks." They did have a point, though. Could she afford to hire someone from the mage security agency in Atlanta run by Chuck Porter, a fellow member of Griff's old team? He would probably cut her a deal, maybe even offer her free protection. But either would make her beholden, and she hated that.

She glanced from Val to Carter and Deke and blew out a breath. "I'm not suicidal or, I hope, stupid. Until we know what the ghouls want or can conclude they've given up, I'll spend my nights here." Reluctantly, she added, "I'll look into hiring a bodyguard."

Maybe staying here would also keep her house in Savannah from being demolished as the cabin had been. The ghouls could look up the tax records on the river cabin and get her name and address. They could lie in wait at her home or office. Or, for the fun of it, vandalize them.

Jones said, "Whatever it is they believe you know, Ms. Murdock, could be critical. The ghouls are worried enough about it to track you. I want you safe until we can figure out what it is and act on it."

"Meaning what?" she asked.

"I want one of my staff to serve as your bodyguard. Short-handed as we are, I can spare only one deputy reeve, but you're potentially a material witness. We protect our witnesses."

"Do you have someone in mind?" she asked. Having a deputy reeve as a guard would save a lot of money.

Deke nodded. "I'll look over the roster and see who I can spare. Then—"

"I'll do it." Carter's face wore a look of grim determination.

Had he gone crazy?

At Tasha's side, Val raised her eyebrows.

Deke said, "You command the Wayfarer unit, Carter. I can't spare you."

"Dixie Blaine can handle that until I get back, and we can rotate someone else in there to fill her slot. Maybe give one of the rookies some experience."

Deke frowned. Before he could say anything, Val put in, "We can take care of her, Griffin and I, with an assist from some others."

Shaking his head, Deke said, "You and Griff are supposed to be focused on outreach to other shires. Besides, everyone I think you're referring to has a day job already. In addition to being civilians who ought to stay out of this."

They also had lives Tasha wasn't willing to disrupt. Reluctantly, she said, "You know Will is saving all his vacation to spend with Audra. Ditto for Stefan and Mel."

Eying Carter carefully, she continued, "You can't really want to do this. Be sure before you commit."

He shrugged. "I'm the only deputy with extensive experience in construction. I can blend into your business better than anyone else. We worked together fine last year. We can do it again."

CARTER BRACED himself as Tasha studied him. In a cool, even voice, she asked, "Do you really think this is a good idea?"

"You need a bodyguard if you won't stay here."

She would agree to keep from imposing on her friends. He knew it in his bones. Whatever her reason, he would run with it. He wanted to, crazy as that might be. The breach between the two of them was long overdue for mending.

So was that fresh start, which he was coming to realize he wanted more than he'd imagined. No matter how unlikely that seemed. Anyway, keeping her safe came first.

"You can explain me as someone starting up a company. I can talk to the people on your job sites in their language if I need to," he said.

"You're an interior designer now, are you?"

She smiled with an evil glint in her eye that called up all the dumb stereotypes about male decorators. Carter kept his gaze level on hers. "If necessary."

In fact, he would do whatever was necessary to protect her. That might be idiotic in light of their history, but he couldn't just walk away.

"Do you have problem with Deputy Lockwood?" Deke asked.

"No," Tasha answered quickly. Maybe a little too quickly, considering the interesting way faint pink washed over her cheeks. "One deputy or another, it's all the same to me."

When Deke just stared at her, she shrugged. "We served in the navy together. I was just needling him."

"So you're old friends?"

Hardly. But she only shrugged again.

"Then we're set." Deke looked from Tasha to Carter and back. "Ms. Murdock, Carter will meet you outside. I want to talk to him for a minute."

Val and Tasha walked out. Deke closed the door behind them and sat on the couch. "I hear there was some friction between you two. What's the story?"

"We weren't exactly friends in the service. I was her CO, and there were times we clashed. There was a particularly bad one right before she left the navy."

He wasn't going to explain that, though. Tasha'd owned up to her mistake and taken the punishment. She didn't deserve to have knowledge of an old misjudgment spread.

"Will she cooperate with you?"

"As much as she will with anybody. We worked together okay on Will Davis's situation last year." With a wry grin and an unwelcome feeling of pride, he added, "She has a thing about not hanging back while other people defend her."

"Like a good sailor?"

"Or a combat veteran." Which she and all the members of Dare's old team were.

With a nod, Deke told him, "Keep her out of trouble. If you need backup, yell, and if things get too sticky, I'll replace you."

"Okay." Carter headed out to meet Tasha.

He cut through the big bullpen with its desks, some of them occupied but most vacant because reeves were patrolling the grounds. Val Dare stood just inside the double glass doors to the lobby.

She stepped forward to meet him. "I have something for you." She drew him aside and fished something from her jeans pocket. "This deflects scrying. It struck Griffin and me as something whoever guarded Tasha would need."

"So you figured somebody would?"

"If today's op didn't yield what we hoped, it seemed likely. This is a loaner, but keep it as long as you need it."

She opened her hand and revealed a flat, golf ball-sized

pendant of lapis lazuli on a black cord. Its stylized eye shape looked vaguely familiar.

"I've seen that symbol somewhere," he told her.

"It's the eye of Horus, the Egyptian god of justice." She held the pendant out to him. "It won't defeat what Griffin likes to call the Mark I Eyeball, but it deflects most scrying."

Ghouls couldn't magically spy on anyone at a distance but, as with so much, traitor mages could.

"You should give that to Tasha," he said. "Nobody's looking for me."

"They will once they figure out you're with her. Besides, she has one."

"Okay, then. Thanks." Carter accepted the pendant, put it on, and tucked it under his shirt.

"Griffin and I want to have a strategy session over dinner tonight in our apartment here. We'd like you to come if you can, along with a few other people. But first Tasha wants to go to her house, pack a bag, and grab things for work. Griffin, Lorelei, and I can meet you there as backup."

Carter frowned, but Tasha would need clothes if she stayed here. She was right about keeping up with her work. He knew from hearing his dad talk that an independent business owner had to stay on top of things. *You don't own the business as much as it owns you*, Dad had always said.

"Okay. Dinner sounds great. Thanks."

"One more thing." Val regarded him solemnly.

When he raised his eyebrows, she continued, "I don't know what happened between you and Tasha, and I figure it's not my business, but if you need a buffer—or even some more bodies on guard—you can call on Griffin and me anytime."

He thanked her and pushed through the lobby doors. Standing by the glass outer doors, Tasha eyed him with a wary expression that stung.

Best to keep things businesslike, and maybe she'd relax. "I've been thinking about why they could be after you. Stands to reason it's because of something that happened in the last couple or three days."

"Makes sense."

"Maybe this won't take long," he said. "So, while we drive to Savannah and get you clothes or whatever you need, let's discuss what you've done the past few days and see what we can come up with."

The smile she gave him brimmed with relief. "I'm down for that. Let's go."

CHAPTER SIX

<small>THIS HAD BEEN A HELL OF A DAY.</small>

The air in Griff and Val's apartment was rich with the aromas of grilled salmon and apple pie, but the homey scents didn't soothe Tasha. As the conversation flowed around her, she longed for her big claw-foot bathtub in Savannah, a cold beer, and some light jazz on the CD player. More than anything, she wanted to close herself off for a while and pretend today hadn't happened.

To cap off the day's trials, Carter Lockwood had ended up sitting by her on the sofa. She could hardly relocate without being rude and ungrateful, but that damn sizzle popping between them made the wreck of her day even worse. Why in blue blazes couldn't she stifle this idiotic attraction?

The Dares didn't usually entertain here because their dining table was too small to seat a big group—in this case, the two of them, Tasha, Carter, Lorelei, Will, and tall, dark-haired Stefan Harper—so the guests had settled themselves at the small bar and in the living room area. Val and Tasha had furnished it together, with burnt sienna tweed furniture, glass coffee and end tables, and a distressed-pine dining table. All that represented a considerable upgrade from the standard-issue stuff.

Good thing this was a two-bedroom unit and thus came with a larger kitchen and living area than the guest suites offered.

Tonight, because they were so crowded, Val and Griff served from the pots in the kitchen.

Too bad Tasha didn't have much of an appetite. The image of her ravaged cabin had haunted her while she phoned clients, rescheduled meetings, and checked with job supervisors.

"You okay?" Carter asked in a low voice that wouldn't carry, even to mageborn ears. "Can I get you anything?"

He was tending her. The realization surprised her into looking at him. Heat turned his gray eyes smoky, but his face held only polite interest. So the sizzle was chafing him too. Yet he was trying to help anyway.

She mustered a smile, feeble though it was. "I'm good. I just want to get this done so I can crawl into bed, pull the covers over my head—"

Chagrined, she stopped abruptly. What the hell possessed her to bare her soul to him? Or to agree that he could stay in the guest suite with her? His argument that there could still be traitors here who hadn't been uncovered had swayed her, but was that really necessary?

"You want to forget this day for a while." He nodded. His fingers closed over hers in a warm grip.

Awareness crackled up her arm and into her body, tightening her nipples. Tasha's breath caught.

Because she hadn't been prepared. That was why. Had to be.

Carter's eyes darkened. His throat moved in a hard swallow, and he jerked his hand back. "I'll see what I can do," he muttered.

"Hey," he called. "This has been a long day, so let's get to business and pack it in."

Tasha bit her lip. She could speak for herself and would have in another minute or two. But she couldn't berate him for being kind.

"I've been thinking," Tasha said as the room fell silent.

"Since I don't know what I did to attract this attention, maybe scrying the specific sites and clients I saw in the three or four days before the attack would give us a clue."

"See if anyone looks or acts suspicious." Stefan nodded.

"It's a good starting point," Will said, exchanging a glance with Griff. "Maybe some of us should scry what happened at those places after you left. And the same again for wherever you go tomorrow."

Tasha didn't tell him Deke's edict about using deputy reeves only. That wasn't her fight to wage.

Carter said, "I'll run the scrying thing by Deke." He turned to her. "Who knew you were going to Fargo? Especially, who knew you would take that route instead of the northern one through Waycross?"

"I mentioned Fargo to a couple or three clients I saw yesterday because I had to build time into my schedule for that drive. I can give you a list. As for the route, everyone knows that's the best way to reach Fargo. I don't know anybody who takes the northern road. On top of that, anybody could've scried my whereabouts at any time yesterday. I don't ward my truck when I'm driving around. Who does?"

"Yeah, nobody." Carter grimaced. Maintaining a ward while driving around took too much energy to be worth it without a strong reason. "That doesn't tell us much, though. We need to narrow that down."

"I'm open to suggestions," she replied, her voice dry.

Will shifted on his bar stool. "Email me your client list for the past few days. I'll check them all out. I can also get Javy to run a deeper check."

He referred to Javy Ruiz, the ace hacker who'd been a member of Griff's team. The clients would hate that if they knew, but the guys would be discreet. Tasha nodded.

"While we drive around, we can go over the past few days," Carter offered. "See if that shakes anything loose."

"There was one thing," Tasha said. "It's probably nothing,

but my last appointment before I went to Fargo was with Geneva Collier, south of Brunswick. The housekeeper showed me into the library, and Geneva was initially annoyed at my being in here. But then she seemed to shrug it off, so it's probably nothing."

"We'll check them first," Will said.

"Anybody have other approaches to suggest?" Val asked.

No one did, so the party broke up. Everyone's hugs were meant to be supportive. Tasha appreciated that, but she really needed some alone time.

When Carter got on the elevator with her, she said, "It was a long day for you, too, and now you're staying here instead of going home."

He watched the lighted display over the doors. "I'll rest fine on the sofa bed."

"I hope so, but still... Let me buy you breakfast in the morning to make up for a night on the pullout." This might be his job, but she didn't want to be any more beholden to him than she could avoid.

He shrugged. "I've slept in worse places."

"For saving my butt, then."

He studied her for a long moment, as though he knew she was trying to balance the scales. Then he nodded. "I'm not one to turn down a free meal."

They reached the unit assigned to her. Carter laid his palm on the plate above the lock and released a trickle of magic. The lock clicked open. "It's keyed to me too," he told her.

The apartment had a tiny kitchen, a sitting/dining area with hotel-grade furniture, and a bathroom across from the kitchen. The bedroom lay beyond the kitchen and bath. Good thing she and Carter wouldn't be here much because they'd be right on top of each other in the cramped, eight-by-ten living area.

A small, tan duffel that must be his sat beside the loveseat that pulled out to make a double bed. At least a bag that size wouldn't hold a lot. He probably shared her hopes for a fast resolution.

"I'll grab the linens from the bathroom closet," she said. She and Lorelei had made the bed in the bedroom earlier, before Carter convinced her to let him stay.

"You don't need to bother. I can handle it."

"It's faster if we both pitch in." She hurried into the bathroom.

∼

DAMN. Doing anything that involved any kind of bed with her was masochistic. Sitting by her through dinner, like a good bodyguard, had made him too conscious of her. Her profile had stayed in his peripheral vision, and the angle had reminded him she had very nice, very cuppable breasts.

Not that he was likely ever to have the chance to test that observation.

Maybe that was for the best. It was hard to think clearly around her because of the damn current that seemed to spark between them all the time.

The sooner they nailed these ghouls who were after her, the better. Same went for getting the bed made since she seemed inclined to be stubborn about it. He set sofa cushions aside and unfolded the mattress.

Tasha hurried back into the sitting area with her arms full of bedding and pillows. She set the bedclothes on a chair and shook out the bottom sheet.

As she and Carter made the bed, he couldn't help watching her smooth the linens, thinking of how those feminine, capable hands would feel on his skin.

And now he was fighting wood. If he could come up with some jokes, that would distract him. But his stock of humor deserted him.

Smooth, dude. You dumbass.

To cover, he grabbed a pillow and a case. Holding them in front of him to put the case on, he visualized kicking back on his sailboat, the *Delta Doll*, nursing a beer and watching the waves. The image helped. He clung to it until he and Tasha finished smoothing the blanket over the sofa bed.

He thanked her. Going for a brisk, professional footing, he asked, "What time do you need to be out and about in the morning?"

"I'm due at job sites between about eight and noon. Then I have my rescheduled client meetings from today and the follow-ups on the places I visited yesterday. Those start around one. I'd like to swing by my office in Savannah and introduce you to my staff."

"So breakfast at six thirty? The dining hall does a good breakfast, actually. Real eggs, not powdered or anything."

"That'll work."

They stared at each other across the bed, and that irritating sizzle sparked in the air again. Tasha's throat worked in a hard swallow.

"Uh, good night," she offered, turning away. "Mind if I take the first bathroom shift?"

"Fine by me. Good night."

The bathroom door closed quietly behind her. She could have first go there and not have to come out of the bedroom later in her PJs. If she wore PJs.

Was it too stupid for words to hope she slept in something sheer and lacy? And black? And that he might get to see it?

Dumbass.

Carter swallowed a groan. At least she wasn't here to see the results of that line of thought. He stepped into the kitchen, out of sight from the bathroom doorway, stripped, and donned a pair of black gym shorts.

As he walked back to the cot, Tasha emerged from the bathroom. "Well, I guess..."

Their eyes met, and her voice trailed off. Her lips parted.

Yeah, baby, Carter thought, crossing his arms over his chest. Nice to know she wasn't as immune to him as she usually seemed.

She wrenched her eyes to the side, mumbled something that sounded like *good night*, and fled to the bedroom.

"See you in the morning," he called after her, grinning. That went well.

His grin faded. So she'd reacted to him. So what? He and she still didn't get along below the surface, and oh, yeah, he had another boner. And the imagined image of her in lacy, black lingerie to sustain it.

Heading to the bathroom, he resisted the urge to slam his hand into the wall. This was going to be one damn long night.

IF THE REST of the day went like this, Tasha decided, it was going to be a very long one. She and Carter were seated on the brown leather sofa in the Colliers' family room, the one they wanted to extend and redecorate. They'd asked if Carter could see the library shelving, claiming he wanted similar shelves in his house, and Geneva had agreed without an apparent qualm. While he examined at the shelves, Tasha looked at the rest of the room, but nothing had seemed odd. So maybe the little glitch the other day had nothing to do with ghouls, not that she'd ever seriously thought it might.

Geneva Collier sat in the armchair next to Carter, whom Tasha had introduced as Charlie Logan, a navy buddy starting his own company. Someone in the shire reeve's department had backstopped that identity online.

Geneva twinkled at him. "Do have some more iced tea, Mr. Logan."

"Thanks, but I'm good," he said.

Was she bumping her knee up against his? Criminy, yes.

Carter shifted toward Tasha. "I was interested in the plan

you and Ms. Murdock had discussed for bumping out this room," he said, his voice cool.

"Oh, but us girls can talk about that any old time." The woman flicked a glance at Tasha before leaning closer to Carter. "What did you do in the navy?"

"We worked together," Tasha put in firmly. "In the navy's construction arm, the Seabees. My construction manager, Randy Butcher, said he came by today. Did you get the information you needed?"

"Yes, yes." The woman waved her hand. "I still haven't decided whether to go contemporary or period in here, and my husband needs to talk to you about the support for the opening." She slid her foot against Carter's.

The poor guy inched closer to Tasha. The woman was a barracuda, but maybe he thought he couldn't smack her down without jeopardizing this deal. She was also delaying the schedule.

"Mrs. Collier," Tasha said firmly, "this is lovely, but we have other appointments to keep. If we could settle what you want, I can move forward with proposals from there."

The woman set her glass down with a snap. "My husband is coming back from work to speak with you. As I said. He has some questions for you, and I don't see why we can't relax a bit until he arrives."

"I'm sorry." Tasha rose, and Carter stood alongside her. "As I explained," she added, her voice light and easy, "I have a schedule of appointments every day, and we've been here an hour. I'll be glad to talk to Mr. Collier on the phone if you like, but we really can't wait. Do you have anything to add before we leave?"

And please don't let it be the wine cellar.

She needed this job, but if the woman was only going to jerk her around and waste time, she wouldn't get it anyway. Might as well cut her losses.

Geneva Collier leaned back and crossed her legs. Eying

Tasha sternly, she said, "Other contractors have been more interested in the social niceties."

"Perhaps they're not quite as busy as I am." Tasha smiled. "I'm happy to speak with you or your husband by phone, but Mr. Logan and I need to go. Thanks for the tea."

The woman fluttered around them, but they kept a distance so she couldn't accidentally bump the screened swords at each of their hips. When they reached the door, Carter's extended senses brushed across Tasha's, checking the exterior.

She glanced at him and got a slight nod in return, but he still stepped out first. The door closed behind them with a definite *thud*.

They strode down the curving walk to the driveway with him slightly in front. Opening her truck's passenger door, he said, "I hope you didn't do that on my account. I can deal with pushy women."

"I thought maybe you were avoiding dealing so as to not blow my chance at this job."

He walked around the truck and climbed in. "It crossed my mind. But if I'd been truly bothered, I would've gotten up, looked out at the area she wants to expand into, and changed seats."

They buckled their seatbelts. Raising one eyebrow, he asked, "Is the whole day going to be like this?"

"I hope not. Next up is a construction site out in Fancy Bluff. The two women on my crew there will be too focused to annoy you."

He grinned. "Who says all that focus on the work wouldn't annoy me?"

She started to snap back, but the words froze in her throat. "You're teasing."

"Maybe." Still smiling, he started her truck, which they were using instead of his car because the tools and sample books Tasha carried around fit better in the larger vehicle. "I happen to have a weakness for women who wield power tools."

"The Seabees must've offered you a lot of choices, then."

He looked straight at her, his gray eyes intent. "Only one woman in the Bees ever interested me, and she was off limits."

Her mouth dropped open. She shut it abruptly. Surely he wasn't coming on to her.

He'd backed down the driveway and was now peering at the road before pulling out. Paying her no attention at all.

He must've been teasing.

"We'll stop down the road," he said, "and make sure nobody put a tracking device on this truck."

"You think they would try that again?" She and Val had scried, pouring pure spring water into a silver bowl and infusing it with magic, to see who'd placed the tracker on her car. Because whoever it was had screened themselves, the scrying had shown only the truck parked in the driveway of her Fargo client, a Mundane, day before yesterday. So they still didn't know who'd placed it.

Carter shrugged "It worked once. I'll call Deke and see if he got the Council to authorize scrying your clients' houses after we leave."

He was back to business. He hadn't meant anything by the comment about women and power tools.

Not that she was disappointed or anything. It was best that way.

CHAPTER SEVEN

A FIFTYISH, HUSKY BLACK GUY IN A HARD HAT WALKED UP AS Carter pulled into the yard at Tasha's next site. Carter needed a minute to recognize him as the guy he'd met earlier at Tasha's office, Randy Butcher, her company's construction supervisor.

She'd said this was a down-to-the-studs remodeling and addition project. In a sea of red-clay mud generated by last night's rain sat a two-story house. Its old siding was gone, and new sheathing and house wrap were nailed in place, the seams sealed.

The site was tidy, no loose bits of lumber or insulation lying around, and her crew's vehicles were all neatly parked at the property's edge.

Opening his senses, he caught no signs of trouble. The guy now waiting beside the truck was Mundane.

She smiled at him but watched Carter, waiting for his nod before she hopped out of the truck. They'd stopped at a gas station, and she'd changed clothes in the rest room. The short, blue silk jacket and black slacks she'd worn earlier now sat in a bag in the truck bed, replaced by a jean jacket and canvas work pants, and she'd traded black heels for work boots.

Carter climbed out. Thanks to her warning, he'd traded his

blazer for his favorite worn, blue canvas field coat and his dress shoes for work boots. They had yet another change ahead of them. How many times a day did she do this? His dad never changed clothes to meet clients. Why did she?

At least her saber was on her hip, sheathed and screened from Mundane sight. He carried his broadsword the same way.

"Hey, y'all," the big guy said.

They returned his greeting, and Tasha asked, "So what've we got? You mentioned a problem?"

Carter subtly warded the truck while Tasha and Butcher talked. The guy stood close but not in her space, and his tone was relaxed and open. They must have a good working relationship.

"Last night's rain swamped this yard," Butcher was saying. "I'd like to call Paulsen's about putting in some drainage. It needs to go in before we start the patio."

Tasha frowned at the muddy mess behind the house. "How's the foundation? Is the water running close to the house?

"Yard gets runoff from the neighbors," Butcher replied, "but there's slope around the foundation. It's nice and dry. Woulda been good if the clients had thought to mention the standing water, though."

"Yeah. Because they didn't, their nice new patio is going to be a pond in heavy rain unless we do something." Tasha shook her head. "I'll call the Jepsons tonight. You make an appointment with Paulsen."

The older man nodded but told her, "They're already griping about cost overruns."

Tasha sighed. "If they wouldn't keep adding things, there wouldn't be cost overruns."

"I think they know it." Randy grinned. "Mebbe they're just worried about bills addin' up. At least they seem like the type to realize drainage is more important than Eye-talian granite countertops."

"There's that." Tasha gave him a rueful smile. "When I talk to them, I'll remind them some of the upgrades they added haven't been ordered yet. We can cancel if they'd feel better about it. But call Paulsen without waiting to hear from me."

"I'll do it. You want to walk through or around first?"

"Let's go through, then finish up out here to avoid getting any more mud inside."

Carter trailed them through the house, his senses open. Here, too, the place was orderly. Everyone walked on the plastic runners that protected the unfinished oak floors. The three men and two women hanging sheet rock worked smoothly with an occasional *shit* or *damn* or *oh, hell* dropped into cheerful, otherwise smooth banter.

No one got in anyone's way.

The crew's efficiency might be Butcher's doing, but Tasha had said he visited different sites on different days. These people couldn't fake working together so well just when the boss was around. Tasha spoke to each one by name, made jokes, and commented on what was done well.

She had a good crew here. He'd always known she was a competent builder. From what he'd seen so far, she was also a capable boss.

But she looked tired and distracted. That was no wonder. Cheering her up wasn't his job, but he would see what he could do when they left here.

&

"You're a lifesaver," Tasha said, accepting a tall cup Carter passed across to her. After visiting another job site, they'd stopped at the drive-through window for a Fuel Cup coffee shop. "I wish you would let me pay."

"Then I wouldn't be a lifesaver." He set his cup in its holder and pulled away from the window. In a few minutes, they were headed back into Savannah on Georgia 204.

Tasha rolled her eyes but let it go. He wasn't likely to think a four-dollar cup of coffee, even mocha with a shot of mint, created some sort of power dynamic.

He glanced at her. "Can I ask you something?" When she nodded, he continued, "What's with all the changes of clothes?"

"I dress for whatever interests the particular client. When I'm pitching a decorating job, I want to project that I can put together a look. On a construction site, I need sturdier clothes but still something that looks neat."

"Huh. Makes sense."

Of course it did. And she had no business feeling warmed by his apparent approval. He was passing through her life, nothing more.

They drove a little longer in silence before Carter spoke again. "You've got good crews," he told her. "I'm impressed."

"So I guess you don't think I'm stupid anymore," Tasha blurted. Appalled, she gulped. She hadn't meant to say that, let alone sound so hurt. Foolish of her.

Carter frowned at her. "I never thought you were stupid."

"Uh, all right." She should make a light comment, change the subject, but her brain was a mortified blank.

"What are you talking about?" he demanded.

He didn't remember. The comment had shattered her, and he didn't remember. Of course, most guys had lousy conversational memories, but that had hardly been just a conversation.

Tasha mustered a weak smile. "It's not important. Never mind."

"I think it is important. Tasha—"

"It doesn't matter," she said, her voice flat. "Let it go." As she thought she had. "Not to fish for compliments or anything, but what about the crew impressed you?"

He cast her a doubtful look. "If I ever said you were stupid, it must have been momentary frustration, because you almost never screwed up..."

His voice trailed off. The air in the car suddenly felt heavy. Tight.

He remembered now, or else had figured it out. Either way, she got no satisfaction from it.

"Let's not go there." She forced the words through her tight throat. "Tell me what you liked at the job site."

His knuckles on the steering wheel went white. Did he mean to force the issue? She dreaded it but was stunned by a tiny flicker of something almost like hope. She squashed it. Marching back over that ground wouldn't change anything.

He took off his sunglasses and tucked them into his pocket. Slowly, watching the road, he said, "Maybe it's past time we went there."

"No."

He glanced at her, assessing. His lips tightened. After a moment, he said, "We live in the same area. We know a lot of the same people. We should clear the air."

"It's not like we run into each other much." Tasha sighed. "Look, Carter. Although I did what I felt was right, I shouldn't have. You did what you had to. There's nothing to discuss."

After a moment, his voice flat, he said, "I could've been less harsh that day. Less personal."

She'd once wished he had been. Now, though... "It's water under the bridge."

He shrugged, his face set and his shoulders tense.

Fairness forced her to add, "I should've asked for the work to be approved beforehand. You were right. It was a stupid thing to do."

The hard line of his shoulders relaxed. He shot her a grateful look. "That was an aberration. You were one of the smartest sailors in the company, as a rule. The one with the brightest future, I thought. That's why I was so surprised to find that you were the one responsible."

Not only surprised but disappointed, she remembered, and

her treacherous mind flashed back to a short interlude of *almost something* on the shore of the Indian Ocean.

But Carter was continuing. "For what it's worth, I take back the bit about being stupid. And I apologize."

Stunned, she stared at him. Her supposed brains deserted her, and all she could think of to say was, "Seriously?"

"Yes. And I'm truly impressed with your crew. You run a tight ship, as demonstrated by the tidiness of your sites, but treat your employees well. They're comfortable with you and clearly like their jobs. They're capable, and they're not crude or careless. I'd trust them to work in my house."

"Except you could do the work yourself." She made herself relax now that they were on firmer ground. Nothing in her voice would show that his praise had touched her. But it had.

Why did she still care about his approval?

"Well, yeah." He smiled at her, but the smile seemed forced.

"Thanks," she mumbled.

"Only the truth." Carter raised an eyebrow. "So. We square, Murdock?"

He genuinely seemed to care. She couldn't hold back a foolish, shaky smile.

"Almost." As long as they were being fair, she had something to confess too. She took a deep breath, bracing herself. "When you showed up at the farmhouse where Will and Audra were staying in November, I was surprised. I saw you, and, well, all the, uh, difficulty of that day came rushing back. I was short with you. You didn't deserve it. I'm sorry."

He glanced at her, his eyes now smoky gray. "I appreciate it."

Relieved, Tasha nodded. "So now, if you're good with it, we're square."

Carter smiled, sending her pulse into a skippy beat. His smile faded, and his eyes darkened.

Not good. This was so not good.

Abruptly he wrenched his gaze back to the road. "That's, uh, great. Really great." He tapped something on his GPS. "Next stop is on Percy, right?"

"Yes, near Orleans Square. It's the last, thank goodness."

But then they would go back to the Collegium, to that tiny guest apartment. Together. With nothing to distract them.

~

GRADUALLY, the tension in Carter's gut ebbed. The emotional air in the car cleared.

He glanced sideways at Tasha. She was doing something on her phone, probably checking messages.

He hadn't meant to get into ancient history. Bringing it up had seemed pointless before. But he hadn't known his comments that painful day had stuck with her. Hadn't been sure she cared enough about his opinion even to listen.

His mistake. But did that mean anything now? She'd apologized for being short with him in November, and he'd never expected that.

They passed a strip mall, then a subdivision and a gas station. Traffic was picking up, so he needed to focus.

"A text came in from Lorelei while we were at that last site," Tasha said. "She wants to bring dinner tonight. What would you like from Lucia's?"

"What's Lucia's?"

Tasha grinned, and his breath caught. Oblivious, she replied, "It's a hole in the wall on the edge of the historic district with the best Italian food in Georgia."

"Lorelei's getting takeout from Savannah?"

"Umhm." Tasha nodded. "We'll have to reheat it, but anything from Lucia's is so worth it. You'll see."

They'd been in each other's hip pockets all day, though. Some time with her friend would do her some good. The Collegium buildings were all warded so that only line-of-sight translocations inside them were possible. No one could translocate in, not even a damn traitor mage who was too lucky to be mortal. And Carter would be outside her door.

"Carter?" Tasha cocked her head. "If you don't like Italian—"

"I like it fine, but wouldn't you enjoy some time without me at your shoulder? Maybe talk to Lorelei about whatever stuff you women get into when no men are around?"

One corner of her mouth crooked up, and her blue eyes lit with an impish gleam that had always slammed straight into his groin. No loose working-uniform shirt to hide the reaction now, either, damn it.

"What could you possibly mean?" she asked sweetly.

"You're jerking me around, Murdock. Don't think I don't know it."

The sparkle deepened. He tightened his grip on the wheel. It was that or pull off, grab her, and show her just what that glint in her eyes did to him.

Which was a really good reason to give her some space for a while, to the extent he could.

Then she laughed, a bright, delighted sound that reached into his heart and squeezed. She hadn't laughed around him since that godawful day.

Carter grinned at her.

"Yeah, okay," she conceded. "You're welcome to join us, Carter."

But the words were polite. *You're welcome to* instead of *I'd really like you to.*

He stifled his disappointment. "I'll get dinner and guard your door from the outside. I'll eat and chase zombies on my tablet."

"That doesn't sound very comfortable."

"Hey, give me a good burger, and I'm set anywhere." Because she still looked doubtful, he smiled. "Order what you want. Have a girls' night or women's night or whatever y'all call it these days. I've got it covered."

"If you're sure."

"Go for it."

She texted Lorelei while he took the exit for downtown Savannah.

The historic district streets here were narrower, featuring parked cars and distracted tourists. Carter focused on watching the road and heeding his GPS until he pulled into a parking space a few houses down Perry from Orleans Square. Three-story wooden or brick houses in a style he identified only as old lined the sidewalks. So did tall live oak trees draped in Spanish moss.

Shutting off the engine, he eyed Tasha. She looked distracted, maybe planning her pitch.

Lightly, he said, "This guy isn't going to hit on one of us, is he?"

He was only half joking. Forewarned, forearmed, and so on.

Her smile brightened her face. "No chance. Neither of us, not even you, has blood blue enough for Winfield Beauregard Poindexter IV."

"What do you mean, *not even me?*" He wasn't sure he liked the sound of that.

"Aren't you the mayor's son or something like that?"

He checked magically for hostiles as he climbed out of the car. Finding none, he walked around to stand watch while she climbed out.

"Something like that," he answered. She didn't seem aware that his mom had served in the US House of Representatives for the last five years. Maybe that was good.

"It's this house over here." Apparently having forgotten her comment, she nodded at a tall, brick house trimmed in black ironwork.

A flight of concrete steps set on brick led up to the main door. Below the small, square porch, bricks framed an archway with a doorbell at one side, probably access to the ground floor.

Watching the street and keeping his senses open, Carter

followed Tasha. Her tall, athletic frame had nice hip curves—feminine but not overwhelming.

Not that his eyes had any business going there. Or that his hands ever would. Although establishing a friendly rapport could change the dynamic in a big way. Open the door, maybe.

One thing at a time, Lockwood.

CHAPTER EIGHT

As they reached the steps, the door above opened, revealing a short white man whose flowing mane of white hair topped a cheerful face with ruddy cheeks.

At least this client seemed pleasant enough.

Carter nodded politely but kept his senses open while Tasha introduced him under his alias. He trailed her and their host, who insisted they call him Dex, through the house.

The place was shabby, with peeling wallpaper, scuffed floors, and flaking ceilings. The flooring was oak, though, and the walls looked like lath and plaster. Absent something like rot or mold, solid construction like this could always be salvaged.

"This is early 1800s architecture," Tasha was saying. "You can turn this parlor into an area for informal receptions and the one across the hall into a guest lounge. When you have a lot of people, maybe for things like wedding receptions or anniversary parties, you could use them both."

"Well, darlin', I hadn't gotten that far, but you're right." Dex patted Tasha on the shoulder. That heavy, exaggerated drawl was something out of a bad movie. Nobody in Savannah talked like that.

Besides which, Dex should keep his blue-blooded hands to himself.

Carter followed Tasha and her client as they roamed downstairs to the big kitchen and upstairs to the bedrooms, where they embarked on a lengthy discussion of plumbing and how to make each bedchamber *en suite.*

Carter had his own ideas, but he wasn't here for that. He was here to watch Tasha.

Which meant he saw every little touch on her arm or at the small of her back that Dex found an excuse to make. Like when he ushered her into the big walk-in closet. Tasha met his eyes. Giving a slight, quick smile, she rolled her eyes. So this guy was okay.

Carter relaxed.

"Look in here, Tasha, and see whether you think this could be a small bathroom." Dex stepped aside but placed his palm at the small of Tasha's back.

At last, they returned to the entry hall. Tasha said, "Think about whether you want to do everything in the style consistent with the period of the house or do each bedroom in a different style from Savannah's history."

"I'll do that, honey." Dex smiled. "We can talk next week."

Recognizing an exit line, Carter opened his senses, checking the street.

"We're just goin' to have the *best* time workin' together." Dex flung an arm around Tasha's shoulders.

She smiled and slipped out of the old guy's hold. Patting his shoulder, she said, "Let me know about bedroom décor. Meanwhile, I'll start on sketches for the public rooms."

At last, they walked onto the narrow porch and down the steps, Carter in the lead.

Tasha sighed. "He's really a sweetie. You'd never know he's connected to everyone who is anyone in this city. He would stop with the touching if I asked him to, but it's kind of his way with everybody. He never crosses the line of what's socially appropriate."

Hoping to give her a laugh, Carter hooked an arm around her shoulders. "Honey, we're just gonna have the best—"

She gave him a startled look, and stumbled, falling against him. His hold tightened automatically. Awareness of her slammed into him. Tasha's eyes softened, and her hand rose to his chest. When she licked her lips, he almost crushed her mouth with his.

Abruptly, the warmth in her eyes died. Staring down the street, she stepped clear—but with an intriguing wash of red over her cheeks.

"Uh, sorry," he said. "I meant that as a joke. Shouldn't have grabbed you."

Again, she licked her lips, and he thought his control might snap.

"It's okay," she said, "but we should go."

"Definitely." Focusing on the street, he told her, "I could use a change of clothes from my place. If you need anything, let's swing by your house too. Then are we done?"

"Mostly. I have to go by my office for a while—return some calls, be sure there's nothing I need to handle—but it won't take long."

"Let's do that first, then go to your place, and then head to Brunswick." They needed to get back to the Collegium before he did anything else stupid.

～

"HE LIKES YOU," Lorelei decided.

Tasha's hand froze on her beer bottle. She and Lorelei were seated at the little dining table in Tasha and Carter's guest apartment. Tasha had just finished telling Lorelei about discussing That Day with Carter.

That silly little blip of pleasure at Lorelei's claim could just squash itself. Tasha shook her head. "He was trying to clear the air since we're stuck together for a while."

"Nuh-uh." Lorelei said around a mouthful of chicken scaloppini. She swallowed before continuing. "Girlfriend, when have you ever seen a man voluntarily bring up a topic that could involve emotions? They hate that, and they don't do it unless it gets them something they want. I'm telling you, he likes you."

Waggling one of Lucia's amazing Parmesan breadsticks at Tasha to punctuate her point, Lorelei added, "And I mean that in the seventh-grade sense of the word *like*."

Tasha's cheeks went hot. "Not possible." She gulped beer and choked on it.

While she spluttered, Lorelei said, "So the *like* thing is mutual."

"No," Tasha choked out between coughs. "Not."

"Oh, please. You're blushing, Tasha. That's rare." Lorelei ran her fingers along the stem of her wineglass.

Tasha couldn't speak yet. She chugged water to clear her throat.

"The past was a decade ago," Lorelei said gently. "He's smokin' hot, smart, brave, capable, and—underrated though the word is—nice. And you're attracted to each other. Why not give it a shot?"

At last, Tasha's breathing settled. She leaned back in her chair and eyed her friend. "For one thing, I think you're mistaken about his having any serious interest in me. For another, even if he did, it would never work. He's champagne, and I'm beer."

Lorelei shot her a stern look. "He drinks beer. I've seen him."

"You know what I mean." Tasha sighed. "He's a hometown hero, a golden boy, son of a prominent family, star student and athlete, and so on. I'd bet he was the guy tagged Most Likely To Succeed. You know how far that is from me."

Telling the truth shouldn't burn so much. The fact that it did was a sure sign Tasha had lost perspective. Carter was nice, damn it. She'd forgotten how nice he could be, what with That Day overshadowing all the pleasant memories. The fun.

But still—oil, water. She hadn't fit well with the 'in' crowd in the tiny South Carolina town of Watkins Landing. Not at all.

Trying to put the subject behind her, she scooped more eggplant Parmesan onto her fork. "Thanks again for bringing dinner."

"You're welcome." Lorelei raised her glass of chianti and studied Tasha across it. "But we're not done. Tasha, high school labels are a long way in the rearview mirror for all of us. No matter what those people expected from you back then, you did succeed. Handsomely. Even if they refuse to see that. You have a fabulous business and a stellar reputation."

"Because I can hide my rough edges at work. I also stay away from circles where I know I don't fit." Rushing on as Lorelei's eyes fired in indignation, Tasha added, "I enjoy the occasional crude joke. I prefer beer to any kind of wine, and God save me from spritzers. I have to do cocktail parties for business reasons, but I hate cocktails and the small talk that goes with them. A guy like Carter and I don't fit."

"If you think you don't," Lorelei responded quietly, "it's a guarantee that you won't." She sighed. "I'm sorry my divination skills have been on the blink since Ken died. I've tried, and I can't turn up anything about your situation."

"You're here for me," Tasha said quickly. "That counts for a lot."

The two women ate in silence for a few minutes. Tasha eyed her friend across the table. Lorelei wanted her to be happy, but she didn't truly understand.

With a sigh, Tasha set down her fork. "In my wild days, I had a few encounters with hometown hero types. They were crazy about me in the back seat of a car or in the dark down by the river. Never at the prom or in the cafeteria or in the halls at school. I just don't fit in their world. At one point, I was so reckless that Nate asked me to rein it in because anytime one of these guys shot off his mouth—most of them exaggerating— Nate had to fight him, and he wanted to keep those problems to a minimum."

She'd dated two of the soccer players, each in different years, and slept with them. Within days of the second breakup, it was all over school that she'd done it with the entire team.

"High school boys are assholes, but that's all behind you."

"I wish. Those boys talked a lot. And the dirt stuck."

Especially after the mayor's son, angry over being turned down, had reported her for taking money for sex. She'd been charged with prostitution. Only the high school principal's intervention and the judge's willingness to look at the complete lack of actual evidence had saved her. The charges had been dropped, and she'd taken the principal's and the judge's advice and gone into the service. It had been a fresh start.

Until she blew it.

"Tasha?" Lorelei waved a hand in front of her face. "You with me?"

"Yeah." She squared her shoulders. Even Lorelei didn't know about the prostitution charge. "When I went back for my grandmother's funeral, I was so proud to stand by her grave in my dress blues, a US Navy petty officer third class, with Nate next to me in US Army dress greens, complete with the hard-won insignia and tan beret that marked him as a Ranger. Against the odds, we'd made something of ourselves, as she'd always told us we would. She would have been so happy."

"Of course she would."

"The next day, I went into town, to the home furnishings shop where I used to work. When I walked in, I overheard some of the women I knew talking about me. About how the navy must take just anybody. I was just…I froze. All that pride just drained away. One said they probably really wanted sluts, with all those sailors at sea for so long."

Ignoring Lorelei's deepening scowl, Tasha added, "Then they started in on some of my supposed slutty deeds and how that was all you could expect of trailer trash anyway."

Her fist clenched on her knee. "I hate that phrase."

"Me too," Lorelei said. "There's nothing wrong with trailers. Gram and I lived in one for a while, before you and I met."

"I bet yours wasn't ratty," Tasha muttered.

"No, because the people who lived in that trailer park took care of their homes. Just like the people we live among now." Lorelei shook her head. "So the women you grew up with were assholes. There's a lot of that going around."

Those women had started young. Tasha had the claustrophobia to prove it.

Lorelei quirked a brow. "Carter Lockwood, however, does not seem to be an asshole. Or a snob. Besides, plenty of guys and women do asshole things because they're young and stupid but eventually outgrow that tendency."

No way was Tasha touching that bit about Carter. She lifted her beer bottle and forced her mouth into a smile. "Here's to equal-opportunity asshole-ness and outgrowing it."

Maybe the women she'd grown up with had outgrown that phase. One of them, PrissAnn Elgin, headed up a literacy foundation in Charleston. Or so Tasha's mom had made a point of telling her, citing PrissAnn as a paragon of what a woman should aspire to. But that didn't mean she didn't look down on the people her organization served.

"Here's to outgrowing bad habits." Lorelei clinked her glass against Tasha's bottle.

"Last thing I'm going to say," Lorelei added. She waited for Tasha's nod before continuing. "People grow up, and they often leave the worlds they were raised in."

As both Tasha and Lorelei had done.

"If he wants a chance," Lorelei said, "think about giving him one."

Tasha nodded, but that was never going to happen. Even if Lorelei was right, a guy like Carter Lockwood might want a fling with a woman like Tasha, but they could never share anything more. That would be okay if she didn't genuinely like him. But she did. That made him dangerous.

Stepping outside the friend zone with him would be a mistake, and she liked to think she'd left her stupid days behind her.

OUTSIDE THE GUEST UNIT, Carter sat on the floor with his back to the wall and his legs stretched into the corridor, halfway blocking it. He had his broadsword harness on, but with the sword lying in easy reach by his right leg.

With the elevator to his left and Tasha's door about fifteen feet down on his right, he blocked access. The window at the corridor's end was no problem. Mages, ghouls, and the ghouls' allies, demons from the Void between worlds, shared an inability to fly, and nobody could translocate into a Collegium building.

Too bad other things weren't as easy to manage. Like women. Especially a tall, sexy, auburn-haired goddess.

He'd been an idiot this afternoon. But maybe, judging by that wash of red on her face, she hadn't entirely minded.

The elevator dinged.

He turned toward it, his left hand setting aside the takeout box with his steak and fries and his right gripping the sword.

Will Davis stepped into the hall, blue soda can in hand, and strolled toward him. Carter relaxed.

Grinning, the archaeologist raised his eyebrows. "Pissed her off, did you?"

Carter shrugged. "Girls' night. Or women's night. Or whatever they call it anymore. Lorelei brought Italian takeout."

"From Lucia's?" Davis's eyes narrowed. When Carter nodded, the other man said, "Damn. I love Lucia's."

"How come I've never heard of this place?"

"It's a local secret. You need to know people in Savannah to hear about it."

At his hip, Davis wore his gladius, modeled on the short swords of the Roman legions. Carter nodded toward it. "Expecting trouble?"

"Since I was coming up here, I figured I might as well be armed. I'd like to think nothing could come at Tasha here, but there's no guarantee."

"No." Shortly after Carter had started work here, ghouls had attacked the Collegium. They'd been trying to recover a portal orb, a rounded crystal that could open a passageway for Void demons to reach this world. They'd almost managed it.

Putting his back to the wall opposite Carter, Davis drew the gladius and slid down to sit with his legs extended and the sword balanced across his knees. He and Carter now totally blocked the hallway.

"We finished preliminary runs on Tasha's recent clients," Davis announced. "Bottom line is, nothing popped. I emailed you the list. The only one at all odd is that Poindexter guy, who has a rep for patting and hugging every woman he meets but is supposedly so charming that the women just shrug it off. I'm sort of surprised Tasha hasn't killed him, but he's probably not the most obnoxious client she's ever had. There's no sign that he pats areas we might call socially inappropriate or pushes for more contact than that."

"She thinks he's sweet."

"Well, there you go." Davis took a swallow of soda and gave Carter a considering look. "How're you two getting along?"

Crap. Was the guy psychic? Carter grabbed a thick French

fry from his box. "Do I detect the hand of Val Dare behind that question?"

"Maybe. After the tension between you two last November, though, everybody's curious." Davis grinned again. "I wanted to start a betting pool, but Audra threatened my manhood."

"A betting pool?" Carter put a warning edge into his voice. "On what?"

"How long until one of you explodes."

"Funny." Carter scowled and grabbed another fry. But Davis's comment had brought Carter's mind back to his woman problem. Based on the little he knew of her background, he figured she'd struggled as a kid. That rankled. He didn't want that for her, and never mind that both their childhoods were years behind them.

"Hey," Will said. "You with me?"

Carter blinked. "Sorry. What did you say?"

Great. Now the blasted woman was distracting him from conversations. Forgetting her would be so much smarter.

Except that didn't seem to be working.

Dumbass.

Davis spoke in patient tones. "I said for you to call me if you need me to do anything."

"Not if you start a damn betting pool."

"That was a joke." Davis studied Carter for a long minute. "So how are you two really getting along?"

"We manage. It's not like this is a permanent deal."

Regret nipped his heart, but he squelched it. The past was likely going to lie between him and Tasha forever, no matter what either one of them said about it.

The elevator dinged again. He and Will both reached for their weapons, but the tall, sandy-haired man in jeans and a green pullover sweater was no threat. Josh Campbell was a deputy reeve, a helicopter pilot, and a friend.

"Isn't this cozy?" Josh dropped down by Carter. "Am I interrupting your coffee klatch?"

"We're done talking about you now," Davis commented, "so have a seat."

"I dunno." Carter eyed Josh's sweater. "That sweater's army green. This is a navy stronghold."

"Yeah, 'cause the navy always does so well when it's land-locked. Anyway, Davis is Switzerland." Josh grabbed one of Carter's fries. "I hear there was dinner from Lucia's."

"The women are having it," Carter informed him. "Does everybody but me know about this place?"

"It's a family, date night, and chick-group place," Josh noted. "You've never asked me for me for a restaurant reference, or I would've mentioned it."

Too true. And Carter had to wonder whether some subconscious hangup about the woman he was guarding had anything to do with that. He seriously needed his head examined.

"Where's Edie? Is she on duty?" Davis asked. Edie Lang was Josh's girlfriend, a wildland firefighter in the summer and a mage combat medic in the off season.

Josh nodded. "Yep. She's on call." He paused, and the proud light in his eyes dimmed. "Don't know if y'all have heard our news. Edie was accepted for smokejumper training."

Jumping out of airplanes to fight fires. Josh had once admitted this goal of Edie's worried him, no matter how supportive he tried to be.

Carter clapped him on the back. "Good for her. She'll be fine. And she has magic on her side."

"Unlike most of the smokies. I know." Josh smiled. "I'm proud of her. It's just . . . I'll go anywhere my chopper can fit. But without the bird, it's a long way to the ground."

Josh and Will launched into a discussion of smokejumper training. That Davis, an archaeologist and loremaster, should know about something like that no longer seemed odd to Carter. The guy had a range of knowledge an encyclopedia would envy.

Munching the burger, Carter watched Josh from the corner

of his eye. The pilot would be Mr. AttaGirl for his Edie, who would, in turn, do what she could to defuse his fear. Because they loved each other.

Meanwhile, Carter was fixated on a woman he couldn't seem to stay on an even keel with. A woman who, attraction or no, seemed pretty sure she didn't want him. This was pointless. When this was over and she was safe, he was definitely moving on.

CHAPTER NINE

THE NEXT DAY PASSED IN A WHIRL OF CLIENT MEETINGS WITH NO one behaving suspiciously. Going to Griff and Val's to party was a welcome relief from watching everything all the time.

Leading Carter toward their two-story, white farmhouse, Tasha wondered whether maybe the threat had passed. Carter probably wished it had. He'd been very quiet all day. She wasn't going to be the one to ask, though. Yesterday's personal discussion was still making her uneasy.

In the service, she'd focused on how different they were. Figuring any relationship was futile helped her stay on the good side of the regs. Not that he showed any inclination to smash them.

Except for that one moment in India. Which he probably regretted starting.

The new gravel-and-crushed-shell walkway crunched under their shoes. Judging by the crowd on the wraparound porch and the patio, many of them dancing to rock coming from the outside speakers, there would be plenty of people here to keep her mind off him.

Besides which, every guest here was trustworthy. She and Carter could take a break from watching her back all the time. It would be nice to kick back and relax, even enjoy whatever was cooking that sent the aromas of warm beef and tomatoes wafting on the breeze.

"This is great," Carter said, glancing around.

"Have you been here before?"

"No, but I can see why they'd rather be here than at the Collegium."

"It's fabulous inside, too. The barn, where we'll be tonight, used to be Griff's bachelor quarters and has his studio above."

"Hence the skylights," Carter guessed, looking up at them.

"Yep. They fixed up the house last fall, in time for their wedding. Val handled most of the decorating, and it's great. Comfortable and homey."

Stefan stepped onto the wraparound porch from the kitchen, a phone held to his ear. He walked toward the three steps and headed toward the cars with his gaze on the ground. He was probably trying to get far enough from the music to hear.

Carter and Tasha had almost reached him when a big grin split his face. "Yes," he cried, pumping a fist.

Then his voice dropped again, but the tender light in his eyes had Tasha's throat going tight.

Carter stopped in his tracks. "Uh, should we hang back?"

"Maybe." She'd never seen Stefan like this.

Still grinning, he pocketed his phone. He raised his head, seeming startled to see them. "Hey, y'all."

"Hey." As she and Carter came even with him, Tasha touched the doctor's arm lightly. "Everything okay?"

"Better than." Impossibly, his grin widened. Golden lights glinted in his brown eyes. "I'm getting married."

"I know." Tasha eyed him carefully. "I saw Mel's gorgeous diamond, remember?"

Stefan laughed, his idiotically happy expression unlike anything she'd ever seen on his face. He wasn't the type to smoke funny cigarettes, but—

"Yeah, I know. It's . . ." He ran a hand over his face and

laughed again. "Mel got a transfer to the Brunswick office. She's coming down as soon as she can so we can set a date and find a house."

"Stefan, that's wonderful."

"Damn straight," he said, sweeping her into a tight hug.

Carter had walked about ten yards away and was studying the barn, giving her privacy with her friend.

Stefan released her and shook his head. "I guess—after all the barriers we've had to climb, maybe I was afraid there'd be another, y'know? That this was never really going to happen."

"That's understandable."

Stefan and his Mel, FBI Special Agent Camellia Wray, had been lovers in school and had broken up because she thought he'd been cheating on her. He'd actually been studying magical healing but couldn't tell her because she was scornful of anything *woo-woo*. They'd reconnected last year when he consulted on a murder case she was working. Somehow, Mel had found her way to accepting Stefan's magic, not that they'd shared details with anyone.

"I would've moved," Stefan said, "but she said I was needed here more than she was in Atlanta."

"Probably true." Tasha patted his arm. "You would be hard to replace."

"We could've gotten married anyway," he conceded. "Lived apart and commuted. It's just. . . . It took us nine years to find each other again. We didn't want to start our marriage living apart."

"Also understandable." Tasha hugged him again. "Why don't you come on in with us? Have a celebratory beer and share your news."

"Thanks, but you go ahead. I want a minute or three to myself."

"Sure." She nodded. Sometimes having a dream come true could rock a person.

Joining Carter, Tasha said, "You get tact points, Deputy Lockwood."

"Is he okay?"

"He's great. Just had a surprise."

She and Carter climbed the four steps to the porch.

"Hey, Tasha!" came from someone in the back yard. She turned to greet a tall, broad-shouldered guy with long, shaggy brown hair and a wicked grin, one of Griff's old Atlanta team.

"Hey, Tim," she called. "This is Carter Lockwood. Carter, Tim Calhoun."

The two men exchanged nods and lifted hands in greeting. Was that speculation in Tim's eyes? Damn it, yes. But she didn't want to explain to everyone why Carter was sticking so close.

They stepped up on the porch. Rock music filled the air. With no neighbors for more than a mile on any side, Val and Griff didn't have to worry about bothering anyone.

The inner door was open. Carter held the storm door for Tasha. Surprised, she faltered for an instant before walking into the big kitchen.

Why was his courtesy a surprise? He'd held doors for her before.

The room was full of familiar faces. Tim and three other guys and two women, all from the Atlanta division of Griff's old team, had come down to party. So had Will and Audra, visible through the doorway to the big living room.

Audra's shoulder-length, black hair gleamed in the light. It and her light tan complexion could've come from a number of gene pools but actually were because of her Cherokee ancestry. She and Will chatted with Lorelei and Miss Hettie Telfair, one of the few Mundanes who was in on all of Griff's secrets.

Hettie, a retired lawyer who wore her long, gray hair in a braid down her back, had been instrumental in clearing Griff's name. She turned, spotted Tasha, and waved.

Chuck Porter and Javy Ruiz weren't in sight, but maybe they were here somewhere. It would be nice to have the core gang back together, especially since being around Carter kept her feeling so off-balance.

"Hey!" Val stepped out of the crowd on the right and gave Tasha and Carter each a quick hug. "Welcome."

Now Carter looked surprised. Why?

Val continued, "We have beer, hard cider, wine, lemonade, and sodas—and good old water—in the fridge and in the cooler on the porch. Help yourselves."

A woman called out to Carter. Of medium height, athletic-looking, and with short, dark hair and olive skin, she looked familiar.

"Hey, GiGi," he answered. To Tasha, he added, "I'll be right back."

GiGi. The name helped Tasha place her. She'd been part of the deputy reeve unit guarding Will and Audra last year. Which meant there was no reason to be jealous. That little twinge when Carter hurried to greet his comrade could just stifle itself.

"I told him everyone here had been vetted," Tasha said to Val. "He can relax for a while. We both can."

"I imagine that would be a relief." Turning her back to Carter and his friend, Val asked, "How's it going?"

Tasha mustered a smile. "We haven't killed each other yet."

Carter and GiGi were standing close, smiling. Were they more than comrades in arms? Was guarding Tasha putting a crimp in his dating plans?

She didn't want to impose, of course. That was probably why that weird little pang kept pinching her heart.

"Well, not killing each other is progress," Val said.

Tim stepped up beside Tasha and put a hand on her shoulder. "Come outside and dance with me? If I'm not horning in on your date."

"It's not a date," Tasha replied. "Just pals. Sure, let's dance." That would get her mind off Carter for a while.

"HEY, CARTER." Lorelei Martin, Tasha's friend, intercepted him as he and GiGi drifted apart.

"Hey, Lorelei. How's it going?"

Where the hell was Tasha? He'd expected her to stick fairly close, and the house wasn't crowded enough to hide her. Especially with her distinctive hair color.

"Can't complain." Lorelei studied him over her glass of white wine. "Something wrong?"

"Have you seen Tasha?"

"She went outside with Tim." Lorelei jogged his arm with her elbow. "She's fine. Val and Griff personally vetted everyone here so y'all could relax for a while. I thought Tasha would tell you."

"She did, but I should keep an eye on her anyway." It was his duty. No more than that. Tim Whoever had seemed friendly enough, but sometimes guys turned grabby.

Carter started for the porch, only to meet Will Davis and Audra Grayson in the kitchen doorway. The two looked joined at the hip, likely because they had so little time together with her teaching in Atlanta and him living and working at the Collegium.

"Hey," Carter said. He and Audra exchanged hugs before he and Will traded back slaps. He liked these two. He really did. But Tasha was outside unguarded.

"Will told me you're helping Tasha out." Audra's phrasing was elegantly nonspecific. "I think that's great."

"Thanks." Manners compelled him to ask, "How's the teaching?"

She grinned, her dark eyes gleaming. "It's great. Naturally my final semester would be the one when I get my best classes of the last two years."

"At least you'll go out on a high note." Then she would work for Davis's parents' archaeological institute as a consultant. "Listen, I hate to rush, but I want to check on Tasha."

They traded farewells with him. Carter hurried out to the porch.

Dusk had arrived, making the visibility poor despite the fairy lights in the trees, the lanterns around the patio, and his mageborn senses. Where the hell was she?

Finally, he spotted her, dancing with that Tim guy on the far side of the patio.

She was undoubtedly *fine,* as Lorelei predicted. In fact, she was having a much better time than she ever seemed to with him. And that guy was standing way too close.

As he watched, admiration drowned his tension. The woman had moves. Her tall, athletic body rocked in time to the beat and swayed as though she had an elastic spine.

In bed, a woman like that would...remain a mystery. He had about zero chance of going there with her, no matter how much he wished otherwise. But the music was ending, and he could claim the next dance, see her move like that for him.

As he stepped off the porch, another guy, broad-shouldered and with long, blond hair like a Thor movie wannabe, stepped up to her. Damn it.

Carter changed direction to grab a beer. Considering all the potential protection around Tasha, he could afford to have one. He popped it open and watched her. That guy was probably another of Dare's renegade raiders. He sure as hell wasn't a deputy reeve, not with that mane, so he wasn't part of Val's task force.

How was a guy supposed to compete with that kind of camaraderie, that trust born of having each other's backs in a dangerous and, yes, illegal venture?

And...*Whoa. Just whoa. Who said anything about compet—*

Someone poked him in the shoulder. "Problem?" GiGi asked.

"Dance with me." He couldn't ignore Tasha and that guy, but he needed something to do besides flat-out stare at them.

GiGi blinked, maybe at his abrupt tone, but she hopped off

the porch with him and threaded her arm through his. Under cover of the music, she suggested, "You should ask Tasha to dance."

"Excuse me?" Had he been obvious about watching her? To cover his momentary panic, he raised his eyebrows.

"Dancing," GiGi explained with obvious patience, "is an easy way of working together."

When he frowned, she added, "I was part of the guard unit for that excavation, remember? I saw the two of you interact. Which is a generous word for it, by the way. Together, you're the poster children for friction. But right now, you're stuck with each other."

Watching Tasha dance, he silently added, *and we're stuck with that...whatever it is between us.* His pulse kicked up. His body stirred.

His cell phone vibrated.

He yanked it out of his back pocket. Jeremy. Carter swiped the screen, but his gut was sinking. What the hell would he do if the kid needed help?

"Hey, Jeremy. What's up?" With a finger in his other ear, Carter walked away from the music.

"Dad went nuts." The boy's voice was shaking.

Shitfuckdamn. "Where are you? Are you safe?"

"I'm in—in the cl-clubhouse. It's closed. He won't look here."

The clubhouse for his subdivision in Brunswick, he meant. Locked doors were no barrier to a mage, and Jeremy had enough power and control at age thirteen to break in without leaving a trace.

"What did he do, Jeremy?"

"He took out part of a w-wall. Threw dinner—across the k-kitchen." After a pause, as though the boy fought for control, he added, "He chased me out—out of the—the house."

Fucking bastard. The Collegium would say alcohol abuse, even involving magic, was for Mundane Social Services, whose staff were no match for a mage. Nor could they offer a reliable haven for a mageborn kid coming into his powers.

"Are you hurt?"

"Nuh-uh."

"Okay, then. I'm going to make some calls, find you a place to stay tonight." Normally, Carter would pick him up and deliver him to the runaway shelter or whoever they arranged to have put him up. But leaving Tasha was out of the question.

"I'm on duty tonight, Jaybird, so I can't come get you. But I'll find someone, and I'll confirm with you before you get in the car." Maybe GiGi would help him out. "Did you get any dinner?"

Had the meal gone flying before or after—?

"Nuh-uh," Jeremy admitted.

Double-fucking shithead bastard. "I'll call you back. Stay safe."

As Carter disconnected, someone touched his arm. GiGi. Perfect. He swung around to face...Tasha?

Oh, hell. Instantly, he blanked his expression, but the intent look in her eyes said he'd been too late.

"What's wrong?" she asked.

"It's, uh, a friend needs some help." He opted for a partial truth and shrugged, hoping she'd read the gesture as minimizing the problem. He wasn't going to burden her with it, but he didn't think she would accept a glib lie.

"I didn't mean to eavesdrop, Carter, but if you need to make calls and worry about food, is this a kid?"

"Teenager," he admitted warily. "It'll be fine. I've got a handle on it."

"Do you need to go?"

"I can get someone to see to it."

"That wasn't what I asked." Watching him intently, she indicated the house with one hand. "Despite my concerns about bringing danger here, I'm as safe here for an evening as I could be anywhere, probably including the Collegium. There're still about a dozen deputy reeves around as well as some others who can handle themselves."

Dare's old team, she meant. He clamped down on a vicious wave of jealousy.

"I don't desert my post," he told her.

"You aren't deserting it. You're just handing it off for a bit." With a slight smile, she added, "Unless you want to tell me I'm at risk surrounded by all these trained mages."

He couldn't. It was only the presence of so many deputy reeves, along with the Dares, Will Davis, and Stefan Harper, that had made him agree to her plan for spending the night here after the party anyway.

"Or I can go with you," she suggested.

"No." At his quick response, her brows rose. Hastily, he added, "I mean, thanks, but there's no need for you to be dragged into it."

If she learned about his unorthodox way of helping his kids, she might casually mention it to someone, which could lead to the shire reeve or a Collegium Councilor knowing, in which case Carter's ass was grass.

"It's nice of you to offer, but there's no need to spoil your evening. If you're sure you'll be okay, I'll head out. My friend's in Brunswick, so this would take me a while."

Like an hour each way plus time to deal with it.

Tasha shrugged. "It's not like I don't have anybody to talk to. Drive carefully."

She was letting him off the hook. Sending him, even. But leaving her rubbed him the wrong way.

"Are you sure?" he asked. If anyone but one of "his" kids had called, he would've answered with a flat *sorry*. "I'll get GiGi to keep an eye on you."

As a deputy reeve, she was in the loop about the threat to Tasha. And she owed him a favor or two.

Tasha frowned but said only, "If it'll make you feel better."

"Okay, then."

"So go. Be sure you take the moonstone that gets you through the property's wards so you can come back." Tasha patted his arm, sending a flash of heat to his groin. "I'm going to find somebody to dance with."

Too bad he couldn't offer to be the one. Dancing with her, watching her moves up close, would be worth the frustration that followed. "I'll bring your bag in before I go."

And talk to GiGi.

"Just set it in the barn. Val said it's unlocked." Tasha turned toward that guy Tim and some others.

Carter choked down his idiotic resentment. Those guys would help keep her safe while he went to the rescue of a kid who really needed a better solution to his long-term problem.

"WHERE'S LOCKWOOD?" Griff shut the door behind the departing guests. Despite his casual posture and tone, his ocean-blue eyes were keen as he walked into the living room and perched on the arm of the buttery tan leather sofa beside Val.

Only the people scattered around the homey room, GiGi Gonzales, Tasha, Stefan, the Dares, and Will and Audra, remained at the party. There was no way to imply Carter was here but somewhere else.

Besides, lying to these people went against Tasha's grain. Though it would be karmic irony if she lied to protect the man who'd refused to cover for her.

She shrugged and gave irony a pass. "He had a friend in trouble, so I told him to go tend to it. GiGi stepped up in his place."

Griff frowned. Sudden tension crackled in the air, and Val, Stefan, and Will suddenly seemed to have pokers down their shirts.

Val and Griff exchanged a grim look. Griff said, "He had no business leaving you."

"I'm covered." Tasha nodded to GiGi.

"I can stay however long it takes for him to get back," the deputy reeve offered. As Carter's friend—or possibly, girlfriend, something that had no business pinching at Tasha—she naturally would cover for him.

"That's fine," Griff said, "but he should've cleared it with someone senior."

Oh, geez. "Look," Tasha said, "since this all started, you've consistently told me how safe I'd be here. So I'm here and staying the night. Surrounded by people who specialize in kicking ass."

"That's not the point," Stefan put in from his easy chair by the hearth. In the matching chair across from him, Will nodded. On Will's lap, Audra just looked uncomfortable.

Stefan continued, "Carter has a responsibility to you, not to mention his obligation to his fellow deputy reeves, and to Deke, to fulfill his assigned duties."

"We trade off all the time," GiGi put in, her voice even.

"With clearance," Val shot back.

GiGi's expression hardened. Before the deputy could say something she might regret, Tasha stood.

"I'm the person most affected here," she reminded them. "I told him to go, partly because I think a kid in trouble should be a priority and mainly because everybody tells me I'm safe here. If I am, then we need to drop this. If I'm not, no way am I coming here again, maybe leading ghouls to my friends' carefully concealed home, until this is all over."

Val's brows rose. "A kid in trouble? What kid?"

"I didn't ask," Tasha replied. "I trust his judgment."

For a miracle, the words didn't stick in her throat. Maybe she really was getting over what happened all those years ago.

Val looked thoughtful. After a moment, she said, "I don't

guess it matters so much when we're all here. We did want both of you to be able to relax, and he did get you coverage."

"I completely agree," Tasha announced. "Let me help you clean up. Then I'll toddle out to the barn and turn in."

The Dares exchanged a look. "You're not going out to the barn by yourself," Griff stated. His raised hand cut off her protest. "Yes, you should be safer here than pretty much anywhere except the Collegium, but we're not betting your life on that, Tasha."

"Listen to him, amica," Will urged. Tasha's heart softened, as it always did at the reminder that she was part of a de facto family here, as he finished, "Better safe than sorry."

"Okay. All right. And thanks." *Especially, thanks for caring.*

Under cover of the noise as everyone picked up bottles and plates around the room, GiGi said, "Thanks for sticking up for Carter."

"I just told the truth." But the fact she'd done so would probably blow Carter Lockwood's mind. Tasha grinned.

JEREMY HAD BEEN SO RATTLED that dropping him off quickly was impossible. Carter's brief errand had taken almost four hours. Tasha was probably pissed, and he couldn't blame her.

Driving back to the Dares' house well after midnight, Carter found his idiot brain fixated on images of Tasha. Of the way she smiled at those guys tonight. At the sexy moves she'd pulled out for them.

Yeah, his plan of forgetting about her was working so damn well.

That guy Tim had seemed interested. Even proprietary.

Carter set his jaw. Once upon a time, she'd been interested in him. Except that navy regs had first stood in the way and then torpedoed any chance they had to see what they could be together.

He'd hoped that with time, her potential for promotion, and the way the US Navy liked to move people around, their situations would change. That dating wouldn't be banned fraternizing.

But no.

So he was supposed to just stand by while she laughed and flirted with other guys. Even though the sizzle between them was still there.

Damn if he would. She'd seemed to be unbending toward him lately. If he bided his time, maybe . . .

"Stalker, much?" he asked the night. With all the hot women in Georgia, only a nut job would fixate on one who didn't want him.

Except he'd felt her watching him in November. She blushed so easily around him, and she wasn't prone to that.

If he couldn't exorcise her from his mind, maybe he should take his shot. See if she would give him a chance.

Just not until this whole business was over. She shouldn't feel any kind of pressure from someone she was, however temporarily, relying on.

He tapped his blinker and turned into the Dares' long, narrow driveway. The magical ward across the opening and the defenses along its length prickled over his skin but didn't trigger. The moonstone in his pocket did its job and slid him through them.

The house was dark when Carter pulled in.

Thanks to the quick text GiGi had sent him, he knew the Dares had been annoyed with him but had let it go. She'd also said that Tasha had stood up for him. He still had trouble believing that.

He parked Tasha's truck in the space between the house and barn, by Will Davis's silver subcompact. Judging by the cars, someone else besides Will, Audra, and GiGi had stayed the night, likely Stefan Harper.

Lights blazed from the barn's skylights. Dare must be painting. If Carter was lucky, they could avoid a confrontation, if one was coming, until morning.

In the ground floor bachelor flat, a light burned in one window, in the living room area. Maybe Tasha had gone to bed.

For the sake of being quiet, he avoided the crunchy path to the door. He let himself in with the key she'd given him.

His duffel sat by a sofa bed upholstered in maroon and blue plaid. The bed was pulled out and made.

Nice of her.

Staggered bookshelves divided the space, with the workout area next and the sleeping area at the back, by the bathroom.

Magically muffling his footsteps, he crept back to the sleeping area to check on his charge.

The bed was empty. Still neatly made.

What the hell?

Had she gone home with that Tim guy? Or that Thor wannabe?

The idea stabbed into his gut. Scowling, he ran a hand over his hair.

None of his business who she slept with, of course. But seeing as he was supposed to be her bodyguard, she should've let him know—

"As a bodyguard, Lockwood, you suck."

CHAPTER TEN

CARTER WHEELED. GRIFF DARE STOOD BEHIND HIM, HIS FACE SET. How the hell had a guy with no magic moved that quietly?

"Where's Tasha?" Carter asked.

"Where were you?" Dare crossed his arms over his chest.

Carter swallowed the hot retort on his tongue. The guy was Tasha's friend. Of course he was concerned. And he'd undoubtedly helped cover her in Carter's absence.

"I was helping a friend in trouble." Carter kept his voice even. Damn if he'd pull Tasha into this by saying she'd sent him.

"A kid, Tasha said," Dare informed him. "Who?"

"That's confidential." Spacing his words for emphasis, Carter demanded, "Where is Tasha?"

Dare studied him a long moment. Carter's gut knotted. If she'd gone home with—

"She's bunking across the hall from Valeria tonight." The relief that rolled through Carter was out of proportion to the news, but Dare was continuing. "Will and Audra are here, and Stefan stayed over tonight, even though he's on duty in the morning. And GiGi Gonzales, covering for you, is on the downstairs couch. I have painting to do, so you and I are bunking out here."

Carter nodded acknowledgment. "Thanks."

"Next time you need to be spelled, follow procedure. Any of us will stand in for you if we're needed, but you're required to notify someone senior."

"I know." Carter ran a hand over his face. "I screwed up. I admit it." But if he hadn't been there, Jeremy would have cowered in the clubhouse, scared and hungry and upset, all night. Carter had to come up with a better plan for the kid.

Yet Tasha had stuck up for him.

Incredulous and foolishly happy about that, he barely heard Dare add, "She was safe, and GiGi kept an eye out, so it's okay."

Yet just this mild reprimand underlined that he wasn't a member of this tight little group. Not like those guys Tasha'd danced with so enthusiastically.

If she'd actually gone home with one of them, his head would've exploded. It might even have done so if he'd stuck around and watched her with those guys. That was a bad sign for his sanity.

Pretty soon, he was going to have to fish or cut bait about making his move.

Tasha barely tasted the breakfast Val and Griff had assembled. Carter didn't say much while they ate. Although she couldn't wait for him to tell her what had happened with his young friend, he didn't seem inclined to do it in front of everyone. Not that it was her business, of course, but having been a kid in trouble, she felt for others with problems.

At last, they climbed into her truck. Carter drove, as usual. Waving to the group on the porch, they headed out.

"How did it go last night?" she asked, watching him from the corner of her eye.

"It's handled. Sorry it took so long."

"You already apologized. Once was enough. Besides, it was great to catch up with the guys. I never see them anymore."

A muscle worked in his jaw. This had to be a new record. She'd somehow managed to irritate him while talking about something irrelevant.

"Want to grab coffee for the road in Wayfarer?" she suggested. The Dares would've supplied it, but neither Tasha nor Carter had thought to ask. "Serenity's Rainbow in Wayfarer has good coffee. It's on Burke Street."

"Okay."

Getting coffee didn't take long, and they were soon on the road to Kingsland and the interstate.

"Today isn't too busy," Tasha said. "I wish I had some more ideas for checking out various clients. Nobody seemed off yesterday."

"Uh-huh."

"Do you have any thoughts?" she asked.

"Nothing new."

Frowning, she stared out the window. He wasn't usually Mr. Chatty, but this seemed terse even for him. Maybe he was embarrassed about last night, though she couldn't imagine why he would be.

They passed the Kingsland veterans' memorial garden, then crossed the town's main street with its little shops and restaurants. After a stretch with an abandoned church and some small houses, they rolled into the area lined with gas stations, quick stops, and motels usual for areas near a major highway.

When they were on I-95 and heading north, Tasha carefully said, "You know, Griff and the rest weren't really irritated with you last night. They're mainly worried about me."

"I know."

Okay then. They'd intended to discuss the day's itinerary last night but had never gotten to it. Might as well do that now.

"I have to go into the office for much of the day. Tomorrow, I'm due on Cumberland Island to talk to a client about redecorating a guesthouse. I'll call and arrange a time for them to send a boat—"

"No."

"Excuse me?" If he thought he could veto a client meeting, he'd better think again.

"We're not taking their boat. That makes our coming and going dependent on them."

"It's an island, Carter. Unless you can fly—or have access to a Collegium chopper—we don't have any other way to get there."

"I have a boat," he reminded her. "Sailboat with a motor. We'll take that."

"Um, great. Thanks."

"Sure," he grunted, looking out at the road.

If he stayed so testy, this was going to be a helluva long day.

When they reached Tasha's office in Savannah, he pulled into her reserved parking space. Once more, she would try. Once. Then if he wanted to pout, or whatever, for the rest of the day, he could just knock himself out.

His extended senses brushed hers as he checked their surroundings for ghouls or mage power.

When he said, "Clear," she screened her saber and climbed out without waiting for him. She opened her own senses and stood facing him across the hood of the truck.

He looked up from shutting his door. "What?"

"You tell me. You've been Mr. Closed Mouth all morning, and you won't look at me." Which hurt, damn it, even if that was ludicrous. "What crawled up your shorts?"

"Aside from your friends back there pointing out that I abandoned my post?" he demanded, slinging a small rucksack over his shoulder. "And the fact they were right?"

Before she could reply, he added, "And the woman I'm supposed to be guarding had to defend me? You want more than that?"

"Carter, how many times do you want me to say it's not a problem? I was safe, and they all know it. You and I agreed, which is kind of a miracle anyway, so you—"

"Then I came in and couldn't find you."

"What?"

He stalked around the truck and toward the building. She would've admired his broad shoulders and trim butt if she hadn't been so distracted by his weird attitude.

"I couldn't find you," he ground out. He stopped and gestured for her to go first up the metal stairs to the second-floor office level. "You weren't in the barn, and I thought I was going to have to punch Griff to make him tell me where you were."

Hurrying up the stairs, she spoke over her shoulder to Mr. Stoneface. "Well, good grief. I figured you'd just assume I was sleeping in the house."

"No." On the stoop, he stepped close to her.

"No," he repeated, and he actually had the nerve to point at her. "What I figured, based on the way you acted before I left, was that you'd gone home with one of those guys. And how the hell was I going to find you?"

"What?" Old, painful memory rushed to the fore, and she pushed his finger aside. At least he had the sense not to resist that. "Are you implying I'm easy?"

"Of course not, but I—"

"What guys do you mean, anyway?" she demanded around a rush of relief at his answer. "I knew lots of guys at the—"

"You know damn well what guys. Tim Whoever and his buddy who thinks he's Thor."

"They're my friends." Tasha let out an exasperated sigh. "Why would you think I'd go home with one of them?"

"I saw how they looked at you."

"You're hallucinating."

"Okay, play dumb. Fine. Let's just get to work."

He kept watch while she opened the steel door. Both of them checked the building with extended magical senses, and the mingling of that awareness generated bubbly heat in Tasha's belly.

She swallowed hard and walked inside. The door led to the warehouse part of the upstairs, an area crowded with crated furnishings, small carpets, and boxed window treatments. Heavier or bulkier items were stored behind the showrooms and conference room downstairs.

Carter locked the door. Again, magical energy washed over her as he warded it against intruders.

As he swung around to face her, something about his attitude struck her. "If I went home with one of them, or anyone else, why would you care, anyway? I would've texted you, and any of them is great backup."

"Yeah." He glared at her. "Thanks to all of you being on the secret squirrel clubhouse team."

He really was the most exasperating man. "This must be how Alice felt on the other side of the looking glass. Nothing you're saying makes sense."

He shook his head once, hard and stalked past her. "Never mind."

"Suit yourself." Now she was talking to his back. She'd never felt a stronger urge to smack a man upside the head.

"Considering that you left, I don't think you'd be in any position to complain if I did go home with someone," she grumbled.

"Seriously?" He wheeled. She had to stop abruptly. "You really don't get it, do you?" he demanded, his eyes hot as molten silver.

"Get what?"

Carter caught her chin between his thumb and forefinger and kissed her.

Tasha froze, trapped between the urge to shove him away and the heat of the unexpected, long-desired contact.

The heat won, swirling through her brain and body and wiping away everything else. When his tongue flicked her lips, she opened them for him. He deepened the kiss, and the world spun. She clung to him while their tongues dueled, their bodies pressed close, and their arms locked around each other.

Abruptly Carter raised his head. He was breathing hard, as though he'd run a race, and his eyes were as unfocused as she felt.

Tasha breathed his name and reached for his cheek with one hand. He caught and kissed it.

"That's why," he said, his gaze intent but no longer angry. "That's why I care."

He released her and stepped back. "I'll go check the warding on the downstairs doors."

Tasha fought to focus. "Wait. Wait a minute. You can't just kiss me and drop the subject."

"Well, if you want seconds, I can oblige." His level stare said he was dead serious.

"I do not want 'seconds,' or whatever." Except she did, but she wasn't about to admit it to him. "You're jealous."

"I was. The kiss took care of that. At least for now. But don't worry, Cupcake. I'm not a stalker. If you want a repeat, you'll have to be the one who starts it."

"Don't call me Cupcake." She loved that light, flirty nick-name, but it enticed her to want something she knew would never work out. Besides, *Lunatic* might fit better, seeing as how she was already wondering how that repeat would be.

The hot light in his eyes kindled answering heat deep within her. Carter shrugged. "It fits, seeing as you taste good enough to eat. But okay."

The double entendre stole her breath. "What's gotten into you?"

"Years of fighting this thing between us. This . . . whatever you want to call it. Navy regs aren't blocking us anymore. The past may be, but I can't help that. If I'm going to stand by while other men ogle you and flirt with you and maybe go home with you, you're going to know what you're passing up."

"Are you saying you want to date me?" Could this day get any stranger?

"I want to see what happens if we stop fighting this thing. Maybe it gets stronger, maybe it gutters out. After all this time, we should fish or cut bait."

Yes! something deep inside her cried. But he and she were so different. Yet the idea of turning him down created a quiet, sick dread inside her.

Still, facts were facts. "It would never work, Carter. Guys like you . . . women like me are not for you except for a fling. And I'm not up for a fling."

"A fling?" His eyes narrowed. "You think I'm looking for a quick roll in the hay, a few tumbles, and a fast good-bye?"

She had, but maybe she'd been wrong. But they were too different for more. Whatever bee was buzzing around in his head would fizzle out once they tried doing the couple thing in his social circles.

"What do you mean about women like you?" he demanded.

"I'm not the type guys like you go for."

He shook his head once, lips tightening, before he held out his hand. "Give me your phone."

"What?"

"Phone. Your cell."

"What does that have to do—"

"Give it to me, and I'll show you."

Baffled, she fished it from her purse, unlocked it, and handed it to him.

Carter scrolled through her contacts and tapped a number. "Tasha's fine," Carter said, his eyes locked with hers. "It's Lockwood."

The heat in his gaze made Tasha's mouth dry. Her heart beat faster, but she couldn't look away.

Carter continued, "No, I need to talk to you. The thing is, Murdock—"

Murdock? As in Nate? As in the last person she wanted sticking his brotherly nose in this?

Tasha grabbed for the phone.

Without missing a beat, Carter twisted away and blocked her with an outstretched arm. "I want to date your sister, and I can't convince her my intentions are honorable. . . . Yeah. . . . Right. Got it."

Judging by the smug look on Carter's face, Nate was all for this plan. Why wouldn't he be? He and Carter were a lot alike—responsible, shining examples of young manhood. Golden boys, both of them. Nobody'd cared about Nate's home life, not when he'd been able to throw or hit a ball better than anyone on the baseball team. He'd been a sports hero.

"He wants to talk to you." Carter passed her the phone.

Tasha took a deep breath and summoned control. "There's no need for you to worry about this. I have it under control."

"Uh-huh." Her twin's voice was dry. "I'm not butting into whether you should date this guy, but for what it's worth, I think he's on the level. If he isn't, if he hurts you, I go nuclear on his ass. I told him that."

Tasha eyed Carter. Watching her with his arms crossed over his chest, he appeared satisfied, not concerned.

Tasha held his gaze. "If anyone's ass needs kicking, I can do it."

"I know, but it's one of those brother things. Besides, I'm four minutes older than you, which makes it my job."

Tasha sighed, but the words touched her. His loyalty had been as much a constant as their parents' disapproval. No matter what she'd done.

"You okay?" he asked.

"Fine." If baffled and conflicted qualified as fine.

"I have some leave coming. I might mosey up there and see what's up with you and Lockwood."

"There's nothing to check on, but I'd love to see you. Watch your back."

"You too."

They signed off. Slowly, Tasha put her phone away.

When she turned back to Carter, he was watching her, his face wary.

"That was a bold move," she acknowledged. "I guess I have to believe you're sincere."

"But you don't think it can work, regardless." His voice was flat now, his eyes bland.

She wanted it to, but . . . better to listen to common sense.

Before she could say so, he told her, "I don't care about the past. We hardly know each other now, except I know you're kind and strong and courageous. That's enough to build on, to be worth getting to know each other better. For me, at least."

That sounded so persuasive, but she'd taken a chance on a guy like him once, not long after she came to Savannah. It had blown up in her face. Tasha bit her lip. "I don't know what to say, Carter."

"That's not a no." He shrugged. "Up to you, Murdock. And so is the next step, if there is one."

The elevator dinged. Its doors opened, saving her from having to reply. Her office manager, stocky, fiftyish Noel Lane, walked out.

Dodging crates, she said, "Tasha, I'm so glad you're here. Lloyd Liston is on the phone, and he's claiming he can't get the cabinets for the Dorton job to us for four weeks."

"He can claim what he wants, but we have a contract. Tell him I'll be with him in a minute."

For once, a subcontractor with a problem sounded great. He never met deadlines anymore—hence the need for a contract—and this was the wrong day to give her excuses.

∽

DARE WAS RIGHT, Carter decided, watching Tasha pick up her office phone. As a bodyguard, he sucked.

You couldn't monitor the surroundings if you were busy sticking your tongue down your principal's throat. On top of that, he'd put her in the horrible position of possibly feeling pressured to act on these annoying urges rather than risk alienating her protection.

Not that she was the type to cave under pressure. But that was irrelevant. He'd been out of line. Yet he was still sitting here, listening to her and not awaiting a replacement.

"Check your contract," she was saying, kicked back in her black leather desk chair with the morning sun glinting off her gorgeous hair and shimmering on her green silk shirt.

His hands itched to touch. He fisted them on his knees.

"If you're more than three days late," Tasha continued, "you pay any resulting—"

Her eyes narrowed, and Carter swallowed a grin. Damn, she was hot in boss mode.

"You signed the contract. If you didn't read it, that's your problem. Bump back the job that's causing your delay since it's late anyway. Then you can make our scheduled installation date."

Squawking noises came out of the phone. Her gaze met his, and she shook her head. Then she let out a breath that whiffled her bangs. Drumming her fingers on the desk, she waited until the guy ran down.

"I understand your problem," she said. "But it's not going to be my problem. If the Dortons can't cook in their new kitchen, you're going to be looking at a bill for any meals they eat out. Which I can tell you will be many. Having a stove doesn't make food prep without a counter any easier."

They went back and forth in that vein for a few minutes before Tasha signed off.

"Well?" Carter asked. "Is he meeting the deadline?"

"So he claims, which is why I made sure he knows he's on the hook for serious money if he doesn't. I get the feeling he would promise delivery and then just shrug when the time came."

"I was impressed," he admitted.

Pink washed across her cheekbones, and she smiled. "Really?"

"Yeah. Listen, Tasha—"

Her intercom buzzed.

"One sec." She grabbed the receiver. "Yes, Sally. Uh-huh. Okay, I'll handle it." With an apologetic look at Carter, she said, "Client having issues. I need to take this."

"Sure." That was why she was here, after all, to deal with the needs of her business. Not to natter with a bodyguard whose head seemed to have migrated up his ass.

Even though he'd been out of line, he wasn't sorry he'd spoken up. The sentiments had been honest and long overdue. And, unless Tasha went hot and heavy with every guy who laid an unexpected kiss on her, he wasn't the only one feeling the pull. It was only his timing that had been so very wrong.

Jackass, much?

But he wasn't actually surprised. She was the only woman who'd ever gotten under his skin to the extent of making him say or do stupid shit. The day he'd confronted her about the missing supplies, he'd had to be as stiff and cold as an iceberg to stifle the urge to comfort her. To agree that her cause was better.

"You signed off on the lilac mist tile," Tasha was saying patiently. "Aside from the materials and labor costs of laying something new, ripping up what you have will be very expensive. . . . No, I can't use it for something else. Most of it will break, and the thinset mortar will stick to much of it."

Lilac mist? What the hell kind of color was lilac mist? Or sea spray, the one they were now talking about?

At last, Tasha signed off. She put her face in her hands and quietly shrieked.

"You okay?" Carter asked.

A nod answered him. At last, rubbing her hands over her face, she raised her head. "I actually do have happy clients. I swear I do. The people we're going to see out on Cumberland Island are fabulous."

"You're about due for fabulous."

"Damn straight." She picked up a pile of pink message slips and scanned them.

Carter squared his shoulders. "Listen, Tasha, about earlier."

When she looked at him, her blue eyes were wary, her face expressionless. "What about it?"

"I'm sorry."

The corners of her eyes tightened, as though she stifled a flinch, and he hastily added, "The kiss was amazing. And I meant what I said about wanting a shot with you."

She relaxed at that, an intriguing reaction.

Carter plowed on. "But that kind of thing is off-limits for a bodyguard. I should've been monitoring our surroundings, not, uh, putting a move on you."

Unbelievably, she smiled. "Only you would get bent out of shape about that." When he frowned, she shook her head. "Carter, we were in the back room of my business. The door was not only locked but magically warded—by you."

She continued, "I own the whole building, and I not only checked it with my magical senses extended before we came in but felt you doing the same. We were safe. There's no derelic-tion of duty."

At her choice of words, his back prickled. Tasha looked taken aback at what she'd said. Yep, here came the shadow of the past all over again.

"It's not appropriate," he said stiffly. "You're relying on me. You should be able to do that and not feel any kind of, you know, pressure. If we call Deke now, he can have someone new for your Cumberland Island visit tomorrow. I'll take y'all out there and bring you back, then slot into the Wayfarer patrol again."

"We're not calling Deke." Suddenly, she grinned. "I don't feel pressured. If you think I can't put you down if I need to, you should spend some time reconsidering."

That was an invitation to banter, but he couldn't take her up on it, not with his conscience chafing him.

She raised one eyebrow. "Don't believe me?"

"You have no reason to put that kind of faith in me." Maybe he should call Deke on his own.

Shaking her head, Tasha came around the desk and leaned on the edge, facing him with her hands gripping the lip of the desktop. "I have plenty of reasons, many of them spawned in the situation with Will and Audra last year. You know how to handle yourself, in a fight and not, and you do what you say you'll do. You always have."

Even when what he said he would do had been certain to bust her career. Their eyes met, and he knew she was remembering that, too. It would probably always be there between them.

"You're right about the thing, whatever it is, between us," she continued, "but I don't know that exploring it is smart. And honestly, I don't want to think about that until this situation is resolved. I have as much on my plate as I can deal with."

Studying her, he cocked his head, "Just so I know, why aren't you jumping at a chance to be rid of me?"

Color rose in her cheeks again. "I'm used to you. And like I said, you're competent. So let's table the whole dating or whatever issue until this is over."

"Okay. If you're sure." He wasn't, but the idea of someone else becoming her shadow grated on him worse than his slipups did. Those, at least, he could stop.

Tasha nodded. "We're good, then. But before we table it, there's just one more thing."

"What?" He couldn't read her face now, but she was giving off a vibe that made him think he wouldn't like what she was about to say.

"I want you as my bodyguard. I want you around, and here's proof." Tasha leaned down and kissed him.

The contact roared through him like an energy bolt. He was on his feet, holding her, kissing her back, before he knew it. Her tongue flicked his lips, and his brain blanked.

A long time later, he raised his head. Breathing hard, Tasha rested her forehead against his chin.

"Damn," he muttered.

"Yeah." She took a deep breath that pressed her breasts into his chest and stepped back. Smiling slightly, she patted his cheek. "That's also a thank-you for asking and for calling my brother."

"So you'll think about it."

"I will. If you don't bail on me." She walked back around the desk. Seating herself, she grinned. "And, oh, yeah, now we're even."

The high color in her cheeks lifted his heart, but Carter groaned. "I call foul, Murdock."

"Hey, one ambush kiss begets another."

"Double foul."

She shot him a prim, admonishing look. "Just sit tight, and I'll be ready to go in a bit."

Sit tight. Right. Good one. Pretty much described the condition of his pants at that moment.

He took his tablet out of his pack and opened the reading app, but he couldn't focus on his book. The holding pattern he and Tasha had been in during their service years and since their meeting again in November had broken. Too bad he didn't know whether that was going to turn out to be a good thing or a colossally idiotic move on his part.

CHAPTER ELEVEN

DECIDING NOT TO THINK ABOUT CARTER WAS A GREAT PLAN. TOO bad it wasn't working. Tasha glanced through her lashes at the man placidly reading in the corner of her office. He seemed lost in the book on his tablet, but she couldn't manage to dive so deeply into her work. No, she had to keep peeking at him. Thinking about him.

Remembering the coffee taste of his mouth and the solid strength of his body against hers.

Scowling, she turned back to the fabric swatches on her desk. The presentation boards, showing the flooring and paint the client had already chosen along with suggestions for furniture, window treatments, fabric swatches, etc., had to be ready to go to Cumberland Island in the morning. She should be gathering everything she needed to put them together at the Collegium. Not remembering a couple of kisses that likely wouldn't ever be repeated.

Crossing out of the friend zone would be a disaster for them. Someone with her background could only disappoint him. Again. Yet she'd been so dismayed at the idea of his walking away that she'd given in to an incredibly foolish impulse. And then promised to consider a relationship. That was a colossally bad idea.

Lucky for her, he'd been gentleman enough to agree they'd table the subject. Even though one small, secret—and obviously lunatic—part of her wished he'd pushed.

Now, though, she had work to do. Work. Right. Bread and butter for everyone at Murdock Custom Builders.

Carter had suggested—rather strongly, which had been sexier than it should've been, a sure sign he was screwing with her head, even if unintentionally, which was so freaking stupid of her!—that they not be here after dark. At least, not after rush hour, when the street traffic died down. Ghouls didn't much care about Mundane safety, but they were no more eager to have witnesses to their actions than the mages were.

Because ghouls were stronger at night, she hadn't been able to argue. He'd seemed a little surprised at her ready agreement.

So here they were, him reading and her half-assedly working. This was taking longer than it would if she could just focus for fifteen straight minutes.

Darkness came early in late February, and the storm that had moved in had brought it even earlier. She and Carter needed to leave soon. Her desk clock said 5:20. Traffic would already be thinning, and no one would wander the area in this weather.

Soft rain splatted on the windows and thrummed gently on the roof, creating a sense of coziness despite the excellent lighting in her office. Everyone else had gone home already.

She glanced at him again, at the way the lamplight glinted on his chestnut hair. At the strong line of his jaw and his firm, wide mouth. That mouth could be stern or soft . . .

Gah! Stop it. Stupid zone, remember?

Resolutely she turned back to her work. It was simple enough to put fabric swatches, sketches, and photos for each room in a separate folder and slide that into a file box.

Yet her foolish heart kept saying *if only*, joining forces with her body, which was all for jumping his bones. At least her brain was making more sense, insisting, *hormones and wishful thinking are a recipe for disaster*.

So yes, he had the power to hurt her. Not that she would admit it to anyone else, especially him. If she took him up on his suggestion, actually started dating him, though, she would be even more vulnerable. There was no getting around that.

Yet the temptation was surprisingly strong.

She let out a frustrated sigh.

"You okay?" Carter asked, looking up. His intent, concerned eyes were soft as smoke.

Her mouth went dry again, but she swallowed hard and made herself not look to the side, not act skittish. "Just frustrated. This is so much easier when I can just put everything together here."

Frowning, he turned his tablet off and stood. "Tasha, I know this is a pain, but—"

"Not as big a pain as a ghoul attack." She mustered a smile. "I know. I understand."

He walked to the window and peered between the slats of the blind. "We should get going. It would be past dark by now even without the rain. How much longer do you need?"

"I'm about done. I need to be sure I have all the folders and grab the actual bifold boards. And some glue. I'll need glue. There's a printer at the Collegium I can use, right?"

"Yep. While you do that, I'll check the perimeter. Stay away from the window." He snagged his broadsword from the corner behind his chair.

"Uh-huh," she said absently, studying her list as he walked out.

That looked like everything. She closed the file box. The handle on top would make it easy to carry.

Carter's footsteps sounded in the storage room, hurrying toward her. "Tasha, grab your saber," he called from the hallway.

It was leaning against the side of her desk, in easy reach. She gripped it. "What's wrong?"

"Ghouls in the parking lot." His face stony, Carter rounded the corner into her office. "At least six. And the mage, who shielded them just after my probe brushed across them. It probably alerted him."

"You sensed them magically?"

He nodded. "We have to get out of here. I don't know this city, so I can't visualize a destination. How far can you translocate?"

"By myself, about a hundred, maybe a hundred and fifty yards. With another adult feeding me power . . . I don't know. Probably farther." She'd done that once, carrying a wounded Javy Ruiz from a covert raid on a ghoul nest.

"I want these bastards," she added. "Let's translocate to the street and sneak up on them. Pick them off."

"Too risky." As she opened her mouth to argue, he quickly said, "The sonofabitch had to feel my magic probe. He let me know there were six. That could be a ploy so we don't suspect there are more. We might be able to take them, but there's no telling when someone will drive by on the way to a hotel or restaurant or just going to see a friend. Even in this weather. We don't want to risk a running battle that could pull Mundanes in."

"No, you're right." A mage's first duty was the protection of Mundanes.

She quickly grabbed her jacket and the file box, holding them in one hand. "Is your ward holding?" Having set it, he would feel any contact with it or change in it.

"So far, but we can't count on that." Frowning, he rubbed his jaw. "Nearest backup is over an hour away, so choose a safe destination. As far away as you can shift us and preferably concealed. I'll feed you power in the shift. That should help you extend your range. Let's go."

Her breath caught, and her cheeks heated. Sharing power was more intimate than kissing.

"There's closer backup," she told him. "Lorelei will be at her shop. She can come pick us up."

His eyes darkened, and his frown deepened. Probably because of that policy against civilian involvement.

"You saw her in action in November," Tasha reminded him. "You know how good she is, and we don't have time for anyone from the Collegium to get here."

Carter nodded. "I'll fix it with Deke. Call her."

"I need you to carry the project boards," she told him, pulling out her phone.

He gave her an incredulous look. "I can't protect you with my hands full."

"You can put them down when we get there. If we translocate into a fight, we're in trouble anyway."

"In which case we'll both need our hands free. Besides, we need to hang on to each other to translocate together."

He was right. Translocating someone else was tough enough when you were in close contact. Shifting someone or something you weren't touching took exponentially more power—and limited one's range accordingly.

"There has to be a way," she said. "I need those boards for my presentation."

His face set in grim lines. "We can come back for those things after other deputies chase off the ghouls."

"Yes, and what if they break in here and trash everything? The material in those folders took days to put together."

"Then you can take the file box, but no boards." She opened her mouth, and he repeated, "Tasha. Please."

It was the p*lease* more than the fact that he had a point that swayed her. One of them needed both hands free if they ran into trouble. There shouldn't be ghouls at Colonial Park Cemetery, but you never knew.

Tasha called Lorelei's cell. Her friend answered on the

second ring. "I'm in trouble," Tasha said abruptly. "Ghouls surrounding my office. Carter and I are translocating to the cemetery."

"I'll get my car and pull up on Abercorn, as close as I can get to the gate."

"Oh, fuck," Carter muttered. He stepped close and held out his arms. "My ward around the building just dropped."

"Gotta go," Tasha said. Careful of the sword in her right hand, she hooked her right arm around him. Her left snagged the file box handle.

He locked his free arm around her waist, feeding her power. With it came awareness of his anger at the ghouls and his fear for her. And his pleasure at having her in his arms.

The heat in her cheeks ramped up.

Kra-KOW! sounded from the ground floor.

Even with Carter's power boosting hers, they probably couldn't make it all the way to the cemetery. Tasha tightened her hold on him, envisioned the corner a few blocks down Liberty Street, and fed power into the shift. Reality lurched sideways in a rush of icy darkness.

They emerged from transit in the rain on the corner she'd chosen. Two more shifts took them to the center of Colonial Park Cemetery. Rain pelted down on them. In the next heartbeat, his shield flared around the two of them in a nimbus of blue. It deflected the rain.

"Can you screen us?" he asked. No mage could screen and shield at the same time.

"Got it." Tasha pulled power from the live oaks, grass, and shrubbery around them, recharging to create the screen.

"Good job." Carter grinned at her.

Looking up to thank him, she realized they were still in each other's arms. The warmth in his eyes made her heart beat faster, and that little smile of his was sexy as hell.

"Um, you can let go," she suggested, sliding her sword arm away from him.

"Oh. Uh, right." He released her and took a hasty step backward. Averting his eyes, he repeated, "Good job."

So she wasn't the only one affected by that embrace. Good to know. Tasha swallowed a smile. "You helped," she reminded him.

"With the rain," he said, peering into the gloom, "I doubt anyone saw that glow when I formed the shield."

"Won't matter if they did. This place is supposed to be haunted, and I bet we looked like a couple of ghosts. I'll call Lorelei and let her know we made it here."

Carter scanned their surroundings. "That iron fence doesn't offer much cover. Screened or not, we should duck behind a tomb or something."

Following him toward a long, low brick tomb on the far side, Tasha phoned Lorelei.

When her friend answered, Tasha said, "We're here, headed toward the tombstone wall to hide between it and a brick tomb on that side. Call me when you arrive."

"I'm four blocks away. Be there in a sec."

Tasha followed Carter behind the tomb, a rectangle four feet high, six long, and three wide topped with a foot-high, curved pediment that ran its length. Six feet beyond it stood a high brick wall with rows of tombstones propped against it and sitting on a ledge along it.

The two mages crouched behind the tomb. In this position, they wouldn't be visible from the street, even without her screen.

Carter pulled out his phone and reported to Deke. He finished, "We have a ride coming, but somebody should check out Tasha's office. Be sure there aren't any nasty surprises waiting for her. . . . I'll let you know. And someone needs to pick up Tasha's truck from her office lot. . . . Right."

Pocketing the phone again, he said, "Deke's sending two squads by helo. They'll screen the scene so no Mundanes see, secure your office and meet us with your truck."

"I don't want to lead the ghouls to Lorelei."

"We can pick a rendezvous that won't." Carter squeezed her arm, sending a flash of heat into the depths of her body. Her face warmed too.

He added, "I know you'd rather wade in. So would I. But this time it's not smart."

"I know," she muttered.

"What's with the tombstones on the wall?" He jerked his head toward them.

"When Sherman's troops occupied Savannah, they camped here. Knocked over all those tombstones, and no one knew which ones belonged on which graves. So the city set them all up there."

Two feet separated him from her, ordinarily a comfortable distance. Yet she wished he would move closer.

Get a grip, Natasha.

Carter raised an eyebrow. "I wouldn't have figured you were into cemeteries."

"It's quiet here." Tasha shrugged. "Tourists seldom come through more than a scattered handful at a time. This is an easy walk from my office and a good place to think."

He nodded. After a moment, he asked, "Do you always check out cemeteries? My mom's into genealogy, and she does."

"I guess you can find a lot of information in burial grounds, but no, I'm not. I checked out all the tourist sights when I moved here."

After she got out of the navy. *Please let's don't go there. Not again.*

Carter asked, "Why Savannah?"

Tasha's phone vibrated. She pulled it out, recognized the number, and answered it. "Hi, Lorelei."

"I'm pulling up now, first parking space down from the gate."

"Excellent." Tasha stood up.

So did Carter. "I go first, just in case. And why Savannah?"

Following him, she said, "I attended SCAD, the Savannah College of Art and Design. Got my interior design degree here, thanks to the GI Bill and a scholarship."

"So you stayed?"

"I worked construction to help pay my way through school. I liked my job, and the company's owner helped me start my design business while I worked for him."

They reached the cemetery entrance, a concrete arch resting on brick pillars and topped with a bronze eagle, wings spread, perched atop an orb. The iron gates were closed.

Carter's magic prickled her skin as he sent out a magical probe. "We're clear," he said. "Meet you at the car."

So they weren't translocating as a unit. Not that they needed to, with Lorelei's pale green sedan in plain view. Besides, it was better that way. Smarter. Now they just had to stay out of trouble until reinforcements arrived.

WAITING PURELY SUCKED, and Tasha was too quiet. Sitting beside her on a flowery sofa in shades of yellow and green, Carter could feel Tasha's growing impatience. She had to be worried about her business, and only an idiot would blame her. Ghouls never left anything intact.

Lorelei's apartment, above her shop on Broughton Street, had tall windows that overlooked the street but were covered now by white curtains. The sturdy furniture, in yellows, blues, and greens, made the open floor plan seem cozy. Or would, for people who weren't on edge.

The homemade tomato soup Lorelei had pressed on them was great, but he ate with one eye on Tasha. He suspected she was eating, however mechanically, for the same reason Lorelei had offered them food, so they would all have something to do while they waited.

"So tomorrow is Cumberland Island?" Lorelei asked. "The Millers, right?"

Tasha nodded. "I'm redoing their guesthouse. The painting is done, and she wanted to wait for that before choosing the furnishings. Wanted me to make suggestions with the actual colors in mind."

She sounded calm, but worry darkened her eyes. After seeing the wreck a battle had made of her river cottage, he couldn't blame her.

He couldn't do anything to reassure her, either. If her building took damage, it took damage. Nobody wanted that, but containing and eliminating the ghouls and capturing that fucking traitor would be his fellow deputies' priorities.

"I'll get some more iced tea," Lorelei said. She walked into the kitchen area halfway down the loft and around the pale yellow counter that separated it from the dining area.

Tasha glanced at the bright, multicolored rug, but he doubted she really saw it. Her entirely reasonable fear ate at his heart.

Lorelei's phone rang, and she answered it in the kitchen.

"It'll be okay," he said softly. "The Collegium has resources you can draw on if you need them."

Tasha's throat moved in a hard swallow. At last, she looked at him, with eyes so anxious that he couldn't help putting an arm around her. She leaned into him. For just a second, but she did.

Probably didn't count as much progress in the circumstances, but he was gone enough over her to be grateful anyway.

Straightening, she took a deep, shaky breath. "Nothing can replace the hours and hours of work that's in that building. The schematics. The job listings. Some of that's on the computer— and backed up—but not all of it. I'm worried and I'm mad at the damn ghouls and that fucking traitor."

He covered her hand with his. "The deputies are good. They might've contained the ghouls in time."

"They couldn't get here fast enough for that," she said, her tone flat. "They about twenty minutes away, even if by helo. The ghouls were breaking in as we left, and you know what they're like."

"Destructive," he said, since she knew it as well as he did and was doubtless worrying over it.

She gripped his hand for a moment before sliding hers free. "Thanks, Carter."

"For what? Making you abandon your business to the enemy?" She would never know how much running instead of giving battle rankled.

"For not telling me sugarcoated lies. That would drive me totally up a tree."

"I figured. It would me too." The glance she threw him this time held both surprise and pleasure. She patted his hand, sending a bolt of heat into his groin.

Lorelei came back with a frosty glass pitcher of tea. "Sorry, y'all. That was my manager with a question about tomorrow."

"No problem," Tasha said. "Thanks for taking us in."

Lorelei smiled, "Hey, what're friends—"

Carter's cell phone rang. When he answered it, the deep voice of deputy shire reeve Brody Hamilton said, "We've cleared the site. Had a bit of a battle, and now we're doing cleanup. No visits from Mundane law enforcement, so the screen must be working."

"The mage?" Carter demanded.

Tasha straightened. Her gaze sharpened.

Knowing what he would want in her place, he said, "Wait. I'm putting you on speaker, Brody." Doing took only a moment. "Go ahead."

"I hate to tell you this, Tasha," Brody responded, "but the building's on fire."

CHAPTER TWELVE

Ross Graham paced the front room of the ghoul leader's cabin. This colony, or nest, was in the woods west of Jasper, Florida, about seventy-five miles southwest of St. George, Georgia. It had started with around forty ghouls. There were fewer now, thanks to the deputy reeves and tonight's failed show of idiotic bravado, but its leader, a big male named Zarig, acted as though he were on a par with the Governor of Georgia. Hence the delay in seeing Ross.

The shabby furniture, peeling paint, and creaking floors didn't matter to ghouls. Most of them lived to eat, fuck, and destroy. Not necessarily in that order.

Some, however, were smarter. Cunning and capable. Ross tried to avoid that sort, who might figure out he'd joined them for reasons that had nothing to do with fearing them.

But no one had tumbled to that yet. Otherwise, he'd be under guard.

Or dead.

Door hinges squeaked to his left, and Zarig stood in the doorway of what had probably been intended as a bedroom. He glared at Ross, who crossed his arms and returned the favor.

Showing fear to ghouls was fatal.

"Mage." Zarig jerked his head, summoning Ross inside, and turned on his heel. Behind him wafted an acrid current of ammonia, the familiar stink of ghouls.

Ross sauntered in but made sure his claymore was loose in its scabbard. He might need it. Ghouls hated taking the blame for anything, and there was a lot of it flying around tonight.

Broad-shouldered, with scraggly, brown hair and the jaundiced skin tone of his kind, Zarig stood about six four. He leaned on the battered desk under the lone, bare light bulb dangling from an old ceiling fixture. Two plastic chairs, one blue, one green, and both scratched, faced the desk, but the ghoul did not offer Ross a seat.

"You got five of my men killed," Zarig snapped. "And two injured badly."

"No, they did that on their own. I saved three." A misdeed he would probably have to do penance for someday. But he had to look like an ally, at least for a while.

Zarig's eyes narrowed until the brown irises were hard to see against the muddy whites. "If you were not protected by the Teacher, mage, I would kill you where you stand."

Ross smiled. Exaggerating his Scots brogue, he replied, "You're welcome to have a go, laddie."

Killing this bastard would be a pleasure. But the reference to a Teacher was disturbing.

Last November, a demon from the Void between worlds had turned up in Wayfarer, Georgia. Known as the Teacher, it had used its ghoul allies to play merry hell with a bunch of archaeologists there because it wanted magical artifacts they'd found. Ross hadn't overtly betrayed it, but why was it protecting him?

"We need a new plan," Zarig announced. His hard stare dared Ross to disagree with what was coming. "We need Mundane hostages. That'll lure the disgusting mage cow out."

Not this again. Ross laughed but kept a wary eye on Zarig's bunching fists. "By all means, take hostages," Ross told him, "seeing as that worked out so well the last time."

The demon had ordered a similar strategy, snatching people from Wayfarer, holding them hostage at the archaeological dig site, and demanding the mages ransom them with the artifacts it wanted. The mages had brought the artifacts, all right. Then they'd obliterated the ghouls and, Ross had thought, even hoped, the demon.

Maybe it hadn't survived. Maybe its home nest was pretending the demon was in charge so as to maintain superiority over its comrades. He would have to find out for sure, warn the mages somehow if the demon had survived.

"The list that fool Collier left on his desk could sink us," Zarig snarled. "That list of nests he was investing for included the Cogdell one. The mages raided . . ."

Having heard this daily, Ross tuned him out. Yes, Cogdell had been on the spreadsheet or whatever, and yes, the Collegium mages had raided it the day before the Murdock woman saw the list. In theory, yes, she could realize what the list had been.

If she'd seen it.

Which Ross took leave to doubt because no other nest on the list had been hit. The woman built and decorated houses. She wasn't a deputy reeve. She probably didn't even know about the Cogdell raid.

"We need that mage," Zarig insisted, scowling. "Before she realizes what she saw. Before she acts on it. She will surrender to save her workers."

"Most likely." As Zarig started to relax, Ross added, "And then the mages who'll be concealed at her back will kill everyone in sight. As they did on Mystery Island. I'll have no part of such a plan."

"You'll do as you're told."

"Not unless the Teacher orders me to do so directly." Ross shook his head. "The bloody woman doesn't know anything, Zarig. If she did, there would've been mages all over the

Colliers by now. And all over the bank where they're putting your money."

"You do not know that. The woman saw the papers that fool left out."

"That doesn't mean she noticed them."

"We cannot risk it. We will not. You will devise a means to take her. If she has already done her damage, she must be punished." Zarig leered. "Besides, we have uses for her. And for the male you sensed with her."

As breeders no doubt. Ross kept his face bland, hiding his disgust.

"So get her," Zarig roared.

"That might be easier if your men hadn't slagged her computer. We could've used it to log into her accounts, but I'll do what I can." No need to tell the hothead that Ross had downloaded Natasha Murdock's schedule. The woman had guts. It would be a shame to see her become a ghoul slave. Maybe Ross could buy her some time.

Although he could only play a double game for so long.

"Work fast," Zarig ordered.

Ross shrugged. "As you wish." *Until I find the info I need. Then you're dead.*

CHAPTER THIRTEEN

A SMART MAN WOULD NOT GO DOWN TO THE WATERSIDE, NOT WITH Natasha Murdock standing there. Nuh-uh. As Carter knew well. With the Indian Ocean softly lapping the shore, a sky full of diamond-bright stars overhead, and the familiar sounds of the Seabees' camp blurring into white noise, a smart guy would walk away from temptation.

But she was part of his command, alone in the dark, in a country where solo women were not always left in peace and the green and tan camouflage fatigues of the US Navy Seabees' working uniform were a red flag to some people. He couldn't just leave her there.

Hell.

"Be a man, an officer, not a foolish teenager," he muttered, marching down the beach. Even though she often made him feel like such a kid.

He let his magic ripple out until it brushed hers, alerting her that he was coming. She didn't move, just stood staring out at the quarter moon's light silvering the waves. The familiarity of the scene pinged him with awareness that this had already happened. So what he saw now had to be a dream.

Still, he let the memory take him. The encounter had been bittersweet, but he couldn't turn away from reliving it.

It wasn't her fault the regulation trousers hugged her hips in a way that showed they had the perfect degree of curve. Or that the drape of the standard, tan tee emphasized her other curves rather than concealing them.

Natasha Murdock wasn't a waifish woman who happened to have breasts and hips. She was lean, fit, and athletic, but undeniably female.

Setting his jaw, he joined her just out of reach of the tide. To keep that pesky attraction to himself, he locked down his magic. Hers, he noted, was now locked down as well.

"Okay, Murdock?" he asked. This was her first disaster relief posting, and the typhoon had devastated this coastal region. Some people had trouble coping with the wreckage and death.

"Yeah. Thanks, LT." She answered absently, without looking at him.

He waited a couple of beats, but she said nothing else. Feeling his way, he asked, "Something on your mind?"

She opened her mouth as though to speak but shut it abruptly. After a moment, she asked, "How'd you decide to join the navy, sir?"

He shrugged. "Didn't want to join the family business." Especially not the political side of it. "So I joined Navy ROTC at Ole Miss. You?"

"Things were sticky at home. I wanted out."

She'd obviously glossed something over, but that was her business. He took a sip from the cola can in his hand before commenting, "The navy gets a lot of good sailors that way."

Her slight nod acknowledged the implied compliment. "You don't need to babysit me, sir. I'm fine."

"You generally are, but it's not safe for a woman alone around here, especially in an area where looters are always lurking, hoping for an opportunity."

One corner of her mouth quirked up. She shot him a side-long look. "You know I can take anybody who bothers me."

"Yeah, but you might have to use magic, and flashing that around Mundanes always complicates things."

"True." She took off her cap and ran a hand through her hair. Resettling the cap, she said, "Everybody knows I didn't come from money."

When he nodded, she continued, "Before my brother and I got old enough to work, there were some seriously lean times. But we had a roof over our heads and indoor plumbing that, when it broke, my dad knew how to fix. We didn't always have something great to eat, but we always had something. I got an education, then an opportunity in the navy. These people . . ."

She spread her hands in a gesture of frustration. "Where's the opportunity for them? They lived in a slum, jammed in like sardines, carrying their water in, pissing in a hole in the ground, and now the few who survived the floods don't even have that."

"Makes you think," he agreed.

Softly, she added, "Especially about the girls. Just being girls was a strike against them, and most people will allocate scarce resources to their sons first. At least around here."

"No argument." He offered her the soda can. As she sipped, he added, "It's a double reminder to people like us that there are some things magic just can't fix."

She passed the can back to him. Their fingers brushed, attraction sparking inside him lightning-fast. Her eyes widened. She wrenched her gaze away and took a deep breath.

The swell of her breasts under the tee broke the last of his resistance. He was officially sporting wood. The best option was to get both of them off this beach ASAP.

"Murdock—"

"I could've been those girls," she blurted, turning to him. "I know some people back home have it worse than I did. I lived in a town and had a job that paid my bus fare to go fifty miles and enlist. My parents didn't exactly help me, but they didn't get in my way, either. Change just a few of those things, and I would've had no more prospects than these girls do."

"Yes, you would."

When she frowned at him, he shifted to face her fully. "You're smart," he told her, "and determined and stubborn. You would've found a way."

"I'd like to think so." But doubt flickered in her eyes.

He couldn't help himself. He reached out to cup her cheek in his free hand. "I know so," he assured her.

Her eyes darkened. Her lips parted, and her hand rose to clasp his.

"Carter—LT," she choked. The desire in her eyes stopped his breath, and the shared attraction they both tried so hard to ignore suddenly crackled between them.

"Tasha," he murmured. In that moment, he wanted her more than he had ever let himself acknowledge. But he outranked her. The choice to risk career suicide had to be hers. "Green light or red? You call it."

Their gazes held for a long moment. Lips trembling, she closed her eyes. Then she squeezed his hand, released it, and opened her eyes. "I really wish you weren't my LT."

"Me too." He took a deep breath and ran a hand over his face.

Her tone formal, she said, "We should go in, sir."

"Yeah." For lots of reasons. Her formality stung, but she was right to drop into it.

She started up the beach, and the water erupted. From the breakers shot ghouls sporting muddy yellow auras, talons extended and eyes enraged. They charged toward her.

He had no sword. Neither did she. He dropped the soda can and blasted blue magic at the ghouls with both fists. Drove them back. "Get to camp," he ordered.

"Like hell." Her fist-wide, green bolts of magic joined his.

There'd been no ghouls before. No battle. Tasha—

Carter jolted awake. He needed a moment to recognize the living area of the guest suite he and Tasha were using at the Collegium.

Breathing hard, he sat up on the foldout. Helluva dream.

Or was it a warning? Was Tasha okay?

He shoved the covers back, grabbed his sword from the floor by the bed just in case, and padded silently to the bedroom door.

Faint sounds came from within. Not like a struggle, though.

Frowning, he extended his senses.

Not a struggle. Muffled sobs. Shit.

He clamped down on his senses. She wouldn't want him to hear her cry. Or even to know she had.

He should go back to sleep, but he couldn't when she was in there so miserable. Reluctantly, he turned away.

THOUSANDS AND THOUSANDS OF DOLLARS. Furniture, carpets, and window treatments waiting to be loaded into clients' homes. Artwork and framed photos. Sample books. Tools. Office furniture. Showroom stock for the ground floor. All lost through fire or water damage. Thousands and thousands of dollars' worth.

The knowledge pounded a loop of despair through Tasha's brain. Even if insurance covered it all, there would be delays in getting replacements. She couldn't bill people for goods that weren't ready for delivery. Without cash flow, she couldn't pay the employees for long.

Not to mention that some of the destroyed stock had been antiques. Each unique.

The tears trickled off at last, and Tasha rubbed her gritty eyes. She was so tired. So frustrated.

And so damn scared. Might as well admit it. She'd spent years building her business, earning a name. And now everything she'd worked for lay in ruins.

Her cell buzzed, and she grabbed it. Nate. Of course.

"I got your email," he said, "but now I'm thinking you didn't tell me everything."

"Yeah, I did. I'm just tired."

"And discouraged," he added gently.

"That too."

A moment of silence, and then he said, "I'm coming up there. Soon as I untangle this situation."

"You don't need to do that, Nate. I can handle it."

"I know. But I need to see for myself that you're okay. Besides, you can always draft me to help. I'll work for food."

Tasha managed a watery chuckle. "How can I turn that down?"

"You can't, 'cause you're smart. See you soon, Short Stuff."

"Take care of yourself, Beanpole."

Smiling, she broke the connection. At six one, her twin had only four inches on her, but the childhood nicknames they'd adopted to irritate each other had stuck.

The smile faded, and she rubbed her gritty eyes. Nate would do whatever she asked, but he couldn't conjure money out of air.

With a sigh, she rolled over and burrowed into the pillow. Tomorrow's nightmare of coping would be that much worse if she didn't get some sleep.

Sleep, though, refused to come. Try as she might, she couldn't stop thinking of all those thousands of dollars in lost materials or of the employees who depended on her to put food on their tables.

At last, she climbed out of bed. Cold water was better for tear-swollen eyes, but maybe a warm face cloth would help her relax. Her green gym shorts and tank were decent enough, especially considering that Carter was probably asleep anyway. At 2:18 a.m., anyone not working night shift ought to be.

She eased the door open and crept into the darkened suite. The bathroom door was a few feet down on her left with the open-plan kitchen opposite it and the living-dining area across the far end. Reaching for the bathroom doorknob, she glanced toward the sofa bed to check on Carter. The covers were rumpled, but there was no sign of him.

Her heart jolted. Surely he wouldn't have left her alone.

"Carter?" she called.

"Right here." Shirtless, he stepped into view. The corner cabinet had hidden him. Walking around the kitchen counter, he asked, "You okay?"

The sight of his toned torso, then of muscular legs concealed only by those black gym shorts, made her mouth dry. The faint scent of his spicy aftershave teased her nose. If she kissed his neck . . .

Tasha swallowed hard before she could reply. "Yeah, just . . ." *Worried sick.* ". . . couldn't sleep. I hope I didn't wake you up." *Please, don't let him have heard me crying.*

He shook his head and showed her the tablet in his hand. "Bad dream, then couldn't get back to sleep. I was chasing zombies through Atlanta. Want a turn?"

"Not really my thing, but thanks." She mustered a smile, feeble though it had to be. "I was just going to try a warm washcloth on my face."

"Okay. I'm going to get some water. You want any?"

"I don't want to keep you awake."

He shrugged. "Not sleeping anyway."

"Okay, then." She thanked him and stepped into the bathroom. The warm water on her face felt soothing, but it did nothing to stop the whirling in her brain. Somehow, she had to settle. Think of something else.

Like maybe how amazingly kind Carter had been all day. And just now.

And how hot he was in those gym shorts that left him mostly naked. Her hands itched to explore his muscular torso and broad, solid shoulders.

"Geez, Tasha, get a grip," she muttered at her dimly lit

reflection. Instantly, an image of her hand sliding into his gym shorts popped into her brain.

You idiot! Closing her eyes and clenching her fists on the edge of the sink, she silently counted to twenty.

Their mutual attraction didn't change the fact that they were just not compatible. Starting something that couldn't work out would only lead to heartache.

No matter how much he tempted her.

Sitting up to talk to him, even if they drank only water, was a terrible idea. Her resistance was too low. She would make some excuse and go back to bed. If she didn't sleep, even that would be better than sitting next to a sexy, interested guy she couldn't have.

She stepped out of the bathroom, and Mr. Temptation announced, "I've got your water here on the table."

Since he'd gone to the trouble to fix it, she walked over to him. He sat at the square, four-seater table in front of the kitchen counter. Faint light from the lampposts on the grounds filtering through the window behind him limned the sleek, muscular outline of his shoulders and neck and glinted on his hair. His face was mostly in shadow, but mage eyesight made his features visible anyway.

"If you want to talk," he said, "I'm happy to listen."

His tone, sincere and yet not pushy, made her hesitate. "Thanks, but I don't know that talking about it would help. It's just . . . all so much."

"And all on your shoulders." He set his tablet aside. "I'm guessing it looks like a mountain looming over you."

"Pretty much, yeah." Without thinking about it, she sat across from him. "I know I have to take it one step at a time, but . . ." Her throat went tight. She swallowed hard. "I don't even know where to start. Or how I'm going to meet payroll beyond this month. I have a credit line, but drawing too much on that is like diving into a hole."

He cocked his head. "I assume you have insurance."

"Yeah. That's not likely to pay off anytime soon, though, and the documentation for a lot of things burned. And that's if they don't decide I burned the place down myself."

"What? You would never—"

"Happened to a friend of mine. Insurance refused to pay because the fire was 'suspicious.'"

"Shit." He scowled at her. "That's not going to happen to you. For one thing, the deputy reeves set it up to look like faulty wiring. We have a cadre who specialize in making ghoul damage look Mundane."

He'd said something like that to her when they'd surveyed the ruin. It hadn't really sunk in.

"As for your payroll, the Collegium has a fund to help you with that. And to cover the difference if the insurance comes up short. Shire Reeve's office administers it, along with things like repairing your cabin. I can walk you through the steps in the morning."

"That's okay." He'd already done way more than he'd bargained for when he volunteered to be her bodyguard. Besides, she had two friends who'd been shire reeves. "Val or Griff can probably help me."

New tension crackled in the air. For a heartbeat, Carter looked...hurt?

In a voice that was too casual, he asked, "You won't take a friendly helping hand from me?"

Damn. She had hurt him after all. He didn't deserve that. "Nothing has ever been just friendly between us," she blurted.

His eyes glinted. The tension faded as that familiar, troubling awareness flared. Aghast, she fought the urge to clap both hands over her mouth and stuff the words back in. They plopped her and Carter smack into the middle of ground she'd meant to avoid.

～

149

Tasha looked stunned at what she'd said, but she'd eased the sting of her not wanting his help. Maybe there was hope after all. But this wasn't the time to push her. And he'd given her his word that he wouldn't.

Which was why he shouldn't notice the soft swell of her breasts under the tank top. Or think about how they would fill his hands perfectly. Or admire the deep shadow the lights from outside created at the top's neckline.

He wrenched his gaze back to her face. Summoning his most casual tone, he said, "I can be a friend, Tasha. Whether or not that's all you ever want from me."

Her expression softened. "The thing is, I'm pretty sure that's not all I want."

As his heart lifted, she added, "But I'm also pretty sure it's all I should want."

Well, that brought him right back to Earth with a thud. "Why—never mind. I agreed to table this. I didn't mean to get into it now."

"We might as well. Unless that will make things awkward between us again."

She had a point. They'd actually gotten fairly comfortable with each other. But now he would wonder what she meant. "Clearing the air worked for us before. Let's try it again. Why do you think you shouldn't want more than friendship from me?"

Tasha sighed. "We're so different, Carter. You're a hometown hero—"

"Excuse me?"

"You know, a golden boy. Athletic hero, honor society member, student body president, son of the mayor, with a mom who led every important social organization, if I remember right. You're everything anyone could want a son to be."

"Tasha, that's high school. It was a long time ago." This was probably not the moment to tell her about his mom's political career.

"Some things stick." Shaking her head, she looked down at the table. "I grew up on the wrong side of the tracks. The popular girls despised me, and I returned the favor. I also turned up my nose at all their proper notions and ran pretty much wild. I made some incredibly stupid choices."

"Again," he said, "high school."

"My reputation is one of those things that stuck." When he opened his mouth, she raised a hand to stop him. Her gaze lifted to catch his. "Besides all that, you're champagne. I'm beer. Meaning you're cultured, educated, and I bet you know how to behave in any social situation. Even which of an array of fancy forks to use when."

"But you're a business owner. A college graduate. You—"

"I studied things that would help me build my business. I don't know Rousseau from—hell, I can't even think of another philosopher to compare him to. I work with my hands, Carter. Every day. In jeans and work boots."

"Yeah, and you built a respected business that way. What's wrong with that?" Scowling, he demanded, "Did some asshole dump you because your collar's blue? In the navy, everybody's collar's blue, including the brass."

No, he'd dumped her because of that and a prostitution arrest, but she would never share that info.

She flashed Carter an irritated look. "My point is that the worlds we come from, worlds we still live in to some degree, don't mesh. They don't even overlap. There's no common ground to build on."

"We can build common ground. If we both want to."

She studied him for a long moment. "You always go by the book. I value rules, especially about building codes and such, but I also think there's a time to ignore them, as you know well."

She wouldn't think he was so hidebound if she knew about his kids, but he wasn't about to spill all that. Having gotten over her resentment of his role in ending her career, she probably would keep his secret. But if she let something slip, it could torpedo his career.

He had something else, though. "Remember my comment about you and Dare and your friends and the super secret squirrel club?"

"Yes. I was going to ask you what that meant, and then I got distracted."

"I've never told anyone else this." He waited for her nod of acknowledgement before he said, "There's a downside to being all those things you described. I could never put a toe out of line. The one time I did was a disaster." It had been worse for his friend, but there was no need to go into that. "I had to present an image that did credit to my parents. But I envied the kids who sneaked out to smoke and drink by the river."

That was how he'd gotten in trouble, trying to go from envying to emulating.

"I can assure you that's not all it's cracked up to be."

"Regardless, I wanted to try it. To have the solidarity those kids enjoyed. They had each other's backs."

"Like your athlete friends must've done for each other."

"It's not the same. There's no social or legal risk there."

Her brows came together. "What does this have to do with Griff's team?"

"You had each other's backs. You were also doing something that desperately needed to be done, what with the corruption at the Collegium undercutting the shire reeve's office. And I'd bet serious money you all enjoyed the hell out of it."

"You're not wrong, but you'll notice we've been told to stop that. And we have."

"I know." He took a deep, slow breath. "I've only seen it on video, but I'll never forget the way you and Davis and Doc Harper and a couple of other people rushed to stand with Dare when the traitor challenged him. Anyone would envy that kind of friendship. I would've liked to go out and smash those ghoul nests too. To be part of something like that."

"Those were covert ops. Our lives would've been forfeit if we'd been caught by the traitors." Slowly, she added, "And it was so very much against the rules."

"Yeah. But it was the right thing to do."

A light glinted in her eyes.

He held his breath, waiting, while she studied him. Had he finally reached her?

At last, she shook her head. "You say that now, knowing how important those raids were. But if you heard about it before you knew there a traitor in this Collegium, if you still thought Griff was a traitor, would you have been so supportive? Or would you have said we should step aside and let the deputy reeves—the professionals —handle it?"

"I don't know," he admitted.

Satisfaction flashed over her face, but it didn't seem to make her happy. Her expression stayed serious. "I met Will in a bar on River Street. He hit on Lorelei and me."

"At the same time?" Damn, the guy had stones.

A smile flickered over Tasha's face but only for a moment. "He was a player in those days, as he would freely admit. We saw him there sometimes, realized there was friendship potential all around, and gracefully declined his offer. And if you tell him I shared that with you, Lockwood, you're toast."

He nodded acknowledgment.

She continued, "Over the next few months, we got to know him. Long story short, when he asked us if we wanted to do something about the ghouls, we were interested. We met Griff and—"

Carter's brows rose. "You took your lives in your hands, meeting the mage world's most wanted fugitive. For that matter, Davis and Dare also took a risk. They must've wanted to meet you pretty badly."

"Griff wanted to build a team, and he needed allies willing to work outside the box. He was determined that the ghouls wouldn't run riot because a Collegium traitor was betraying the deputy reeves."

"Sending them into ambushes," Carter murmured, scowling.

"Yes. Will swore up and down that Griff was no traitor. And Griff told us his story, the one that came out at the trial. Lorelei and I trusted Will. Partly on his say-so and partly because Griff impressed the hell out of us, we decided to trust him."

She paused, her gaze intent on his face. "We also decided that some rules were best disregarded."

"You still took a huge risk, just on trust."

"Could you have taken the same risk in going to meet Griff?"

The answer pinged inside him. He couldn't lie to her. "Probably not," he admitted. It wasn't the answer she wanted. He was losing the little ground he might've gained. "Tasha—"

"I shouldn't have kissed you. That was leading you on, even though I didn't stop to think about that first. I just didn't want you to walk away. I like, um, having you at my back. And . . . around me. But that's as far as it can go."

She stood and started back to the bedroom.

"Tasha—"

The bedroom door shut quietly.

Carter stared out at the night. He'd meant to distract her, even to offer some comfort. Instead, he'd given her something else to put distance between them.

Smooth move, Lockwood. Way to go.

He got the message, though. Attracted or not, she wouldn't give them a shot.

It hurt in a deep way, one he'd never expected to experience, like a huge, tearing hole in his soul. He let out a long breath.

By morning, he needed to get a grip.

CHAPTER FOURTEEN

FUNNY, TASHA THOUGHT, HOW YOU COULD SHARE A BATHROOM and kitchen with someone, both of you getting ready for the day at the same time, and never speak. Or even make eye contact. Because that, of course, would require speaking. She had no idea what to say and would bet Carter didn't either.

He wore his usual calm expression. In jeans, work boots, and a flannel shirt, he would blend well during her upcoming staff meeting. But he had shadows under his eyes, as though he hadn't gotten any more sleep than she had.

Looking at him hurt her heart. After last night, she couldn't deny, at least to herself, how very much she wanted him. The pull between them was muted, but watching him move still stirred up the warm, bubbling need deep inside her.

Yet she'd hurt him. That was the worst part. Hurt him and disappointed him. Once again, she hadn't measured up to what he thought she was. That burned in her throat.

He'd been willing to accept her, based on what he knew, and his comments about not feeling accepted had touched her. But if he ever knew everything about her past, he would be even more disappointed, even disgusted. She couldn't let that happen.

Today's problem was enough, and her fault. Somehow, she had to make amends.

Pouring a cup of coffee while he folded up the couch, she said, "Thanks for making this."

"No problem. I set it to go last night." He sounded as relaxed and casual as always. But he would. Like her, he had his share of pride.

She set her cup down carefully and turned to him. "Listen, Carter, I—"

"It's okay, Tasha." He straightened from closing the foldout. Finally, he faced her, his eyes tired despite his blank, unrevealing expression. "I'll tell Deke you need someone else. Val Dare offered to help out. I'm sure she'll spell me until Deke assigns a replacement. Of course, I'll still ferry you out to the island."

The offer stung. More than she would've expected. A jolt of panic tightened her throat, but she forced out words. "I don't—I never said—do you want to bow out? I understand if you do."

If he did, she would rarely see him. Maybe that was for the best, but . . .

He blinked. "I thought, after last night, you'd want me gone."

That was the last thing she wanted, and the implications of that were best left alone. "Last night, you said you could be my friend," she blurted. "If that hasn't changed, I—that's what I want." That and so much more she couldn't risk hoping for.

Surprise flashed through his eyes. Slowly, he nodded. "I can do that. You ready to go get some breakfast?"

"Sure."

They took the elevator down in silence. Awareness of his tall form at her side hummed through her, and his spicy aftershave tickled her nose. There was no point in kidding herself. Moving to the friend zone was going to be tough.

≈

JABJABJABJABJAB. In the reeve country gym, Carter pounded one of the six heavy bags with short, hard punches.

"Friends," he muttered. "She wants to be—" *jabjabjabjabjab* "—friends."

He'd walked right into that one. And how pathetic was he, that he would seize the chance so eagerly? Would spend his time around a woman who'd made it plain he wasn't her type?

Even if she did kiss him so enthusiastically.

Jabjabjabjabjabjabjabjab.

Breathing hard, he steadied the bag and wiped sweat out of his face. The kiss was meaningless. She'd all but said so. Damn it.

Val Dare had offered to spell him today so he could have some downtime. Great idea, if he could get his mind off Tasha.

He grabbed his towel and water bottle. The punching bag wasn't helping. Maybe the treadmill would. Maybe he could run off this frustration and idiotic need.

She was an adult. She'd said no. She'd clearly meant it.

Sipping water, he stared at the two mages sparring hand to hand on the big mat in the corner. Somehow, he had to get through the days and—God help him—the nights until his fellow deputies figured out why the ghouls were so keen to grab Tasha.

Running from them last night had rankled. Staying, skewering as many of the bastards as possible, had a lot more appeal. Admitting that to Tasha, though, would be a big mistake. Convincing her to flee her office had been difficult enough, and they weren't out of trouble as long as—

"Hey." Josh clapped a hand on his shoulder. "You're scowling at Phillips and Scott like you think they're secretly ghouls."

"Ghouls on my mind," Carter muttered. "Fucking bastards."

"I heard," Josh said. "I hate what happened to Tasha's shop."

"It might've happened to Tasha if I hadn't been doing a

perimeter check at the right moment." Carter ran his towel over his face. "I'm gonna run for a while." Like as far as he could before he dropped. "You?"

"I'll run."

Together, they walked to the row of treadmills against the back wall. They stepped onto the belts of side-by-side machines and started going. The warm-up jog wasn't helping. Carter nudged up the speed and incline. Nudged it up again.

If he could wear himself out, maybe he could lose the frustration over the whole *friends* business. What the hell had he been thinking?

"You okay?" Josh asked, pounding along at a sane person's pace. Mages were stronger and faster than Mundanes, so he was running faster than a Mundane comfortably could. But not nearly fast enough to match Carter. "You ever hear of warming up, Lockwood?"

Carter shrugged. "Got a mad to work off."

Now he felt it, the burn in his legs and new tension in his chest. Good. Pushing out the frustration would help him endure the cozy dinner Val Dare was, even now, organizing.

"Look," Josh said, "you got her out. She's safe, and that was your job. The rest of us will hunt ghouls."

"Not much . . . progress," Carter ground out. His breath was burning his chest. Good.

"Yeah, but we're on it, and I'd bet her buddies from Dare's old team are on it, too. Even though they're not supposed to be. We'll nail the bastards."

Carter shot him a sidelong glance. "What team?"

Josh shook his head. "I was at Dare's trial. And I'm not stupid."

So he'd figured out what that rush of people to Dare's side meant. Scowling, Carter adjusted the incline again. Yeah, Tasha was safe, and yeah, that was the most important thing. But . . .

Friends. What a vile word. He should never—

"Earth to Carter." Josh's voice yanked him out of his

thoughts. "You were miles away. Is there something else eating at you?"

"Nope." Nothing he cared to share, anyway.

He and Josh ran in silence for several minutes, Josh's pace gradually increasing. Josh glanced over at him from time to time, but Carter pretended not to notice. If he made eye contact, Josh might ask questions he didn't want to answer.

At last, legs burning and breath laboring, he bumped the speed and incline down. That should do it. He could go home to his own house and take a shower in his actual bathroom, where there were no reminders of troublesome women and none of their gal pals hovering around.

As he toweled off, Josh stepped up beside him, also wiping his face. "I backed away," Josh said quietly.

"What?"

"I backed away. From Edie, a few years ago. I'd do anything to have those years back."

Carter stared, and Josh continued, "Maybe I'm reading you wrong, but when a guy sets out to run himself into oblivion, there's usually a woman involved. And I saw the way you looked at Tasha after the battle in the swamp last winter. So if that's—"

Hell if he was going to admit that. He opened his mouth to deflect, and words popped out. "I'm not the one backing away."

Well, shit. That wasn't what he'd meant to say. That was nobody's business.

Josh nodded. "I see. Sorry it's going that way. Let me know if I can help."

Carter nodded his thanks and watched Josh walk away. Home was definitely the best choice. Sitting on the dock, dangling some bait in the water, would help him relax. So what if it was February? The fish didn't care, the temperature was in the high fifties anyway, and he had a good jacket if he needed it.

He could use a little peace before he had to go to dinner at the Dares' place and be Tasha Murdock's *friend.*

TASHA SURFACED SLOWLY. The sunlight slanting through the window implied it was midafternoon. She snagged her phone off the bedside table and turned it on. It showed the time as 3:33 p.m., so she'd slept three hours. Slept like a log.

Rubbing her gritty eyes, she turned onto her back. A sound came from the outer room. Carter? No. Not Carter.

Tasha drew a deep breath to push away disappointment. Of course it wasn't Carter. He was on break, probably delighted to have time to himself instead of guarding a woman he was attracted to but who wanted to be his friend. He'd said he wanted to stay, and she wouldn't hurt him further by sending him away.

Not that you want to do that, a small, persistent voice in her head said.

Scowling, she sat up. Friends. She was going to be *friends* with the hottest, smartest, kindest guy—the navy incident notwithstanding—who'd ever crossed her horizon. What insane impulse had prompted her to ask for that?

More subdued clattering came from the outer area. She pushed her blanket aside and crawled off the bed to check it out.

When she opened the bedroom door, Val poked her head out of the kitchen. "Hey, you're awake. Did you get some sleep?"

"Yeah. Thanks. That hot milk did the trick."

Val shrugged. "Griffin's mom." She turned back to the big kettle on the stove.

"Yeah, you said." Lara Dare had created a concoction of whole milk, vanilla, and a dash of condensed milk that, served hot, was better than a sleeping pill.

Tasha walked around the kitchen counter area and took a seat at the table. A rich, meaty aroma filled the air, and the pot Val was stirring simmered quietly. "What're you doing?"

"Checking my beef stew. It's softening up nicely." Val

160

grabbed a bottle of red wine and splashed a little into the pot. "Want some hot tea?"

"I'd rather have coffee, but I can get it."

"Nope. This is Pamper Tasha Day. Cream and sugar, right?"

Tasha watched Val fix the coffee. She'd made a fresh pot at some point.

"Lorelei's on her way," Val announced, setting a mug in front of Tasha. "We have some time to catch up before the guys roll in. Or, if you're frustrated and want something to pound, we can go down to the gym in reeve country. We could spar if you want."

"I'm too tired." Tasha saluted her with the mug. "Thanks, though."

"Anytime." Val leaned on the counter. "And anything. Anything you need, Tasha, Griffin and I will get for you."

Sudden tears stung Tasha's eyes. "I know. Thanks." But no one could get what she currently, idiotically—probably because she was so discouraged and vulnerable—wanted most, to be able to fit in Carter Lockwood's world.

Val took aluminum foil off a plate on the counter and passed the plate to Tasha. A mound of golden-brown, coconut-sprinkled cookies filled it. "Have a cookie with your coffee. We should eat what we want before the guys show up and devour them."

She grabbed a blue china teapot that must've come from her apartment and poured tea into a mug. Magically warming it between her hands, she held it until faint traces of steam wafted upward.

Tasha bit into her cookie and had to close her eyes to savor the taste. Coconut, chocolate, and something else she couldn't place. "You could open a bakery, Val."

"Thanks, but I like kicking ghoul butt more."

They grinned at each other, and a knock came at the door. Familiar magic washed through the room.

"I got it." Tasha hurried to let Lorelei in. They exchanged hugs, and Lorelei said, "Is that a cookie? I want one. Or three."

"Why do you never gain weight?" Tasha demanded.

Grabbing a cookie, Lorelei smiled. "I have the metabolism of a hummingbird."

"I think you must," Val informed her. "Let's move to the living area. I can monitor dinner from there."

"I thought we were eating at your place," Lorelei said.

"Stew needs to simmer a while. I can carry it up there in a bit. Handy thing about magic is that you can carry hot or very cold things safely."

"Any word from Carter?" Tasha asked as they relocated.

Val replied, "He called about an hour ago to see how you were. Said he was going to his house and would skip dinner if it's okay with you. He has leftovers that need to be eaten."

"Of course it's okay," Tasha said, hoping her tone was casual. "He's doing a lot for me." Yet her disappointment stung. Was he avoiding this idiotic *friends* thing they'd agreed to? Maybe he'd changed his mind about it. Why wouldn't he? She would try, and he'd said he would. But—

"So how are things with you two?" Lorelei turned to her. "Getting along okay?"

"Yeah, it's—" Frustration welled into her throat and blocked it. Tears stung her eyes.

"Oh, honey." Val leaned in, but Tasha put up a hand to stop her.

So now this had happened. *Great. Just great.* Her friends were looking worried, still leaning close. Tasha battled back the tears and took a shaky breath.

"I will barbecue him," Val ground out. "And I'm talking to Deke about replacing—"

"Not—not his—fault," Tasha managed.

"When you're this upset about him?" Lorelei scowled. "Try again, girlfriend."

"It's not." Frustration and despair welled into her throat

again, this time pushing out words. She told them about the previous night's conversation, concluding with the demented notion that he and she could be friends.

"Tasha," Val said slowly, "if you're this upset about turning him down, is it possible you're making a mistake?"

Tasha shook her head. Glancing at Lorelei, she said, "I can't —I don't want it to be Ferrell all over again."

"I'm lost," Val said. "I'm going to get you a cold cloth, and then I want to hear about this obvious jerkwad, Fred or Ferret or whoever he was." She hurried toward the bathroom.

Lorelei squeezed Tasha's hand. "Ferrell really was a jerk-wad. And arrogant. From what I've seen, Carter is neither."

Val passed Tasha the cold cloth and sat beside her on the loveseat. "Okay. Who's Ferrell, and did you make him sorry for his jerkwadness?"

Telling the story was easier with the cloth pressed to her stinging eyes. That way, she didn't have to look at her friends. "Long story short, he was trying to climb the corporate ladder. We dated for about six months, and I was falling for him. Until I found out he'd been taking other women to various upscale events. When I confronted him, he told me he couldn't take a *day laborer* to these classy things. I wouldn't do him credit."

He'd mainly focused on her arrest, but Val and Lorelei didn't need to know about that. If Tasha had her way, they would never hear of it.

"Day laborer, my ass," Val snapped. "You're a business owner."

"I wasn't then." Tasha sighed. Staring at the cloth, she refolded it to bring cooler fabric to the outside.

"I bet if you asked Carter," Lorelei put in, "he'd say being with you does him credit."

Tasha glared. "Get real."

"I've seen the way he looks at you." Lorelei's chin jutted out. "Besides, a guy who isn't proud to be seen with you doesn't announce his honorable intentions to your brother."

Shaking her head, Tasha buried her face in the washcloth again.

Val patted Tasha's knee gently. "You'll never know whether something could work between you unless you try, and if it doesn't, there could be a dozen reasons. But I don't think any of them would have to do with Carter being a snob."

He wasn't one. They were right about that. But he came from circles where she couldn't fit in, and if anyone in those circles, even if they were just small-town politics, found out about her wild child past, they were bound to see her as a problem best shunted aside. Yet he didn't seem either judgmental or superior. Was there a chance he could understand?

Tasha sighed and pressed the cold cloth to her eyes. She desperately wanted something with Carter. Maybe she should think about telling him the truth.

CHAPTER FIFTEEN

AFTER DINNER WITH GRIFF AND VAL, TASHA WENT BACK DOWN TO her guest apartment with Carter, who'd arrived in time for dessert. In the elevator, he watched the floor number above the door change as he said, "You're awfully quiet."

"Just tired," she replied, shrugging. A conversation about her past wasn't for an elevator. "I'm glad you got some time off. Nobody wants to be on duty 24/7."

"I don't mind." But his gaze remained on the readout.

"Did you have a good afternoon?"

"Yep. Did some fishing, zoned out on the dock." With a grin, he added, "Ate leftover chicken that probably wasn't as good as whatever you had upstairs."

Tasha only smiled. The beef stew had been melt-in-your-mouth tender.

The elevator reached their floor. They walked out together. Was this the time to tell him the truth? Could she risk it?

But what would be the point? They'd settled, however irrationally, on being friends. Stirring that up, especially since she still didn't really believe he could accept her, didn't seem wise.

They reached their door, and she suddenly couldn't stand to go in. With all this churning in her head, she would never sleep.

"Can we take a drive?" she asked.

Ushering her inside, Carter frowned. "It's risky for you to be outside the grounds after dark. After the attack in the fall, I'm not convinced walking around the property is much better."

At least he was looking at her. "I really need some fresh air," she said. "I'm feeling trapped and pressured and . . ." scared of what might happen if she shared, but she couldn't say that to him. "I'd really like to go down to the water. Maybe over to Jekyll Island." Thanks to the causeway, they could drive there, unlike with Cumberland Island. "It's only nine thirty, not that late."

"I know, but—"

"Besides, considering nobody's attacked us when we left the last couple of mornings, they probably don't know we're here. If they do, they'll think we're in for the night anyway."

"That's not the point." He ran a hand over his face. "We're going out on the water tomorrow, sailing over to Cumberland Island to meet your clients. You'll get plenty of fresh air then."

Tasha blew out an impatient breath. "Those are all good points, but if I'm willing to risk it, you should—"

"No." His face went stony. "I couldn't stand it if something happened to you on my watch." The anguish in his voice stabbed into her soul.

"I know," she said, realizing she did know it. "It means a lot."

At that, his expression grew tender. The warmth in his eyes wrapped itself around her heart and tugged. She couldn't help taking a step closer as he murmured, "Tasha—"

His back pocket buzzed. Carter muttered something soft and vehement, and the moment was broken.

Just in time, too, as she'd been about to make a big mistake.

A glance at his phone, and his face closed over again. He shot her an apologetic look. "I'm sorry. I need to deal with this."

"Sure." She strolled into the kitchen for a glass of water while he texted. To give him privacy, she walked back to the bedroom and straightened up the bed. She'd left it a mess after her nap.

Carter knocked on the doorframe. She looked up. Wearing a worried frown, he said, "Please don't ask me to take you off the grounds, Tasha."

"Was that bad news on the phone? Has something happened?"

"Nothing to do with you." His brusque tone had her stiffening.

"Okay." She cocked her head to one side. "I need to talk to you." Feel him out. See whether telling him the truth could be safe. "I'd rather do it down by the water, but we can do it here."

His frown deepened. "Can it wait? I need to make some calls."

"Uh, yeah." Not like she was eager to dive into those waters. But she'd seen him so evasive and perturbed once before, at Val and Griff's party. He'd been planning to *make some calls* then too. Except he hadn't exactly taken a call a minute ago. "Are you making calls or sending texts?"

The frown became a scowl. Before he could reply, she added, "You're acting like you did when that kid needed your help."

Guilt flicked over his face, only to disappear behind a blank expression a heartbeat later.

Gotcha. "If you need to go, Carter, it's okay. I can go back to Griff and Val's."

"Yeah, right." He shook his head. "We did this dance once before, and your friends were right to be pissed. This afternoon was downtime. Now I'm on duty, and I'm not leaving you."

"Then I guess you'll have to take me with you." The words popped out before she thought. This would be a great reason to delay any kind of serious talk.

He glared at her. "Were you not listening when I explained about going outside the grounds at night?"

"If this is like before, it's a kid in trouble. Are you really going to turn your back?"

"You come first," he snapped.

She really shouldn't let those words make the middle of her chest all gooey. "I know you take your duty seri—"

"Not duty. You. You come first, Tasha." As she gaped, struck speechless by the vehemence and the fact she believed him, he added, "We'll go talk to the Dares. You'll stay with them while I handle this, and if they want to be pissed because I'm leaving again, they can."

While she let him go out alone to handle something that worried him. "You might need backup."

"Your job is not to be backup. It's to stay safe."

"We had a great evening with Griff and Val, but you were off all day. This will make them ask questions, and since you're so tight-lipped with details about what you're doing, I don't think you want that. And I don't want static between you and them."

"Not your decision."

"Well, it should be," she snapped. "You—" *come first* popped into her head, but there would be no going back if she said it, so she substituted, "—matter to me, you idiot."

He blinked, looking stunned.

"Don't you trust me?" she asked. Dirty pool, but she didn't want to risk Val or Griff being annoyed with him. The only way to avoid that and let him follow his conscience about this kid was for her to go with him.

CARTER YANKED his scrambled wits into some kind of order. "Of course I trust you. That's not the point. It. Is. Dangerous."

"We'll see." She fished her phone from her purse and punched in a number. "Hey, Griff. I'm putting you on speaker. Carter and I need you to settle something for us."

No, they didn't. "What are you doing?" he mouthed.

"See, the thing is," she began, ignoring him. "I really want to get out of here for a while. I've got cabin fever, and I want to go

168

for a drive. Carter thinks we shouldn't leave the grounds after dark."

"He's right," Dare stated, his voice flat. "Anything else?"

Checkmate. Carter fought to keep from smiling. Now she would have to go wait with them while he handled this problem.

Tasha's brows knitted. "Everyone else leaves when they want, and don't tell me everyone else isn't a target. I know that. But I also know I really need open space and fresh air, or I might just have a screaming fit."

A moment of silence, then Dare said, "I'm sorry, Tasha, but it's too risky."

"If the ghouls knew where I am, they'd be staking out the front gate," she argued, "and we likely would've been jumped already. Even if they do know, they probably figure we're in for the night."

Carter stifled a snort. That wouldn't work any better on Dare than it had on him.

Again, silence came over the phone. "Okay," Dare said, stunning Carter. "Valeria and I will follow you in our car so you have backup. Where are we going?"

Shit. This was bad to worse. No way the Dares would keep quiet about it if they met Jeremy and Mila, the girl who was the one in trouble this time. That Carter had been unofficially helping the kids would quickly become apparent, and then his career was toast.

But Tasha held up a finger, signaling him to silence. "Griff, I appreciate that. Really. But I need some semi-alone time."

"You had that this afternoon."

"Yes, but I had it here. Surrounded by walls and, much as I love you all, people. I need clear space around me, a minimum —as in just one—of energy intrusion from others, and fresh air on my face."

"I'll call you back," Dare said. He disconnected.

Carter shook his head. "He's not going to agree to that, Tasha, and I won't leave you."

Her phone rang. "Speaker again," she warned.

Griff Dare said, "I don't think this is a great idea, but you have a point. Can you take this alone time in Brunswick, maybe at Mary Ross Waterfront Park? If you can, Valeria and I will drive into town and park over by Old City Hall. That should give you privacy, but we'll be close enough to help if you need it."

Tasha nodded at Carter, who said, "That works."

They could meet the kids there. Across the narrow inlet beside the park, Oglethorpe Bay, lay only vacant land. No prying eyes to call the cops about people in the park after dark.

"Got it," Dare said. "You won't see us unless you need us. If you do, shoot a bolt into the air. We'll see it."

Before Carter could thank him, he disconnected.

Tasha tucked her phone away and smiled at Carter. It was one of the few smiles he'd seen on her face since all this started, and it made his pulse skip.

"All fixed," she stated.

In a dry voice, he commented, "Including the fact that you've arranged it—or think you have—so I have no one to leave you with. I can find somebody."

"If you do, what will you say when Griff and Val ask me whether I had a good outing? I hate hauling them out when they've done so much already. I'm not going to lie to them when they're giving up their evening."

He stared at her. "That's blackmail. And you just lied up one side and down the other."

"I told the truth about what I wanted," she replied, unperturbed. "I just left out the part that's your business. Consider it a compromise. You get to help your young friend, I get out in the fresh air, and we have backup in the unlikely event of a ghoul attack. It's all good."

She paused, her expression suddenly vulnerable. "Unless you really don't trust me."

He was a sucker for that look. "You'll need a jacket," he replied.

~

THE STREETS of Brunswick were dark and mostly deserted. This late at night, the shops in the center of town were closed. Anyone wanting something to eat would need to head out to the chain restaurants near the interstate, but he and Tasha had made sandwiches for the kids.

Driving wasn't a challenge, so there was nothing to keep his mind off the woman beside him. Whatever perfume she was wearing smelled like ocean breezes, faint and fresh with a little salt to it. Even without looking directly, he couldn't help noticing the way the streetlights outlined her straight, narrow nose, curvy lips, and determined chin.

"Tell me about this kid," she said.

In for a buck, in for a bundle. He'd better hope he could really trust her. "Jeremy's thirteen," Carter said, "and mageborn. I met him on an investigation. His mom took off a few years back. Jeremy should've had magical training at the Collegium this year, but there's no one who cares to see that he gets it. His dad's a drunk who rarely notices the kid unless he's on a bender and Jeremy happens to cross his path. Then he gets pissed off. When I met the kid, I talked to him, then I bought him dinner. He said it was the first meal he'd had that day."

"Not even lunch at school? That's awful."

"It was a Saturday. Anyway, when Jeremy gets jammed up or his dad's on a tear, he calls me. I make some calls, see that he's fed, and find him a place to stay. There's a shelter for runaways up in Glencoe."

He glanced at her. The distress in her face encouraged him to

171

trust her further. "That's what happened the night of the Dares' party. His dad was lit and chased him out of the house."

"I can't imagine living like that. Can't the Collegium do something?"

"I checked. That's not in their purview, apparently."

"Well, it should be," Tasha snapped.

"Agreed, but it is what it is. I try to help him study when I have time."

"That's really nice of you, Carter. Very kind."

He shrugged. "He needs help. No one else stepped up, so I did. Anyway, the girl with him tonight is named Mila. She's a friend of his, a Mundane, so no magic. She's fourteen. They go to the same school. She has two parents who can't seem to decide whether they want to stay married, so one or both of them is always jetting off or bringing somebody home or whatever else floats their boats. Mila's on her own most of the time."

"Do both of them have a problem tonight?"

"No, just Mila."

The waterfront park looked desolate in the streetlights. Carter pulled in and parked her truck beside the big lawn. Next to the lawn on the right, a long, white open-sided shed ran from the parking lot almost to the walkway near the water. Local markets were held there. To its left stood a white, two-story structure that looked like a house with a gazebo on one corner of the porch. It had openings where windows and doors should be. A round, white tower with an open area below its pointed roof topped the building. What the tower was for, he'd never figured out. The kids would be in the house part.

"Mila's folks aren't home," he said, watching for her and Jeremy to emerge. "Haven't been for days. Some kid followed her when she left school. Harassed her."

"By 'harassed,' you mean what, exactly?" Tasha frowned at him.

"Sexual insults and taunts. And vague threats. She took

refuge in the library until it closed. By then, the guy had given up."

"And she has no one to turn to. The Mundane cops can't do anything about that stuff." Tasha's voice rang with disgust. "What are you going to do? Besides feed them?"

"I'm going to get the details and show her some escape moves, which I hope she never needs. Then, tomorrow, I'm putting the fear of God into the little shit."

"That sounds good, but I think you should also teach her some purely retaliatory things."

"Why?"

A grim smile curved Tasha's lips. "Because a girl—anyone, really—who knows she hurt an assailant, that she can make him sorry, has more confidence. And enough confidence can sometimes ward off the need for the rest."

"You sound like you know," he said before he realized it wasn't smart.

"Of course I know." She turned to him, but her face was unreadable. "Thanks to the United States Navy."

A smart man would let it go at that, so Carter did. Grabbing the sandwiches and sodas from the rear seat, he said, "The kids should be in the fake house. Let's go get them."

"Right. But Carter, one more thing."

"Yeah?"

She looked uneasy, so he braced as she said, "You shouldn't be putting your hands on a girl that age who's not a relative. For any body-contact stuff, your demonstration partner should be me."

In his arms, with his hands on her. Just the idea was arousing. How the hell would he cope with doing it?

But he had to. She was right.

Before he could reply, Jeremy's head poked out of the open doorway. The boy waved tentatively.

Carter opened his door. "Let's get the kids."

TASHA HUNG BACK, letting Carter take the lead while she carried the food and their screened swords. The boy, Jeremy, was about five four, too thin for his age, and had haunted, brown eyes below a mop of dishwater blond hair. His companion was about an inch taller, with medium brown skin. Although she also was too thin, she had noticeable breasts, probably what had attracted the harasser, though you never knew what turned on those vile creeps. Tight, black ringlets framed a face that would've been pretty if her eyes weren't puffy, as though she'd cried a lot.

Tasha's parents hadn't been much on smoothing their kids' way. Her hands fisted with memory and sympathy. If only magic could fix things for these kids. Really, it was unconscionable that the Collegium wouldn't step up.

Jeremy flung himself into Carter's arms. The deputy reeve caught him, gave him a quick hug, and stepped back. He kept one hand on the boy's shoulder and said, "You did right to call me, Jaybird. Don't ever worry about that."

Releasing Jeremy, he turned to Mila. "Rough day, I hear."

She nodded, her lips trembling. "I don't—I'd rather not, you know, talk about it."

"Sure. Y'all, this is my friend Tasha. You can trust her. She's going to help me show you some things."

Tasha lifted a hand in salute. "Hey."

Jeremy gave her a nod, but Mila looked doubtful. Carter crouched, so she was taller than he was. "Just one thing I have to know, Mila. Did he actually touch you?"

Her lips trembled again, and her throat worked. At last, she said, "Just flipped the edge of my jacket. Tugged my hair. That stuff."

"That's a crime, Mila," Carter said. "It's assault. You know that?"

"What difference does it make? He'll just say he didn't do anything, and his parents are important. Big in the PTA."

"Got it," Carter told her.

Tasha understood, too. When you had a wild rep or were disadvantaged and up against someone with pull, nobody wanted to hear you complain. Mila's parents apparently had money but didn't look out for their daughter.

If she had to pull a move on this guy, would anyone believe he deserved it? Or would she just get into deeper trouble?

"Okay," Carter said, rising again. "Let's go out the back so we're not visible from the road. Then we'll go through some things."

They walked up the empty structure's steps, through it, and out the back, where a narrow border of grass separated the building from a wide, concrete walkway. Letting the others go ahead, Tasha laid her saber and Carter's sword down just outside the door, keeping them screened. Another narrow, grassy border lined the area by the water. Moonlight silvered the narrow blackness of Oglethorpe Bay.

Tasha and Jeremy sat on the steps behind the fake house while Carter showed Mila how to break a wrist grip by kicking an assailant's knee, rotating her wrist to slide out of the grip at the thumb, then kick or punch to get time to run. From there, they moved to breaking fingers.

"A ballpoint pen can be a weapon," he said. "So can keys between your fingers."

Mila looked doubtful. "I don't know if I could, you know, hurt him."

"When it's him or you, always choose you," Carter replied. Glancing over his shoulder, he said, "Right, Tasha?"

"Absolutely," she replied.

"Tasha knows how to fight," Carter said. "Nobody messes with her."

Nobody now, but those guys in high school who'd had the

wrong idea . . . Yeah, she knew how Mila felt, and Mila didn't have a Nate to stand up for her.

I can stand up for myself now. This girl can learn to do that too.

Carter beckoned to her. "Mila," he said, "have a seat with Jeremy. Y'all can eat while Tasha and I demonstrate some other moves."

As Tasha handed out sandwiches and sodas, Mila asked, "Can't you demonstrate with me? How will I learn?"

"You and Jeremy can practice," Carter said. "You and Tasha can run through some of these moves, but I'm a lot older than you, Mila, and not a relative. It's best for us both if I'm not grabbing you the way I need to for some of these lessons."

Tasha stood in front of him on the grass. "What's first?"

"We'll go with a hair grip from the front," he said. Reaching out, he grabbed her hair with his right hand. Tasha slapped her left on top of it so he couldn't pull her hair, used her right to lightly punch the nerve center above the elbow on his extended arm, and mimed a kick to his groin.

His grip broke. She danced away.

"Good job," he said, his eyes warm with approval that made her breath stutter. "Now we'll do it slowly."

They ran through it several times. Then Tasha rehearsed it with Mila while Carter called instructions.

"You're gettin' it," Jeremy cried. "Way to go, Mila!"

Tasha and Carter exchanged a smile, and she was ready for the flutters in her tummy this time. Working with him felt good. Much better than the awkwardness of the day.

"Okay," Carter said. He offered Mila a high-five. Grinning, the girl slapped his palm.

To Tasha, he said, "Let's go with back bear hug."

With his arms around her and their bodies close. A recipe for trouble.

His face looked calm, but the wariness in his eyes revealed his misgivings. "Like in boot camp."

They hadn't learned this in boot camp, so he must mean the attitude. She gave him a brisk nod. "Right."

He stepped behind her. His arms closed around her, pinning hers and pulling her back against his solid frame. Tasha ignored the sudden rush of heat in her blood. Grabbing his arms, she dropped her weight. That forced him to bend forward. It also brought her breasts into contact with his muscular forearms, something she liked far too much. She mimed stomping on his foot and then kicking her heel up into his groin.

"Then you run," she told their students.

"Watch the process, kids," Carter said. His voice sounded tight, so maybe she wasn't the only one affected.

He continued, "Again, Tasha, and call it out as you go."

They ran through it three more times. Each time, she felt more conscious of his closeness. When she turned to face him the third time, he looked tense. At least she wasn't the only one.

Practicing with Mila helped get her mind off the way he'd felt against her. And how much she'd liked it. If there was a chance things could work out, even a slim one, it would be intoxicating.

If.

"Now we'll do it with your arms free," he said.

Tasha raised her eyebrows. "Hip throw?"

"Roger." He stepped behind her and grabbed her around the waist. Tasha twisted in his hold, grabbed his shirt, and pulled him across her hip. Carter did a slo-mo tumble to the grass.

"I like that one," Mila crowed.

Tasha smiled at her "Putting the bad guy down is always fun."

"Now from the front," Carter said. His arms encircled her. Her breasts flattened against his chest, and the pressure at her groin made her breath catch. She and Carter jerked their hips back at the same moment.

A muscle worked in his jaw, but he looked over her shoulder instead of at her. "Okay?" he asked, his voice gruff.

"Yeah," she managed. "Ready?"

At his nod, she bent, pushing her hips back, and swung her clasped hands toward his groin. He jerked his hips backward. His grip loosened. She mimed a kick that would've slammed her shin into his groin. Now she had enough room to get her hands up, so a forearm to his throat shoved him back.

"And then you run," she repeated.

"You always say run," Jeremy commented.

Carter nodded. "Because these moves are designed to help you get away. To open a can of whup-ass on this guy, you'd need years of martial arts lessons. And lots of practice."

They ran through the sequence twice more. Each time, her awareness of Carter's body, of the strong line of his jaw and the way his hair waved over his ears, became more intense. By the third time through it, her breasts were tight and her panties damp. She managed to focus anyway, but just barely. The sooner they stopped this, the better.

At least, despite their mutual reactions, they were talking to each other without awkward pauses and evasions. If she told him the truth, the whole truth, she could lose that.

A lump blocked her throat. She swallowed hard. "Mila, let's practice."

They ran through the sequence several times. The girl's fierce expression boded well for her remembering this if she needed it.

"Okay," Carter said at last. "A few more basic moves, and we're done. Tasha, I got this."

"Right." Maybe he was as relieved as she was that they could stop pressing against each other. The closeness raised too many thoughts best ignored.

She joined Jeremy on the steps. They watched while Carter ran Mila through a forearm shove to the throat, an elbow to the solar plexus, and a groin kick. They did that three times too.

"Carter's awesome," Jeremy confided in a low voice.

"He's a good guy," Tasha agreed.

"Better than good. He found me practicing blood spells. Trying to help my dad, y'know."

"Is that so?" Although she kept her tone casual, her mental ears were perking up.

Jeremy nodded. "He told me I was in a world of trouble, but he didn't report me. He talked to my dad, for all the good that did, and told me to call him if I was tempted to step out of line again or if I was in trouble."

"That was good of him." And, she would lay odds, very much against Collegium regs.

Maybe he was more willing to bend the rules for a worthy cause than she'd realized.

"Yeah. He really helps me out. Me and some others. I dunno what I'd do without him."

Carter glanced at his watch. "That's a wrap for tonight."

"Already?" Mila glanced at Jeremy for support. She'd lost her distressed look, but learning to kick ass could do that for a person.

"Carter's tough about school nights," Jeremy said.

Carter looked from one to the other of them. "Y'all need a ride?"

Tasha raised her eyebrows. "What about, um, our other friends?"

The *oh, shit* look on his face said he'd forgotten them. "We'll need to explain a detour."

So the kids must not live in the direction of the Collegium. They would fit in the truck's extended cab, but there would definitely be questions. Damn it, she'd meant to help Carter, not create problems for him by having Griff and Val come along.

"Explain to who?" Jeremy asked.

"Some friends of ours in town," Carter said. "Nothing to worry about."

Jeremy looked from one to the other of them.

"We'll walk," Jeremy said. "We do it all the time."

"I don't—" Carter rubbed a hand over his face. "Okay. You call me when you get home, Jaybird."

"Roger that." The boy grinned. "Thanks, Carter."

Mila gave Carter a quick hug and then gave Tasha one. "Thanks, you guys. Thanks loads." She and Jeremy trotted off across the park.

Carter and Tasha retrieved their swords and walked to her truck. There, they waited until the kids were out of sight. She and Carter were alone. The darkness of the bay and the unoccupied land across it lay behind them. Aside from the wind rustling the palmetto trees, there was no sound. In the silence, all the awkward awareness of him rushed back. Add in the memory of how he'd felt against her, how he'd reacted to that, and it was no wonder she felt so fidgety.

"I guess we should go," she said in a voice so bright it sounded fake. She barely managed not to wince. She shouldn't make a decision about talking to him when she was so antsy. Once the truth was out, there was no taking it back. Before she spilled to him, she had to be sure it was the right move.

CHAPTER SIXTEEN

WOULD TASHA AND VAL NEVER GET OFF THE PHONE? CARTER glared out at the road. Tasha had already covered the fact that they were on the road and headed for the Collegium. What was all this crap about the weekend? They had the rest of the week to iron that out.

He really, really needed her to stop talking. Until she did, he couldn't forget she was here. Couldn't get his mind off the way she'd felt in his arms. Or how much he wanted her there again. Having her in his peripheral vision was bad enough. It fed the awareness that always crackled between them.

He couldn't do this friend shit. It was just that simple.

He could ride it out until his fellow deputies found the people after her—and that seriously better be soon—but then he needed to step back. Get some breathing room. Maybe when he and Tasha weren't around each other so much, he could find the head space to bring this . . . whatever it was . . . between them under control.

He could move on.

Finally, she and Val signed off. Carter focused hard on the road.

"Can I ask you something?" She glanced over at him. At his nod, she said, "Jeremy told me how you met him."

Oh, shit. What would she think about Carter's choices back then?

"I was wondering," she continued, "were you supposed to report him or arrest him or some such?"

"Yeah."

She waited, maybe hoping for an explanation. Finally, she asked, "Why didn't you?"

"He needed help, not lectures and confinement, even for a couple of days." Maybe if Carter kept his answers brief, she would drop it.

Why the hell couldn't her psychically-or-whatever-linked brother call now? Except then she'd be talking and Carter's idiot brain, the one in his cargo pants that had been standing to attention most of this evening, would stay focused on her. If she'd noticed, she hadn't said anything. Maybe she didn't want to notice.

What a lowering thought.

She cocked her head. "I won't tell anyone, if you're worried about that."

"I know."

They rode a couple of miles in merciful silence while both his brains persisted in rerunning the feel of her breasts against his arm—and against his chest—and the way her body—

"I never thought you would go against the book, even for a good cause," she told him quietly. "I was wrong."

Did that mean—? No. Not going there. No point. She hadn't said anything about changing her mind.

"Told you," he said.

"Yeah." She turned toward him. "Is anything wrong?"

"No." He pulled out to pass a slow-moving pickup.

"Then why won't you look at me?"

He flicked her the briefest of glances and swung back into his lane. "I'm driving."

"With no traffic."

True. Headlights that probably belonged to the Dares' car lagged far behind. Carter shrugged because what could he say?

Tasha bit her lip. "Did I do something wrong?"

"You were great."

"Then why . . . never mind." She faced front again, her face set.

Damn it. He'd hurt her. But saying anything would take them onto ground they'd already traveled. Fruitlessly. Frustratingly.

Yet that awareness still hummed in the air. And now that she wasn't talking, memory and desire were tormenting him together. Well, so be it. Carter set his jaw and drove.

CARTER'S PROFILE looked chiseled in stone. He hadn't said anything for the last five minutes. The earlier, easy rapport was gone. Tasha bit her lip. She had to have done or said something to set him off. Maybe she shouldn't have asked him about meeting Jeremy.

Surely he couldn't be afraid she would turn him in. They'd moved past that incident in the navy.

But maybe he wasn't sure about that.

He turned into the Collegium, and Darren Hale, a young, dark-skinned deputy reeve with a ready smile, checked the car. "You're good, Carter," he said. "Hey, Tasha."

"Hey, Darren." She mustered a smile for him. They'd met when he, too, had helped guard the farmhouse that was HQ for Will and Audra's excavation.

Carter thanked his fellow deputy and drove on. Tasha texted Val to tell her that she and Carter had arrived safely.

"Long day," Tasha said, giving him a last chance. "With a lot to do tomorrow."

He responded with a curt nod that felt like a slap.

Enough. Enough, already.

As soon as the car stopped, Tasha grabbed her sheathed saber from behind the seat and hopped out. She and Carter met at the rear bumper. He held his sheathed broadsword in one hand.

"You wait for me," he snapped. "Even here."

He was looking across the parking lot, not at her. Her free hand balled into a fist.

"Tell me what I did, damn it."

"Nothing," he ground out. "Let's get inside."

"No. Just no." Fighting frustration, she stated, "We're standing right here until you tell me what I said or did that's got your shorts in a wad."

"I told you. Nothing. Now—"

"Then why won't you even look at me?"

He made a low sound like a growl and slammed his hand against the truck's tailgate. Tasha recoiled from the *bam*.

"I can't be your friend," he roared. "I can't."

Breathing hard, he turned his gaze to her at last. The heat and the yearning and the pain in his eyes tore into her soul. The pain echoed in her heart and shattered her restraint.

"I can't be friends either," she blurted. Reaching for his face, she took a single step toward him. "Carter—"

He made a strangled sound, dropped his broadsword, and yanked her into his arms. Tasha gasped. His mouth came down on hers, tongue sliding inside, plundering, and thought fled. She kissed him back. Kissed him harder.

His hands roamed, caressing her hips, her back, her breast, raising heat and pleasure and aching need. She dropped her saber so she could explore him, too, the hard muscles of his shoulder and back, the planes of his chest. His firm butt. He kissed his way down her neck, his beard stubble scraping the skin and adding more heat. Her left hand slid into his soft, thick hair as her right pulled him closer.

His erection pressed into her. When she looped a leg around

him, bringing his center flush with hers, he groaned and took her mouth again.

The kiss broke. Breathing hard, they stared at each other. He smiled, and her heart melted. He bent to nibble her ear. His lips were soft and warm on her skin.

Pleasure flashed into her core. She moaned and arched into him.

A tiny voice in the back of her brain insisted, *NoNoNo. All hands to battle stations.*

She ignored it. The pain in his eyes had been the last straw. She was done resisting this thing between them. Nothing mattered now but finally having Carter in her arms. In her bed. She tugged his head up for another kiss.

"No," he said, his breath rasping. "We're exposed out here. Let's take this inside."

Only then did she realize he'd turned them, putting her between himself and the truck. "Okay. Inside. Fast."

"You bet." He kissed her again quickly.

The voice of sanity objected, but so what? She and Carter had waited a long time for this. They would have tonight, come ghouls or demons or earthquakes. They could worry about anything else tomorrow.

They picked up their swords. With their arms around each other, they started for the building. His hip bumping hers as they walked deepened the craving inside her. As soon as they had privacy, his hips could bump hers in a different, better way.

Tasha's heart was singing, and her body hummed with awareness of him beside her. Despite the misgivings now roaring in her head, she would stand by that impulsive, heart-felt choice. She needed this with him. Whatever came of it, she couldn't turn back now.

Still holding each other, they hurried inside and down the hall to the elevator. Carter pressed the button. The car arrived. They stepped in and had it to themselves.

With his eyes on hers, he caught her hand. He raised it to his lips and kissed her knuckles, his eyes hot. The bubbling inside her deepened.

"If you want to call me Cupcake," she said hesitantly, watching his face, "I'm okay with it."

Carter grinned. He lowered his head as she stretched up to kiss him. His mouth opened on hers, his tongue teasing, and his arms locked around her waist. The hard bulge pressing her groin made her crave more.

The elevator dinged. Arms around each other, they rushed down the hall. Tasha laid her palm on the lock plate on their suite. The door clicked.

They stepped inside together, and Carter locked and warded the door. Then he kissed her again, hard and deep. Tasha's back hit the door. Her hands roamed his back, warm and muscular under cotton knit. Still kissing her, he took her sword and tossed it aside with his. She barely heard the *thunk* as the weapons hit the carpeted floor.

Carter pulled back. Watching her face, he slowly unbuttoned her shirt. The desire in his eyes made her throat close. She slid her hands up his chest, over the firm muscles, and up to his neck to draw his head down. She kissed him, nipping his lower lip, teasing him.

With a groan, he crushed her against him and took the kiss deep. Hard. Tasha broke it and licked the muscular column of his neck. He slipped a hand down the back of her pants, his finger sliding along the cleft between her buttocks. Shuddering with pleasure, she yanked the bottom of his tee upward. He finished ripping it off, then bent to nibble her neck while he pushed her shirt off her shoulders.

Tasha shrugged out of it. Carter flipped the catch on her bra and tugged it clear. She pressed kisses over his broad chest, flicking her tongue against the warm, sleek skin. He made a choked sound.

Then her bra was gone, and his head swooped down to take

her breast in his mouth. Pleasure flashed through her, blinding her.

When she surfaced, they were on their knees on the floor. Carter cupped her breasts in both hands, sending a flash of heat through her "So damn perfect," he told her as she gasped. "I knew you would be."

She blew lightly into his ear. His muscles went rigid, and she brushed her lips over the ridges and hollows. Of his abs She stroked his soft, curly chest hair. "Nice," she whispered as his muscles tensed. "Just right."

Lightly, she stroked her nails over one of his nipples. He jolted, his grip tightening, and she exulted in giving him pleasure.

He suckled the other breast. Craving throbbed deep inside her. She arched toward him. He lowered her to her back. The carpet felt rough beneath her as he whisked off her running shoes. Her jeans and panties came next.

Before she had time to feel shy, his head was between her thighs. "Beautiful," he murmured. His tongue flicked over the sensitive nub there, and Tasha cried out, clutching at his head. Carter's hands slid up to her breasts. Playing with her nipples, he licked and sucked between her legs until she was whimpering.

"Carter, please . . . please."

He drew her upright for a long, deep kiss. His hand replaced his mouth between her thighs, stroking. With his other hand, he fumbled at his belt. "You're . . . not getting . . . rug burn," he said between kisses.

Tasha grabbed his belt and batted his hand away. Barely able to focus because of the waves of pleasure and craving shooting upward from his hand, she managed to get his pants open. To shove them down.

"Condom," he groaned as she reached for his briefs. "Hang on." He crawled toward the couch, then stretched to reach his bag beside it. "Condom," he repeated as he handed it to her. He pushed his briefs down.

His penis jutted upward. A bead of liquid dotted the tip. Tasha licked it off. Stroking the soft mounds between his legs, she explored his erection with her lips and tongue while he shuddered.

"Tasha—need you."

She tore the condom open and sheathed him. Falling backward, he drew her with him. She straddled him and looked down at his intent face. He watched her grip his cock and ease down onto it. As she sank down, the flood of pleasure was so intense that her head fell back in a long gasp.

He rocked beneath her, and she cried out. Meeting his smoky gray gaze, she slid up, then down. So good. Too good. She might die of it.

Yet she couldn't look away from him. Not even when he cupped her breasts again, squeezing them. His hips thrust in time to her movements.

The tension inside her built until it was almost pain. At the same time, Carter's thrusts sped up. His hands dropped to her thighs, holding her as he surged upward.

Close. She was so close . . .

He pressed that sensitive nub, and the tension inside her burst. Tasha's eyes closed. Her head fell back with a cry. Carter groaned her name, thrusting hard and shuddering.

Tasha slumped as the aftershocks of release rolled through her. As they finally eased, she opened her eyes. Carter smiled and tugged her down for a kiss.

"So damn perfect," he murmured.

"Yeah." It had been. And that was scary. But she wasn't going to think about that now.

She settled onto Carter's chest, and his arms locked around her. Idly, his hand stroked her back. His spicy scent filled her nose, and her hand lay in the center of his soft chest hair.

Carter sighed. He tipped her chin up for a soft, tender kiss.

"Gotta deal with the condom," he told her. "Then I think we try out the bed."

"No rug burn there," Tasha noted, climbing off of him. The moment when his flesh slid out of hers was almost sad. She already wanted him again.

He curled upward to sit and kissed her again. "Be right back, Cupcake."

When he stood, his pants dropped to his ankles. Shaking his head, he leaned over.

"I got it," Tasha said. In moments, she had his sneakers off and his briefs pulled down with his jeans. "Step out."

Naked now, he loomed over her, all gorgeous male and finally hers. *For now*, the little voice in her head whispered. Tasha shrugged it aside and smiled up at him. Stroking one finger along the inside of his thigh, she suggested, "Meet you in the bedroom."

He tugged her to her feet. A light pinch on her ass sent need flashing through her. "Deal," he agreed. "I have more condoms."

"Excellent."

While he disposed of the condom, she turned the bed back and climbed onto it. Round two needed to start fast, and she meant to make that happen. With pillows behind her back, she angled herself toward the door and spread her legs wide.

The toilet flushed. Water ran and shut off, and Carter's footsteps sounded outside the bathroom. Tasha slid one hand into the soft, damp hair between her thighs, stroking lightly. With her other hand, she caressed her nipples.

Carter stepped into the doorway and froze, his expression stunned.

Tasha gave him a teasing smile and arched her back. "What's the holdup? Don't you like what you see?"

"Oh, yeah," he said in a strangled tone. His body confirmed his words, also proving he had the fast recovery time of most mages.

Like a predatory cat, he strolled toward her, way too slowly. "Keep going," he added, his eyes hot and his voice husky.

He dropped some condoms on the bed, then climbed onto it between her legs. His big hands gripped her ankles, tugging them farther apart. He slid his hands up the insides of her thighs to her knees, then back to her ankles. Up again, an inch farther and back down. And again.

Craving built within her. Why was he dragging this out?

His hot gaze roamed her body. His sliding hands reached her crotch, but he didn't touch her there. Instead, he traced the creases between her legs and hips with a finger on each side.

Tasha bit her lip to stifle a whimper.

When his hands reached her ankles again, he lifted her foot and kissed the bottom. A bolt of heat shot straight to Tasha's core, and the whimper escaped. He kissed and licked and nipped her foot until she was writhing. Then he switched to the other one.

Tasha thrashed on the bed. The intensity of sensation forced her eyes closed. Because she couldn't reach him, her hands clenched on the sheet. The scent of her musk filled the air.

Something ripped. She opened her eyes in time to see him roll a condom down his erection.

Finally.

He leaned over her, his weight on his forearms. The tip of his cock teased her aching flesh. Tasha wrapped her arms around him. "If you—stall anymore—"

"Can't," he groaned.

His hard thrust sent pleasure roaring through her. As his weight settled on her, she locked her legs around his waist. He slid partly out and then, fast and hard, in again. And again. She dug her fingers into his taut buttocks, urging him on.

Carter buried his face in her neck. "So good," he groaned.

Tasha kissed the side of his face. "Don't stop."

Again, the tension built inside her. Carter's hips pumped,

pushing waves of alternate pleasure and craving into her, building that tension . . .

Until it burst into fireworks behind her eyes.

When the fireworks faded, she realized Carter was lying still atop her. Was still hard within her.

"Carter?" she asked, stroking his hair and fighting drowsiness.

"Not—stopping," he panted. He thrust again, and Tasha moaned.

The spiral of need built again, bigger this time. Tighter. Clutching him with arms and legs, she bucked beneath him.

"Tasha," he groaned, "I'm—"

She squeezed with her inner muscles. He gave a wordless shout, thrusting hard. The spiral within her exploded and wiped away everything.

When the world came back they were still joined, both breathing raggedly, both their hearts pounding. Carter kissed her, a slow, sweet caress, before he headed to the bathroom.

Tasha waited for him in a pleasant daze. When he returned, he pulled the covers over them both and reached for her. She settled against his side.

Nothing had ever been this good.

Danger, danger, red alert, the troublesome little voice screeched. *Are you nuts? Bail while you can.*

It was already too late.

She should've known that in the parking lot. That pained look in his eyes had been more than she could stand, and now it would be worse if she backed away after what they'd shared.

"You're tensing up," he murmured. Stroking her arm, he drew his head back to look at her. "We waited a long time for this, Cupcake. Don't overthink it."

Meeting his gaze, she answered, "I'm trying not to." Gently, she cupped his cheek, beard stubble rasping against her palm. "I care about you, Carter, but I'm nervous."

He kissed her hand and pressed it into the soft hair at the

center of his chest. "I get it, Tasha. I'm no longer young and stupid enough to think a couple of rounds of great sex would torpedo your misgivings. But please talk to me if you're worried. That's all I ask."

"I will," she promised, settling her head into the hollow between his neck and shoulder. "We have Cumberland Island tomorrow. We should get some sleep."

"Yeah." He turned off the bedside lamp. "Can't wait to show you my boat. Ever made love on the water?"

"Nuh-uh."

"It'll be great," he assured her, his voice drowsy again.

That was what she was afraid of.

CHAPTER SEVENTEEN

"You can't be serious." Seated in front of Deke's desk, Carter stared at the shire reeve. "There has to be some progress. Can you put more people on it?"

"I already have three deputies working this, plus Val and Griff Dare and, whether I want him or not, Will Davis. And probably others of Ms. Murdock's civilian friends."

"Is there anything I can do?"

"Keep her safe," Deke said.

"Working on it," Carter muttered. "If that's all, I should get back to her. Val's keeping her company while I'm down here, and she has things to do for her task force."

"Yeah. Too bad other shires don't take the threat of traitors as seriously as we do."

Carter shrugged. "Helps to have your face jammed in the truth, like happened here last summer."

"Too true," Deke said. "Let me know if you need help."

"Will do. Have a good one." Carter walked out to the bullpen. Behind him, Deke's intercom buzzed.

Leaning back against a desk by the lobby door, Griff Dare had his arms across his chest and his gaze locked on Deke's door. Wasn't that just great? The last thing this morning needed was someone warning Carter away from Tasha. 'Cause that wasn't going to happen.

He stopped beside the former shire reeve. "You waiting for me?"

"Yeah. Let's walk."

Together, they pushed through the glass doors to the combination lobby and staging area and stepped out into the wintry sunlight.

"I need to get back to Tasha," Carter said.

"This won't take long." Dare raised an eyebrow. "Valeria tells me you and Tasha are together now. Can you guard her effectively when you're involved with her?"

As Tasha's friend, the guy had a right to ask, so Carter swallowed his irritation. "If I can't, I'll get a replacement."

Studying his face, Dare nodded. "I'll hold you to that. There's one other thing. Hurt her, and it's you and me."

Despite Dare's lack of magic, the threat wasn't toothless. After the southeast shire's own traitor mage had crippled Dare's magic, he'd killed that traitor in magical combat anyway.

"Tasha's got that covered," Carter assured him. "If she doesn't, her brother promises he does."

"Good enough." Dare clapped him on the back. "If you need us, we'll rearrange whatever we need to and be there."

"Like last night. Thanks for that." Though *thanks* didn't begin to cover it. If not for last night's work with the kids, he and Tasha might never have—

"Carter!" a woman behind them called.

He and Dare wheeled. Annie Wilson, a fellow deputy reeve, leaned past the door she was holding open. "We got a tip. Boss wants you."

With Dare at his side, Carter rushed into the building and to Deke's office. The shire reeve beckoned them in before Carter could knock.

"We got an anonymous phone call," Deke said.

"Like the ones we had last year?" Dare demanded.

"Exactly like. Same voice. Said if we wanted to save Natasha Murdock, we should look at the world of finance. I had Peterson check her client list, and there's a broker on there. Hewlett Collier. We're bringing him and his wife in for questioning. One team will go to the brokerage house in Savannah while the other hits the house outside Brunswick."

"Does Tasha know?" Carter asked.

"Yes. She wants to come along, but that's not happening. Val offered to stay with her, so if you two want in, suit up. Fast."

"You got it." Griff dashed for the equipment lockers, but a sudden thought stopped Carter in his tracks. "Deke, let me be the one to knock on the door. A bunch of mages in combat gear will spook them, but they think I work with Tasha. I'll be inside whatever defenses they have, able to open them for the rest of you."

"It's a good idea," Deke said, "but no. If these people really are traitors, they could have nasty surprises waiting. We're going in hard and fast."

"Okay," Carter said. He raced after Griff. Maybe they could bring Tasha's nightmare to an end today.

"CLEAR," a man's voice called from the back of the Colliers' house.

"Clear," a woman echoed from the basement.

"All clear," a man shouted from the bedroom level. "Looks like someone packed in a hurry up here."

Standing in the great room with Deke, Carter, and Griff exchanged disgusted glances. Deke's lips tightened, as though he held back the same curses that burned in Carter's mouth. He touched a stud on his mic. "Be sure there are no hidden rooms or tunnels."

"Roger" crackled over the comm. "We checked for that, boss, but we'll check again."

"Damn it," Deke muttered, hands on his hips.

"Let's hope the brokerage house team has better luck," Griff said.

"They didn't." Deke scowled. "I got a report right before we came in here. They went in screened, as planned, right back to Collier's office. The guy was gone, but his email was open. The team checked the latest message, which read, 'They're onto you. Get out now.' Just to be sure, one of the women glamoured herself into civvies and went to the front desk. Collier left unexpectedly."

"Well, shit," Carter said.

Deke turned to him. "Do you want to tell her, or shall I?"

"I'll do it," Carter said. He'd hoped to bring good news. Instead, he was going to ruin her day. Maybe the Cumberland Island client visit would cheer her up.

A romantic distraction might be even better. If he could set it up under her nose. He pulled out his phone and texted Josh.

"Well, there's one good thing," Dare said.

"What's that?" Carter demanded. He sent the text.

The former shire reeve shrugged. "Now we know who we're hunting."

Carter nodded. "Yeah. And we'll get 'em."

FIVE HOURS LATER, Tasha and Carter stood on the wraparound porch of her client's rambling Victorian house on Cumberland Island. He'd confronted the kid who harassed Mila, leaving the guy seriously worried about ever seeing him coming again. So maybe that was solved.

If only he could solve Tasha's problems as easily. She had faked an upbeat mood extremely well this afternoon. Her client's behavior had probably helped. In contrast with Geneva Collier or Dex The Toucher, Julia Miller had been both friendly and businesslike, even when she served them iced tea and thin, homemade lemon cookies.

Off to his left, Tasha and Julia were saying their farewells.

They needed to hurry. The sun was dropping toward the west, and he wouldn't put money down that the ghouls or their pet mage hadn't learned Tasha was with him. If the bastards had, they probably knew where he lived. The mage traitor could scry, and that meant he could see back in time. Possibly to the days before Carter had started wearing that lapis lazuli eye of Horus amulet.

Encountering an ambush when he and Tasha pulled alongside his dock would just suck.

He had his senses open, with one eye on Tasha and one on the expanse of green yard carved out of what appeared to be primeval forest. Live oaks draped in Spanish moss mixed with head-high clusters of saw palmetto, the blade-like leaves fanning out to make discs bigger than his head. Lots of wildlife in the bushes but nothing magical. He was ready, though. He wore his sword at his hip. It was easier to conceal with a glamour there than in the shoulder harness, which puckered his shirt. Tasha's sword also hung at her hip, hidden by a glamour.

"So you'll give me a call when you decide?" Tasha prompted. "Or if you have any questions or want to see some more options, don't hesitate to ask."

The woman really was a genius with customer service. How she was going to provide options when all her sample books had been destroyed, he had no clue. But he was sure she wouldn't let that stop her. Tasha had gumption. The word had gone out of style, but it was perfect for her.

Her client, a petite, sixtyish woman who dressed with casual elegance, smiled. "I'll make Fred sit down and give me his opinions tonight. You know, Tasha, we're very impressed with your service. Your crew is prompt, polite, and tidy, and you have fabulous taste. We're having a dinner party next week and would like you to come."

Carter went on alert. Dinner party? As in at night? When ghouls were strongest? Oh, hell no.

Julia smiled at Carter. "Mr. Logan is also welcome, of course. You could showcase your plans for each room in the guesthouse —I promise I'll make my choices by then. My mama was a famous ditherer, but I like to get things done—and we could let people see the space and your plans for it. The flooring will be in by then, won't it?"

"It should be laid tomorrow. What day is the party?"

"Thursday. I'd love to introduce you to our friends." With a sassy smile, Julia added, "Then when they hire you and rave, I can remind them I discovered you."

Tasha laughed. "I'll check my schedule, but I think I'm free."

If she wasn't, she likely intended to change that. He would rather not fight with her, and he understood her need to pull in income, but the business wasn't worth her life.

Carter kept the scowl off his face with an effort and pretended to study the three brown horses, wild residents of Cumberland Island, wandering across the yard. The horses mostly roamed the southern part of the island, rather than heading up to the northern end. Up there lay most of the private residences that predated the island's becoming a national seashore. But the animals could go anywhere they pleased.

Tended by the park rangers when they needed help, grazing and roaming wherever they chose, they had a cushy deal, at least for horses.

He wanted to give Tasha a cushy deal. To protect her. If things worked out, maybe even cherish her. But he shouldn't get ahead of himself. She was still skittish.

Maybe Carter could make all that go away, though, at least for a while. Josh had set up everything, even enlisting Edie for finishing touches. Having Josh so deep in his business burned, but he'd had little choice. At least he and Edie were discreet.

The clothes Carter wore, trousers and a button-down, would

fit right in once he added the tie and sport coat Josh had retrieved from Carter's house. Good thing a mage didn't really need keys. Tasha's pale green silk blouse, black slacks, and heels would be perfect for the occasion.

Unless he'd gone too far.

He'd assumed a romantic gesture would please her. A woman who was still holding back might resent that.

He was committed now. He would just have to hope he hadn't put his foot in it.

They said their farewells and walked down the porch steps. As they crossed the yard, heading for the dock and his boat, Tasha murmured, "Don't start about the dinner."

"We can talk on the boat." He put some steel in the words.

The stern, even pigheaded, glance she threw him spoke volumes.

Yeah. Definitely might've put a foot in it.

How could she make him see? Mulling it over, Tasha hurried down the wooden dock, her heels beating a quick tattoo on the planks. Jutting out from ground level, the dock rose about six feet above the water. A short stairway led down to the floating platform where his sleek, white sailboat, the *Delta Doll*, was moored.

Carter stepped onto the teak decking first and offered her a hand. "You were great, Tasha."

"I thought that went well," she said, taking his hand and stepping down, "but we should probably head out."

He slid his arms around her waist and drew her against him. Nuzzling her ear, he said, "Or we could take a little break."

A delicious shiver ran through her. The thirty-footer's cabin was small and cramped, but they'd managed on the way here.

But the house's upstairs windows were visible, which meant anyone looking out of one could see the deck.

"Not here," she said.

When she tugged, he released her. "Tasha? Hey, what is it?"

"We're visible from the upstairs windows. If Julia saw us go below together and stay a while, she might make assumptions I'd rather my clients didn't make." Tasha swallowed hard. "I have to think of my reputation."

"Of course," he said. "We can sail back to Brunswick, head to the Collegium, get a good dinner we don't have to cook, and maybe enjoy a recreational break before we call it a day."

Tasha's cheeks blazed with heat. "Is that what we're calling it now, recreation?"

Carter grinned. "Well, it's fun."

"No argument from me. Our little stop on the way here was, as promised, a lot of fun." It had also gotten her mind off the Colliers' betrayal, as she would bet he'd intended. "Cast off, captain, and let's head back."

On the way, they could talk about Thursday's dinner party. She had to do this. It was too big an opportunity to pass by if there was any way to minimize the risk.

He had the lines cleared in no time. Since the late hour meant they needed to hurry back, he used the motor instead of the sails.

He sat by the tiller, and she perched on his left. "I have to go to this party of Julia's, Carter."

"I understand your concerns, but—"

"Hear me out. The Collier job was going to mean big money. And a shot at a prestigious charity event I've tried to get into for five years with no luck. The exposure would've generated more business. If I was lucky, a lot more."

"Why can't you get into this thing? Surely you've given a great pitch."

So he had faith in her. Surprised, she smiled at him. No other guy she'd dated—not that there had been very many— had said such a thing to her.

"Someone the committee members trust has to vouch for

you," she explained. "And I was hoping it would be Geneva Collier. I can kiss that goodbye now. On top of that, there are my cash flow problems. I need, really need, the business this could generate."

"I get that." The worry in his eyes flicked guilt over her heart as he continued, "You also need to keep breathing. Leaving aside your friends' and your brother's concerns, your employees need you to run the company. To keep them paid. Something happens to you, then what?"

That hit uncomfortably close to home. Tasha shrugged. "I don't know. Nate has no interest in taking over something so low-adrenaline, and even if he did, he hasn't worked construction in about fifteen years."

"Anybody on your staff who could step up?"

"If there were, I wouldn't be the owner now."

Surprise flashed over his face. "I don't believe that."

"Thanks for that." She squeezed his near hand and held on to it. "The man who owned the company before me already wanted to retire when he hired me. He liked that I could drive a nail one day and put together a window treatment the next."

"Window treatment." Carter frowned as they glided past the Sea Camp ranger station, a small, one-story building of weathered wood with a screen porch. "Is that like curtains?"

"Sometimes. Anyway, he fed me business. Took a cut of the decorating services I provided but let me take the bulk of the fee. On top of my salary."

"How'd you manage that?"

"Worked nights. Between working construction and occasionally seeing decorating clients during the day, going to school, and working on interior design projects at night, I worked most of the time."

His expression thoughtful, Carter said, "He saw you were a go-getter."

"Maybe." Tasha wrinkled her nose at him. "I never let an opportunity pass me by. When you grow up—" Before the word *poor* could pop out, she substituted, "When you don't have much of a cushion, you grab any work you can do."

"Work you're good at," Carter said. "How did that translate into owning the company?"

She nodded her thanks for the compliment. "None of his kids wanted it, and the only other person on the crew he thought could generate clients was also looking to retire. So he gave me a shot." She sighed. "I still owe him for that shot. I bought him out in installments. Next one's due later this year."

"You'll make it."

"I wish I felt as sure as you do."

Tasha turned her face into the breeze. Across the water on the right, a couple of jutting piers marked the edge of the Kings Bay submarine base. One of the big, white hangar-like structures was partly visible beyond them. On the left, driftwood lay scattered on Cumberland Island's narrow beach. Mixed with clumps of saw palmetto, live oaks draped in Spanish moss lined the shore above the sand. The lights of a house appeared through the trees. The island looked so peaceful. It would be nice to come back someday just to look around.

Judging by Carter's slight frown, he still wasn't convinced. "I'm scared, Carter. Seriously scared."

He slid an arm around her shoulders and tugged her close. "Cupcake, the Collegium will help you if you get in a jam. It's going to be okay."

"Murdock Custom Builders is all I have." She locked her arms around his waist and laid her head on his shoulder. The faintly audible beat of his heart offered comfort, as did the warmth of his body through his dress shirt. "Keeping it going is like rolling a ball. You have to keep it moving. If it stalls, work doesn't get done. Your rep doesn't spread. New clients don't seek you out. I—"

The fear clamped around her throat, stopping her. She blinked to clear her stinging eyes. This dread of failure was why she tried not to think about this when she didn't have to.

At least he wouldn't see her wet eyes with her head on his shoulder. He'd grown up with family money behind him, probably still knew it would back him if he needed help. How could he possibly understand what it was like to board a bus for boot camp with thirty dollars in your pocket and know that had to last until whenever the navy paid you? To be scared that if you didn't work hard, you'd end up in that situation again?

His arm tightened, and he kissed the top of her head. "I get it. I'll see if Deke can spare a couple of deputies to come with us as backup."

"It can't be much fun to sit in the boat while we're at dinner. Who'd want to?"

He shrugged. "I can pull in a couple of favors."

"That'll make you popular."

"Val and Griff didn't complain last night."

"Because they're the next thing to family. You said you didn't like hauling them out. Neither did I, but once I knew why we had to get to the kids, I completely understood. If Griff or Val knew, they would—"

"Bust my chops," he said. "Tasha, you can't say anything."

"I won't," she snapped. If he really trusted her, he wouldn't need to remind her. "I told you I wouldn't. I'm just saying they were already okay with it. They would be doubly okay if they knew it was to help someone. That's all."

"Right, but I still need to arrange backup. I want to call Deke. If he doesn't have anyone, I can find someone."

"I know you're right. I just hate to be beholden."

"You're not beholden to people for doing their jobs."

"I'll leave it to you," she agreed.

He looked closely at her but didn't press. After all, she'd accepted his argument. There was no way around needing backup if she meant to come to this party, and she couldn't pass it up.

Hauling her friends out last night still made her feel guilty.

Hauling out people she didn't even know, regardless of it being their job, just felt wrong.

But Carter was right, and if the ghouls came after her, he would be in danger too. Putting him at risk was a poor way to repay him for all he'd done. The idea of fighting ghouls with bad odds made her shudder, but she still hated to be beholden to yet more people.

The deputy reeves weren't the mean girls she'd gone to school with, who'd rubbed her family's charity-dependent lean times in her face, nor were Val and Griff. Still, nobody wanted to be giving all the time.

CHAPTER EIGHTEEN

"I will kill that mage cow," Zarig roared. "She has ruined us."

He wheeled and slammed his fist into the support post for the porch roof. It cracked halfway across.

Standing one step below him, in the dirt patch that passed for a yard, Ross shook his head. "Collier can still invest for you. He'll just have to do it differently. Besides, you still have your dummy account at his brokerage house."

"If the mages haven't found it."

"Look," Ross said in his most reasonable tone, "she's obviously revealed whatever it was she knew. It really wasn't that much in the grand—"

"She interfered with my plans," Zarig bellowed. "I will have her under me screaming in agony. She will beg to die." Breathing hard, he narrowed his eyes at Ross. "It will be a lesson to all her kind when we dump the pieces of her at their Collegium's gate."

Well, fuck. Ross's big plan had become an epic fail. He'd hoped to take the heat off Natasha Murdock by making the ghouls think she'd done whatever damage she could. Moving on was the logical move for Zarig. Unfortunately, Ross had forgotten that ghouls much preferred revenge and destruction to logic.

The ammonia stench of ghoul stung his nostrils. From the rundown breeder hut thirty yards away came a man's cries of pain.

Ross crossed his arms over his chest. He was bloody sick of these vile—

"You will find her," Zarig ordered. "Find her, mage, and bring her to me on her knees. Or I will make an example of you, Teacher or no Teacher." Zarig stomped into the house.

Ross set his jaw. He'd waded in shit up to his armpits since starting this—would swim in it if that was what it took to find the man who was his brother in all but blood—but he could no longer abide the idea of sacrificing Natasha Murdock. The woman's brains, guts, and drive compelled his respect. There were limits, even for a desperate man.

Still, he'd better turn up something useful. The ghouls barely tolerated him as it was. If they had any inkling of his divided loyalties, he'd be doomed. Then there would be no one to save Angus.

He paced across the packed-earth yard to his quarters, a big shed probably stolen from a garden supply place. It was too small for pacing, so he turned and strode back to the shack that was Zarig's HQ.

Scrying hadn't worked to find the woman. If she was inside a building at the Collegium, it wouldn't, not without some kind of power boost or a charm to defeat shielding. She had a schedule, though. While the ghouls with him at her office had been busy wrecking everything in sight, he'd downloaded her schedule and the mail program, with its contents, off her office computer.

The fire—not his idea but one that filled his nasty companions with great glee—had screwed up that plan, though. Of course Murdock had changed her schedule to deal with the aftermath. Too bad Team Destruction hadn't thought of that, but there again, logic.

Still, she had a staff. Had to keep them updated. Especially her office manager.

He had her schedule and a handful of emails. With those, he could determine which ISP the office manager used at home. If he were a hacker.

He stepped onto the porch and knocked on Zarig's door.

Opening it, the big ghoul snapped, "What?"

"You got a Mundane here who can hack?" Ross's buddy Neil Bruce, back in Edinburgh, could crack any server anywhere. But no one else Ross cared about was going to be pulled into this mess.

Zarig's lip curled in a sneer. "We don't give them weapons, fool."

Weapons? Oh. Carefully, Ross said, "I meant computer hacking. Do you have a Mundane who—"

"I heard you. Why do you want one?"

Because ghouls lacked the patience to succeed at that, but saying so would be fatal. Ross explained about hacking Murdock's office manager's email.

Zarig nodded, a mean smile curving his lips. "If we don't have one, someone will. Don't fail me again, mage."

Ross nodded. Soon he would know how to find Murdock. Then he had to figure out how to set an ambush that wouldn't get either him or her killed.

CHAPTER NINETEEN

D<small>ARKNESS WAS FALLING WHEN</small> T<small>ASHA AND</small> C<small>ARTER REACHED</small> Brunswick. They rode back to the Collegium in silence. Carter was probably figuring out which of his friends he could draft for backup. Tasha owed too many people already, and now she was going to owe more. But he was right. They shouldn't go to the dinner party without backup.

Walking into the building, she asked, "Should we get dinner in the dining hall? I just realized I never really stocked our place —" sweet, dangerous words "—with much beyond breakfast stuff."

Carter shook his head. "Sure, but I need something from upstairs first."

Tasha nodded, and they went up to the guest unit together.

Carter opened the door, and she froze on the threshold. The sofa bed was neatly made, as usual. In case they had company, Carter folded the bed into its storage space every morning.

But beyond it, by the window, the small dining table was draped in a white linen cloth. Brass candlesticks and a low vase of multi-colored flowers sat atop it. Two places on adjacent sides were set with the standard-issue blue stoneware, wineglasses, and stainless steel utensils. Beside the table sat an ice bucket on a stand, a bottle of white wine protruding from it.

Stunned, she turned to Carter. "What's this?"

He looked tense, almost nervous. "Do you like it?"

"It's very pretty, but why—?"

"Because you deserve a break. We shouldn't go to the Marsh Heron while these ghouls are on your tail, but the Marsh Heron's food can come to us." Watching her eyes, he added, "You and I were busy all afternoon, so I had a couple of friends see to it."

Her throat burned. No one else had ever gone to so much trouble for her.

"I have a coat and tie in the bedroom," he said. "But we don't have to do this. The fancy bit, I mean. I just thought you might enjoy it."

"You thought right," she managed. She tugged his head down for a kiss.

His arms encircled her waist, drawing her against him. When the kiss broke, he rested his forehead on hers and sighed.

Tasha raised her eyebrows. "Did you really doubt I would like it?"

"With everything that's happened lately, it occurred to me that you might not be in the mood."

She cupped his face in her hands. The light stubble along his jaw teased her palms, and the solemn, tender look in his gray eyes was a balm to soothe her worries. For now, at least. That brought worries of its own, but she would deal with them later.

"I was in a mood," she confessed, "but I'm happy to put it aside for now and enjoy a romantic dinner. Thank you, Carter."

"My pleasure." He kissed her quickly. "Let's go in, shut the door, and put everything else aside."

He ushered her to a chair, pulled it out for her, and ordered, "Stay here while I get everything ready."

"I can help you."

"Some other time. This is my surprise for you, so I do the legwork. What there is of it, anyway."

Tasha let him seat her. He snapped out her napkin and laid it across her lap.

"Wine?" he asked.

When she nodded, he drew the bottle out of the ice bucket, dried it with the towel draped over the stand, and pulled the cork out. Someone had considerately opened it.

Carter poured a glass for her and one for himself. "You go ahead, but I'll wait until we eat."

Then she would wait too.

He lit the two candles magically and dimmed the lights. Picking up the plates, he said, "We might as well have a little atmosphere." He set the plates on the kitchen counter and hurried back to the bedroom.

Tasha watched him go. Even distracted, he moved with easy, almost predatory grace. And the back view—wide shoulders, lean waist, and sculpted butt—had her thinking about what came after dinner. She knew the contours of his body so well, though she'd spent only a single night and a quick stop on the way to Julia's exploring them. He and she had checked each other out pretty thoroughly, after all.

Carter came back into view. He'd donned a dark blue tie and a gray sport coat. Stepping into the kitchen, he spoke to her across the counter. "You have your choice of scallops in lemon cream sauce with asparagus and a salad or grilled salmon in dill sauce with the vegetable medley and glazed carrots. And to go with both, brown-bread rolls."

"The scallops, please." She cocked her head as he transferred food onto plates. "Did you know they're my favorite?"

"You mentioned that once or twice. I remembered."

She gaped at him. "I haven't talked about food around you since—well, not since we were in the service. That was a long time ago."

His gaze on her was warm and intent. "I told you, only one

woman in the Bees ever seriously interested me. When I'm interested, I remember."

Her cheeks warmed, and the sweetness of it rolled through her. "I guess you do."

Their gazes held. Abruptly, he turned back to his tasks.

They needed a safe subject. Like the kids he'd befriended. "You told me how you met Jeremy. How did you get involved with Mila?"

"She's a friend of Jeremy's." Carter shrugged. "One thing led to another."

"There's more to it than that, isn't there?"

"What do you mean?" he asked, keeping his eyes on the food.

"You're so conscientious, but you've broken the rules, maybe even mage law, for these kids. I think it's admirable, and I'd like to know why."

He said nothing for a long minute before he looked up at her. "When I was seventeen, a friend and I went joyriding in his folks' car. He'd gotten his hands on some beer. We thought we were hot shit."

Because, as he'd said, he'd envied the kids who broke the rules?

"He went around a curve too fast," Carter said. "Rolled the car. We were lucky not to be seriously injured." He shook his head. "We were both such habitual straight arrows that we'd made sure to buckle our seatbelts. That and the car's heavy steel frame saved us from anything worse than bumps and bruises."

"You were lucky." But what did this have to do with those kids?

"We were also lucky we hadn't yet cracked open the beer. I got community service," he said, "seeing as my parents were such fine, upstanding members of the community and promised to keep me on the straight and narrow. Stan's parents told him he'd gotten himself into this and could get himself out. He got convictions for reckless driving and underage possession of alcohol, seeing as it was his family car, and way more community service than I did. It would've been worse, except several teachers vouched for him."

When he looked up, his eyes burned with outrage. "Yeah, he was the driver, but the difference between his treatment and mine wasn't fair. Not even almost."

"No, it wasn't. So you help Jeremy and his friends because of the way those teachers stepped up for a kid who had no one else on his side?"

"That and a few lessons from the sheriff's deputy in charge of the bratty kids doing community service. He was ex-navy. Had a lot to say about privileged kids thinking they could get away with anything. He rode me hard, made sure I knew how lucky I'd been, and purely by an accident of birth."

"Some people would've resented that," Tasha noted.

"At first, I did, but I knew deep inside that he was right. I started to listen, to really hear what he was saying. He's one of the reasons I decided to be a deputy reeve while I figured out what was next for me."

"Have you figured it out yet?" When he did, would he leave?

He shook his head. "Still working on it."

So he would be here a while longer. But when he left would be a natural time to break this off, a no-harm, no-foul reason. "How about teaching?"

His grin flashed. "Don't have the patience."

"What about counseling? You were great with those kids."

He paused what he was doing. A thoughtful expression came over his face. "That's a possibility," he said as he went back to preparing the food.

"Don't get the wrong idea about my parents," he added. "We had chores, were expected to study and get good grades, and didn't have fat allowances or a lot of expensive toys. I had a car because I got a job and paid for it."

"In your dad's construction business?"

"Yeah, in the summer. In the winter . . . " He grinned. "Waiter."

On the counter he set a bread basket lined with a napkin, then the plate of salmon, then one of scallops. "Order up," Carter announced. He walked out of the kitchen and transferred the food to the table.

Taking his seat, he informed her, "I warmed it magically. I hope it's okay. That usually works on leftovers."

"I'm sure it will be fine." She glanced over the candlelit table and the flowers and at his warm, intent expression. Nobody had ever thought she was the candlelight dinner type. Not until him. The gesture was absurdly moving.

Tasha cleared her throat. Raising her wineglass, she said, "Here's to beautiful evenings."

"And beautiful women." Carter clinked his glass on hers, and they drank.

"I'd like to give you a lot of evenings like this," he added.

She wanted that too. Yearned for it. Even though he and she could never last. Pointing that out, though, would ruin the evening, so she settled for saying, "We'll see."

Disappointment flickered over his face, and he turned his attention to his salmon.

The guilt that nagged her could just stop. If she told him her secrets, he might accept them. He also might be embarrassed. Disillusioned about her. She couldn't bear it if he was.

But that could wait. She wouldn't risk spoiling this beautiful evening he'd planned. Instead, they could make beautiful memories for later in case this thing they had blew up.

Tasha cut into a scallop and tasted it. Creamy, tender, with slight, lemony tartness, it was perfect. "This is wonderful, Carter."

"So's this. Do you mind if I try a scallop? I'll trade you some salmon."

"Sure." She started to push the plate toward him but went with impulse instead. Cutting off a piece, she stirred it into the sauce. Then she offered it to him on her fork with her free hand under it to catch any drips.

Carter's face lit with a heat that echoed deep in her body. He wrapped his hand around hers to steady it and closed his mouth around the scallop. The calluses on his hands marked him as a workman. And, she knew, as a swordsman. She liked the feel of them.

When he'd swallowed the scallop, he murmured, "Delicious," but his eyes were on her face.

He copied her gesture with the salmon. She copied his when she accepted it. As she had been in bed, she was acutely conscious of his sturdy hand and the fine hair on the back of it. Of how that hand felt on her body.

Having him give her food this way, having him take it from her fork, was sexy and tempting. Doing it again wouldn't be wise, but, oh, she wanted to.

"Want to share?" he asked, his voice husky.

Yes, but that wasn't smart. "You know this is my favorite," she said lightly.

"And you're my favorite. Tiny tastes are fine, as long as you give them to me the way you just did. Or we could trade plates."

Eat the entire meal off of each other's forks? His gaze roamed over her. Tasha's nipples tightened, and heat bubbled in her belly. She should say no, dial this back, but she couldn't. Instead, she slid her plate toward him.

He traded the plates. "Share a wineglass too?"

Her heart thudded. The little voice in her head yelled, *Danger! Danger! Incoming!*

It probably was right, but there was no point in being with him if she couldn't store up memories to savor later, to ease the hurt when he was gone.

Tasha poured the contents of her wineglass into Carter's and pushed hers aside.

Every bite of food, every shared sip of the cool wine,

ramped up the desire spiraling between them. Magic crackled in the air. With it came awareness.

She knew how much he liked the feel of her smooth hand under his bigger one. How savoring the fish he'd taken from her hand made him want to savor her. How the candlelight glinting on her hair made him want to plunge his hands into it.

She was in so much trouble.

"It will be fine," Carter murmured, holding her hand.

Of course he'd sensed her misgivings in the magic spiraling between them.

Before she could reply, he brought her hand to his lips and kissed it. Against her knuckles, he repeated, "It will be fine."

She licked her dry lips, and the magical current between them sizzled with his awareness. "I want it to be," she said. No matter how impossible she knew that was.

"It will be," Carter insisted.

The plates were empty. So was the wine bottle.

"Is there dessert?" she asked. Preparing more food would require an intermission, a chance to let this aching desire fade.

"There is. If you want food, there's cheesecake with chocolate sauce. I'd rather have you, but this is your evening. Your call."

Green light or red? he'd asked once, long ago. *It's your call.*

She'd hurt him then. She couldn't do it again, not when he'd given her such a romantic evening. Especially not when he was looking at her so intently, as though she were the only thing that mattered.

"The food can wait," she said, and the heat that kindled in his eyes made her panties go damp. "But if this is my night, I want to plan my own dessert."

"Deal," Carter agreed, his voice husky again.

"Push your chair back."

When he had, she shifted onto his lap. Carter's arms slid around her waist. He nuzzled her neck. "Want me to unbutton your shirt?"

Twisting her head, she caught his mouth for a kiss. As usual, it caught fire. The magic around them surged, driving his intense desire into her and sharing hers with him.

Both of them were breathing hard when she raised her head. Tasha grabbed the knot on his tie and tugged it free. The tie hung loose around his neck, and she reached for his buttons.

His hands rose to hers, but she said, "Wait."

He dropped his hands, but the strain in his face would've told her how impatient he felt even without the shared magic betraying him. She had his shirt open in moments, pulling it out of his trousers so she could caress the sleek, contoured lines of his chest and abs and comb her fingers through the reddish-brown hair in the center of his chest.

His hands tightened on her thighs, stroking. When she reached for his belt, he groaned.

When she had him free of his pants, she sank onto her knees between his thighs.

She kissed her way down from his collarbone, over that soft patch of hair, down the center of his hard abs, and lower. Each time her lips brushed his skin, the muscles tensed, then relaxed.

Surprise kindled on his face and in the magic around them. "Tasha, you—"

"Sshh." He deserved good memories for later, too. Reaching onto the table, she sank a finger in lemon cream sauce. It had cooled, but warming it magically was easy. She dabbed it on the head of his erection.

Carter groaned. His hands tightened on her shoulders, but his gaze stayed locked on hers.

When she'd covered the head, she licked him from base to tip. His head fell back. He made a strangled sound. She stroked his thighs, and his hands speared into her hair, not controlling but caressing.

He thrust into her grip, his eyes locked on her, and his breath coming fast. "All clean," she whispered, her breath feathering over his hard flesh, "but let's be sure."

Watching his face, she sucked him into her mouth. Carter gave a wordless shout, thrust upward, and climaxed.

Tasha waited until he stopped shuddering before she rose. The stunned, grateful look on his face made an act she'd never especially enjoyed into a true pleasure.

Holding his gaze, she slowly unbuttoned her shirt. Carter's eyes heated anew. Not surprisingly for a mage, his body responded.

His control lasted until she shrugged out of her shirt and bra and cupped her breasts, the nipples peeking between her fingers.

"That's it," he announced, reaching for her. "Time for my dessert."

Tasha gave him a teasing smile. "You agreed—"

His mouth captured hers, and thought fled. Without breaking the kiss, he stood, drawing her upright along with him. She had to cling to him to stay on her feet. His tongue darted into her mouth, caressing and stroking. She sucked it, and he palmed her breast, rolling the hard nipple against his hand.

Tasha whimpered. Her hips rocked toward his.

Carter nibbled her ear, sending shivers of need through her. All around them, the magic crackled again. He opened her pants, and they dropped around her ankles.

"When I said you tasted good enough to eat," he murmured, his breath teasing the sensitive inside of her ear, "I meant it."

Tasha gasped at the image that evoked.

He slid her panties down. Reaching around her, he pushed everything on the table to the side. He couldn't mean to take her on the table.

But he did. He eased her back onto it and tugged off her shoes, pants, and panties.

Spreading her wide, he murmured, "Gorgeous."

Tasha reached for him. "Carter."

"It's my turn, Tasha." He caught both her hands. Watching

her face, he kissed one palm, flicking it with his tongue, and then the other.

Her back arched, hips rising. "Hold onto the table," he said, "and don't move."

He walked around her. A few seconds of clattering signaled that he was clearing the table. When he returned, he stood between her thighs and leaned over her, his weight on one elbow. His free hand traced slow lines around each of her nipples in turn.

"So gorgeous," He murmured, and licked them.

Again, her back arched. Her grip on the table tightened. She wanted to hold onto him, not this—

He drew one breast into his mouth and sucked. Aching for more, she locked her legs around him, pulling, but he wouldn't let her draw him against her.

He switched to the other breast, licking and nipping and sucking. She couldn't stand it anymore. Her grip on the table failed, and she flung her arms around him.

Carter pressed the sensitive nub between her legs. The tension in her exploded in a flood of heat. Tasha shrieked, tightening her hold, and then drifted in sweet, warm, darkness.

Sliding back into the world, she realized Carter's head rested between her breasts. Her arms encircled his shoulders, but most of his weight was still on his elbows. She stroked his thick, soft hair and found it damp at the ends.

He turned his head to look at her and smiled. "I want seconds."

Her protest died when one of his fingers slipped inside her. With a whimper, she rocked against his hand. He kissed the underside of her breast. Working his way down with a kiss here, a flick of his tongue there, a tiny nip after, he ratcheted her anticipation to feverish heights.

His breath stirred the tight curls at the junction of her legs, and Tasha moaned. Carter knelt between her thighs. Still watching her, he drew his finger out of her and sucked it. Then he replaced it with his mouth.

He licked and kissed and sucked. "So sweet," he murmured, his breath teasing her. His hands rose to knead her breasts.

Writhing under his hands and against his mouth, Tasha clutched him. "In me," she panted. "Want you—in me."

His already-hot eyes burned. The magic around them filled her with the sense of his pleasure. Of the salty taste of her in his mouth.

He straightened long enough to grab something out of his trousers pocket. A condom. Finally! He sheathed himself and lifted her legs over his arms.

"Hurry." Tasha bucked against his hardness. Unable to reach him, she gripped the table again.

"Oh, yeah." He spread her legs wider. Still watching her, he slid slowly inside. The hot, gliding fullness of him and the need throbbing in the magic made her sob with pleasure. Her hips rose, taking him in.

He released her legs so he could fondle her breasts. Tasha locked her legs around his lean waist and pulled. With a groan, he pulled almost out and surged into her again.

They rocked together, the table creaking madly. Carter's thrusts sped up.

"Yes," Tasha gasped. "Yes, I—"

His mouth on hers stopped the words. Shuddering, he roared the pleasure of his release into her mouth. His body ground down on hers and pushed her over the edge.

The darkness behind her eyes was warm and sweet, but it slowly faded. She and Carter were still joined, their hearts pounding together and their breathing ragged. With her cheek against his temple, Tasha stroked his hair. Nothing had ever been this good.

He was an experienced and inventive lover. A considerate one. She'd been with other men who could claim all three, but the magic hadn't sparked with her and the only other man who'd been mageborn, and the craving to never let go hadn't ever caught her by the throat as it did now.

There was only one explanation. The release and the closeness were so exquisite because he was Carter. That she was all wrong for him didn't make any difference.

WHEN TASHA WOKE the next morning, Carter was sitting up beside her, looking down at her with solemn eyes.

"What is it?" she asked. He looked so serious. A tiny, cold wisp of fear poked her heart. She pushed up to sit too.

"We didn't talk last night," he replied. "Not that I'm complaining, but there's something bothering me. I don't get why you're uncomfortable about asking for help from people whose job is protecting mages. Like you."

"But if Deke can't spare anyone, you'll ask your friends who have next Thursday off. And I can't imagine how boring it will be to sit on the boat while we're at a prolonged dinner party."

He raised an eyebrow. "Do you think they've never done stakeouts? My friends will do this for me as a favor if they can. I would do the same for them. Why does that bother you so much?"

He just didn't get it. She was going to have to explain, preferably without giving away too much of her sorry past. "I know you're right about needing backup. It's just that I don't—I don't like to be beholden. In fact, I hate it."

"Tasha—"

"I know it's their job, but it can't be an assignment anybody wants. And if Deke can't spare anyone who's on duty, we'll be imposing on your friends."

Frowning, he said, "Would you rather ask the Dares?"

"I don't want them doing this on top of everything else they've done."

He still looked baffled.

Frustration pushed words through her tight throat. "You impose on people enough, and they don't want to see you coming."

Or else they rubbed your nose it, but no way was she sharing that. It would only emphasize the vast, probably unbridgeable gulf between his life and hers.

"You think you imposed on Griff and Val the other night?" he asked.

"Well, duh. Of course."

Again, he shook his head. "Tasha, you had Griff Dare's back when damn few people did. If you asked him, I'd lay down real money that he'd say he owes you, not the other way around."

"But we were doing something necessary. All in it together."

"Yeah. And one of you, Dare, lived on the run because he was already condemned. Getting caught with him would've been a death sentence for all of you."

He was right. But that didn't change her feelings.

"Let me ask you something," Carter said. "Do you think you're beholden to me?"

Yes, but he would explode if she said so. Tasha wrinkled her nose. "Sort of. But you asked for this job, and now you're—"

"If you say 'sleeping with me,' we're going a few rounds," he warned.

"Well, you are." His eyes flashed, and she hastily added, "But that's not what I meant. You care about me, so you have an interest to protect."

He studied her, his expression thoughtful. Tasha's heart pounded in her throat. She didn't want to talk about this. It led to territory she still hadn't worked up the nerve to visit with him.

At last, Carter said, "I more than 'care' for you, Cupcake."

What? Had he said—? He couldn't mean it. They were too different.

Yet the words reached into her heart and grabbed. Tasha gaped at him. Carter drew her close and kissed her. The warmth of his mouth on hers melted the protest she'd been forming. She slid her arms around him and kissed him back. The kiss grew deeper, and they slipped down into the bed together.

When the kiss finally broke, Carter held her against his side and kissed her forehead. "I'll take care of Thursday. Please stop worrying about owing people. I promise you, nobody else looks at it that way."

"I hope not."

Her doubt must have shown on her face, though, because he cocked his head and studied her. Quietly, he asked, "Do you care for me, Tasha?"

Oh, way more than, a terrible realization she would deal with later. Admitting it, besides laying her heart out like a door-mat, would be like handing him a weapon if he couldn't deal with her past.

"Yes," she said, a huge understatement.

Carter caught her hand again. "What do you think it would do to me if the ghouls captured you on my watch? Or worse, killed you in front of me? Do you see why I don't care about trading favors, about owing my friends, if that helps me protect you?"

"That's dirty pool," she muttered, her gaze sliding to the side lest he read more in her eyes than she wanted him to. "But I'll try to look at it that way."

"Thank you." He kissed her hand and held it to his heart. "I know there are things you aren't saying. I can see them in your expression."

The claim gave her a jolt of panic, but he continued, "Some-day, I hope you'll feel that you can say them. That you can tell me what's behind your worries."

"I'll try," she said.

He kissed her quickly, releasing her hand, and stood. "Thank you, Cupcake. I'll make my calls and we can grab breakfast."

Attentive as he was, he might truly have seen evasion in her face. Or he could be playing her, trying to draw her out. She didn't have the nerve, not yet, to tell him why she valued her independence. That revelation would lead to others she was still working up to share.

～

THE NEXT FEW days passed in a blur of insurance claims, client visits, and site inspections. Before Tasha knew it, Saturday had arrived, and she and Carter were in Wayfarer with the Dares.

Now she sat in their cozy living room with Audra, Val, Lorelei, and Mel Wray, Stefan's fiancée. The guys had gone out to the barn to watch some sort of sporting event. Tasha hadn't paid much attention.

"What are the guys watching again?" Audra asked.

"Some world skiing thing," Val answered with a shrug.

"Skiing?" Lorelei frowned. "Not one of them skis, and they're unlikely to learn as long as they live in south Georgia."

"They're guys," Mel put in, her voice dry. "It's a sporting event. I suspect that's enough for them."

"Besides," Audra added, grinning, "I bet they think we're going to start talking about weddings, and they're allergic."

"Aren't we going to talk weddings?" Val asked as everyone laughed.

"Stefan certainly would avoid that," Mel agreed. "He told me whatever I want is fine as long as it includes exchanging 'I Dos.' But we put the house first, so I haven't really thought much about the actual wedding."

The smells of baked chicken, fresh bread, and chocolate cake from dinner had faded. Everyone had a beer or a glass of wine, and the munchies on the table included not only Val's various cheese offerings but Tasha's homemade salsa and a big bowl of chips.

"Tell us more about the house," Tasha urged Mel.

The FBI agent's gray eyes glowed below the bangs of her

dark brown bob. "It's perfect. Exactly what we wanted. Late Victorian, four bedrooms and a bath upstairs with a living room, dining room, parlor, half bath, and kitchen downstairs. And a screened porch across the back. It needs a lot of work. We can see the potential, though."

Smiling broadly, she shook her head. "I can't believe we found something that we could both love so quickly."

"That was the plan, after all," Val reminded her. She clinked her wineglass against Mel's.

Smiling, Audra leaned forward to snag a chocolate cake pop. "Can I ask if you've set a date, now that you have the house?"

Mel blushed. "May. Early May. We're getting married in Brunswick, where we want to begin our life together, so we have to check venues there."

"You'd better handle that," Lorelei advised. "Stefan will probably pick the first thing he sees that's clean, weathertight, and convenient."

"Too true," Mel agreed, grinning. "I'll find the venue and the caterer. He's in charge of finding a hotel for the out-of-town family and friends."

"Sounds great," Val said. "Do you need any help?"

"I'm sure I will when things get rolling," Mel replied.

"We can cover that," Lorelei assured her.

"Thanks." Mel leaned back, blew out a gusty breath, and took a gulp of wine. "It's kind of surreal, you know? Us getting married after all this time."

As Stefan had said the night of Val and Griff's party, when he'd been so happy. Tasha smiled at his bride. "When it's right, it's right," she said.

If saying it gave her a little twinge because she was probably going to lose Carter when she told him her story, that was her problem. She and Mel were on the way to becoming friends, and friends reassured each other when even the smallest need arose.

Mel peered down into her wine glass. "I'm going for a refill. Anybody need anything?"

"I'll come with you, grab some more salsa," Tasha said, snagging the glazed terra cotta bowl.

They walked into the big kitchen together. Mel took the salsa container out of the refrigerator and passed it to Tasha. Spooning more into the bowl, Tasha said, "Actually, Mel, there's something I wanted to talk to you about. "

Mel put the wine bottle in the refrigerator and leaned back against the island. "Shoot."

"Whatever you need to do to the house, I'd like to help you with as my wedding gift."

"What?" Both Mel's eyebrows shot up. "Tasha, we're talking refinishing floors, getting rid of wallpaper, window repair, gutting bathrooms and the kitchen, new appliances—that's too much."

"It's not too much." Though the current cash flow situation would make it a tight squeeze. Tasha couldn't not offer, though, not on something for Stefan and his bride. "I'm a contractor and interior designer. I get huge discounts. Anything that has to be made or bought, I'll get for you at my cost. Any labor, again, is at my cost, and my services are free."

Looking dazed, Mel pulled out a stool and dropped onto it. "Tasha, I can't. That's a wonderful offer, but I can't let you do that. You barely know me."

"No, but I hope we'll get to know each other, seeing as how you're marrying a guy who's had my back time after time. Stefan's like a brother to me, Mel, and you make my brother happy. It's that simple."

Mel's eyes glistened. "I'm . . . stunned. Tasha, are you sure?"

Tasha nodded. The look on Mel's face was worth the financial bob and weave this would require. "Val wanted to do this place herself, and they wanted to use local builders. Making a place in the community, you know? I understood that and will understand if you go the same route. I helped Val with just a few things. However much or little help you need from me, I'm happy to give you. Really."

"I should probably talk to Stefan, but I bet I know what he'll say." Mel stood, reaching for Tasha. "Thank you, Tasha."

The hug was brief but tight and heartfelt. Stepping back, Mel repeated, "Thank you so much."

"Anytime. When things settle down, I should probably meet you and Stefan there so you can tell me what you need done."

"That sounds wonderful." Mel grinned. "I'm not exactly what we might call a homemaker. I know what I like, and I know how to buy curtains and furniture and such, but I'm not creative with it. I don't nest, exactly."

"Everything in its time," Tasha said. "I am pretty creative, but I also know when to step back and do what the client wants."

Tasha picked up the salsa, but Mel said, "Speaking of things settling down, Stefan told me what's been going on. I'm so sorry. If there's anything I can do, just ask."

"I figured. Thanks, Mel."

They pushed away from the counter. Heading into the living room, Mel commented, "I'm glad you have Carter. I hear that, despite a hiccough at first, he's really watching out for you."

"He is." Tasha was also glad she had him, in every sense, even though the odds were so stacked against them. As he'd said, they'd waited a long time for this. Maybe that was why she hadn't walked away after that first, passionate night.

"Do you know where he's from?" Mel asked.

"Some town near Gulfport, Mississippi. Why?"

"Interesting. There's a Congresswoman Lockwood from that area, a big supporter of the Bureau, as it happens. She and Carter have the same hair color."

Congresswoman? Oh, no. "It's not a common color," Tasha managed.

"No, and her website says her son is a navy vet living in south Georgia. He looks a little like her. The eyes are similar."

"Huh. Interesting." And galling, that he hadn't told her, and terrifying because this so widened the chasm between them. No politician wanted to be linked to someone with Tasha's past. Political opponents researched candidates and their families and their families' associates. If the prostitution charge came to light, so would the circumstances of her enlistment. And the disaster with the girls' school and the supplies. Just thinking about it made her queasy.

They walked back into the living room, but Tasha let the conversation about bridal showers swirl around her. Why hadn't Carter told her? Because he didn't think she was good enough to meet his mom? Or because he knew his mom wouldn't think she was?

Or because he was trying to minimize the gap between them?

What would the press do if Tasha was with Carter and they uncovered her background? What would his mom's opponent do in the next election? A candidate's son dating a woman labeled as trailer trash and a slut in her hometown?

She'd known what she was risking when she went to bed with him. Had even known how things between them would go. So why did getting smacked in the face with more evidence of it feel like a rip in her heart?

This relationship was so doomed.

SOMETHING WAS EATING AT TASHA. Holding her close in the darkness of the Dares' renovated barn, Carter stroked her hair lightly, but she didn't relax. Didn't snuggle against him as she usually did.

"What's on your mind, Cupcake?"

"You mean besides the usual?" she asked.

"Yeah. Besides."

"Isn't that enough?"

"Sure. Except you seem distant, like you're with me but not."

Tasha sighed. She pulled away to turn on her bedside lamp. Sitting up, she looked down at him. "You didn't tell me your mother was in Congress."

"It never came up." He sat up too. Was this what had kept her so quiet this evening? "Where did you hear about it?"

"Mel." Tasha shrugged. "It seems your mom is a big supporter of the FBI. And you have her hair and her eyes."

"Yeah, but why does it matter?"

Irritation flared in her eyes. "Don't play dumb, Carter. You know I'm not at ease in the world you come from. You had to know your mom being a congresswoman would underline that."

"So you grew up in a trailer. So what?" At her stunned look, he said, "Moreland mentioned it, just a passing reference, one day when we were deployed. And you told me you didn't have much growing up. Do you think anyone in my family, including my mom and me, is so shallow that we'd care about any of that?"

"Maybe you should," she said quietly.

The sick dread in her eyes ripped at his heart. "Don't do this, Tasha. Don't seize on this info as a reason to bail. Maybe I should've told you, but I was afraid exactly this would happen. That you'd pull away when we'd barely started to get close."

She shook her head. Desperate, he added, "It's a job, like any other job. It's not that different from being in the Women's Community League back home."

"It certainly is," she snapped, "being on the national stage and all."

Tasha sounded as though she were gearing up to break it off with him. He couldn't let that happen. Quickly, he told her, "The only difference that makes is a bigger, nosier press corps that doesn't already know everything about her."

Tasha paled. Carter touched her shoulder. "Tasha, what is it?"

"It's—it's nothing. Carter, I don't fit in the world of fancy receptions. I hate small talk and would far rather have a beer than a cocktail."

"Nobody cares what you drink, for fuck's sake. As for small talk, all you have to do is ask people about themselves. It's simple."

"I hate that kind of thing."

"You're doing it at Julia Miller's next Thursday."

Tasha gasped. "That's low."

"Yeah, it is, but you know you can do the chit-chat thing when you need to. Besides, being with me does not mean you need to. I don't do campaign events, not unless there's one when I'm home and even then, not always. When I can, I join my mom for election night. That's it."

She still looked pale, even faintly ill. Her lips trembled.

Carter's heart plummeted. Gripping her shoulder, fighting fear, he asked, "Tasha, honey, why does this scare you so much?"

Pain flashed in her eyes. She opened her mouth, then shut it.

"Tasha?"

"It just does," she insisted. "Not for anything would I embarrass you or your family."

"You're not making sense. Nothing about you would be embarrassing. Tasha, I'd be proud to have you at my side anywhere. Any time. Any event."

Biting her lip, she shook her head.

This was crazy. It didn't make any sense at all.

Except he'd already guessed she wasn't telling him everything. A ball of fear knotted in his gut, cold radiating out from it. He scarcely recognized his own voice when he demanded, "What aren't you telling me?"

"Nothing." Her voice sounded hoarse, and her eyes slid to the side. "I've told you what worries me."

And now she was lying to him.

Pushing back the fear, he cupped her face in his hands. "Tasha, there isn't much I wouldn't do for you. Please trust me. I'm begging you."

Her expression shuttered. Her back stiffened. "Not much except save my navy career."

"I—" No. He'd sworn never to tell her about the letter he'd written on her behalf during that awful time. If he told her now, it would only seem self-serving. Instead, he replied, "You said you were over that. Are we really going back there now?"

Her shoulders sagged. "No," she said, her voice soft and her eyes full of regret. "That was low. I shouldn't have said it."

"But you meant it," he pressed. If she did, he really had no shot at all.

"No," she repeated. "I did what I shouldn't have done, and you did what you had to. I came to terms with that, like I said."

"Then why bring it up?"

"Because I need you to back off, Carter. I've told you my concerns. Anything else doesn't matter."

"But there's something," he said.

"Nothing that concerns you."

But that was still something, and she wouldn't be evasive if it didn't matter. Pushing her now, though, would only drive her away.

He blew out a breath and kissed her gently. Her hands rose to his forearms, and she kissed him back. Thank God.

"Okay," he said.

Tasha kissed him again. "Thank you."

When they lay down together, she snuggled close. She traced the center line of his abs with one hand, sending heat washing through him. His body hardened instantly.

"How thick do you think these walls are?" she murmured.

Trying to focus, he said, "Pretty thick. Lath and plaster, most likely."

She stroked his erection, and his hold on her tightened. Her whisper sent her soft breath wafting into his ear. "The bed doesn't squeak. I tested it earlier."

He caught her wrist. "Do you want me? Or do you want to distract me?"

Tasha froze. Looking straight at him, she said, "Both. Please, Carter, don't push this. Let's just enjoy what we have."

For now hung in the air unsaid, and foreboding dimmed desire. "Tasha . . ."

"Please, Carter."

The quiet words and the plea in her eyes were a warning. So he would back off. Also *for now*.

He let go of her hand and rolled her above him. As long as they were together, he had a chance to break through. He meant to fight for it.

CHAPTER TWENTY

Thursday evening, Tasha and Carter shared a loveseat in Julia and Fred Miller's comfortable living room. She missed his arm around her. Missed it very much, which was a terrible sign. Because she was here in a professional capacity, they didn't touch at all. The awareness crackled between them, though, as usual.

Julia had only antiques in the dining room, a beautiful, mahogany Chippendale suite, but she'd gone for upholstered comfort in here. The warm jade greens and golden browns, with accents in deep blue, came together nicely. The roughly semicircular arrangement of furniture also made conversation easy. Whoever decorated this room had known their stuff.

The fire crackling in the hearth at the semicircle's open end added a cozy note to the evening. Not as cozy as Carter's arm around her would have been, but she would have that later. The thought generated fizzies deep inside her.

Her project boards for the guesthouse stood on a distressed-oak buffet along the far wall. They'd been set up before dinner, so everyone could get a look.

A fiftyish woman, Sarah Brewster, asked, "Tasha, where do you start when you have a project like this guesthouse to do? At dinner, you said you go by what the client wants, but surely you make suggestions."

"I do," Tasha said. Just like she recognized a planted question when she saw one. *Thank you, Julia.* "We start with whether the client wants a contemporary or a historical vibe."

"What if the client doesn't know?" a silver-haired man, a lawyer if she remembered correctly, asked.

"I do some rough sketches, and we see what clicks." Smiling at him, she asked, "What do you do if a client doesn't know what he or she wants?"

He grimaced. "Most of 'em know, even if what they want is wrong-headed or just impossible. Then I have to talk them out of it."

"What do you do, Mr. Logan?" a young, blonde woman asked.

Carter replied, "Mostly shadow Tasha." To their blank looks, he added, "I've worked construction and am thinking of striking out on my own. Tasha and I know each other from our days in the navy, so I've been following her around and picking her brain."

"He also has some good ideas when we go around job sites," Tasha said. He never offered them until she asked, though. He respected her ability to handle her business.

They talked for a while longer before Tasha caught a meaningful look from Carter. Turning to her hostess, she said, "I'm very sorry, but we need to go. I have to be over in Fargo early in the morning." Which had the merit of being true.

"You sailing back, son?" the silver-haired lawyer asked.

"Probably not," Carter said. "This late, I'll probably use the motor."

"You have running lights, though, right?" Fred Miller, their host, asked. "If you don't, we can have our boat take you."

"We're good, Fred," Carter replied, "but thanks."

Everyone said good night, and the Millers walked them to the door. Under cover of getting jackets, Julia whispered to

Tasha, "He's a sweetie. If I were single and your age, I'd make a play."

Stunned, Tasha stared at her. Julia patted her arm. "Just a word of advice."

"Um. Uh, right."

Carter unwittingly saved her by extending his hand to Julia. "Thanks very much for a great evening. The food and the company were terrific."

Fred grinned. "That's what people are saying about the two of you when you're not listening."

"Yes," Julia said, beaming. "Tasha, I'll be surprised if your phone doesn't ring."

"Thank you, Julia," she replied, offering her hand. "I really can't thank you enough."

Julia evaded the hand and stepped in for a quick hug. "Don't be silly. Friends share great discoveries with their friends."

They stepped outside to finish their farewells. The days were fairly mild this far south, but the evenings were chilly. Tasha huddled into her jacket.

When their hosts were back inside, Carter slid an arm around Tasha's shoulders. "You were terrific, Cupcake."

The words warmed her. "You think so?"

Roland Wade and GiGi Gonzales waited on the boat, but Tasha and Carter had privacy now. Glad for it, she slid her arm around his waist.

"I know so. While we were getting our coats, Fred said you wowed 'em."

"That's good to hear." She wouldn't count the proverbial chickens, though, until she had commitments and start dates.

Carter squeezed her shoulder. Gently, he said, "You were great. Really. You can do this kind of evening, Tasha, and if you don't like it, you hide that well."

"Dinner's different from those meet-and-mingle things. I do them, but I'm never comfortable, and there are always people who don't want to talk much to me because there's no social advantage in it."

They walked a few more steps in silence. Maybe he would drop the point he'd been aiming for with his remark. She wanted to enjoy being outside, close to him, and bask in a successful evening.

It capped off a successful week. Dex liked the sketches she'd done for him and had offered help, should she need it, through a connection on the insurance board. But so far, things were going well. All the other projects were on schedule, more or less. And this evening had been pleasant even if nothing else ever came of it.

"Did I tell you," Carter asked in a low voice that wouldn't carry over the water, "you look sexy as hell tonight? In a professional way." He brushed a kiss over her temple, and pleasure flashed down into her core.

"It's a silk shirt and slacks, but thank you."

"That's why I said professional. But don't forget those sexy heels." Nuzzling her jaw, he added, "Maybe you'll wear those for me tonight. Just those."

At the thought, her breath caught. Tasha swallowed hard. At least the darkness would hide the heat blazing in her cheeks. Until they got to the boat.

"Behave," she muttered. "We have company."

"Only for a while. But yeah, inconvenient. I need something to tide me over."

"Tide you . . . oh," she said as he tugged her to a stop. They were under the live oaks near the water now, shaded from the yard lights and truly in darkness.

Carter's mouth caught hers, and his arms locked around her waist. The kiss was hot, almost fierce. She sucked his tongue, and he made a low sound in his throat.

Breathing hard, he raised his head. "So sexy," he murmured. "But yeah, we got company."

The kiss this time was soft, even tender, and it wrapped

itself around her heart. When it broke, she leaned into him with a sigh. Neither of them spoke for a few moments.

Tasha raised her head and stroked his cheek. "Will that tide you over, deputy?

"Yeah." But he kissed her again quickly. As they started walking again, he said, "Deputy. Sounds a lot hotter coming out of your mouth than anybody else's."

When Tasha and Carter stepped onto the dock, it was clear. So was the sailboat's deck. Carter leaned over the railing on the side where the boat was moored. "Roland?"

"Yo." The burly, blond deputy reeve poked his head out of the cabin. "You rang?"

"Just checking," Carter said as Tasha lifted a hand in greeting. "Anything to report?"

"Nope. Quiet as a night in early March on a mostly deserted island."

He and Tasha headed down the dock again. "Can one of you help me cast off? Tasha's wearing heels, and I'd like to get underway as quickly as we can."

"Are you worried?" Tasha asked.

They'd reached the ramp down to the boat. He gestured for her to go first, but she waited for his answer.

Carter shook his head. "Not particularly. But we're out of the Collegium after dark, and a traitor mage is hunting with however many ghouls they'll give him. I'll feel better when we're away from land."

"Because they can't swim?" she asked, trying to remember where she'd heard that.

"They could, but they mostly don't bother to learn. Let's get aboard, Tasha."

They hurried down the ramp to the dock and climbed onto the boat. Roland, whose sword hung at his left hip, passed Carter his sword in its harness. Carter shucked his jacket and put on the harness. Because of the crowd at the dinner party and the nearness of their backup, he and Tasha had opted not to risk having someone bump into their screened, and thus invisible, swords.

Tasha ducked into the cabin, where GiGi sat on one of the two facing benches that converted into beds. Like Roland, she wore civilian clothes—jeans, a turtleneck, boots, and a medium-weight jacket. Her broadsword hung at her left hip. A space heater warmed the cabin, and a little kitchenette and toilet filled the alcove beyond the beds.

They greeted each other, and Tasha said, "I really can't thank you enough, GiGi. This was an important event for my business." She grabbed her sheathed saber from its place in the corner and strapped on the belt.

"Carter said." The deputy reeve nodded. "I'm happy to help, Tasha. That kind of ghoul destruction, burning your business, could happen to any of us if we landed in their crosshairs. We have to stick together."

Was that how she saw it, as sticking together, rather than giving up her evening as a favor to a friend? "I hope you and Roland weren't bored."

"Nah. We played a few hands of gin rummy and streamed a superhero show about an acrobatic blind guy. And ate the snacks you brought. You make wicked salsa, Tasha."

"Thanks. It's my one of my few accomplishments in the kitchen."

GiGi grinned. "Not my favorite room either. I'd much rather be training to kick ghoul butt and take names."

Tasha grinned back and offered her a high-five. Her past sort-of jealousy of GiGi seemed absurd now. Carter had made it plain where his interest lay.

Roland ducked under the low opening. "Carter says we're heading out. Tasha, he wants you to stay in here where it's warm."

"I'll just go speak to him," Tasha said, ignoring the look his fellow deputies exchanged.

She stepped out onto the deck and into the magical awareness of Carter's extended senses. Even now, he was looking out for her. If only . . . but that was a pointless wish.

Moonlight laid a silver path over the water and gave the buildings of the navy base ahead a faint glow. Dolphins roamed these waters, but they were probably doing whatever it was dolphins did at night.

Carter sat by the tiller in the stern. "You should stay in the cabin," he said. "It's warmer."

"While you sit out here in the cold? I don't think so." She walked toward him.

"It's not just warmer in there, Cupcake. It's also more protected. Dare gave me those stones you mentioned, the ones that can keep a small place from being scried. They're in the cabin, and you can shield the cabin magically when you're inside. I saw you put on your Eye of Horus pendant, but there's no such thing as being too careful."

"Carter . . ."

"I would appreciate it. A lot." He looked earnestly back at her.

He'd done nothing but think about protecting her for days. She could give him this. She should. "Okay, then."

"Thanks. It—" Carter stiffened and drew his sword. His magic flared around the boat, shielding it in a blue aura. "Roland," he called. "GiGi."

They were already rushing onto the deck, swords at the ready.

"You felt it too," GiGi said, peering into the darkness off the bow with Roland.

"Oh, yeah," Carter said. "Fucking ghouls. One of you screen us, and—"

"On it," Roland replied.

GiGi added, "I've got the shield," as Carter finished "take over the shield."

Tasha's heart thudded into her throat. "How did they find us?"

"None of these protective devices will defeat eyes. Or magical proximity," Carter reminded her, staring at the running lights now visible behind them. "What's important is, the bastards are here."

A magical screen, however, would defeat eyesight. Maybe Roland's screen would buy them time to get away.

Carter looked at Tasha. "Please go below."

A protest formed on her lips, but he was right. If the screen or the shield failed for any reason, she was a visible target. The traitor mage had made her shield wink out. If he was out there, he might be able to do it again, to the screen or the shield. She ducked into the cabin but left the door open.

"We're almost to Drum Point Island," Carter said. "If I get there in time, put the island between us and them—"

The roar of an engine split the quiet. "Outboard," Roland said, his voice grim. "A big one. How much juice does this baby have, Carter?"

"Not enough," he replied. "It's intended to supplement the sails, not win races. If they get close enough, they'll sense our magic. They already know we're here."

A flare of silver magic illuminated the mages on deck, the trees beyond, and the water outside the cabin. If Roland's screen held, the light wouldn't matter. The mage was showing off for the ghouls, who couldn't screen.

Another flare shot toward the boat. It fizzled out before it reached GiGi's screen. When the ghouls came within range, though, it would sizzle against the shield and betray their location.

Tasha moved to the cabin steps. She had to know what was going on. If she were out there—No, Carter was right. Everything that could be done now was being done. She would only be an additional worry.

Still, the outboard motor grew louder. The pursuing boat's running lights drew closer.

Carter swung his boat about. "I'm going to see if I can gain us some distance. If we can make it out of their magical range, we might pull this off."

Again, his magic flared blue, hidden by the magical screen. This time, he focused the energy off the stern, pushing the boat faster. The gap between them and the pursuers stayed steady. How long could he keep it up?

"I could help you," Tasha called softly. "Lend you energy."

He hesitated but finally said, "Okay. But stay low."

With Roland busy screening them from view and GiGi shielding them, there was no one else to boost him. Tasha crept over the deck to sit by his knee on the side away from the tiller.

His hand cupped the nape of her neck, and she funneled power into the contact. The boat surged ahead.

Behind them, though, the other boat started gaining.

Carter veered around a land mass even Tasha's mageborn eyes could barely see in the darkness. "Drum Point Island," he said. "Mill Creek and a bunch of little inlets where we might hide ahead."

"Let's hope they guess wrong," GiGi said. She and Roland knelt in the stern, watching the other boat.

The pursuers' engine roared more loudly.

"They're following," Roland announced. "And closing."

"Damn it," Carter muttered. He drew more power from Tasha, who drew it in turn from the trees and grass on either side of the water and the fish beneath it.

With a *kra-kow*, muddy yellow ghoul energy hit their shield and fizzled. Now the ghouls knew where they were.

"That's it," Carter said, tugging Tasha to her feet. "New plan. Abandon ship. Tasha, pick a good spot on the shore."

She couldn't run in these heels. They had to go. She kicked them off and magically shielded her feet. The shield wasn't quite as good as an actual shoe, but it was close.

"When you come out of the shift," Roland said, "drop flat. We'll let some magic show as we form our shields, see if we can draw them off."

"I'm calling for a ride," GiGi stated. "You should, too, so the reinforcements know where to find you."

"Will do," Carter said. "Be careful."

"You, too," Roland said. "See you soon."

With a nod, Carter hooked his arms around Tasha's waist. "I'll do the translocation," he said. "You got a spot?"

She pointed to a clearing on the shore. His tightened his hold. "Got it. Going in three . . . two . . . one . . . mark." His magic flared around them as he reached for the space between life and death and fed power into the shift.

Reality wrenched sideways in a wave of icy darkness. An instant later, they emerged in the clearing. They dropped flat immediately. To the north, a flare of green, almost too quick to spot, as though released by accident, marked Roland and GiGi's destination.

"Let's get to cover so we can stand up and go again," Carter said. "I want us away from these bastards."

Silently, they crept toward a thick stand of saw palmetto. "I scried this island," he told her as they both drew their swords. "There are ruins to the south. It's open ground, so a helo can land there. There's also a potential LZ north of here, near a museum, but Roland and GiGi went that way."

"South works for me."

Swords in their hands, they made their way through the darkness.

Carter continued, "The campgrounds are on the other side of the island, so no Mundane witnesses. The helo crew will screen against sight and sound, which will keep the few Mundanes in the private residences around this part of the island from hearing the helo."

They might hear ghouls, of course, but there was no helping that.

Crouching in the cluster of saw palmettos, Tasha and Carter listened. The usual insect noises were the only sounds. Somewhere, an owl hooted.

"We should recharge," she whispered, opening herself to the life energy in the forest around her. "You used a lot of power to propel the boat. I'm sorry about the boat, by the way. I know it was your grandfather's."

"It's a boat." Also recharging, Carter shrugged. "The choice between it and you was easy."

When he said things like that, she could almost believe—

Magical energy crackled off to their left. Through the blade-like palmetto leaves to the north, the muddy yellow of ghoul shielding flared.

CHAPTER TWENTY-ONE

"SPREAD OUT," THE MAGE ORDERED. "FIND THEM."

"Oh, fuck," Carter whispered as Tasha's heart jolted. He wrapped a screen around them but kept it tight, likely so the mage wouldn't sense it easily. With a hand on her shoulder to remind her to stay down, he peered above the leaves. "I count ten, so—shit. He just brought more in. We gotta go, Tasha."

Still on his knees, he drew her close. "Going . . . now."

She braced herself for the wrenching transition. Still kneeling, they emerged into reality on a white-sand road about ten to fifteen feet wide.

Rising, they looked back the way they'd come. "How many do you think there are?" Tasha asked.

"Last group looked like another nine or ten."

"So about twenty."

He answered with a curt nod. He didn't have to say those odds sucked. She knew it as well as he did.

Carter pulled out his phone. "I have the phone on night mode to darken the screen. It's also on silent. I'm texting the dispatcher, telling the flying squad where to meet us. They'll text back."

"So you have a plan."

"Yeah. We're heading down to the Dungeness ruins."

"The what?"

"Used to be a mansion. Lots of history there, but we can get to it later. There's plenty of open space around the ruins for the helo to land. We'll get off the road, walk alongside it." Glancing at her, he asked, "Screen or shield?"

"I'll screen." Envisioning the road without them, she spun the magical aura.

Magic brushed over her senses as Carter's shield formed. "Stay close. We should keep the shield and screen tight."

"Yep. Got it."

Magically muffling the sounds of their footsteps, they moved off the road and into the semi-cleared area under the trees that bordered it. In a low voice, Carter said, "The undergrowth is thick through here. It'll offer more concealment if we need it, but walking through it would slow us down a lot."

And the saw palmetto and other undergrowth would rustle. Tasha commented, "At least the shadows are deeper here."

"There's that."

They walked in silence for several minutes. Behind them, rustling sounded in the undergrowth. A quick backward glance revealed a pair of shielded male ghouls.

"If we fight them," Tasha said softly, "the noise will draw the others."

Carter nodded. "We need to evade."

Magic crackled over Tasha's back. She and Carter wheeled to meet it. A wide flare of muddy yellow scythed across the forest, crashing into trees and kicking up dirt.

It sizzled on their shield.

"Fuck," Carter breathed. "Going again."

Tasha grabbed him, and he translocated. This time, they landed about fifty yards from where they'd been, under a pair of big live oaks. "We need to stay under cover, not get to Dungeness too soon," he whispered.

Another flare of magic ripped over the area, just missing

them. His lips tightened. "Then there's that," he muttered. "Hang on."

He shifted them to the other side of the road, about thirty yards farther along it.

"What's the helo's ETA?" she asked.

He pulled out his phone, glanced at it, and put it back in his hip pocket. "Taking off now. The pilot will firewall it. Be here in seven."

Another muddy yellow blast flared across their shield. More shielded ghouls crashed through the undergrowth and into view. "Eight out there," Tasha said.

"It's like they know where we're headed," Carter muttered, reaching for her.

Tasha wrapped her arms around him "Go."

They emerged from transit at the edge of the clear space, really a wide lawn, around a ruined mansion. Standing side by side, they surveyed the structure. The roof was gone. Some of the walls had crumbled. Others jutted upward into the moonlight. In them, starlight showed through gaping, empty windows.

Off to the right stood a low, white cottage with gabled windows on the second floor. Farther away on the wide lawn, a herd of gray, white, and brown horses stood in clumps, probably asleep.

Through the trees, the muddy glow of ghoul shields, more of them than before, rushed down the road in a clump. The horses' heads snapped up, turning toward the road.

The ghouls fanned out along the lawn on both sides of the road, more than twenty of them now, and prepared to blast the tree line.

"Hang on," Carter whispered. He grabbed her, and Tasha steeled herself.

When they came back to the world this time, they stood in a small, square area with stone walls. Tasha's stomach knotted.

Quickly, she looked up, to the open sky. He'd taken them inside the ruin.

Not trapped, not trapped, she repeated silently, gazing at the stars.

Carter's shield dropped. "Let the screen go," he whispered. "They can sense our magic more easily than they can sense us."

With a nod, Tasha did as he asked.

Outside, muddy yellow magic flared, so intense that it crackled over their skin despite the thirty or forty yards between them and it. Hoofbeats sounded as the horses fled en masse.

"Spread out," a rough, female voice ordered. "They could be here, screened."

Magic crackled, muddy yellow flaring. The ghouls were sending random blasts around the lawn. Good thing the horses had gotten clear.

"If they look in here from the right angle," Carter whispered, "they'll see us."

While drawing the ghouls was no longer an issue, since all of them seemed to be here, Tasha and Carter were badly outnumbered until reinforcements reached them. Still, they had to do something. "Running fight?" she whispered back.

"Don't like the odds," he muttered. "There's a cistern on the far end. It's partly underground with thick stone walls and a wooden roof. I scried the interior. We can hide in there. It's far enough inside the walls that the ghouls won't sense us if we don't use our magic and stay huddled. Unless they probe it specifically."

Tasha barely heard him. A cistern. A cramped space. With a roof.

Her teeth chattered. Fighting for breath, she said, "No. I can't."

"What?" He peered closely at her. "You're claustrophobic."

Too scared to be embarrassed, she nodded. Clenching her teeth stopped the chattering.

He stroked her hair back gently. With his lips close to her ear, he said softly, "Honey, if I had a better choice, I'd offer it. We rush out there, we're likely to get killed. This is a last-ditch option."

Shivering, she shook her head.

"No choice," he insisted. "I'll hold on to you the entire time."

Rough ghoul voices crew nearer. Carter tensed against her, and Tasha's hand clenched on her saber's hilt.

"Cupcake, trust me. Helo's due in about four. I'll keep you safe."

Four minutes could be an eternity.

At least he wasn't taking her into that thing against her will. The tiny part of her brain that wasn't terrified gave him credit for that.

"You've trusted me this far. Trust me a few minutes more." Cupping her face in his hands, he touched his forehead to hers. "It's that or we die here. Both of us, because I won't leave you. Please, Tasha."

He might die if she didn't agree.

That penetrated the shroud of fear muddling her brain. She couldn't let him die for her. Clutching him with both hands, she nodded. Carter locked his arms around her waist and translocated.

Into utter darkness. Not so much as a sliver of light penetrated. Tasha's stomach lurched. Her hands clawed at his shoulders, and she battled back a scream.

"I've got you," he murmured, his cheek pressed to her hair. One of his arms stayed tight around her waist. With his free hand, he rubbed her back in long, soothing strokes. "I've got you."

He said other things, all softly so the ghouls wouldn't hear. Mage ears were keener than theirs. But Tasha couldn't make out the words through the haze of terror chilling her from head to toe.

Cold. She was so cold.

She groped for his face, tipping hers up. In the darkness, their lips met. Tenderness wouldn't do this time. She needed heat, fast. Lots of it. Tasha nipped his lip.

Carter exhaled a soft groan and deepened the kiss. His hand dropped to her butt, holding her against his hard groin.

The chill and the fear and the world faded. There was only Carter, with his body close, his arms around her, and his mouth so very hot.

He broke the kiss abruptly and tucked her head into the curve of his neck and shoulder. "Wait," he whispered, sounding breathless.

Eyes closed, Tasha clung to him, trying to focus on his scent, spicy aftershave and sweat, and the warmth of his embrace. Cold was climbing up her feet. She couldn't let it paralyze her.

"Helo's inbound," he said softly. "We're going to have to translocate out, near the helo if we can, and run for it. The helo will be shielded, so we can't translocate into it. When we get close enough, the mages shielding it will extend the shield around us, too."

Tasha nodded.

"Okay." Again, he stroked her back. "When they text us, we go."

That couldn't be a moment too soon. Again, she nodded.

Carter wrapped both arms around her. "They'll try to come down between us and the ghouls," he whispered. "Between here and that little white house that was off to the right."

He pulled his phone out again, dimmed. The glow from the screen was barely visible.

The faint *chukka-chukka* of helicopter blades penetrated the cistern. The sound grew steadily louder.

"Any minute," he told her quietly. "Ready . . . now!"

Reality wrenched sideways. They reentered it near the corner of the white cottage. Carter shielded them both for the moment Tasha needed to get her head in the game again.

The helo was there, between them and the ruined mansion, with the hatches on both sides open. On the far side, flares of green and blue magic clashed with muddy yellow ghoul power. The crackling clashes of energy bolts, the angry roars of ghouls, and *chukka-chukka* of the deputy reeves' Black Hawk roared in the night. Deputy reeves in combat gear surrounded the helo, shielding it and blasting at their foes who tried to flank them. In the far doorway, a longbowman fired shaft after shaft at the ghouls.

The noise was deafening.

Crouched in the open hatch, another deputy reeve in combat gear beckoned.

Carter squeezed Tasha's shoulder. "Go."

Shielded, she darted for the helo. Instead of running beside her, though, he stayed a step behind her, shielding her doubly. They were going to have to discuss that.

The mages' shield reached out to envelop her and Carter, just as he'd said it would. They dived through the hatch. The mage kneeling by it shouted into her headset mic, "Package is aboard. Let's go."

Deputy reeves scrambled back through the hatches and slammed them shut. The woman who had greeted Tasha and Carter motioned to seats for them and handed them headsets.

"Thanks, Jill," Carter said. She clapped him on the shoulder and strapped in beside him. The helicopter rose straight up with ghoul magic crackling against its shielded underside.

Tasha twisted to see who was behind them. "Where's GiGi? And Roland?" she shouted over rotor noise.

Jill answered. "Most of the pursuit followed you. They killed theirs and are on the beach farther north."

"Darren got the traitor," a man said over the comm. "Sizzled him."

"He was standing near the tree line but exposed," Darren Hale said in his soft drawl. "I got in a lucky shot. I think he survived, though."

Tasha glanced at Carter. That mage was too powerful for a single blast to take him. Unless he'd been almost out of power.

A stocky man in combat gear crouched in front of them. His dark brown face creased in concern. The medical caduceus was embroidered on his vest above his name, Parkhurst. "Anybody hurt?" he asked.

They shook their heads, but he frowned. "Look at me," he told Tasha.

He lifted his right hand, palm out, and held it about six inches from her forehead. Pale green energy trickled out to play over her face. "Your magic's good," he said, "but you're pale. You're showing signs of an acute stress reaction."

"I'm tired," she said. Not for anything would she admit her claustrophobia over a commnet.

He looked unconvinced. Standing, he took a blanket from an overhead compartment and draped it around Tasha "If your lips are still white when we get back, we're detouring by the infirmary." To Carter, he added, "Let me know if her status changes."

"Roger. Thanks, Doc." He slid his arm around her.

She burrowed into his shoulder. He felt good. Solid and warm and dependable. All of that, especially depending on him, was dangerous. He wouldn't always be there.

He switched off both their mics. "Tell me the truth, Cupcake. You okay?"

"I will be. It—this hasn't happened in a long time."

"Because you avoid triggering situations," he guessed.

She nodded again. Carter's arm tightened, and he laid his cheek against her hair. "We'll be back at the Collegium in about ten minutes. They don't push the speed when they're not headed to an emergency. Until we get back, just lean on me and rest."

She couldn't do much else. How embarrassing.

One thing she could do, though, was think. In a vague, semi-focused way. Carter's heartbeat sounded faintly in her ear. He'd not only comforted her but distracted her. Driven the claustrophobia back.

Not even Nate had ever been able to do that. Carter had taken her out of herself. She'd never kissed a man during a panic attack, but she knew in her bones that no other man could've given her the same level of reassurance.

That could only mean her feelings for him were stronger than she realized. And the fall, when it came, would be even worse than she'd expected.

HE COULD HAVE LOST HER. The knowledge beat in Carter's veins and jabbed into his heart. She could've died out there.

Now she sat beside him on the loveseat in their Collegium apartment, sipping hot tea Val Dare had made for her. Val, Griff, Will, and Stefan had all been waiting when the helo arrived. Stefan had insisted on checking her over himself, agreed with his colleague's diagnosis of acute stress, and prescribed rest and warmth. Then he'd shooed everyone out. To be fair, though, they'd all said they weren't staying, just wanted to be sure she was okay.

"Val brought fudge," Tasha said. "With walnuts. Want some?"

No. No, he did not want any damn fudge. He wanted to wrap his arms around Tasha and hold her close so he could stand between her and anything that ever threatened her.

The realization momentarily stopped his brain.

When it kicked in again, he thought, *So that's the way of it. Hell, Lockwood. Nothing like falling for a woman who believes you're wrong for each other.*

He had, though, and there was no helping it. He would have to proceed even more carefully than—

"Carter?" Tasha frowned at him. "You okay?"

"No." Careful of the tea, he drew her onto his lap. "I

could've lost you. If we'd been just a little less lucky, it could've been all over."

She was warm and breathing in his arms, her familiar ocean spray scent wafting into his nose, her hair soft against his cheek, her free arm around his back. She was very much alive. He had to keep her that way.

Cuddling closer, she sighed. "It wasn't luck. It was your excellent planning. If you want to say you told me so, okay. You can say it. Once."

"No need," he answered, his voice deliberately dry. "I think we both get that."

She leaned forward to set her half-full mug on the coffee table. "Val thinks tea is a remedy for everything and this peach kind is soothing."

"You don't like it?" he asked, his lips against her soft hair.

"No, but I didn't want to hurt her feelings. It was obvious they'd all been worried."

"So you decided to be a friend."

"Sure. I mean, that tea, honestly, is just nasty. At least to me. But she brought fudge too. It balances out."

"So you're a chocoholic." Another thing he hadn't known. Could he use it to make a dent in her armor?

"Um."

They sat in silence for a few minutes. He could do this every night, and he would've given his sailboat—which the ghouls apparently had sunk—to know whether this brought her as much comfort as it did him.

"Carter?"

"Hm?"

"Why do you think the mage was right on our heels?"

"I was wondering about that. He must've figured a helo could be coming and known we'd need a wide LZ for it. The ghouls were between us and the museum, so that left the area around Dungeness. He was reasoning logically, not tracking us. Or that's my guess, anyway."

"It makes sense."

"In the battle at the farmhouse," he began. Pausing, he waited for her nod before he continued, "Will fought that mage. Said he thought the guy was pulling his punches. And he walked through a section of warding like it wasn't there."

"I remember." Lifting her head, she frowned up at him. "Griff says Darren's really good, that he knows what he's doing. Still, it seems odd that a single blast could penetrate that guy's shielding and take him down."

"It does. I wonder if he deliberately took that hit."

"Why would he?"

"I dunno. Maybe he's had too many screwups and wants to look like he isn't waltzing clear. He's missed you three times now."

"Yeah." She grinned. "Thanks to you."

"You did your part. And I gotta tell you, you look sexy as hell with that saber in your hand."

Her eyes narrowed. "I didn't fight anybody tonight. Or when they came to my shop. And don't I wish I had? I'd really like to hurt those bastards."

"I know. Me too. But sometimes the smart move is running away."

"I guess." With a sigh, she nestled against him again. "I liked those shoes."

The shoes he'd asked her to wear for him, with nothing else, tonight. "I forgot them," he admitted, "but I liked them too. I was looking forward to liking them better."

Tasha looked up at him with mischief in her eyes. "Why, Carter, I think you're what my gran would've called a naughty young man."

"Guilty as charged." He nipped her lower lip. "Let's be naughty together."

"Great idea." Bracing herself with her hands on his shoulders, she straddled him. "I know just where to start," she whispered in his ear. Then she licked it, and his already-hot blood ignited.

Ripping her silk shirt wouldn't gain him any points, so he unbuttoned it quickly. At the same time, Tasha was working on his shirt.

Her bra came next. Bare-chested, they leaned into each other. Carter palmed her breasts, kneading firmly, and she moaned into his mouth. Her lips traced a hot path along his jaw to his ear, where she sucked the pulse point.

His hips bucked. He fumbled the catch on her pants, and she helped him get rid of them. In a moment, she had his trousers open and her hand around the hard, throbbing part of him. "I can't wait," she told him.

He could smell her musk, and her nipples were hard nubs beneath his palms. He ached to oblige.

"Condom," he gasped.

Tasha lifted up enough for him to lean over the little sofa's low arm and snag one. They sheathed him together.

"Now," she said.

"Now. Look at me, Tasha."

Her eyes locked onto his as she sank down, taking him inside her. The heat and desire there matched his own. Was he imagining the tenderness?

Her head fell back. She rocked atop him, and he thrust in time to her movements.

"Carter—I—I need—"

He took one rounded, firm breast as deeply into his mouth as he could and sucked hard. Tasha gasped. Bucked against him. His vision started to fog.

She caught his cheeks and tugged his head up to kiss him. Holding her thighs, he thrust upward.

Tasha shrieked into his mouth. A moment later, he shuddered, thrust again and followed her into the warm oblivion of release.

When he surfaced, they were still joined. *I love you*, he thought, but he knew better than to say it. At least not yet.

THERE WAS nothing like really good sex to reassure a woman that she was alive. Nothing like lying in the arms of an ardent lover to savor the aftermath.

But Tasha's lover didn't seem to be savoring the way he usually did.

She propped herself up on her elbow and looked down at Carter. Idly, he stroked her back. They'd moved to the bed for round three and cuddled for a while when it was done. Whether there would be a round four remained to be seen.

"Are you okay?" she asked.

"Fine. Why?"

She laid her hand over his at his waist. "You seem . . . I don't know . . . distracted."

"Is that a complaint?" He raised an eyebrow.

"You know it's not. In between, I mean. Not during."

"Well, good." His lips curved in a faint smile that didn't reach his eyes. "I try to focus when I'm doing something important."

"Not complaining," she assured him, "but I'm concerned. Your forethought saved us tonight. You know that, right?" Squeezing his hand, she added, "You did good, Deputy Lockwood."

"Maybe," he said, "and maybe we're just lucky they didn't probe the ruins magically. If they had, we would've had to translocate out and take on really terrible odds."

"But we didn't." Cocking her head, she studied him. "You've never been one to focus on what could've gone wrong but didn't. Why is this bugging you so much?"

He looked back at her without changing his expression. She couldn't read his face. The temptation to push a little niggled at her brain, but maybe he needed some space to get his answer together.

With one finger, he traced the line of her short hair down the side of her face. "You could have died," he said.

"So could you." Fear for him had given her the courage to endure the claustrophobia.

He shook his head. "You wanted to know what's on my mind, and that's it. Knowing I could've lost you."

The tender words wrapped themselves around her heart. Better to ignore that warm, squishy feeling, though. Not get too used to it.

"It wouldn't have been your fault," she said. "You were ready. There was no way to know they'd bring so many—"

"No," he said gently. "No, Tasha. When I say I could've lost you, I'm not talking about tactics or responsibility. I'm talking about not having this, the two of us together. About losing that."

The squishy warmth around her heart pushed up into her throat. The tender look in his eyes made hers sting. "Carter, I—I don't know what to say."

He drew her hand to his lips and kissed it. "You don't have to say anything. I'm not trying to start a big thing, only to let you know how I feel."

With his body relaxed and his voice quiet, he seemed sincere. She couldn't pick up any vibe in the magic, though.

"Okay." Going with instinct, she let the subject drop and nestled into his embrace again.

Carter lightly stroked her hair. "Can I ask you something?"
"Sure."

"Have you always had trouble with small spaces?"

"No." She shifted to look into his face. "When I was eight, I went to a slumber party. I didn't know the girl who was having it didn't want to invite me, that her mom made her." Out of pity for the poor little girl from the trashy trailer, and that impulse had sure as hell gone wrong. "The girls locked me in a closet in the unfinished basement all night."

Carter scowled. "You're not kidding me. They really did."

"Yeah. And when I got out . . . well, I was claustrophobic."

"Where were the parents? Didn't they hear you?"

"I didn't call out. I was scared to. They threatened to have their brothers beat up Nate if I told anybody."

"I'm guessing he wasn't an Army Ranger-level badass in those days."

"He was a bookworm. I was scared for him."

"Of course you were." Carter kissed her hair. "I'm sorry I brought it up."

"You got me through it tonight, Carter. Of course you can ask."

"I wish I could fix it."

Tasha shrugged. "I cope with it well enough. But now you know why I was a Seabee and didn't try for the submarine corps."

The crack got the smile she wanted. Stroking his hair, she said, "I'm kind of tired. Let's postpone round four until morning and get some sleep."

"Whatever you want."

She turned onto her side, and he spooned behind her, his arm over her waist. They laced their fingers together.

His breathing gradually slowed and deepened. He soon slept.

Tasha lay awake, remembering what he'd said about losing her. Whatever their differences, he was as straight-arrow honest as a man could be. He cared for her. That meant learning the truth about her past would not only disappoint or disgust him. It would hurt him. He didn't deserve that, but it was far too late now to prevent it.

CHAPTER TWENTY-TWO

THE DOOR TO ROSS'S HUT CRASHED OPEN. ROSS JERKED UPRIGHT ON his cot as Zarig stormed in.

"You lost twenty of my best fighters," Zarig roared, yanking him up by his collar. He backhanded Ross across the face, sending him flying into the wall headfirst.

Dazed, Ross fought to clear his brain. Zarig could kill him before Ross could magically summon his claymore from the floor beside the cot.

"Give me one reason I shouldn't gut you now." Zarig had him by the collar again, the ghoul in his face, with the reek of ammonia around him and on his breath threatening to turn Ross's stomach.

"Or," Zarig said, smiling, "once you've been taught your place, we can use another breeder."

The words sent a chill rippling down Ross's back. Bloody hell, no. He would rather die.

He glared up at Zarig. "We've been close to catching her three times. Because of me. I'm the one who caught her on South End Road. I had her until the other mage arrived. I got us past her shields and into her business. Not my fault if she sensed us and fled."

"Last night, you cost me too much." Zarig slammed him into the wall.

"Last night," Ross replied, infusing as much contempt into his voice as he could, "the supposed heroes you sent me bolloxed the operation. Some of them thought we'd lost the Murdock woman and wanted to go after the Mundanes in the campgrounds. Others disagreed, and they attacked each other." As ghouls tended to do, but this wasn't the time to point that out. "I had to kill the last three to stop them and then burn the bodies."

Actually, he'd triggered the fight and killed several himself. A good night's work, all in all.

"You had no right," Zarig thundered, slamming him into the wall again.

Quickly, though his vision was unfocused, Ross snapped, "I had no choice. If they'd run amok on Cumberland Island, the mages would've put everything they have into finding this nest."

"Pah! Do you fear them, mage?"

Ross shook his aching head. "But why buy trouble?" With a jerky nod down at the rough, red magic burn on his chest, he said, "I was injured trying to get her. I'll try again, but I'll need fighters who can follow orders and stick to a plan."

Yeah, and good luck finding those among the ghouls.

Zarig glared down at him, and Ross kept his own face blank. His fate hung on a sword's edge. If he had to fight his way out of here, it would be rough going.

Zarig's eyes narrowed. "I will give you one more chance, mage. One. If you fail me, you will die regretting it."

CHAPTER TWENTY-THREE

S<small>EATED</small> <small>AT</small> <small>THE</small> <small>DINING</small> <small>TABLE,</small> T<small>ASHA</small> <small>RAN</small> <small>THROUGH</small> <small>THE</small> morning's email on her laptop. Across from her, Carter did the same. Sitting there together with coffee and bagels felt good. Homey. Right.

But there lay dragons.

She'd been trying not to think about what he'd said last night, how he would hate to lose the two of them. Yet the words kept running through her brain, tempting her.

With a small shake of her head, she pushed the memory aside. The next email was interesting, considering the company she was currently keeping.

"Carter?"

"Hm?"

She waited until he glanced up at her. "I got an email from Joe Moreland." The wiry, Puerto Rican electrician had been a whiz at his job. Anything he wired was done right and quickly.

Too bad she couldn't hire him away from the navy.

"He was such a quiet guy," Carter commented. "I never would've figured him for a daredevil. How's he doing? Still jumping off anything he can find?"

"Not anymore. He took up parkour—you know, that sport

where people run around and jump and somersault off things?
—a few years ago and hurt his knee. The navy docs were very
stern about what he was allowed to do after that. Since he
wanted to stay in, he listened."

Carter's brows rose. "Must've been some injury."

"Yep. He had to have an ACL replacement. And since he
means to be career navy . . ." Tasha shrugged.

"What's he doing these days?"

"He's stationed in San Diego and really enjoying it. He and
his wife just had a little boy. Their third."

"Great news about the baby. If you have his address, I'll
send a card."

"He would like that. Hang on, and I'll get you the info."

She pulled up the contact and sent it to Carter's email before
typing a quick response to Moreland. He was a Mundane, so
there was very little he could know about her current problems.
That was just as well. There was nothing he could do to help.

She sent the email. The top one now in her inbox was from
Liston Cabinetmakers. Odd. Liston usually called with updates.

Tasha clicked on the email. "Tasha," it read, "really sorry, but
I can't make that deadline. It'll be another two weeks. Maybe
three."

"Sonofabitch," she muttered.

Carter's head snapped up. "What?"

Heading into the bedroom to grab her phone, she explained.

In an irritated tone, he asked, "Is that the guy you were
arguing with when we were in your office?"

"The very same."

She dug the phone out of her purse. Punching Liston's
contact, she headed back to the table. The phone rang five
times, then rolled to voicemail.

"Coward," Tasha muttered. When the beep sounded, she
said, "Lloyd, I got your email. We still have a contract, and I still
mean to hold you to it." Shaking her head, she disconnected.

"Can you fire him?" Carter asked.

"On the one hand, I'd like to. If he's pissed off, he won't do his best work, and I want the best for my clients. On the other hand, they'll be eating out a lot if their kitchen isn't put together by the move-in date."

"Which requires cabinets."

"Exactly, and the contract requires him to reimburse any such expenses. He must think he has an out."

Carter opened his mouth and shut it abruptly.

"What?" Tasha asked.

"I know a cabinetmaker," he said. "He's in Mississippi, but—"

"He works with your dad." Oh, this would not do. Nothing that led Carter's parents to take an interest in her could be good in any way. They would ask questions. Maybe not accept the evasive answers Carter still tolerated because of their affair. His parents, wanting the best for him, would want no part of her.

"Used to," Carter replied, eyeing her warily. "He's semi-retired now. I could see if he's free. The cabinets would need to be shipped up here, which would eat into your profit margin, but I may be able to get you a deal on that. Anything Langston makes is beautifully done. He's the best."

"That's very generous, Carter. I appreciate it. But that's a lot of trouble and, as you point out, adds the shipping expense. I'll figure something out."

His brows knitted, but he said, "Okay" and turned back to his screen.

"I need to call my clients," she said, and headed for the bedroom. At least she sounded relaxed despite the tension in her neck. Carter had made a generous offer, one she would've pounced on from anyone else. Yet she'd given him a lame excuse and refused. How much longer could she keep this going?

Probably not long. Their physical intimacy deepened daily, but she knew he wanted more emotional intimacy. Sharing. Trust.

She couldn't outright lie to him about her past, but the truth would shatter his view of her. Heartbreak would be easier to bear than seeing disillusionment and shock in his beautiful eyes.

A smart woman would break up with him, and soon.

∽

DRIVING BACK to the Collegium that evening, Carter watched Tasha out of the corner of his eye. Last night had forced him to recognize his love for her. The passionate, tender sex, with magic crackling around them, had only strengthened his feelings.

But she'd been distant all day. On top of that, she was in a jam with this cabinetmaker and refused Carter's help. Was that pride? Or something else?

Instead of talking to him, she stared out the window or talked or texted on her phone.

"What's on your mind?" she asked. "You're awfully quiet over there."

"So are you." What would happen if he pushed? Just a little.

"Tired, I guess." Not looking at him, she said, "I have to call Lloyd Liston again. He hasn't responded to texts, so I'm now going to be a pest until he shapes up." She tapped the contact on her phone.

"Lloyd, it's Tasha. Yes, I know you're very busy. . . . Uh-huh." Her brows drew together, a bad sign. When her eyes narrowed, Carter braced himself.

In a voice that could've chilled the Arctic, Tasha said, "I see. Thank you so much for your cooperation and support, Lloyd. Don't get too comfy, because you absolutely will be hearing from me."

She disconnected, banged her head back against the head-rest, and quietly shrieked.

"What?" Carter demanded. "What happened?"

Tasha turned to him, her face tight with fury. "He said he doesn't think we had a contract, but if I can produce it, of course he'll reconsider."

"And you can't produce it because it burned."

"Got it in one." She banged her fist on her knee. "Sonofabitch."

"Does anybody else have a copy of the contract?"

"Lloyd does," Tasha bit out. "Unless he destroyed it. Y'know, I was reluctant to hire him because he hasn't been keeping up with things lately. But he begged for the job, and he always did a good job for my old boss. The contract was even his idea. And now this. I have a backup copy in the cloud, but it doesn't have an original signature. I think that could be important."

"Maybe lawyers can sort it out." Though that, of course, would mean legal fees at a time when she needed money flowing in.

Tasha shrugged. "I'll figure something out."

They drove a few more miles in silence. "At least that drainage problem is taken care of," Carter said. The project that had had the problem was rolling along. Exterior siding was up, and they'd almost finished the sheetrock work.

"Yeah, that's a bright spot."

More silence. They were headed back to the Collegium and dinner with Will Davis. Carter would have no chance to talk privately with Tasha, and her refusal to let him help was still bothering him. He'd had enough of evasions. Of not being trusted.

So why not clear the air now? Why not push and see what that got him?

"My offer on the cabinets is still open," he said casually.

She shot him an irritated glance. "Thanks, but I'll figure something out. Like I said."

"Will you? Or will you spin your wheels with lawyers,

hunts for new cabinetmakers, and trying to appease frustrated clients who have no kitchen?"

"That's my problem," she snapped.

"If you'd let me call Langston, it might be a solved problem."

"Yes, by dragging even more people into my situation. Thank you, but N-O, no, thank you."

"Is it the beholden thing again?"

"Yes," she answered, far too quickly. She was lying. Hell if he would take that anymore.

Carter pulled into a grocery store parking lot and parked. "Don't lie to me," he ordered.

"Don't butt in."

She hadn't denied she was lying, and that stung. He kept his gaze locked on her stubborn face. "I'm trying to help you, Tasha, and I don't believe it about the beholden thing. Not this time. You're not beholden to anyone for what you pay for."

"You are when you couldn't get it without their help."

A hint of fear shadowed her eyes. He was onto something.

"Bullshit," he said. "You and I are involved. That means we help each other. At least in my corner of the universe. I help you, you help me, and it evens out in the long run."

"This isn't the long run," she insisted. "This is right now."

"And right now, you're turning down my help. Why? Is it pride? Or something else?"

The fear that flashed over her face was his answer. Her lips trembled, but her face otherwise went blank. "No one's forcing you to stick around. If I'm so unsatisfactory—"

"You're not," he cried. "You're terrific. You're brave and kind and strong and sexy, and I wish you would just trust me."

"I'm telling you what I can," she responded, her voice flat and her expression now completely shuttered. "Whether it's enough is up to you."

So much for pushing. She'd thrown up even harder barriers.

He was a jackass, had let his impatience push him into a mistake. Now he had even more ground to make up.

Looking directly at her, he didn't try to hide his feelings. "You," he said quietly, "just you, are more than enough for me."

Her lips trembled again, and she pressed them together. Unshed tears glistened in her eyes in the moment before she shut them. "I don't—I don't deserve you, Carter. And someday, when you figure that out . . ."

"More bullshit," he said gently, and he risked laying his hand over hers on her knee. When she gripped his hand, tension he hadn't been aware of flooded out of his neck. He drew her into his arms. Tasha pressed her face into the hollow between his neck and shoulder.

"I'm sorry I pushed," he said with his lips against her hair. "I meant what I said. You're enough. Just you."

At least for now, but at some point, she would have to trust him. If she couldn't or wouldn't, the relationship couldn't survive. But he could give her time.

She made a choked sound into his collar, and he tightened his hold as best he could with the console between them. "Nothing you could tell me would change my mind," he added. Tipping her chin up, he gazed into her damp eyes. "Nothing, Natasha. I mean that."

"Okay," she choked. She tugged free and grabbed a tissue out of the glove compartment. "Thank you for the offer of help, but I'll work this out."

He nodded acceptance and started the car. When they were on the road again, she laid her hand on his knee, the first time she'd reached out to him all day. He entwined their fingers and hoped the gesture was a good omen.

They were nearly back to the Collegium when Tasha's phone let out that brass and drum thing that heralded her brother. Her face lit up, and she grabbed the phone from her purse.

"Hey, Beanpole," she said. "What? You're where? Hang on." She turned to Carter. "Nate's here. He's at the Collegium. I

266

knew he was coming, but I wasn't sure exactly when. You don't care if he joins us for dinner, do you?"

"The more, the merrier." Carter meant it, but he hid a trace of foreboding. Would Tasha trust him not to push her again? Or would she use her brother as a barrier between them?

∼

"I'M SO glad to have you here," Tasha told Nate. They'd eaten in the dining hall and were heading back to her guest unit. Will and Carter, probably giving them space, lagged behind. She knew she wasn't out of Carter's sight, though. She could almost feel his attention on her.

"So what's with you and Lockwood?" Nate asked quietly. Despite the keenness of mage senses, the two behind them wouldn't overhear.

Tasha matched his tone. "I guess you could say we're involved."

"It's not making you happy."

Tasha shrugged.

Nate turned to their companions. "I want to talk to Tasha. Give us a half hour or so."

Carter's expression hardened. "I'm responsible for her. I stay with her."

"Yeah, yeah. I know the navy has its merits, and no offense to deputy reeves either, but I'm an Army Ranger with magic. Do you want to tell me you can protect her better than I can?"

Great. Macho posturing. Tasha rolled her eyes.

Carter looked at her with a question in his eyes. When she gave a slight nod, he said, "Okay, Murdock, but I'm waiting down the hall. You may be a serious badass, but I'm responsible for Tasha's safety."

"Granted," Nate said.

Will offered, "I'll wait with you."

They all rode up in the elevator together. Will and Carter

stopped in the hall between the elevator and Tasha's door. Tasha and Nate went inside together.

"You want coffee?" Tasha asked, heading into the kitchen.

"Sure." Nate sat in one of the two armchairs. "Define 'involved,' Short Stuff."

She stuck her head out to give him her *Seriously?* look. "We're not in high school, Nate. I'm sure you can figure it out."

Tasha dumped the old coffee and rinsed the pot.

He came as far as the doorway and leaned on the frame. He had blue eyes like hers and hair the same auburn as hers but worn longer, brushing his collar. His face, so like hers except with a masculine cast, was twisted in a frown. "You're sleeping with him. Your business and all that, but why are you doing it if you're not happy about it?"

Spooning coffee into a fresh filter, she weighed how much to say. This was Nate, who knew her better than anybody. With him, there was a lot she didn't have to say.

"You know what home was like, Nate. How people looked down on me." She ran water into the pot and poured it into the reservoir. "What they said."

"All of it was bullshit, and a lot of it was outright lies."

"Lies that were believed," she reminded him. "And it's not like I was completely innocent. I made bad choices. We both know it. Carter comes from a leading family in his town. He's a golden boy, a hometown hero type. Like you."

Nate shot her a wry look. "I was never a golden boy, and you know it."

"What I know is that everyone contrasted me with you. I heard a lot about how great you were. How responsible, how smart, and how I should try to be more like you."

"From Mom and Dad, and you know what I think about that. As for the rest of the town, I was tolerated because I could throw and hit a ball."

"And drive a nail. At least you were allowed to work construction." Which paid way better than the home furnishings store. "But you were the only reason anyone accepted them."

Their parents had resented both of them, first as the cause of their shotgun wedding, and then because the twins had possessed more powerful magic than their parents. If not for Gran, they wouldn't have gotten training at a Collegium satellite class.

Nate shook his head. "Mom and Dad could have a better life if they worked at it, the way we have. You know that, and you're too smart to swallow their crap."

Eyeing her closely, he added, "We've had this conversation too many times to go over it again, so let's bottom-line it. You like Lockwood enough to sleep with him, so why isn't that making you happy?"

"Because it can't last," she said simply, taking four mugs from the cabinet. "Sooner or later, he's going to find out what everyone in Watkins Landing thinks about me and what I was like growing up."

Nate opened his mouth, but she rushed to forestall him. "I know what you're going to say, so save it. Carter's dad runs a family construction firm and served several years as mayor of the town. His mom is in Congress. The US Congress. The one in DC. Do you honestly think a family like that is going to want to be linked with the wild child of Watkins Landing?"

"I think if they care what you did in high school, they're idiots. And I know you won't hear that because you refuse to. As usual." Scowling, he demanded, "Are you telling me this thing between you and him is doomed because of crap most people have long since forgotten about?"

"Not everybody, Nate. The mud stuck, even if you don't want to hear it."

Nate studied her. "So he doesn't know."

"No, and when he finds out . . . " Tasha shrugged.

"Then why get involved in the first place?"

Because of the pain in his eyes. But she would sound sappy

admitting that. Instead, she sighed. "This has been building a long time. Once we started spending time together, it just kind of happened."

"Uh-huh." He shook his head. "You really like this guy. If you didn't, you wouldn't care what he'd think."

"Yeah. But that's not likely to matter in the long run."

"He looks at you like you're all he cares about."

Tasha flinched. "I'm sure that's an overstatement." But Nate was a keen observer. He might be right, and if he was, the disillusionment waiting for Carter would be horrible.

The longer she let this relationship go on, the worse the end would be for him too. She'd been so concerned about protecting herself, so sure he would get tired of her and bail, that she hadn't realized until the other day that the end would also be painful for him.

"At least I know why I kept getting the urge to call you," Nate said. "Chased by ghouls, upset with Lockwood. First I wasn't in a position to call, and then I was in transit. I could feel that you were okay, but still, I wish I'd taken the time."

"You couldn't have done anything," Tasha said.

"I could've been here." He drew her into his arms.

"Yeah." Tasha leaned on him gratefully. In all their lives, Nate's presence had never failed to comfort her. He was a bulwark against any problem.

"Do you think Lockwood is shallow?" Nate's voice rumbled in his chest.

"Of course not."

"Then maybe you should try trusting the guy. I mean, he's navy and all that, but everybody's entitled to one mistake. A mistake you shared, y'know."

Tasha rested her forehead on his shoulder. "I can't, Nate. I just can't."

She could almost feel him thinking. On the counter the coffeemaker burbled, the only sound in the room.

At last, he said, "Your choice, Tasha. Can we let Lockwood and Davis in now?"

"Okay. I know how they take their coffee, so I'll fix it. But Nate—one more thing."

"What's that?"

"When this goes south . . ."

"I'll be here," he assured her, and Tasha nodded her thanks. She'd worried so much about how she would cope that she hadn't thought about what a breakup would do to Carter. He would have a fit if she tried to end things before they solved her ghoul problem.

Once that was done, though, the kindest thing she could do was set him free.

CHAPTER TWENTY-FOUR

IF SOMEONE HAD TOLD CARTER A WOMAN COULD MAKE PASSIONATE love to him in the shower and then be uneasy and distant ten minutes later, he wouldn't have believed it. But that was what Tasha had done. Now, while he shaved, she was bustling around the kitchen in gym shorts and a T-shirt, fixing breakfast.

And not talking.

If he tried to tear down that aggravating, invisible barrier of hers, he could lose her.

Maybe he was going to lose her anyway.

The idea burned, but maybe it was time to face it. He was running out of things to try.

Unplugging his razor, he ran his free hand over his face to check the shave. Good enough. His hair was neat enough too.

His phone chimed with the theme from *Steel Magnolias,* his message tone for his mom. He swiped the screen.

Coming your way, she'd written. *Event in Charleston in 2 wks. Want to bring mystery woman 2 lunch w/me and event organizer? Newsletter in your inbox now. Love you!*

Did he want to bring Tasha? Absolutely.

Did he think she would come? No, and maybe that said a lot.

He stared down the screen. Was it possible Tasha's uneasiness over having Langston make her cabinets was due to his dad's involvement? If so, how would she react to his mom?

His parents were both great people. There was no reason anyone would want to avoid them.

Unless Tasha's reason had to do with the things she wouldn't tell him. A sick feeling clamped around his gut. He might not be a precog, but he had pretty good hunches, and this one was telling him, *right on.*

He couldn't be with a woman who wouldn't meet his folks. Not just his parents but his sister and her family. His terrific nieces and nephew. He needed someone who could care about them too.

Could Tasha?

Maybe it was time to find out. Not pushing had achieved exactly zero. He'd meant to give it more time, but maybe that was a mistake. She was more distant this morning than she'd been yesterday.

Pocketing the phone, he walked into the dining area. Tasha sat at the table with her laptop open. She'd put coffee and a bagel with smoked salmon by his computer. He took his seat and thanked her.

"No problem," she replied, focused on her screen.

He opened his email and looked for his mom's newsletter. It was the second message, no surprise since he didn't have a lot of email buddies. He clicked on it. The details she'd left out of her text were all there.

He glanced across the table at Tasha. Once you put something to the test, you had to live with the results. Whether you liked them or not. But if you didn't try, you never knew what you had on your hands.

So be it.

He pasted on his best approximation of a happy smile. "Tasha?"

"Yes?"

He waited until she looked at him. "My mom's coming to Charleston. Meeting with the head of a local literacy foundation." He turned his laptop so she could see the newsletter.

Her gaze dropped to it, and she paled.

"You okay?" he asked. The sick feeling was churning now.

"Sure. Fine." But her voice sounded strained.

"Anyway, Mom wants us to come up and have lunch with her and this Priscilla Elgin, the event organizer. Think we can make that work?"

"I can't—I can't be gone for the whole day. You know how much ground I have to make up." Now she looked not only pale but scared.

"I do, but the event's not for another month. You have a great staff—"

"I can't dump my job on them," she protested.

Despite the fear now pushing into his throat, he somehow kept his voice even. "You know as well as I do that they can manage for a day. I want you to come with me." Leaning forward, he added, "I want you to meet my mom, Tasha."

"I—this is not—we don't have a meet-the-family kind of relationship."

She might as well have slapped him. Quietly, he said, "We agreed we weren't having a fling."

"And we're not, but we—I don't feel that way about you, Carter. I'm sorry, I—I just don't. It's not in the cards for us."

Now she had the panicked look of a trapped animal. He was almost sure, only almost, that she was lying. He had one more card to play, a humiliating one if it didn't get through to her. But she was worth the risk.

"I'm sorry to hear that," he told her, "because I'm in love with you."

～

For the space of a heartbeat, joy roared through Tasha's veins. Then reality crashed in. He wouldn't love her if he knew everything. Then that scornful look she knew so well from back home would cross his face, and she would have no pride left at all.

Priscilla Elgin, née Priscilla Anne-Elizabeth Pomeroy, head of the mean girls at Tasha's high school, would take one look at Tasha and tell Carter and his mother everything. While Tasha sat there and watched his feelings for her die.

No. Walking naked through the Arctic would be easier than that.

Looking into his eyes and lying about this was a sin. But she had to do it for both their sakes. "Carter, I—That's very flattering, and I—"

"It's not flattery if it's true," he said quietly, and that horrible pain was back in his eyes.

How could he love her when she'd inflicted that on him? It was all her fault for having started this in the first place. She should've resisted his pain that night in the parking lot, as she had to resist it now.

"I'm sorry," she choked. "I don't love you."

As she said the words, she knew they were a lie. She did love him. She always would. Maybe she always had.

But loving him meant doing what was best for him, and that was sending him away. How would he feel if he knew he'd fallen in love with such a disaster of a woman?

He looked at her for a long moment, his gaze probing. Gradually, his expression closed over. "Maybe you don't," he said, "and maybe you just don't have the courage to fight for what you want. I guess we'll never know."

He pushed back from the table and stood. "I'll ask Deke to send a replacement. While we wait, I'll pack. I'll leave the Horus pendant on the dresser."

Tasha nodded. Carter picked up his laptop and headed into the bedroom.

Fighting a pain too deep for tears, Tasha put her face in her hands. Every breath seemed to shred part of her chest. This was the right thing, though. It was.

Someone pounded on the door. Familiar magic seeped into the room, and a familiar voice shouted, "Tasha!"

Nate. He must've sensed her distress, and this time, he was close enough to act on it. "I'll get it," she called to Carter.

"The fuck you will," he snapped, and he translocated to beat her.

"Damn it, Carter, it's Nate."

He threw her a furious look and opened the door. Nate bulled his way into the room. "What the fuck, Lockwood?"

"Stop it," Tasha cried, grabbing Nate's arm. "It's not his fault. Nate, listen to me."

Carter's jaw set, and Tasha repeated, "Listen to me."

Nate turned a narrow-eyed glance on her. Their eyes met, and comprehension bloomed in his. "Short Stuff, you didn't."

"I did," she whispered.

Nate's lips tightened. He shook his head. "Sorry, Lockwood."

"What just happened here?" Carter asked. "What was all that about?"

"It's private," Tasha said. Rocks blocked her throat, but she pushed words past them. "You don't have to wait around. Nate can stay with me until your replacement arrives."

"I'll grab my bag and wait outside," Carter replied, "but I'm staying there until I'm relieved."

Tasha and Nate waited in tense silence while Carter went into the bedroom for his gear. When he emerged, he walked straight to the door. He hesitated with his hand on the knob.

Turning to her, he said, "I know they'll catch the ghouls soon, and you'll be safe. Whatever happens after, I hope you'll be happy."

Tasha's throat closed. "You too," she managed.

Carter walked out. The quiet click of the door closing behind him might as well have been a dagger driven into her heart.

Nate took a breath, and she held up a hand. "Don't. Please. It's done. This was inevitable, and at least I have my pride."

"Ah, hell," he grumbled, holding out his arms. Tasha went straight into them, but this time, the bulwark failed.

She should never have given in to her longing for Carter. The stunned, devastated look on his face when she'd said she didn't love him was seared into her soul. He might eventually forgive her, but she wasn't at all sure she could ever forgive herself.

~

"Could you do me one favor?" Tasha asked Val, Carter's replacement for the day, as they drove toward Savannah. "Is that offer to use your guest room still open?"

"Sure. We can move you in when we get back."

"Great. Thank you. Staying in the guest unit with someone I really don't know would just be weird." Not to mention that staying there, in the bed she'd shared with Carter, would make the pain of missing him so much worse.

"I can see that," Val agreed, but she looked as though she were considering adding something.

"You can say whatever you're thinking," Tasha told her, watching the road ahead. "Nate's already been very free with his opinion."

"Just like his sister usually is," Val pointed out.

"Maybe. Sometimes."

"I don't have anything to say, Tasha, except that I'm so very sorry. The two of you seemed to really click."

"That's not the problem. He wanted me to meet his family. I can't, so I sent him away. And before you say anything, I've already heard it all from Nate."

Val shrugged. "When Deke called me, Griffin was pretty pissed at Carter. I'll call him and tell him to stand down."

"I wish he would." Tasha sighed. If she'd ever felt this tired, she couldn't remember when. "I appreciate everyone who has my back, but there's really nothing to be done."

"Except find these ghouls who're after you. Any ideas?"

"I'm thinking it has to be related to Hewlett Collier's brokerage deal. Geneva didn't have anything ghouls would want. But Hewlett's a self-made man. He made their money. Maybe he's making money for the ghouls. But I don't see how that ties to you."

"That's what Deke said. One of the rookies is a computer genius, so Deke had him hack the brokerage house server and get a list of Collier's clients. Deputies are checking them out."

"Legwork, I guess."

"Or phone work, in this case." Val patted Tasha's knee. "We'll get them. You just have to be patient until we do."

Tasha blew out a hard breath. "I hope it's soon. I really need to get back to my actual life." At least rebuilding the warehouse and office space would keep her too busy to think about Carter Lockwood.

Eventually.

"Close the door," Deke said as Carter stepped into the office. Deke gestured to the chair in front of his desk.

When Carter was seated, the shire reeve said, "What happened?"

"We got involved," Carter answered, the words rough in his throat. "It went south. I can't be as effective as I need to be."

"You've done a good job so far."

"Thanks." He would have preferred to keep on doing it, but maybe it was better to cut his losses. "Who's replacing me?"

"For today, Val Dare. Since you know Tasha, I wanted your input. For the long run, who would you suggest?"

"Sybil Harrison or Wes Hardin." Harrison had been Valeria Dare's chief deputy and had stayed on under Deke. She was young but tough, with a lot of experience. Hardin was a veteran with a no-nonsense attitude and a lot of experience against the ghouls.

Deke drummed his fingers on his desk.

"The 'long run' can't be very long, Deke. This is starting to wear on Tasha."

"We're doing our best. We have an alert out for Hewlett and Geneva Collier, and mages scry for them regularly. So far, no luck."

They were probably inside a shielded nest, hidden from scrying.

Carter said, "Collier had to meet with his ghoul client at some point. If we could scry that, follow the ghoul back to its nest, we might be able to solve this thing."

"That's tough, as you know, but worth doing. I have Althea Park, one of our best at scrying, looking along with two others. If she spots Collier with a ghoul, she'll follow up."

"I guess I'm going back to the Wayfarer patrol," Carter said. Saying it felt like he was abandoning Tasha, but she'd already abandoned him. Hanging around was pointless.

"I need you down there. No one's better than Dixie at enforcement, but she despises paperwork even more than I do."

"And look where you ended up," Carter responded.

"Yeah, but I have minions to do the paperwork. It helps. And speaking of paperwork, we recovered your boat." Deke pulled a folder out of the pile on his desk.

"That's great." Finally, a bright spot in the day. "How badly was she damaged?"

"There's a big, charred hole in the left side, or whatever you navy people call the left. Looks like she took on water through that hole and sank. The good thing is that the water put out the fire." Deke slid the folder to Carter. "Let us know where you want it towed. Then get an estimate on repairs and bring it in. You're eligible for reimbursement."

Carter accepted the file. "There was some nice woodwork in the cabin. It'll probably take magic to fix that up. Good thing I've got that."

"Yep. Anything else I need to know about Ms. Murdock's situation?"

"No, but I'd like to be kept posted."

Deke kept his face expressionless. "We can do that."

"Any word on my proposal for non-magical self-defense lessons and counseling for kids?"

"I was going to wait to share that." Deke drew out another folder. "The Council turned it down. Too expensive when we're already short on personnel, and they think the legal liability if something goes wrong could be huge."

"I see. Thanks for trying, Deke." He hadn't expected success, but he'd put together a solid proposal.

"I agree with you, you know, but the decision is above both our pay grades."

"Right." But the kids were left out in the cold again. Great. Just great.

Deke studied him for a long moment. "You look like you've been through the mill. Take the rest of today off. You can resume command in Wayfarer tomorrow. Dixie won't mind subbing for one more day."

A day off would give him too much time to think. He should take it anyway, though. Get his head back in the game before he stepped into a command position again.

He thanked his boss and walked out.

Val Dare was one of the best deputy reeves. She could take care of Tasha. But if a threat arose, could she keep Tasha from charging toward it?

Not your problem anymore.

It wasn't, and that was obviously the way Tasha wanted it.

Val knew what she was doing. He would have to trust her to handle things.

Meanwhile, he would go sit on his dock, let the fish chase a hook-free lure, and find some way to stop thinking about what was happening with Tasha.

CHAPTER TWENTY-FIVE

Despite the problem with cabinets, the Dortons' house was coming together nicely. Tasha stood in the kitchen with her construction manager. "You've all done a great job, Randy."

She looked around at the new light fixtures, the smooth wooden banister on the stairs, and the big, open kitchen with its island now in place. A family would be comfortable here. She loved this part of a job, when everything was coming together. Giving people a comfortable, attractive place to live.

She turned to share that with Carter . . . but he wasn't there. Solid, fiftyish Wes stood behind her, looking around the room.

Carter's absence pinched her heart, but she would eventually stop expecting him to be there.

She and Randy said their farewells, and Tasha followed Wes back to her truck. His open senses checked for ghouls, and he gave her an *all clear* nod. After she climbed in, he shut and warded the door.

Climbing in, he asked, "Where to?"

"I'm meeting Dr. Harper in town, over on Gloucester Street." She gave Wes the address, and he started the car.

Mulling cabinetmakers, Tasha drummed her fingers on her

knee. She'd told the Dortons she meant to fire Liston, and they hadn't objected. But she needed someone to replace him.

She looked over at Wes. "You don't happen to know any great cabinetmakers who have time on their hands, do you?"

"Sorry."

Okay, so now what? The other cabinetmakers she knew all did good, solid work, but she needed someone extraordinary for high-end clients like the Dortons.

Who had her old boss, Harley Whitaker, used? She'd been a carpenter at first and hadn't paid much attention to where the furniture came from. But later on, when she'd started the decorating side of the business, there'd been a Black guy with bad acne scars on his face and, as Harley'd put it without knowing such a thing was actually possible, magic in his hands.

Slater. That was it. Enoch Slater.

A quick web search turned up two Enoch Slaters and one E. Slater. Might as well start at the top.

"We're here," Wes said, parking by the curb. "I don't need to follow you around the house if you're with the doc, but I should be close. Tell me where you want me to be, and I'll wait there."

"Right. Thanks." She could make those calls after she and Stefan finished.

Wes checked the surroundings and came to let her out of the truck. Mel hadn't mentioned that the house had a porte-cochère, a fancy type of carport, on one side. Stefan's blue BMW sedan sat under it.

Stefan opened the front door and called, "Hey, come in."

He held the door wide as they entered. When he closed it behind them, Wes warded it.

Tasha asked, "Stefan, is there somewhere Wes can wait while we wander the house?"

"Ground floor is better," Wes put in, "just in case."

"Sure. The kitchen's straight back. There are a couple of folding chairs and a table back there. We put some bottles of water in the refrigerator. It's antiquated but works okay. Help yourself."

Wes thanked him and headed off.

Stefan offered Tasha a piece of paper. "Mel's very organized. She made a list."

"Great. Saves time." Tasha pulled out a pen. "Let's get started."

As they walked through the house, Mel's warning that it needed a lot of work came to mind.

"It's solid," Tasha told Stefan. "The floors are cypress hardwood and in pretty decent shape. A couple of the bottom sashes on the living room windows seem to have some water damage, but everything else looks good. I'm guessing it passed inspection."

"Yep. The owner replaced a couple of pipes in the basement and knocked some off the price because others need work. He'd inherited the place, and I think he wanted to unload it. He lives in Tulsa, so coming back here to tend to it would be a pain."

"Umhm. His loss."

They walked through the house, and Tasha could see it taking shape. Could envision it offering warmth and hominess and filled with love.

She wanted that, too, someday, so it would be best if she and Carter both moved on. No matter how much that hurt.

"Long day," Wes commented as he started the truck three hours later.

"Yep." After leaving Stefan, she'd met with a prospective interior design client, one of Julia's friends, and checked on a jobsite. "I'm sorry to make you so late for dinner."

He grinned. "Comes with the job." He pulled away from the curb and into the street.

Tasha looked over her list from the day. Most items had

check marks beside them. One very important one, however, did not. "Shoot. I never did call that cabinetmaker. I need to do that."

"Won't bother me." Wes swung off of Albany and onto Gloucester Street, heading for Glynn Avenue. The four-lane, limited-access road would take them north to Charles Taine Parkway and the Collegium faster than going through town.

Tasha tried the first Enoch Slater she'd found. The number was disconnected.

When she tried the second, she got voicemail. "Mr. Slater, this is Natasha Murdock. I used to work with Harley Whitaker, and I remember you supplied cabinetry for him on various jobs. I need some work done if you're available. If you're not the right Mr. Slater, I apologize. If you are, please call me back. Thanks." She rattled off the number.

"So much for that," she said.

"It's about dinnertime," Wes responded. "Some don't pick up during meals."

"There's that."

They were almost to Glynn. Up ahead lay the emptiness of Howard Coffin Park and the vacant lot across from it. Beyond lay the dark salt marshes and, in the distance, the lights of St. Simons Island.

Spring was coming, the days growing longer. A month from now, anyone who drove onto Glynn Avenue here at this time of day would see the wild, beautiful wetlands as well as the distant lights.

Bang! came from the rear of the truck. The vehicle shuddered.

"Blowout," Wes said, wrestling it back into its lane.

Bang! came from the other side of the back.

Wes set his jaw and glanced at her. He didn't have to say what they were both thinking. One blowout might happen by accident. Two, not likely.

Pulling off at the park entrance, he flung a magical shield

around the truck and stepped out, where he had room to draw his sword. "Stay in the truck," he said, shielding himself. "Call this in."

Much as she hated to leave him to fight alone, he was right. Tasha shielded herself and fished for her phone.

The shield around the truck winked out. Ghoul shields flared into being on both sides of the vehicle, and muddy yellow clashed with blue on the driver side. *Oh, shit.*

Tasha punched the passcode into her phone and hit the contacts. At her side, the window vaporized. She slammed a magically powered elbow strike toward the traitor's smug face and flung a bolt at him with her free hand. He dodged both strikes, grabbed her arm, and destroyed her shields. The next instant, silver magic flared around him. Pain roared up her arm and into her head, and everything went dark.

CARTER DROPPED his keys on his kitchen counter. It was good to be home. If the house felt too empty, well, he'd go sit on the dock. Bundle up, grab a beer, and watch the stars.

It wasn't like he had anything better to do. Laundry didn't count as better than anything, except maybe cleaning the bathroom.

His phone buzzed with the shire reeve's office tone. He pulled it out and swiped it. "Lockwood."

"Carter, it's Deke." The grim tone in his boss's voice made Carter's heart plummet.

"Hardin missed his check-in. Have you heard from him or Ms. Murdock today?"

"No. Deke, I can come in."

"Stay where you are until I know whether we need you. Do you know what her schedule was today?"

"No clue. At some point, she had a conference with Doc Harper in Brunswick, but I don't know when." Because he would have to be in her inner circle to know, and she'd kicked him out. And he'd let her. *Jackass.*

"I'll get back to you," Deke said. They disconnected.

Scowling, Carter paced the kitchen. If he'd been more stubborn, resisted more or argued her around, maybe. . . . But that wouldn't have made any difference. She was done with him.

That didn't mean he would abandon her, though. He pulled up the message app and sent a quick text to Jeremy, asking if he could talk.

A moment later, his phone rang.

"What's up, Carter?" Jeremy sounded good. The stress level at home must be down lately.

"You remember Tasha, right?"

"Sure. Me and Mila think she's really cool."

"That's great." How to put this so he didn't scare the kid? "Listen, Jaybird, Tasha was in Brunswick today. You didn't see her, did you?"

"No. I've been hanging at home since school."

"Right. The thing is, she isn't answering her phone, and we're getting concerned."

"Did something happen to her?" Jeremy sounded worried. "I could go look for her."

"No, you stay home and do your homework." If ghouls had her, that was the last thing Jeremy should walk into.

If only they knew where these ghouls' nest was, but they'd had no luck tracing it. Hadn't even narrowed down the area, damn it.

"Well, okay," Jeremy said. "But you help me a lot, Carter, and Tasha helped Mila. I can go look if you want."

"That's great, very generous. It's better if you don't for now, though."

"I could put the word out. Describe her and ask if anybody saw her or her truck."

"Just among the kids you know, right?"

"Sure. Just them." Scorn crept into his voice as he added,

"My dad never notices anything anyway."

"That would be great, Jeremy."

"I'll call you if I hear anything."

"Thanks very much."

They signed off. Carter laid his phone on the kitchen counter. Too worried to sit, he rose to pace the room.

It was all very well for Deke to tell him to stay put, but the woman he loved had been targeted by ghouls, and now the veteran deputy guarding her was late checking in.

In no set of facts imaginable did that bode well. None.

If he'd been with her, the result probably would've been the same. But at least he would be with her now. He should've been with her.

He had to do something. But what?

He had Nate Murdock's phone number. The guy probably didn't want to hear from him, but he would know what was going on.

It was worth a try.

Carter's phone buzzed with the office tone. He lunged for it. "Lockwood."

Val Dare said, "Wes Hardin phoned in. He and Tasha were ambushed on Gloucester Street, near Howard Coffin Park. He fought ghouls but was overwhelmed. He's got puncture wounds and venom sickness. When he came to, the passenger-side front window of her truck no longer existed, the passenger door was open, and Tasha was gone."

"Why the hell is he there to call in? Ghouls don't leave unconscious mages behind." Their supply of mageborn breeders was too small to waste a prospective one.

"He thinks they left him for dead."

Yeah, he would say that, wouldn't he? "Val, do you believe him?"

"I do. There's no taint of dishonesty in his words. He at least believes what he's saying." Val paused. Gently, she added, "Her phone and purse were all still in the truck."

Of course they were. Ghoul captives weren't allowed phones and had no need of money. His mind flashed to a ghoul breeder hut he'd helped liberate last fall, a ramshackle shed full of broken, frightened people who bore scars inside and out.

Oh, Tasha.

Carter closed his eyes and forced the image away. They had to stop that from happening to her. "What about her saber?"

"No sign of it. That could be good."

If she can get her hands on it. With ghouls, that was a huge *if.* "Is Wes coming in?"

"Deke sent a couple of deputies to pick him up. You're coming in too, fast as you can."

"You bet I am. And Val, ask Nate about the weird, kind of hoo-doo thing he and Tasha do. From being twins. Don't know if they've ever used it to get a directional fix, but it can't hurt to try."

"No, it can't. See you when you get here. Hurry."

TASHA HURT EVERYWHERE. As though she'd been zapped.

"We should have taken her to the nest," a woman's unhappy voice insisted. "It's dangerous to have her in our house."

"Then you and your fool husband should've been more careful with important papers," a guttural voice snapped back.

"The mages have looked here," a man's Scottish brogue said. He must be Ross Graham, the Scottish traitor mage. "They won't look again. They would never think you would come back here."

A sour-ammonia taste coated Tasha's tongue, and she felt queasy. And completely drained. *Venom sickness,* she thought. *Great.*

Memory came flooding back, and with it came fear. Poor Wes. He'd died for her, and here she was anyway.

Tasha swallowed, trying to think. Her friends would miss

her eventually, would scry for her, and if the house wasn't shielded, they could . . .

Oh, crap. It wouldn't make any difference whether the house was shielded against scrying. The eye of Horus pendant she wore, meant to keep the enemy from finding her, would now conceal her from her friends. If they scried for her, they would come up empty. Only if they scried this house, this room, and happened to see her saber would they know where she was.

Shit, with a triple-fuckety damn thrown in.

Trying to move her arms and legs failed utterly. As she roused, she realized restraints confined her upper arms and ankles.

Cold fear rippled down her back. How many was she up against?

She opened her eyes a slit. She lay near a doorway, looking out into a carpeted room furnished with upholstered chairs and sofa and a huge TV. Looked like somebody's man cave. Geneva Collier stood by the sofa, looking both nervous and annoyed.

Oh, shit. Shit with a triple fuckety fuck.

"Zarig will do her here," another ghoul, a female, rasped. "As a lesson to you."

"Do her?" As in me?

Terror clawed into Tasha's throat. She closed her eyes and breathed deeply to fight it. If there were only two ghouls and the sniveling Geneva, she could hold them off long enough to grab her sword. Bladed weapons conducted magic best, but anything could become a weapon.

Maybe she could loosen her bonds magically without being noticed. She tried, but nothing happened. No power answered her call.

How could that be? The little fight she'd had time to put up had barely tapped her magic. She should be able . . . Except the ghouls' mage ally could drain power, at least from wards. Had he done that to her?

The male ghoul grumbled, "I could soften her up for Zarig. Give her taste of what's coming."

No. Oh, fuck, no. If she could recharge, she might—

Silver mage power banged her head against the floor. "The bitch is awake," the Scottish man's voice announced. "Pay attention. Why is she not collared?"

"We had no collar with us, fool mage," the female ground out.

"We didn't need one to capture her, now did we? There's one here, however," he said with exaggerated patience. "In the gear by the door."

The female disappeared from view. Footsteps went up the stairs.

Overhead, cabinets slammed. Heavy footsteps clomped.

The mage leaned over Tasha. "Try to recharge again, bitch, and I'll let Horux over there play with you. He's good at making breeders more cooperative."

Was that disgust in his eyes? No, she had to be imagining it.

The female strutted back into view. She held a metal collar with a long tongue jutting down near the clasp. Stefan had described those collars after his captivity. The tongue kept the collar from turning to bring the clasp in front.

If they put that thing on her, she couldn't recharge. She was as good as dead. Tasha shifted, trying to kick, and the female kicked her in the stomach, knocking the wind out of her.

Gasping for air, Tasha could do nothing. The female grabbed her hair, yanked her head up, and slipped the collar on. It clicked into place. The cold metal bit into her neck where she lay on it.

"Problem solved," the female said.

"Any word on Zarig?" The mage sounded bored.

The bastard. She wouldn't be in this fix if not for him.

"Due in an hour, maybe a little more," the male ghoul responded. He leered down at Tasha. "Then we teach this cow her place."

"Pull her back," the mage ordered, "so we can shut the door."

He reached up to flick the lights off. The only light now came from the man cave. They were going to shut her in here. Wherever here was.

The female sank her claws into Tasha's shoulder. Tasha gasped at the blinding pain. As the female dragged her backwards, she fought the agony in her shoulder and caught a view of the walls. Walls lined with wine cabinets. Racks. A wine cellar.

She shot a panicked look around. The room wasn't more than four feet wide and five deep. Terror sizzled in her bones. "Don't," she gasped.

She thrashed against her bonds. "Don't, please don't." Wrong thing to say to ghouls, but the words roared out of her soul. "Please, no. I'll do anything. Please."

"Yeah, you will." Grinning, the female slapped her.

Tasha's head jerked sideways, and her ears rang. "Please," she whispered.

The female ghoul stepped over her, heading out.

Chuckling, the mage knelt beside her. His finger brushed her cheekbone. It felt weird, but she couldn't think through the terror strangling her.

"You once told me, 'Fuck you.' I told you that could be arranged," he said. "I look forward to it." He stepped out and shut the door.

The room was utterly dark.

Tasha gasped. She couldn't see anything, but she could feel the walls pressing in. They were a cold, crushing weight on her chest. She couldn't breathe.

Her teeth chattered, and she shivered, fighting a scream. Carter had gotten her through last time. If she could summon his image, the memories . . .

But the fear and the venom and the darkness blocked out everything. Cold and terrified, Tasha shuddered on the floor.

CHAPTER TWENTY-SIX

CARTER BLASTED UP GLYNN, HIS CAR SCREENED TO AVOID SPEEDING tickets. He was almost to Howard Coffin Park. Tempting as it was to pull off and check the crime scene himself, he was needed at the Collegium.

His phone rang. Carter glanced at in-dash screen, which read, "Jaybird."

Could the kid have found something already?

Carter pushed the steering wheel button to engage the phone. "Yeah, Jaybird?"

"I might have something. This kid Leon, little guy who lives over by Howard Coffin Park, was near the park. He's a Mundane, and it was dark, so he didn't see real good. But he thought he saw a couple of guys and two women putting a woman in the trunk of a car. There was a blue pickup truck beside them that had a sign on the door. He couldn't read the sign until they pulled out, but then he saw it was for Murdock Custom Builders."

Carter's pulse kicked. He made himself wait as Jeremy continued, "He said one woman and one of the guys looked weird. Not the woman in the trunk."

Carter's heart leaped. He bit down on wild hope. "Weird like ghouls?"

"It sounded sorta like, but him being a Mundane, he wouldn't know what to look for."

"Sure. Did he see the hair color of the woman in the trunk?"

"He saw it was short. It scared him, so he ran home. By the time he got up the nerve to tell his mom, there was nobody at the park."

Shit. That delay had cost Tasha precious time. "How long did he wait?"

"Maybe an hour. He's not supposed to be out after dark, but he sometimes sneaks over to his friend's house to swap comic books."

Comic books. Didn't seem like that was worth breaking the rules for, but these days, neither did the once-tempting idea of going joyriding with beer.

"Did he get any details on the car?"

"He saw it drive away. He thinks it had four doors. It was red, and from what he said about the hood logo, a Mercedes."

Hot damn. The deputy reeves could work with that. "That's a great lead, Jeremy. Thanks."

"Hey, I'm glad I could do something. Leon said there was a guy on the ground beside the truck."

That would be Wes, who was getting treatment now. "Thanks. Your homework done?"

"Mostly. Then I stopped and made phone calls. But I'm gettin' to it."

"Fair enough." The kid was good at speaking up for himself. It was really too bad his dad spent so much time in a drunken stupor and couldn't appreciate his boy.

"You gonna get her back, Carter?"

"I am." And the ones who took her were never going to trouble anyone again.

Carter and Jeremy signed off. Carter called Deke's direct line.

"Jones," the shire reeve said.

"Lockwood. I just got a tip." He explained what Jeremy's friend had seen. "Can we find out whether Geneva or Hewlett Collier drives a red Mercedes?"

"Hang on."

Carter turned onto Charles Taine Parkway. The shops and apartment complexes zipped by in a blur he scarcely noticed. Finally, after what seemed an excruciatingly long time but actually was only a few minutes, he took the turnoff to the Collegium. He was almost there. What was taking so—

"Lockwood, you there?" came over his radio.

"Yeah, boss."

"Geneva Collier drives a red Mercedes sedan. I have deputies scrying the Collier house now."

"I can turn around, head there, and keep an eye out until you arrive."

"Deputies are scrying," Deke repeated. "We need you here, so come on in. Gear up and meet us in the conference room."

"Roger." Though standing back and waiting went seriously against the grain.

"One more thing, Lockwood. You're involved with the hostage, so you do nothing without my go. Do you copy that?"

He did, and it sucked majorly. But it also made sense. "I copy," Carter said.

"Good. What's your ETA?"

"I see the gates ahead, so three minutes to get to the building, one to grab my gear and come to the conference room."

"See you there."

WHEN CARTER RUSHED into the conference room, he found it full of deputy reeves. Deke stood on the dais at the front, against the wall. At the edge of the dais, deputy Althea Park stood before a large, silver scrying bowl set on a table.

In the depths of a three-foot-diameter crystal magically suspended over the bowl, the Collier house appeared. A red car sat in the driveway along with a black, boxy SUV.

Deke acknowledged Carter's arrival with a nod.

Nate Murdock, seated in the back of the room by Val Dare, flicked a dismissive glance at Carter. He worked his way over to them. Along the way, he passed GiGi, Roland, Josh, Darren Hale, tall, dark-haired longbowman Brody Hamilton, Griff Dare, and blonde, curvy Sybil Harrison, the chief deputy, in the crowd of about thirty deputies.

Kneeling by Val, he set his sword harness, helmet, and gloves on the floor. He'd already shrugged into the torso protection, a waist-length vest with wide protective flaps that hung down from the waist in front and the back. Now he strapped on the thigh and shin guards. Adjusting the sword harness over the vest would take time. He could do that on the way.

"Lockwood," Deke said, "You've been to this house. Anything about the site we should know?"

"No. I've also been inside the house. I can translocate in if need be." Translocation required visualizing a destination.

"Roger." Deke gave him a look that said he'd better not do that on his own initiative. "Deputy Park has also been able to break their screens and scry inside the house. She'll give us visuals for translocation while I talk. Park, go ahead."

The slender, Korean woman nodded, her eyes on the crystal above the bowl. The scene shifted to the Colliers' living room.

Deke said, "We'll seal off the street on both ends with deputies dressed as utility work crews." He used a pointer to indicate the placements.

Sybil Harrison asked, "Why would they take her there when they know we're on to them? The mage, at least, has to know we'll be monitoring the place."

Deke shrugged. "Maybe the ghouls figure we've already looked there. They may have overruled the mage if they have some reason for using that house. It might not be a logical reason by our standards, but they don't think the way we do."

Roland asked, "What about the neighbors?"

"We're not evacuating the neighbors. If we tell them we're US government, one of them is likely to call the Feds to confirm, which will draw those Feds, who are the last thing we need. Squads on either side of the house will erect magic screens to keep the noise and any light show contained." Again, he used the pointer.

"There are two ghouls, plus two traitor mages, Geneva Collier and this Ross Graham, inside," Deke said. "Unfortunately, we haven't been able to find Ms. Murdock."

"Oh, hell," Val muttered.

"The eye of Horus," Carter breathed.

Deke looked at them. "Do you have something to share?"

Val replied, "Tasha is wearing a pendant that defeats scrying. As long as she does, we won't be able to find her that way."

Dismay rippled through the room.

"What about a magical probe when we get close enough?" Deke asked.

"That would work," Val confirmed. "Or if we scry the location and see anything of hers, that could be a clue.

Carter asked, "Did anyone scrying the house see ghouls or that mage walk as though they were carrying something? Something that wasn't visible?"

"Yes," Park answered. "Stand by."

The images in the crystal stopped showing the house. Shifting back in time, she presented a view of the driveway. Geneva Collier and Ross Graham climbed out of her car. The SUV pulled in behind them, and two ghouls, male and female, emerged.

Collier popped her trunk. The mage reached in and lifted out something invisible. Whatever his burden, his arms had the configuration for carrying a person.

Tasha. Carter shared an angry glance with Val. That Scottish sonofabitch had lived much too long.

On Val's other side, Nate Murdock's face went expressionless. Except for his eyes. They radiated determination to murder.

An Army Ranger who had magical powers wanted the bastard's ass. Everyone else might as well step to the rear. That fucker wasn't going to live out the day.

"The bigger problem," Deke continued, "is that this is not our kind of operation. We go into nests in force, destroy them and the ghouls who inhabit them, and free captives. Even last winter, when we rescued the hostages on Mystery Island, we knew where the hostages were and had a way to get reinforcements on the island specifically to rescue them. What we face here, however, is like a Mundane hostage rescue situation. We don't know where the ghouls have Ms. Murdock, assuming she's here. If anyone shields that property, we have no stealthy way in, and in the time we would need to force entry, the ghouls could kill her."

He looked around the room. "Any questions before I tell you the plan?"

Nate raised his hand. "If I can get inside the house, I can get a directional fix on Tasha. I have to be within twenty or thirty yards of her for that to work, though."

"Noted," Deke responded. "If the property isn't shielded, one squad will sneak in the front, one in the back. They'll fan out, magically probing for Ms. Murdock. Whoever finds her will translocate to wherever she is, grab her, and translocate out immediately."

Park had gone back to showing rooms of the house. One, dark at the moment, was a wine cellar. Carter nudged Val and whispered, "Perfect place to stow a prisoner."

Nate's eyes narrowed. His jaw set, and a hunch pinged in Carter's head.

If Carter got the chance to go in, that room was his target.

He hoped they hadn't put Tasha in there, though. If they had, her claustrophobia would've kicked in. She would be terrified.

"If the property is shielded, that's tougher. We open negotiations." Deke's stern gaze swept the room. "We all want these fuckers, but if we have to let them walk to save one of our own, they walk. Is that clear?"

Half-hearted yeses drifted up from the watchers.

Deke put his hands on his hips. "Is that clear?" he repeated, his tone harsher.

"Yes, shire reeve," came back to him in a chorus.

"Any questions about the plan?"

Everyone shook their heads.

"We're taking helos for the speed. If Ms. Murdock is at the Colliers' house, they could move her at any time. Lockwood, Murdock, you ride with me. I'll hand out assignments on the way. Move out, everyone."

Chairs scraped as people stood. Mages streamed toward the door.

Carter turned to Nate. "How is she?"

Nate hesitated. "You're not with her, so it's not your concern." He started to brush by Carter.

Carter moved into his path. "I love your sister. No matter how she feels about me, I'm going to see her safe. So how is she?"

Nate studied him with unreadable eyes. Finally, he gave Carter an abrupt nod. "I'm getting nothing. I think she may be unconscious. Before that—" He shook his head. Heavily, he finished, "she was terrified."

CHAPTER TWENTY-SEVEN

Everything was so dark. Where were the lights?

Tasha blinked, trying to reach for a light, and then she remembered. She was trapped in a wine cellar. A prisoner of the ghouls.

Her heart thudded. Her teeth chattered, and cold rolled up her legs. The ammonia taste of venom and the nausea from venom poisoning made it all worse.

There was no Carter to hold the fear at bay this time. No Carter, and one of the last things she'd said to him had hurt him. "I didn't mean it," she whispered through her chattering teeth.

You're strong, he'd once said to her.

If only. But she had to think. Find some way out of this.

There was no way out.

Her teeth started to chatter again. She ground them together. There had to be something she could do.

She must've passed out before, from hyperventilating. She hadn't had a chance to prepare for being locked in, not that there was much she could do, but the shock had made the panic worse.

How long had she been out? How much time did she have?

Despite the shivering and hyperventilating, she did feel slightly stronger. Her power must've recharged a little. But how was that possible when she wore this collar?

The mage had threatened her if she tried to recharge. But ghouls couldn't sense that unless they were close. Most mages had to be fairly close too. Were Geneva and Ross Graham too far away?

Shivering, she reached out carefully with her power. When it answered her call, her heart leaped. The collar was defective. If she could recharge enough, she could get rid of it and the restraints.

She let the power seep a little farther out. Behind and above her, there was plant energy. The back of this place must be an exterior wall.

A wall that was very, very close. The weight pressed down on her chest again. Cold inched over her feet.

Tasha forced herself to take a slow, deep breath. *Recharge. Have to recharge.*

She closed her eyes, trying for self-generated darkness, and envisioned plants. Sunshine was the easiest source of a recharge, but she'd been grabbed at night. Unless she'd been here a very long time, there would be no sun. Closer to the floor than the plants, earthworms and tiny creatures lived in the earth. Drawing from them could kill them, so she carefully drew life energy, a little at a time, from the plants.

Strengthened by it, she reached farther in that direction. Found grass and trees. Birds. Squirrels and chipmunks.

The power flowed into her veins, warming and soothing. A recharge couldn't cure venom poisoning, but it lessened the effects.

She wasn't back to full strength, but she might not have time for that. Lying still, she strained to listen, to not think of the darkness around her or the walls closing in.

Voices came from upstairs. The floor muffled them, but mage senses were keener than Mundane ones. Straining, she caught the conversation. Talking about future raids. Investments. Something about all the way from Jasper. Sounded like a town.

Could the nest be in a place called Jasper?

Later for that. Focus.

Nothing about when the other ghouls were expected. That could be anytime, so there wasn't a minute to waste. Her heart pounded, and the small room pressed in on her. She had to hold the terror back for a few seconds. Just a few seconds to work on her restraints.

Envisioning one side of one of the handcuffs she wore dissolving, Tasha fed a minuscule amount of magic into them. Then more, and more.

Suddenly, the tension was gone. She slid her hand out.

The same technique worked on her zip-tied ankles and the collar. As she recharged again, the room pressed in. Tasha swallowed hard. *Pretend it's a big space, just a dark one. Big. Dark. Very big.*

Still listening, she groped until she found the door. In the house there'd been two ghouls, the traitor mage who was so powerful, and the sniveling traitor, Geneva Collier, who might or might not have combat training. The ghouls and the Scottish bastard certainly did.

Outside the wine cellar had been a man cave with a big TV. No sound came from that area. A ghoul would never just sit and think. If one were on guard, it would be using the TV.

Best guess, Tasha was alone down here. She felt for a doorknob and found a handle. When she tried to ease it down, it moved. Not locked.

She grinned in the darkness. *Score one for the home team.* Using a little of her small store of power, she muffled the hinges so they wouldn't squeak. Then she gently pushed the door.

It opened a crack. Light seeped in, and Tasha's teeth stopped chattering. The weight on her chest eased. She put her eye to the opening and peered out. The TV was off, and no one was on the sofa facing it.

But her saber was leaning against the sofa's arm. If she could get her hand on the hilt, the weapon would amplify any magic she poured into it. If she had to fight her way out, that could save her life.

Right now, she hadn't recharged enough to translocate. That took full power.

If she could get to her sword and suck in as much power as she could, as fast as she could trees and shrubs at the back, would she have enough to translocate out?

Whatever she did, she had to hurry. The enemy might come to check on her at any time.

Getting to the sword would be a lot harder if a magical being blocked the way. Okay, then. No choice.

Steeling herself, she shoved the door open and lunged through it.

∽

A DOZEN MAGES, screened from view and with swords in hand, took positions in front of the Colliers' house. As expected, a red Mercedes sedan and a black SUV sat in the driveway.

Carter and Nate crouched with Deke in the bushes across the road, supposedly so he could call on them at need. Carter suspected it was actually so Deke could be sure they didn't do anything he considered rash.

The worry was unnecessary. Neither man would do anything that put Tasha in danger. Unless they faced a choice between her death and an insane move that could possibly save her. Then all bets were off.

"Team four, status. Over," Deke said into his radio. Once magic started flying, radios would be useless.

"She's sick," Nate told Carter in a low voice. "Queasy. Still scared, but not as badly."

They'd discussed this on the short hop over from the collegium. Both of them were sure Tasha was in the wine cellar. That was their joint target.

"That's good," Carter said. "Thanks."

"Team four moving into position at the rear," GiGi's voice said over Deke's radio. "Stand by."

Nate nodded. "I'm sorry it didn't work out."

"Thanks. Me too."

"Team four in position. Over."

"All right," Deke began. "Team one will make their way up the front to the windows. Two—"

Silver magic and muddy-brown ghoul power flared around the house. Shields. The mage attack force had been detected.

TASHA'S HAND closed over the hilt of her saber. *Oh, yeah.* Things were looking up. She stood directly under the window and sucked in life energy as fast as she could.

With a crackle like static, magic rolled outside. Its energy grated on her open senses. That was ghoul magic mixed with mage power. They'd shielded the house.

If a fight started, she would be a prime hostage. *Time to go.*

Translocating in through shielding was impossible. Translocating out, though, was entirely doable. She just had to be sure she emerged past the shields so the ghoul magic in them didn't fry her. Tasha sucked in a last bit of energy.

The big, male ghoul charged down the steps. He gaped at her for an instant, and Tasha blasted him with green magic from her sword. He stumbled backward. Footsteps pounded on the stairs.

No time for more of a recharge. Good thing she didn't have far to go.

The shield probably was fairly near the house to conserve magical energy, and the front lawn was half an acre deep. Visualizing the monkey grass that edged the lawn by the road, she reached for the space between life and death.

The big mage appeared in front of her.

She fed power into the shift and was gone in a flash of wonderful cold.

~

"GOING WITH PLAN B," the shire reeve said into his radio. "We'll hail them and open negotiations."

Nate shared a grim glance with Carter. Once the ghouls knew they were here, anything could happen to Tasha. Nate's insistence that he could magically tunnel under the shield and the lawn to the wine cellar had been met with flat refusal.

A figure winked into view by the edge of the road. It dived, rolled, and regained its feet with a green shielding aura forming around her. Tasha! With her saber in hand.

She ran full out for the tree line.

Carter and Nate broke cover, heading for her. Both men flung out shielding to reinforce hers.

Tasha looked stunned and delighted. Carter reached for her, but she flung herself into Nate's arms. Clinging to him, she buried her face in her twin's neck.

A kick to the balls wouldn't have hurt so much.

"Cover us?" Nate asked, turning for the trees.

"Roger." Carter swallowed hard and let them go ahead of him. He added his shield to theirs. Only when they were safely in the trees did he step off the road.

Tasha hadn't once looked at him. She really must be done with him.

Wearing full battle gear, Stefan knelt in front of her.

"Plan C," Deke announced into the radio. "Ms. Murdock has escaped and is safe. Repeat, Ms. Murdock is safe. We're back to business as usual. We need a prisoner to try to find out where their nest is. That's the only restriction. Otherwise, take that house and every being in it down. We're not going to leave so much as a brick standing. Damage adjustment team, stand by."

The jubilation of Carter's fellow deputies washed over his magical senses. This, they knew well how to do. The attacking force would demolish the place, and the damage adjustment team would make it look like a gas explosion or some such.

He walked up to Deke. "I want in."

The shire reeve raised an eyebrow. "What part of 'wait for my go' did you not understand, Deputy Lockwood?"

"I thought the hostage might need cover, sir."

Deke stared at him, a clear sign that his bullshit, however logical it might be, was not fooling his boss. "I'll let it go this time, but don't make a habit of it."

"No, sir."

With a nod, Deke said, "Fall in with team two."

"Thanks, boss." Carter walked over to Sybil Harrison, Darren Hale, and Val Dare. "I'm with you."

"The more, the merrier," Harrison said.

"All units," Deke said over the radio, "open fire on my mark. Three . . . two . . . one . . . mark."

The mage squads channeled magic through their weapons, blasting the shield around the house from both the front and the back. The clash of energies sizzled, filling the air with the stink of ozone, and glowed as brightly as sunlight.

Val's face was set, intent. Because she was so domestic, it was easy to forget she'd been shire reeve and was tough as any mage when it came to fighting ghouls.

Suddenly, the shield winked out. The mages' blasts slammed into the house. Gaping holes appeared in the walls. The second story shuddered, sagging in the middle where load-bearing walls below had been blasted away.

Magical probes shot out from the squads surrounding the wreckage. Sybil Harrison frowned. "Odd. I'm not detecting anything alive in there."

"Fine with me." Darren Hale scowled at the house. "Other than needing to find that nest."

"Recon," Deke's voice said over the radio. "Squads two and four, take point. Let us know what you find."

Harrison thumbed her radio. "On it, boss. Moving out."

With their senses open and ready for trouble, Carter and the others followed her into the building.

WITH THE DANGER handled and darkness approaching, the screened helos moved in closer, one in the driveway and the other on the front lawn. Tasha sat in the open door of the one on the lawn. Stefan had tended her wounds and drawn out the venom, so she felt almost normal. Nate leaned against the Black Hawk's side next to her. From there, they could see the mopping-up operations.

With his distinctive hair covered by the helmet, wearing the same clothes as everyone else, Carter should have been indistinguishable from his comrades. But she knew the way he moved. The way he carried himself.

Running to Nate and not to him had been a hard choice. She had no right to seek comfort from him, though, when she couldn't give him what he wanted.

Watching him made her heart hurt. So did the fact that, while he glanced at her from time to time, he never made eye contact. Maybe that was just as well. No matter how much she regretted hurting him, that was only because she hadn't handled things better. Leaving him had been the right thing to do.

"Sure you don't want to climb in and sit?" Nate asked. "Seats in these things aren't great, but they beat the decking."

"In a minute." Tasha took another deep breath of clear air. "I need to be outside a little longer."

They said nothing for a few minutes, both watching the

deputy reeves. They really were taking the house down to the ground. Inside, they'd found the corpses of two ghouls and Geneva Collier, the ghouls gutted, as though by a mage's sword, and Collier bearing a magic burn mid-chest. Of the Scottish traitor, there'd been no sign. Had he killed them?

Casually, Nate said, "We figured you were in the wine cellar. Lockwood and I both knew what that meant." He paused before adding, "He was really worried about you."

She flashed back to the dark, close room and shuddered. Nate squeezed her hand.

Carter walked back toward the helo with Roland Wade. Softly, Nate said, "He's a solid guy."

"Yeah." She knew that, and she owed him an apology.

When he glanced her way, she braced herself and held out a hand. Looking wary, he came over to clasp it. The warmth in his eyes was banked but still there. It was a painful reminder of all the things she wanted that could never be.

"You okay?" he asked, pressing their clasped hands to the body armor over his heart.

"Stefan says so. He wants me in the infirmary overnight."

"Probably smart," Carter said.

"Yeah." Out of the corner of her eye, she spotted Nate drifting away. Had he been closer, she would've smacked his shoulder. "Thank you for coming for me."

A tender look flitted through his eyes before he squashed it. "Of course," he told her, and she was sure that wasn't what he really wanted to say.

What she had to say next wasn't what she wanted to say, either, but it was the only thing she could offer. "I'm sorry, Carter, about the clumsy way I handled things the other day. I could've been more tactful."

He shrugged. "There wasn't much of a way to cushion that, and it's done now. I hope you'll be happy."

"You too. I want that very much."

Again, he started to say something. His mouth closed

abruptly. He looked at her for a long moment before he squeezed her hand and let it go. When he walked away, he took her heart with him.

Tasha's eyes stung. She blinked to clear them.

Nate strolled around the helo, and she frowned at him. "Thanks so much for your moral support."

"You know I didn't belong in that conversation." He sat down beside her and hooked an arm around her shoulders.

"No, I guess not." Tasha sighed and rubbed her eyes. "It'll be good to have this over, to go home again."

"Don't count on that too soon."

Her head snapped up. "What does that mean?"

"We didn't get the ghoul who wants you dead. We're pretty sure, from what you told us, that we got minions. The Big Bad is still out there."

"You are kidding me."

"I don't kid about this shit, Short Stuff. So unless you know where we can find these guys, this isn't over."

"Jasper," Tasha remembered. "Someone said the head guy was coming 'all the way from Jasper.' Maybe that's where the nest is. Wherever Jasper is."

"Maybe so." Nate beckoned to Sybil Harrison and passed on Tasha's information.

The chief deputy nodded. "Good work. We'll definitely scope it out." She walked back to the team working in the house ruins.

"They'll move on this fast," Nate said. "They know if they wait, the ghouls could slip away."

"I hope this pans out. I'd really like to go home." And start on life after Carter.

CHAPTER TWENTY-EIGHT

NEAR DAWN TWO DAYS LATER, CARTER WAITED WITH A DOZEN other deputy reeves outside a ghoul nest near Jasper, Florida. Similar squads waited on every side. A tiny yellow flag marked each of the land mines the ghouls had planted all around the rusted chain-link fencing. When the go signal came, the strike force would explode those landmines and open the way to the fence.

After so many years of finding themselves outnumbered on such raids when they had expected not to be, the veterans from the area radiated tension. Trusting that no one had betrayed them to the enemy was going to take time.

Carter's gloved hand clenched on his sword hilt. There was only one traitor he wanted, and if there was any justice in the world, the bastard would be inside this nest.

Inside the fence, ghouls meandered to and from the shack recon had said was a breeding hut. Stronger and more active at night, they generally slept mornings away.

The gray sky brightened. In the east, the edge of a big, red orb that was the rising sun slipped above the trees. Almost time. Mages preferred to fight when the sun was up, partly because it made recharging so easy and partly because the ghouls were weakest in full daylight.

The sun rose higher, the light turning yellow. A flight of two dozen arrows, six from each side of the nest, arced into the sky and dropped toward the buildings around the packed-earth yard. On every rooftop except that of the breeding shed, explosive arrowheads detonated on impact.

Deke's voice crackled over the radio network, which was already disrupted by the mages' magical screens. "Go," he snapped.

The mages in the front rank detonated the land mines. With a near-deafening *boom*, dirt, pine needles, and palm leaves spewed into the air. The next moment, blue and green bolts of magic vaporized the fence. The ground force held back, though, waiting for three more flights of explosive arrows.

Ghouls rushed outside. Many of them blasted fist-wide beams of muddy yellow magic at random. Another flight of explosive arrows arced through the sky and dropped into the open space. Before those landed, another flight was inbound.

"That's three," Carter said. "Go."

The squad followed him as he charged into the compound. The *rat-a-tat* and *brrr* of automatic weapons fire added to the din. The ghouls had gotten to their guns. Shielding as heavily as they could, Carter and the others dropped to lie flat. The mages scrying the battle should help target the gunners.

Arrows streaked toward the gun emplacements. Judging by their lower, flatter flight paths, the archers had moved closer to shoot directly at their targets.

Explosions rocked the ground. The guns fell silent.

Carter raised his head. Ghouls who'd avoided the gunfire were charging the attackers. Carter pushed to his feet, sword in hand, and engaged the nearest, a big, pug-faced male. Not the big male he wanted, but a target nonetheless. A blast from the ghoul's fist glanced off his shielded body armor and knocked him back a couple of steps. Drawing more power, channeling it through the blade, Carter ducked a vicious swipe of talons and slashed upward.

"Morere," he cried, pouring magic into the command.

The strike penetrated the ghoul's shields and sliced it open from crotch to neck. As it fell, Carter wheeled to find another foe.

There, a tall, wiry female with shaggy, black hair. She pulled out a handgun.

Fuck. He used a sidewinder slap of blue magic to whip her hand aside. Before she could bring the weapon to bear again, he shouted, "Morere," and stabbed her.

Glaring, she collapsed, but she tried to bring the gun up. With her shields gone, kicking it away was easy.

Carter fought this way across the yard, always heading for the shack that recon had labeled the HQ. Every mage had an image of the ghoul who'd been giving orders. Ziggly, or something like that. The name didn't matter. Only the fact the bastard had ordered the hit on Tasha did.

The only enemy Carter wanted more was the fucking traitor who'd helped the ghouls capture her.

"Carter," GiGi Gonzales shouted before she clapped him on the shoulder. With her gory sword, she pointed to his left.

There was the big sonofabitch ghoul, flinging a wounded deputy aside. Carter pounded toward him. Behind Carter, GiGi shouted, "I got your back. Get the fucker."

There was a true friend, letting him have first shot because she knew he craved it.

The big ghoul shrugged off another mage attack. Blue and green magic sizzled on his muddy yellow aura but didn't penetrate it.

That shouldn't happen. The memory of last fall's super ghouls flashed into Carter's head, but he had no time to worry about it. Whatever it took, he was bringing this fucker down. Waving his blade so the mages blasting would keep it up, he pulled all the power he could into it, everything he could safely draw from the sunlight and from the woods around the camp.

The ghoul's back was to him as it blasted the mages. Shields holding, they gave ground slowly, still firing green and blue bolts at it.

Stabbing the bastard in the back was the smart play, but Carter wanted it to see its face when he killed it. He took two big steps to his left and shouted, "Hey! Fuckwad!"

Smirking, the ghoul turned. Carter and GiGi added their power to their comrades' blasts. The big ghoul actually staggered sideways a couple of steps. Good. Its resistance was down.

Angling his left side toward the ghoul so momentum would add power to his right-handed strike, he kicked it in the stomach. It grabbed him as it fell, talons sinking into his leg. The pain was blinding. He fought to stay conscious as the ghoul pulled him off balance.

Going with the pull, he gasped, "Morere," and stomped on the ghoul's sternum. Bone cracked, audible over all the noise of combat. The ghoul made a strangled noise, and its grip relaxed. Its breath whooshed out.

The other mages ran to engage more ghouls. Only GiGi stayed close, guarding Carter's back as she'd promised.

Carter skewered the ghoul just below the heart, driving his blade through the male's barrel chest and into the dirt below. His *morere* hadn't been fatal because it hadn't been timed well with the impact of his foot, but the power it carried had gotten his foot through the ghoul's shields.

Its eyes were glazing. Better hurry.

He dropped to his left knee to take the pressure off his wounded leg. Careful to stay out of reach, he said, "That's for Natasha Murdock. You lose, and I hope you burn in hell."

The ghoul's lip curled as though to sneer, but it didn't finish the gesture. Its eyes blanked, and its face went slack.

"Clear," someone called behind him. Answering shouts

came from around the compound. Thanks to the explosive arrows, the mop-up wasn't going to be nearly as tough as it might've been.

"Hey, Carter," Brody Hamilton, one of the longbowmen, called. Once the hand-to-hand action started, they'd put down their bows and joined in, as usual.

Carter wheeled toward his comrade's voice.

A grim smile split Brody's tanned face. He shook the man he held by the collar. "Look who we got here."

Thanks to the briefing before the unsuccessful raids on the Colliers' home and this guy's office, Carter and every other mage couldn't help recognizing Brody's prisoner. Hewlett Collier, Geneva's husband, cringed in the tall deputy reeve's grasp.

Carter stalked toward them. At his back, GiGi said, "I guess we'll get some answers now."

"Damn straight." The penalty for a mage engaged in treason with the ghouls was death. Hewlett would undoubtedly do anything he could to avoid that. Despite being surrounded by ghoul corpses, he probably thought he could talk his way out of this.

"Carter," Brody said in a warning tone.

Carter stopped him with an upraised hand. "Did you sic them on Natasha Murdock, Collier?"

"N-nn-no, no."

"Then who did?"

"Z-Zarig. He was so angry."

"Why?" Carter roared, crowding the man. "Why did he target her?"

Roland shoved in front of him, his back to the prisoner. "Easy, bro."

"You did something," Carter ground out. "Otherwise, they wouldn't have taken her to your house."

"P-please." Sniveling, Collier said, "My wife is dead. I've lost everything. Please—"

"Not everything," Carter replied. "You're still breathing."

The man's eyes widened. Shoving up against Roland's bulky form, Carter demanded, "Why her?"

"I-it-it's not my fault. Geneva . . ."

Words spilled out in a confusing babble. As it continued, the disgust swept over the faces of Carter's fellow reeves.

"Please," Collier said. "Please, I've told you everything."

Carter glared at him. "So Ms. Murdock was put in the wrong room to wait for your wife, where papers you carelessly left out lay on the desk. Papers that could reveal your treasonous dealings with the ghouls. So you—or Zagbag, or whatever his name was, I really don't give a flying fuck—decided she must've seen the papers and would report you, so you had to kill her. Do I have that right?"

"She-she was by the desk."

"So you assumed she was a snoop. Even though days went by and nothing happened about the info on those papers."

"She reported us. Ruined me."

Carter shook his head. "Whoever reported you, it wasn't her. She didn't even notice your fucking traitorous papers. I should kill you right here." Or at least drive his fist into the slimy bastard's face.

"Watch it," Roland rumbled.

"Carter," GiGi said, stepping up to his side, "Enough."

"Yeah," he agreed, "more than."

He turned away to join the mop-up and found Deke watching him. The shire reeve walked toward him, and everyone else found something to be busy with.

"I understand the impulse," Deke told him, "but there's a reason we have trained interrogators."

A rookie could've gotten that weasely traitor to spill, but Deke was right. "Understood, boss."

With a nod, Deke said, "I need to see you after debrief."

Carter almost asked about what, but Deke's closed expression didn't seem hospitable. Wondering what was up now, Carter went back to work.

The mages lost no one, though about a dozen were wounded, wiping out the ghouls. They freed nineteen captives from the breeding shed and liberated several dogs and goats and a horse from pens. The animals were fodder for creatures who could eat only fresh kill.

But Ross Graham, traitor mage from Scotland, was not onsite. Nor had anyone seen him.

At last, debrief ended. Carter reported to Deke's office. Knocking on the open door, he asked, "What's up?"

Deke regarded him solemnly. "Close the door and have a seat."

That didn't sound good. Carter complied.

"I hate to ask you this," Deke said, "but how did you know about the red Mercedes?"

"I got a tip."

"From . . .?"

Fuck it. He would evade, but he wouldn't lie. Maybe it was time to come clean on the whole business anyway.

"From a kid I know in Brunswick."

He told Deke how he'd met Jeremy, gotten involved with the kid's friends, and met a couple of mageborn street kids in Savannah. As he talked, Deke's face grew increasingly less sympathetic.

"Is that the only case where you didn't report someone you should've?" Deke demanded.

"The only serious one. There was a shoplifting incident in Savannah."

"And you didn't do your duty because you didn't trust the system?"

"It had already failed them both. What was the point of setting them up for that again?"

"Lockwood . . ." Deke sighed. "I see your point, but I have a duty, too."

"I know. If you want me to resign, I will." Though what he'd do then, he had no clue.

Deke shook his head. "Jeremy Hayes's dad overheard the boy talking to you. He found your name in the kid's phone."

Oh, shit. If that drunken assclown had gone off on Jeremy . . .

Deke continued, "He scried you and saw you with his kid. In uniform. He's making noises about undue influence."

So now the drunkard had decided to care. "I can make noises about alcoholism, emotional abuse, and neglect. Serious noises."

"None of which changes the fact you stepped outside the lines while acting in an official capacity. Neither the Collegium nor its Georgia Institute for Paranormal Research alter ego needs a lawsuit."

"No, they need to do something so kids like Jeremy don't fall through the cracks."

"You know I agree with you, but that's not for us to decide." Deke cocked his head. "Council elections are coming in the fall. Why don't you run?"

"I hate politics." Despite his parents' baffling love of the field.

"It's how things get done around here." Again, Deke shook his head. "Regardless of your reasons, you broke the regs and could have exposed this institution to huge liability. But I do agree with you, so I'm opting for the lightest penalty I can give you, a thirty-day suspension without pay."

Carter blew out a relieved breath. "That's more than fair. Thanks."

"Get some rest. No offense, but you look like you could use it. Get your boat fixed. Until we can smooth this over, stay away from those kids."

Carter nodded, but there was no way he was turning his back on those kids if they needed him.

As he walked out through the bustling bullpen, Deke's words echoed in his head. They followed the same lines as the speech Carter had given Tasha all those years ago. *Sauce for the goose*, he thought wryly.

Too bad he couldn't share that with her.

He could do something else, though. When he reached the parking lot, he called Will Davis's cell. When Will answered, Carter told him about his exchange with Hewlett Collier.

"I expect Deke's going to give her the all-clear when he's sure," Carter said. "But I thought she had a right to know."

Silence came back to him. At last, Will asked, "Why call me? Why don't you tell her?"

Because even though he desperately wanted to hear her voice, the distance she'd put between them would still be there. "You're a smart guy, Will. You know why. Can you pass the word along for me?"

"Sure. Take care of yourself, Carter."

"Right. Thanks."

They disconnected. Carter climbed into his car. Somehow he needed to get a conduit to the kids who relied on him, a way to be in touch and not leave their parents room for complaint.

There was one possibility. He pulled his phone out again and called Reverend Alice Withers, the head of Home for the Night, the local shelter for runaways. When she answered, he explained what he needed.

A long pause had him on edge before she said, "Those kids need you. Come on by, and let's see what we can work out."

CHAPTER TWENTY-NINE

"It's good to be home," Tasha told Lorelei. They stood in Tasha's cream-and-pale-green kitchen assembling plates, utensils, and glasses for a potluck buffet. Tasha was providing chicken curry and rice, and everyone else was bringing sides, drinks, or dessert.

From the eat-in kitchen, they could look through the dining room windows and across Whitaker Street to Forsythe Park, its fresh green leaves and grass heralding the coming of spring. The river cabin was still a wreck, but at least the house had survived intact. Maybe because she'd stayed away from it.

"There's nothing quite like your own space," Lorelei agreed. "When Nate gets back with the wine, we'll have everything."

"I've enjoyed the quiet. Nate's given me my space." Maybe too much space, because memories of Carter tended to pop up in idle moments—the silvery brightness of his eyes when he was amused or intent, the storm cloud gray when he was angry, the smoky softness when he felt affection. Or made love.

Tasha swallowed against a lump in her throat. "I'll just put these plates in the dining room."

She picked up the stack and took it to the long table she used as a buffet. The furniture in here was a hodge-podge, but that was okay. She'd refinished the table, the buffet, and the mix-and-match chairs in warm oak shades. They would do until she could get the sleek, contemporary set she wanted. Tasha set the table with forest-green placemats and napkins.

When she walked back into the kitchen, Lorelei looked up from thin-slicing Brussels sprouts and cauliflower for a salad. "How are you holding up, Tasha?"

"I'm okay." Tasha shrugged. "Two nights in my own bed have been great." Even if the queen-sized bed now seemed much too large.

Lorelei pursed her lips. After a moment, she laid down her knife. "There's something I think you need to know. Not everyone agrees."

"I'm thrilled," Tasha said, raising an eyebrow, "to know you've all been talking about me. What's going on?"

"Carter's been suspended," Lorelei said.

"What? Why? He's great at his job." Had someone uncovered his deal with the kids?

"I don't know. The suspension is common knowledge, according to Will, but the reason isn't. I think Val might know. She isn't telling, though. It's a personnel matter and thus confidential, she says."

"It's not confidential from me." But it was, because she had sent him away. Her heart hurt again at the memory.

"If you can get it out of Val, good luck. I couldn't."

Tasha glanced at the stove clock. "They'll be here in about fifteen minutes. And Nate should be back anytime."

"Do you mind if I ask you something before they get here?"

"Shoot." Tasha grabbed her beer and slid into one of the chairs at her white-enamel-topped kitchen table.

Again, Lorelei looked directly at her. "Are you in love with Carter?"

Yes. Always. For all the good that does either of us.

Around a pained breath, Tasha asked, "Why?"

"Because giving up a guy you're in love with isn't the same as giving up one you like a lot."

Lorelei would know. She and Ken had been in love, new to the realization and not sure it would last, but giddy with it all the same. Until the wreck that claimed his life.

"If you love him," Lorelei continued, "you could drink some silly cocktails and munch finger food and make chit-chat for an evening now and then. If I'm smart enough to know that, so is he."

Yeah, he'd figured that right out. "Your point is?"

"He's bound to know there's some other reason."

"He does. He just doesn't know what it is. And he's never going to know."

"Because you don't trust him? Or because you don't believe in yourself?"

That stung. Tasha's brows knitted. "What does that mean?"

"I think you don't give yourself enough credit. I also think you put way more importance on the distant past than anyone else ever would."

Anyone else who said that, Tasha would've shut down fast. But this was Lorelei, whose concern was beyond doubting. "You're wrong," she said evenly. "I know exactly what I've done, all along the road. Don't make light of my concerns."

"I'm not." Bracing both hands on the island, Lorelei blew out a hard breath. "Girlfriend, I'm just trying to get you to look at things from another angle."

Tasha shook her head. "I know you mean well, but you weren't the one in the relationship. I was, and I know it wouldn't have lasted. So can we just drop this?"

Lorelei met her earnest look with a frustrated one. At last, she replied, "Sure. Just one more thing, and I'll shut up about it."

Tasha sighed. "And that is?"

"If Carter died tomorrow, would you be glad you turned

away? Or would you regret it?" Lorelei's eyes glistened with unshed tears.

"Oh, Lorelei, I'm sorry." Tasha sprang from her chair and hurried to her friend. "I didn't mean to remind you."

Lorelei shook her head. Wiping her eyes, she said, "I don't need reminders. It's with me every day."

"You just fake it well," Tasha said. She knew how that was. Boy, did she!

"Yeah." Pain shadowed Lorelei's eyes when she looked up. "Ken and I had a good thing. Maybe it would've lasted, maybe it wouldn't, but I would crawl unshielded over hot coals to have the chance to find out. He's the first one who I thought, *maybe*, and those don't come along often. I don't want you to blow your shot with a really good guy."

Tasha hugged Lorelei. "I appreciate that. I don't know what I'd do without your friendship. But I need you to trust me on this and stop worrying. I really do know what I'm doing."

"I hope so," Lorelei muttered.

The doorbell rang. "I'll get it," Tasha said. Lorelei could use a few minutes to get her face in order.

Griff and Val stood at the door, Griff holding a six-pack of Wayfarer's local beer, Bar Brew, and Val carrying a cake box. Behind them, at the curb, Stefan and Will got out of Stefan's blue BMW sedan and reached back in for food.

"Come on in," Tasha said. "Just set those down anywhere in the kitchen. The curry's almost ready."

She waited for Will and Stefan, who'd brought more Bar Brew and what looked like fruit salad. Following them into the kitchen, she eyed Val. The deputy reeve was too conscientious to spill in front of everyone. How could Tasha get her alone?

AFTER DINNER, Tasha and Griff cleared plates while Val served cake. Tasha had a big kitchen, but it didn't feel like one when everyone was in it. Nate rose to help, but she shook her head at him. This might be her best chance to get Val alone.

Val opened the cupboard for plates. Tasha glanced backward. Griff had gone back to the dining room. Good.

"Val, I really need to know what happened with Carter."

Val sliced into the chocolate Bundt cake before she replied. "I really can't tell you." She put a slice on a plate and looked at Tasha. "I know you're worried, but I can't tell you. It's confidential. If you want to know, you'll have to ask Carter."

"But Val—"

"No buts." Val laid another slice on a plate. "I will say, though, that unpaid suspension for thirty days is a slap on the wrist as such things go, and the least Deke could give him in the circumstances."

"I really need to know those circumstances."

"To do what?" Val asked. "You can't change anything, Tasha, and honestly, do you think Carter would want you poking in his business?"

That stung, but it was true. It did nothing, though, to ease her ache to know.

Coming back into the kitchen with serving bowls, Griff said, "He was suspended for stepping over the line to help some kids."

"Griffin!" Knife in hand, his wife glared at him.

He shrugged. "It's not like she'll spread it around, and I think she has a right to know."

"There's a lot of that going around," Val muttered. Looking from Tasha to Griff, she pointed with the chocolate-coated knife. "The subject is now tightly and irrevocably closed. Sealed with Super-Glue. Or else. Got me?"

Tasha nodded. Griff grinned at his wife. "Damn, but you're sexy when you're pissed."

She shot him an exasperated look. Waving the knife, she reminded him, "I know how to use this for more than slicing cake, y'know."

But the love in their faces spurred Tasha's envy and made her miss Carter even more. She grabbed the two plated slices. "I'll just leave the two of you to finish here."

There would probably be kissing involved, so she hurried to give them privacy. Walking into the dining room, she announced, "First piece to my rarely-here brother," and set a plate in front of Nate.

"Next piece to the woman of the hour," Will said. "That's you. Sit down with your cake. If Val and Griff need any help, I'll handle it."

"No need," Val said from the doorway. "It's done." She and Griff passed out the remaining plates.

While Tasha's friends got coffee from the pot on the sideboard, she hardly listened to the conversation. Carter had been suspended for stepping out of line to help some kids. Talk about dejá vu all over again!

Those kids were a worthy cause, as the girls' school in Bangladesh had been. She'd thought he should've stepped up for her, for those kids. Could she do any less for him now?

BETWEEN SITE VISITS and client calls, Tasha couldn't get to the Collegium before noon the next day. She'd called ahead, though, and had an appointment with Shire Reeve Deke Jones.

A deputy reeve escorted her to his office, and he stood to greet her. "Come in, Ms. Murdock. Have a seat. The letter you wrote thanking us for our help wasn't necessary, but we all appreciated it."

"It was entirely deserved." Tasha settled into one of the two chairs in front of the desk. "That's not what I'm here about, though."

"What can we do for you today?"

Now that she was here, she wasn't sure this was entirely the best idea. But she owed Carter and his kids her life. What would they do without him to stand behind them?

"I want you to reverse Deputy Lockwood's suspension," Tasha said.

Deke's face closed over. "That's a personnel matter. I can't discuss it with you."

"I'm not asking you to. I only want you to listen to me. I met a couple of the kids Carter worked with. They look up to him. Respect him. Most important, they need him. They have literally no one else they can count on."

"And you know this, how? Because he told you?"

"The two I met did. And yes, I know they could've been playing me, or even both of us, but neither of us is stupid, and the kids came across as genuine. Regardless, the Collegium hangs mageborn kids with neglectful or abusive parents out to dry. I asked around about that, and there's nothing. We just slough the problem off on the Mundane courts. It's wrong. So you should cut Carter—Deputy Lockwood—a break."

Deke's face was expressionless. At last, he asked, "Did he send you here?"

"No, of course not. He doesn't know I'm here, and I doubt he would welcome my poking in his business, but I had to let you know there was more to this situation than you maybe knew."

"I knew," he said firmly. "Ms. Murdock, it's kind of you to come in, but this really is not your concern."

"It should be all of our concern." Tasha stared at him.

"Thank you for coming in." Deke stood. The gesture ended the interview.

She gave him a stiff nod. "Thanks for your time."

Walking out, she felt like banging her fist into a wall. That had done so much good.

Maybe about the same as Carter intervening on her behalf years ago would have done?

It was something to think about.

She walked out into the sunlight. Being able to go where she wanted, when she wanted, still felt like a joy. She tipped her face up to the light, the better to absorb the sun's power.

At the edge of the parking lot, she looked ahead, and her heart leaped. Carter was walking away from his car.

Her mouth felt dry, and she couldn't seem to draw a good breath. She waited for him. "Hey. How are you?"

"Good." His eyes held no warmth, no welcome. He was completely closed in, and the change hurt more than she would've imagined.

"I, um, I heard about your suspension. I'm sorry. You don't deserve it."

He shrugged. "Under the regs as written, I do. I'm only here because I'm meeting some friends for lunch."

"I see. Well . . . I asked Deke to cancel the suspension." He might as well hear it from her so she didn't add sneakiness to interfering.

He blinked, looking flabbergasted. After a moment, his face set in hard lines. The shadow in his eyes might or might not be pain. "Thanks for the thought, but you shouldn't have interfered."

"Maybe not, but I wanted to help."

"If you want to help," he said slowly, "don't come to reeve country again."

The rebuke burned, but he had a right to it. She'd butted into his business and forced him to see her again, though she hadn't intended the latter.

"I'll stay out of your way," she promised. Judging by the ache in her chest, that was best for them both. "Goodbye, Carter."

TOO MUCH WAS RIDING on this. Seated in Alice Withers' office on the third day into his suspension, Carter tried not to think about what this could mean to the kids he considered his. They needed him—or some kind of support—and he'd come to care for all of them. He didn't want to be cut off.

After losing Tasha, he couldn't take another loss.

She'd looked good yesterday. Obviously, their separation wasn't a problem for her. He should've realized sooner that it wouldn't be. Meanwhile, he couldn't sleep, and she was on his mind constantly.

If he'd told her he'd written a letter to the battalion commander asking for leniency after her stunt in Bangladesh, would it have made a difference? Probably not, but he wished she knew he'd done it, no matter how irrational that was.

Alice walked in with Benson Hayes, Jeremy's dad. The man was scowling. Carter stood.

Benson Hayes was of medium height, with brown eyes and disheveled brown hair. His clothes looked rumpled and not quite put together properly. His sallow complexion and too-thin build didn't look healthy. Especially not next to Alice, whose sturdy five six frame was attired in neat pants and boots with a green tunic. Below her close-cropped natural hairstyle, her dark brown face radiated intelligence and optimism.

"You," Hayes said when he spotted Carter. Pointing, he continued, "You stay away from my boy, or I'll have your badge."

Carter kept his mouth shut, but only just. He'd agreed to let Alice, who was also mageborn, lead this meeting.

"That's what we're here to discuss," she said in a low, firm voice. "Mr. Hayes, take a seat."

The man's eyes narrowed. "This pervert was setting my son up, and you want me to sit down with him? Oh, hell, no!"

Carter clenched his fists, his nails biting into his palms, to keep from erupting.

Alice gave Hayes a cold look. "You will sit down, or I will report you to the Mundane social services department for child abuse and neglect. Then I'll file a complaint with the Collegium about misuse of magic."

At the man's blank look, she added, "During drunken rages. Now sit down."

Scowling, Hayes complied. Carter sat too.

"You think Deputy Lockwood has targeted your son for abuse? Deputy, I know you've discussed this with Mr. Hayes before, but please remind him how you met Jeremy."

"We got a report of someone dabbling in blood magic. Investigating, I found Jeremy drawing sigils in blood in the woods outside your house."

"That's a damn lie!"

Alice shot Hayes a quelling look, and he closed his mouth.

"He got the blood from the meat department at the store," Carter continued.

The kid had to be the most inept dark magician ever. He loved animals, so he wasn't about to sacrifice any for this. "He told me about your drinking and your rages, and how he never had any food. I investigated and found he was telling the truth. If I'd reported him, as I should've, he would've been confined and undergone mandatory counseling at the Collegium. But that didn't seem to me to be what he needed. So I stepped in."

"To set him up," Hayes snapped.

Alice shook her head. "Deputy Lockwood brings Jeremy and other kids here to spend the night. I've checked him out, by both Mundane and magical means. He's reliable and decent. So we need to decide what we're going to do about your problem."

The conversation went back and forth for nearly an hour. Finally, Hayes agreed that he would get his drinking under control, and that Alice would supervise Jeremy while he did.

When he left, Alice turned to Carter. "I know you hate not seeing Jeremy, but this is the best I could do."

"I know." It wasn't what Carter wanted, but for now, it would have to do. "Next time you see him, how about tell him I miss him, huh? Maybe when his dad gets clean, assuming he actually follows through this time, I can see him again."

"I'll tell him. I'll be sure he knows to call me if there's a problem, and I'll ask him to spread the word among his friends. I'm not an adult male mentor, which is what he needs, but maybe we can get his dad shaped up."

Neither of them was naïve enough to think that would be easy, but Carter said, "I hope so." He exhaled heavily. "Jeremy's thirteen. He should be going to the Collegium for training."

Families who lived far away often relied on satellite programs. Some tried to train their children at home, despite the warning that they were missing out. Someone living in Brunswick had no excuse. No one could claim cost as a factor because the training was free.

Carter shook his head. "Thanks, Alice." Her organization was supposed to work only with runaways, and she'd warped the definition of that to squeeze Jeremy and a couple of others in. Carter could trust her to keep an eye on the kids he still thought of as his.

"Sure." She leaned back in her chair. "I know you don't volunteer anywhere regularly because your job is so unpredictable. Mundane first responders don't get called back to work off-shift unless something extraordinary happens, but deputy reeves do."

"That and the fact parents have to agree for kids to participate in adult mentor programs. Parents like Hayes and some others won't do that because they don't want the world to know their kids need help. Those are the kids I worry about."

"The ones who look like all should be well." Alice nodded. "Maybe you should consider a career change, Carter. Go into a field that lets you work with kids. You could set things up so your door was open to anyone."

Like the counseling job Tasha had suggested.

"Maybe," he said, thinking it through. He'd talked to Marc Wagner, the director of the community shelter down in

Wayfarer, about setting up something focused on kids. That needed someone to spearhead it, though. Marc already had his hands full, and Carter's unpredictable hours made him unsuitable to take charge of something like that.

He and Alice said their goodbyes, and Carter walked out into the spring sunshine.

At least Jeremy would be taken care of. On the one hand, Hayes's concern was understandable. On the other, such a neglectful parent had no room to throw stones. Maybe this would lead to his straightening up, though the odds on that weren't good.

If so, this would prove to be a relatively easy fix. Too bad there was no such thing for the situation with Tasha.

Except there was no situation. They were over. Done. And he'd better get used to it.

CHAPTER THIRTY

CARTER'S SUSPENSION WAS ALMOST UP. HE SAT IN THE COLLEGIUM clubroom with Roland and Josh. With Edie visiting her family in Colorado, then heading to Montana for smokejumper training, Josh was unusually on edge. Carter had recruited Roland to help distract their fellow deputy.

The guys had a pitcher of beer. In the background, a spring training exhibition baseball game played on the muted TV.

"So," Carter said, "did you see Doc Harper's report on that big ghoul who was shrugging off our bolts?"

Roland frowned at the bowl of peanuts on their table. "Let's hope that mutation he said was responsible doesn't spread."

"Absolutely," Josh responded. "At least the thing wasn't a superghoul. Even with the blade coating Doc Harper came up with, they're still harder to beat than the usual. I'd hate to see a bunch more of them crop up."

"It's weird there's no sign of that Scottish traitor." Roland shook his head. "It's like he's a ghost. And the sumbitch is powerful."

"Too powerful," Carter put in. "I asked Will Davis to look up mages with that kind of power. He found nothing on that, but he did see a study reporting an increase in ghouls who'll actually reason, rather than just mindlessly smashing whatever they come across."

"Oh, great." Scowling, Josh noted, "Those bastards already outnumber us. Our brains, along with our ability to move around during the day or the night, have given us an important edge."

"Don't forget working together," Carter said. "Whatever they're doing or however they're changing, they still suck at that."

"It's a good thing too," Roland commented.

Carter announced, "I still want that Scotsman. There's too much about him that doesn't add up. Why would he put a defective collar on Tasha, then leave the wine cellar door unlocked? Why did he let the ghouls go back to the Colliers' place? On top of that, Tasha told me the hung back when the ghouls attacked her on South End Road."

Saying her name hurt, but he had to get used to it.

"All good questions," Josh told him. "Did we ever hear why the Collier guy was working for the ghouls? Was it greed and fear that we'd lose, as has been the case for others?"

"No." Carter said, "Ghouls accosted the pair of them one night. Collier convinced them to spare him and his wife because they could make money for the ghouls."

"And now they're dead," Roland noted. Hewlett Collier had been tried, convicted, and executed a week after his capture. His was the first mage execution in almost 200 years.

Josh took a handful of peanuts. "Yeah. He should've made his escape, played along for a while, and then called us in. But I heard they paid him well."

"Yeah," Carter confirmed softly. The ghouls had paid the bastard well, and he'd had no qualms about sacrificing Tasha to keep his sweetheart deal.

At least the two Colliers had paid for their misdeeds. Finding the slimy Scotsman would cap the deal. They had to find a way to nail him.

A MONTH WENT BY. During the day, rebuilding the business kept Tasha's mind occupied. The nights were lonely, but that was very slowly getting better too.

Some projects were done. Enoch Slater had come through with the Dortons' kitchen cabinets and counters, and the young couple were happy in their new home. The Jepsons' drainage problem was handled, and they'd moved in two weeks ago.

Unfortunately, Tasha's building was a total loss. Heat damage to the cinderblocks made the structure unsafe, and the ground-floor furnishings that hadn't burned had been destroyed by water damage. Leaning on the hood of her truck in the parking lot, which at least was unscathed, Tasha sighed. The insurance was coming through, but rebuilding would draw crews away from generating profit. She was going to have to hire more people.

Enough of that, though. She was due to meet Mel at the house. With the wedding in ten days, both Mel and Stefan were eager to know the timetable for finishing.

Tasha took an appreciative breath of the scents rising from grass and trees and flowers. Spring had rolled out in full force. Beautiful, comfortable, and welcome. All too soon, it would give way to hot, muggy summer and leave everyone wishing for fall.

She hadn't heard from Carter, nor had she expected to. Will had let slip that he was taking night classes to get a degree in counseling. Stefan had said, when he didn't think she was in earshot, that Carter was lobbying the Council to get a program for kids who fell through the cracks. She wished him luck. There was a desperate need, both among mageborn kids and Mundanes.

She climbed into her truck and was about to start it when her phone rang. *Dex calling*, the screen read. Tasha swiped it. "Hey, Dex. How are you?"

"Not bad, honey. Not bad at all. But I had an idea that might help you make up for all the disruption from the fire."

"I'm all ears."

"You know about the Savannah Christmas Cavalcade, right? You should apply for a slot."

Oh. So much for the great idea. "I appreciate the suggestion, but I've applied several times. I've never made the cut."

"Oh, pshaw. Those women, I declare, they're the clubbiest bunch I ever did see. And I oughta know because my second cousin twice removed, Suellen Lee, heads up the danged thing. It's a Christmas display deal, not the cure for cancer. They need to get over themselves."

Maybe, but that didn't help her. "It raises a lot of money, and they have a right to be proud of that."

"Sure, sure, but it's always the same designers. Anyway, Tasha, you know I love what you've done with my house, and I'd be happy to put in a word with Suellen. If that's okay with you."

"Okay? Dex, that's wonderful. I can't thank you enough."

"You're welcome, honey. Suellen'll see your proposal gets a fair shot."

"I appreciate that more than I can say."

"I'm glad I could help. You take care now, y'hear?"

"You too."

They disconnected, and Tasha grinned out at her currently empty parking lot. The Christmas Cavalcade. And she didn't have to suck up to Geneva Collier for a shot. That was all she had, a shot, but it was more than she'd had a few minutes ago.

She reached for her phone but froze when her fingers touched it. She'd wanted to share the news with Carter. When would she get it through her fool head that they were done?

❧

AN HOUR LATER, Tasha and Mel sat in folding chairs in what would be the master suite. By taking the huge linen closet out of the hall, they'd been able to give the room its own bath. The deep teal walls had a lush feeling to them. The dark walnut furniture Mel and Stefan had chosen, a sleigh bed with matching dressers and nightstands, would add to that.

"I love it all," Mel said. "So does Stefan."

"I'm glad to hear it. The furniture for this room will be here early next week, and the window treatments for this room and the downstairs parlor by Tuesday." Her temporary storage was filling up with projects, so installing some would be a big help. "We'll get things loaded so you and Stefan can stay here after the wedding. The rest will come in while you're away, and we'll load it."

"Do you think we're being silly?" Mel ran her hand over the notebook Tasha had made instead of presentation boards. A notebook was much easier to tote to and from Atlanta. "Wanting to spend our first night here, I mean?"

"I think it's romantic." Mel and Stefan had stocked breakfast supplies. They didn't know their friends were assembling a hamper of champagne and munchies for after the reception. Because Tasha had a key, she would sneak it in before the wedding. Neither Mel nor Stefan would be here beforehand.

"There's something I have to talk to you about," Mel said. "We should've done it sooner, but, well, I'm not here much and Stefan can't, or won't, or whatever, because he's a guy."

"Is there something wrong with the work?"

"Oh, no, everything's wonderful. This is about the wedding. In the interests of keeping it small, we didn't invite many people from my office or the Collegium. Stefan did invite the medical staff, the Council and the department heads. Unfortunately, as head of the Wayfarer patrol, Carter came up on the list. Snubbing him didn't seem right, and, well, he's coming."

"Oh." Tasha's chest felt suddenly tight, and her pulse fluttered. "Is he, um, bringing anyone?"

Mel shook her head. "When we do the table seating, I'll be sure he's not anywhere near you. I just thought you should know, and this is the first chance I've had to talk to you in person since the RSVPs started coming in."

Through a suddenly dry mouth, Tasha managed, "Thanks for the warning."

"Sure." Mel hesitated, then said, "Is there anything I can do, Tasha?"

"Not unless you have an amnesia pill handy."

"I'm fresh out. Sorry. If you ever want to talk, though, I'm a good listener."

"I bet. I appreciate it, but there's really nothing to talk about.'

"Okay." Mel turned the notebook page to the upstairs bath.

Before she could say anything, words tumbled out of Tasha's mouth. "The thing is, though, everyone thinks I made a mistake, and I really wish they would just see that this is how it has to be."

Mel looked up at her and asked, in a mild tone, "Why is that?"

"I don't fit in his world. And his mother's a politician, which means news media and snoopy reporters and opposition research by her opponents, and I have a terrible past."

Why was she even talking about this? Mel wasn't some stranger on a plane. She was going to be in Tasha's life. A lot.

But she was also logical, a computer whiz, and an FBI special agent. Maybe she could come up with a way to make everyone stop looking at Tasha with such regret.

"Do you mind if I ask what's terrible about your past?" When Tasha hesitated, Mel said, "You may or may not know that I broke up with Stefan because I didn't believe I fit in the mage world."

"You fit just fine."

Mel nodded. "Which everyone knew except me. Tasha, I grew up in a small town, and my mom was the town freak. She was heavily into New Age theories, always talking about her powers, celebrating the Solstice instead of Christmas. Worse, she invited people to those celebrations. On top of that, I was a geek girl way before that was cool. Some of the girls in that town made my life a daily trial."

"I can relate. I'm so sorry, Mel." Was it possible Mel *would* understand?

"Thanks, but that doesn't bother me anymore. What did bother me, what stuck with me, was feeling as though I were always being tested. Always had to prove myself. Music was my ticket in at school, music and good grades."

"I've heard you sing, and you're amazing."

"I appreciate that." Mel gave her a quick nod. "Then, with the Bureau, I earned a place with computer skills. In the mage world, I'm Mundane. Ordinary. So how could I ever earn a place? I finally realized that the feeling of being tested was coming entirely from within me. Other people accepted me because they liked me, but I couldn't see that."

"What changed? If you don't mind me asking."

"Stefan offered to move into my world and leave his on the periphery. When he did that, it meant so much. No one had ever put me first, and there he was. But I couldn't let him do it. He's needed in the mage world, especially with the ghouls so active. I couldn't ask him to turn his back on that need. I figured I would just have to deal."

With a smile, she added, "To my surprise, everyone has been welcoming, and I don't feel like an outsider at all. Is there any chance it could be that way for you?"

Tasha sighed. "My past isn't just not fitting in. It's really bad, and dirt sticks."

"Sometimes unfairly. I finally decided I didn't care what people back in Essex, North Carolina, thought about me. Later, I discovered they'd stopped thinking anything about me long ago." Mel paused, studying Tasha, before she said gently, "You know, I work for the FBI. I've seen a lot and heard about more. My threshold for *really bad* is pretty high."

"I guess." Tasha's fists clenched under the table. Could she risk telling Mel?

What did she have to lose?

Tasha took a deep breath and explained about the wildness and the boys and the trailer trash rep and her grandmother's funeral and even jerky Ferrell and his disdain for her work. She stopped at the prostitution charge, but Mel's sympathetic expression hadn't changed. Maybe it was time to share that too. Tasha took a deep breath and plunged in. As she talked, Mel's brows drew together.

"What a bastard," Mel said.

"Yeah. He was the mayor's son, like Carter, so maybe I unconsciously let that color my view of Carter. Anyway, I didn't know the judge was going to dismiss the charges, no matter what I did. Principal Joyner implied that would only happen if I signed up. Nate was already in the Army ROTC, so I picked the navy."

When she finished, Mel said, "You know, most of those guys probably don't live there anymore. Some of them have probably forgotten shooting off their mouths, and some of them are probably ashamed of doing it."

"Maybe, but like I said, Mel, dirt sticks."

"It does, but grownups can also see jealousy and spite much more clearly than kids. Those girls have probably moved on the like the guys did by now, and if they haven't, so what? You have a successful, respected business and a tight circle of friends who all, as you put it to me a while ago, have your back. What do you care what a bunch of childish bitches think?"

"I care what they would tell reporters, what could be used against his mother." Through an ache in her chest, she added, "I care if Carter doesn't want me anymore."

"I guess you haven't talked to him about this?"

Tasha shook her head. To her great embarrassment, her lips

trembled. She pressed them together and breathed in before she could reply. "I can't risk it. He knows I'm not telling him everything, and he says he doesn't care what it is, but how could he not?"

Gently, Mel answered, "He's a grownup." Before Tasha could think how to reply to that comment, which seemed vaguely insulting, Mel added, "Let me ask you something. Who knows Carter's mom better, him or you?"

"He does, of course, but he's not thinking straight."

"Are you sure? Tasha, do you think Carter's a wimp?"

"No, of course not!"

"Then why do you think he would fold at the first sign of very old trouble?"

"Well, because he loves his mom, and she can't possibly accept someone like me."

"There again, if he's not a wimp, that'll be her problem. And before you say you don't want to cause a rift, consider whether you're doing her justice. She's a sharp woman. She can understand jealous girls and spiteful, thwarted boys. She probably even went to high school with those types. It's not like our generation invented them."

Tasha couldn't muster a smile at the mild joke. "You're not giving me a way to make everyone accept my decision. You're telling me to take the leap."

"I expect I'm not the first."

"No, but . . ." Tasha shook her head.

"Is he trustworthy?"

"Of course."

"Then aren't you insulting him by not talking to him about your concerns?"

"Maybe." *Definitely*, the uncooperative little voice in her head announced.

Leaning closer, Mel asked, "Do you plan to stay single forever?"

"No." Tasha frowned at her. "Why would I?"

"Because the arguments you've given me could fit, in some way, every guy you might ever come to care about."

Stunned, Tasha stared at her. Mel was right. "I never thought of it that way."

"I imagine not. Why think of other men when there's a guy you love filling the horizon? You do love him, don't you?'

"Very much," Tasha admitted.

"I thought so." Mel's eyes were kind, full of sympathy, and her voice was gentle. "I know how scary that leap can be, Tasha. But if you've got to make it sometime, why not jump for a guy who loves you, says he doesn't care about the past, and, because he's not a wimp, deserves to be trusted? When are you going to have a better shot?"

Never.

Heart beating fast, Tasha raised an eyebrow. "I bet you're hell in interrogations."

"I hold my own, but—"

"Hey," Stefan's voice called from downstairs. "I hear there are beautiful women in this house. Where are they?"

Mel's face lit up like a kid's at a carnival. "Upstairs," she called, pushing back her chair. "Coming down." She rushed out of the room and down the stairs. Her flats clattered on the newly refinished wood.

Left alone, Tasha couldn't avoid thinking of what Mel had gotten her to admit. Carter did deserve to be trusted. But did she have the courage to try?

Even if she did, would he still want her?

CARTER'S red bullet and his truck sat side by side in his carport. He was probably home. She could've scried to find out, but that seemed intrusive.

Tasha pulled in and parked. Her throat tightened, and her heart pounded. She wiped her clammy hands on her jeans.

What if he wouldn't forgive her? What if he didn't want a woman who'd slept around and had been charged with prostitution?

But what if he really didn't care about all that? There was only one way to find out.

Taking a deep breath, she grabbed the plastic container of cupcakes from the passenger seat. Red velvet with cream cheese frosting ought to at least get her a hearing. A chance to grovel.

He'd said he loved her. Surely he wasn't the kind to toss that aside because she'd been an idiot.

Then again, idiot . . .

She could sit here dithering all day.

Tasha squared her shoulders, climbed out of her truck, and marched to the door. With her thumb, she pressed the doorbell. It chimed.

Seconds passed, and no one came to the door.

Hmmm. Maybe he wasn't home after all. Or maybe he was out on the dock and hadn't heard the bell.

Going around back uninvited was nervy, but she'd come this far. Eager to see him, yet dreading the conversation to come, she walked through his carport.

There was the boat, so maybe . . .

There he was. Her heart spasmed. Damn, she'd missed him.

At the end of the dock, Carter slouched in a low beach chair, a navy blue ball cap with NAVY in gold lettering above the bill tipped down over his eyes and a loosely held bamboo pole in his hands. A beer sat on the deck beside him, and headphone wires snaked from his lap into his ears.

The sunlight gleamed on his bare chest and gilded the hair there, on his arms, and on the legs bared by his cutoff jeans. His bare feet were crossed at the ankles.

Love welled into Tasha's throat and brought tears to her eyes. He had to forgive her. That was all there was to it.

Okay, Tasha. Game on.

Best to look confident but be humble. Blinking her eyes clear,

Tasha strode onto the dock. She'd taken three steps when Carter pushed up the ball cap. He'd probably sensed her magic.

Wraparound sunglasses hid his eyes, but she knew he was watching her. So why the hell didn't he say something?

"Hey," she called.

"Hey." He didn't move, but at least he was talking to her. Then again, he'd been raised to be polite.

"I'm glad you're here," she said. "I need to talk to you."

Shrugging, Carter tucked the earbuds into his pocket. "As long as you don't scare the fish."

"Are they biting?"

"Not so far." He tipped his head back to look up at her but didn't stand or offer her a chair. Politeness apparently had gone as far as it was going to.

"I made you cupcakes," she blurted, thrusting the container at him.

He made no move to take it. "Why?"

"They're part of my apology." Suddenly cold with dread despite the warm morning, she rushed onward. "I let myself get trapped in the past, and I didn't see you—or even myself—as we really are. What I said to you about high school was true. I never really felt that I belonged anywhere, and I envied you because you so obviously did."

Frowning, he straightened. "Tasha—"

"Please let me finish." He might send her away, but she was going to take her best shot first.

Without waiting for his nod, she dived into the worst part. "I have a terrible reputation back home, really awful. I slept around—well, with two guys, but that morphed in the gossip into the whole soccer team. When I wouldn't sleep with the mayor's son, he had me charged with prostitution."

"Sleazeball." Carter scowled and came to his feet. He tugged off the sunglasses. Searching her eyes, he said, "And I was the mayor's son."

"Yes, but I didn't even think about that, not consciously."

"Glad to hear it. I'd still like to pound that guy." He dropped the sunglasses into his chair.

Hope unfurled inside her. "Me too," she told him, and then she explained how she'd come to enlist in the navy.

"That's what was eating at you, what you were afraid to tell me," he said quietly.

"I was working up my nerve to tell you when I found out your mom was in Congress. If we were together, her opponents could turn up the prostitution charge and the navy disciplinary action and use me to smear her. I didn't think you could accept that. I was afraid that if we had lunch with her, the event organizer, Priscilla Elgin, who's from my hometown, would tell your mother everything. Then she would see right through my education and manners to the angry, alienated, wild girl underneath. Or that your dad would see the same thing if I got involved with him over the cabinets. They wouldn't want you to be with someone like me. Worst of all, if you knew all that, you wouldn't want me anymore. And I—I couldn't bear—"

Her voice shook, and she had to press her trembling lips together.

"Tasha." This time his voice was gentle. He laid the pole by his chair.

He was going to cut her off. She couldn't let him.

"I love you, Carter. I think maybe I always have."

The grin that flashed onto his face smashed her fear. Her heart soared. He closed the distance in a single step and drew her close. She burrowed into his shoulder. He was warm and solid and smelled faintly of sunblock.

"I love you, Natasha." His hold tightened, and her tears overflowed. Clinging to him, she tried to catch her breath.

"You're getting me wet, Cupcake."

"S-sorry."

"Well, seeing as you brought me cupcakes, it's okay." He raised his head.

When Tasha looked up at him, he kissed her. The kiss

ignited in an instant, and the pressure of his body against hers wiped everything else away.

At last, breathing hard, Carter broke the kiss. His lips brushed over her forehead, her eyelids, and the tip of her nose, ending with a quick peck on her mouth.

She was grinning like an idiot by the time he finished, but that was okay. He still loved her. Next to that, nothing else mattered.

He used his thumbs to wipe away the tear tracks. "My mom's a smart woman. She and my dad understand how things get twisted. They'll understand this too."

"Are you sure?" She wrapped her fingers around his warm, sturdy wrists. "I would hate to be the cause of trouble—"

"There won't be trouble. If anyone tries to make anything of that, my mom will squash them. She's not afraid of a fight." Searching her eyes, he said, "Trust me on this, love of my life. I wouldn't lie to you about it."

Love of my life, he'd called her. The sound of that wrapped around her heart. Tasha let out a breath that seemed to carry all her worries with it.

Carter smiled. "As it happens, I have the day off. Can you take it too? Hang with me?"

"I already gave myself the day." Stroking his cheek, she said, "I would love to spend it with you. Catch up."

When he waggled his eyebrows, her cheeks heated. Hastily, she added, "And other things."

"Definitely. Just so you know, it means a lot that you stood up for me with Deke, but I'm okay with how things worked out. I did some maintenance chores around here and got the boat repaired. I even decided to go back to school, get a degree in counseling. As you suggested."

"I heard about the counseling. I think it's great."

"Yep. It's all good." Glancing downward, he said, "I think the cupcakes are gonna be a total loss, though."

"What?! Oh, no!" Her hands were empty, and the container

lay on its side by his bare foot. She must've dropped it during that hot kiss.

Still holding her with one arm, Carter leaned down to scoop up her peace offering. Tasha peered through the clear plastic and winced at the jumbled shapes inside. "Maybe they'll still taste good."

"You bet. Stand by a sec." He handed her the box. Then he grabbed the pole, pulled the line out of the water, and tossed the rig into the boat.

"You know," she said, watching him, "there's this wedding coming up, and I need a date."

"What a coincidence. Me too." He scooped her up in his arms. As she laughed, he started for the house.

"So that's settled," he announced. "Meanwhile, have you ever had cupcakes in bed?"

"Not so far."

"Stick with me, darlin', and I'll show you a raft of new experiences."

Tasha tightened her arms around his neck. "I'm counting on it."

EPILOGUE

"They're here, they're here!" Mel's eight-year-old second cousin, Jimmy, jumped up and down. Rushing to his mother, he cried, "They're coming!"

Outside Brunswick's Old City Hall, car doors slammed. A few moments later, voices drifted up the stairs to the second-floor banquet room.

The wedding party had stayed behind to take photos at Mary Ross Waterfront Park. Now they were here, so the celebration could start.

Tasha stood with Carter by their assigned table. Grinning up at him, she said, "After this rough spring, it's nice to have such a happy day to celebrate."

It wouldn't have been nearly so happy for her if he hadn't been there beside her. She'd told him everything, he'd told his parents, and none of them had cared. His mother had made a point of calling to invite her to come for a long weekend with Carter. Tasha still could scarcely believe it.

"I've always liked Doc Harper," he said. "Looking forward to getting to know Mel."

Waiters quickly distributed flutes of champagne or sparkling cider to everyone. The wedding party, along with Mel's and

Stefan's parents, streamed into the room, their shoes clattering on the dark, hardwood floor. The men still wore tailcoats, and the women, the sleeveless, floor-length sheath dresses in rich blue.

Griff, as best man, stopped in the doorway. Val stood beside him, and a waiter brought them champagne. Behind them, a bit of Mel's white skirt showed in the opening.

When everyone but the bridal couple had reached their tables, Griff called, "Can I have your attention? Your attention, please."

As the room quieted, he lifted his glass. "Friends, please welcome, in their first public appearance as a married couple, Camellia Wray and Stefan Harper."

Everyone applauded. Mel and Stefan entered, Mel's right hand nestled in the crook of his arm and her left holding her bouquet. The newlyweds radiated such joy that looking at them made Tasha's throat tight.

Stefan took Mel's hand from his arm and twirled her. At the end of the spin, still holding hands, she curtsied while he bowed.

"Kiss! Kiss! Kiss!" the teenagers chanted.

Laughing up at Stefan, Mel stepped into his arms. The kiss was quick but emphatic, and they were both beaming when it was done.

"To Mel and Stefan," Griff called.

The toast echoed around the room, and everyone drank.

"Thanks, everybody," Stefan said. "Now let's sit down and eat."

Carter pulled out Tasha's chair, as she'd come to expect. They shared a table with Lorelei, Will and Audra, Dr. John Parkhurst, and Dr. Bonnie Dunn and her husband. Quietly, Carter said, "Mel didn't change her name?"

"For professional reasons," Tasha replied. "She has a rep under her own name and wanted to keep things simple."

Carter nodded. "She looks great."

"She does. I love her dress. It's cut on princess lines." Which Tasha knew only because Lorelei had gone on about the details. Long-sleeved and close-fitting, the white silk gown had a gored skirt and a simple, scooped neck. White lace covered the skirt gores. Instead of wearing a veil, Mel had caught her shoulder-length, dark hair back with pearl and crystal combs, a wedding gift from Stefan.

"The flowers are gorgeous," Tasha told Lorelei. "In the bouquets and on the tables. You did a great job."

Lorelei beamed. "Thanks. It's hard to go wrong with the white roses and spring flowers she chose."

Waiters served salad, and everyone devoted their attention to passing condiments and bread. Carter looked preoccupied, though.

"Everything okay?" Tasha asked him.

"Hm? Oh. Yeah. I was just thinking."

"Anything you want to share?"

"Yeah." He reached under the tablecloth to clasp the hand she had in her lap. In a low voice, he said, "I was thinking you'd be dynamite in a dress like that."

Did he say—? Tasha blinked at him. "Carter?"

His eyes were soft as mist and intent on her face. "Not popping any questions, Cupcake. It's a little too soon for that. I wanted to let you know where my mind's going, though."

Relieved, because it was too soon, Tasha smiled at him. "I like the direction."

His eyes lit. "I hoped you might."

Leaning close, she whispered, "You do realize you're now officially in the super secret squirrel club?"

He grinned as another chant of "Kiss! Kiss! Kiss!" broke out.

"That demand's not for us," Carter said, "so I'll owe you one." Neither of them was a big fan of public displays anyway.

"I'll owe you back," Tasha assured him.

His grin flashed. "I'm counting on it."

The End

AFTERWORD

Thank you for reading *Mage's Nemesis*. I hope you enjoyed it. If you care to leave a review on the vendor site of your choice, I would appreciate it.

For information about upcoming books and other news, please visit my website, www.NancyNorthcott.com.

Thanks again!

ALSO BY NANCY NORTHCOTT

<u>Paranormal Romance</u>

The Light Mage Wars

Sentinel Mage

Renegade Mage

The Deadly Orb, a novella

Embattled Mage

Warrior Mage

Also Coming in 2023 & 2024

Mage's Nemesis

Magic & Murder

Traitor Mage's Fate

Mage Paladin

Mage Crucible

Firelord

Short Stories

"Magic & Mistletoe"

"The Magic Christmas Guy" *Warning* ~ contains spoilers for *Renegade Mage*

"GiGi's Magic Christmas"

<u>Romantic Suspense</u>

The Arachnid Files

Note: This series consists only of novellas so far. No novels yet.

Danger's Edge

(first published in the *Capitol Danger* anthology)

Danger's Dance (forthcoming)

The Last Favor

(Also available in the *Christmas at Caynham Castle* anthology)

Mr. Never Again

(Also available in the *Trick or Treat at Caynham Castle* anthology)

Worth the Wait

The One Who Got Away (Available in the *Love and Valentines at Caynham Castle* anthology)

Romantic Spy Adventure

The Deathbrew Affair

The Fabulous Fakes Affair (forthcoming)

Fantasy

The Boar King's Honor Trilogy

The Herald of Day

The Steel Rose

The King's Champion

The Merlin Club

The Merlin Club

The Hussar's Bane (forthcoming)

Conspiracy's Web (forthcoming)

The Devil's Chariot (forthcoming)

Science Fiction

The New Badge, a novella in the *Welcome to Outcast Station* anthology

Scorpions for Christmas, a novella in the *Christmas on Outcast Station* anthology

"Justice for Tillie," a short story in the *Predators in Petticoats* anthology

The Speaker for All, an Outcast Station novel (forthcoming)

Eden's Secret, an Outcast Station Novel by Jeanne Adams (forthcoming)

ABOUT NANCY

Nancy Northcott's childhood ambition was to grow up and become Wonder Woman. Around fourth grade, she realized it was too late to acquire Amazon genes, but she still loved comic books, mysteries, science fiction, fantasy, history, and romance. A sucker for fast action and wrenching emotion, Nancy combines the romance and high stakes (and sometimes the magic) she loves in the books she writes.

She's the author of the Light Mage Wars paranormal romances, the historical fantasy Boar King's Honor Trilogy and related Merlin Club novellas for Falstaff Books, the Arachnid Files romantic suspense series, and the Lethal Webs romantic spy adventures. Together, she and Jeanne Adams cowrite the Outcast Station space opera mystery series.

Nancy's website is www.NancyNorthcott.com